...im for The Time of My Life

makes for a w...g... ...r style ..."
Independent on Sunday

"Unique and magical."
Heat

"A warm and thought-provoking read."
Good Housekeeping

"A surreal and witty treat of a novel
that will have you gripped."
Woman & Home

"A funny, very poignant, and truly original tale . . .
a thoroughly enjoyable read."
The Sun (UK)

"This latest from the bestselling author won't
disappoint her legion of fans."
Bella

"Gripping from the first page."
Best Magazine

"A wonderfully enchanting, tender,
and beautifully penned tale."
Candis Magazine

By Cecelia Ahern

ONE HUNDRED NAMES
THE TIME OF MY LIFE
THE BOOK OF TOMORROW
THE GIFT
THANKS FOR THE MEMORIES
THERE'S NO PLACE LIKE HERE
IF YOU COULD SEE ME NOW
LOVE, ROSIE
P.S. I LOVE YOU

Cecelia Ahern

The Time of my Life

HARPER

An Imprint of HarperCollinsPublishers

This book was originally published in Great Britain in 2011, in a slightly different form, by HarperCollins Publishers.

Extract from *Down On Me* reproduced by kind permission of Aslan—Christy Dignam, Billy McGuinness, Alan Downey, Joe Jewell and Rod O'Brien.

HARPER

An Imprint of HarperCollins*Publishers*
10 East 53rd Street
New York, New York 10022-5299

Copyright © 2011 by Cecelia Ahern
ISBN 978-0-06-224862-6

First William Morrow paperback printing: May 2013
First Harper mass market international printing: February 2013

HarperCollins ® and Harper ® are registered trademarks of HarperCollins Publishers.

Printed in the United States of America

Visit Harper paperbacks on the World Wide Web at
www.harpercollins.com

10 9 8 7 6 5 4 3 2 1

For my precious girl, Robin

"You used to be much more . . . 'muchier.' You've lost your muchness."

The Mad Hatter to Alice in the film of
Alice in Wonderland (2010)

CHAPTER ONE

Dear Lucy Silchester,
You have an appointment for Monday 30 May.

I didn't read the rest. I didn't need to, I knew who it was from. I could tell as soon as I arrived home from work to my studio apartment and saw it lying on the floor, halfway from the front door to the kitchen, on the burned part of the carpet where the Christmas tree had fallen – and landed – two years ago and the lights had singed the carpet hairs. The carpet was a cheap old thing chosen by my penny-pinching landlord, a grey worn industrial yarn that looked as though more feet had trodden over it than the apparently 'lucky' testicles of the bull mosaic in Galleria Vittorio Emmanuele II in Milan. You'd find a similar kind of fabric in my office building – a more appropriate location as it was never intended to be walked on barefoot, made only for the steady stream of on-foot shiny leather-shoe traffic moving

1

from cubicle to photocopier, photocopier to coffee machine, coffee machine to emergency exit stairwell for a sneaky smoke, ironically the only location which failed to alert the fire alarm. I had been a part of the effort to find the smoking spot and each time the enemy had located us, we began efforts to find a new safe house. The current place was easy to find – hundreds of butts in piles on the ground to mark the spot, their lives sucked out of them by their users in panicked distressed frenzy, their souls floating around the insides of lungs while their outsides were dropped, stamped on and deserted. It was a place more worshipped than any other in the building, more than the coffee machine, more than the exit doors at six p.m., most certainly more than the chair before the desk of Edna Larson – the boss lady – who ate good intentions like a broken dispenser that swallowed your coins but failed to spit out the bar of chocolate.

The letter lay there on that dirty singed floor. A cream woven envelope with grand George Street font declaring my name in certain no-doubt-about-it black ink, and beside it, a gold embossed stamp, three swirls joined together.

The triple spirals of life. I knew what it was because I'd received two similar letters already and I'd Googled the symbol. I'd failed to make an appointment for either of the requests to meet. I'd also failed to phone the number supplied to rear-range or cancel. I'd ignored it, swept it under the rug – or would have if the Christmas tree lights hadn't set fire to the shagpile that used to be there – and forgotten about it. But I hadn't really forgotten about it. You never forget about things you've done that you know you shouldn't have done. They hang around your mind, linger like a thief casing a joint for a future job. You see them there, dramatically lurking nearby in striped mono-chrome, leaping behind postboxes as soon as your head whips around to confront them. Or it's a familiar face in a crowd that you glimpse but then lose sight of. An annoying *Where's Wally?* forever locked away and hidden in every thought in your conscience. The bad thing that you did, always there to let you know.

A month on from ignoring the second letter and this one had arrived with another rescheduled appointment, and no mention of my previous fail-ures to respond. It was like my mother – its polite failure to acknowledge my shortcomings was making me feel even worse.

I held the fancy paper at the corner between my thumb and forefinger and tilted my head to read it as it flopped to the side. The cat had pissed on it again. Ironic really. I didn't blame him. My illegally owning a pet in a high-rise apartment block in the middle of the city and holding down a full-time job meant the cat had no opportunity to go outside to relieve himself. In an attempt to rid myself of my guilt I had put framed photographs of the outside world around the apartment: the grass, the sea, a postbox, pebbles, traffic, a park, a collection of other cats, and Gene Kelly. The latter obviously to service my needs but I hoped the others would dispel any longing he had to go outside. Or to breathe fresh air, to make friends, to fall in love. Or to sing and dance.

As I was out five days a week from eight a.m. often to eight p.m. and sometimes didn't come home at all, I had trained him to 'eliminate', as the cat trainer had phrased it, on paper so he would get used to using his litter box. And this letter, the only piece of paper left lying on the floor, was surely just a confusion to him. I watched him move self-consciously around the edge of the room. He knew it was wrong. It was lurking in his mind, the thing he'd done that he knew he shouldn't have done.

I hate cats but I liked this cat. I named him Mr Pan after Peter, the well-known flying young boy. Mr Pan is neither a boy who will never age nor, oddly enough, does he possess the ability to fly, but there is a strange resemblance and it seemed appropriate at the time. I found him in a skip down an alleyway one night, purring as though in deep distress. Or perhaps that was me. What I was doing down there shall remain private but it was raining hard, I was wearing a beige trenchcoat and after mourning the loss of a perfect boyfriend over too many tequilas, I was doing my best to channel Audrey Hepburn by chasing the animal and calling out 'Cat!' in a clear and unique, yet distressed tone. Turned out it was a day-old kitten and it'd been born a hermaphrodite. Its mother or owner, or both, had shunned it. Though the vet informed me that the kitten had more male than female anatomy, naming him felt as though I alone took the responsibility of choosing his sex. I thought of my broken heart and my being passed up for a promotion because my boss had an inkling I was pregnant – though it was after the holidays and my annual gorge-fest had been a wild boar short of a Tudor banquet – I'd been through a particularly horrific month of stomach cramps; a street bum had groped me late one night on the train; and when I had enforced my opinion at work I'd been called a bitch by my male counterparts and so I decided life would be easier for the cat as a male. But I think I made the wrong decision. Occasionally I call him Samantha or Mary or something feminine and he looks up with what I can only describe as thanks before sloping off to sit in one of my shoes and gaze wistfully at the stiletto and the world he's been deprived of. But I digress. Back to the letter.

I would have to attend the appointment this time. There was no way around it. I couldn't ignore it; I didn't want to irritate its sender any further.

So who was the sender?

I held the drying page by the corner and again tilted my head to read the flopped paper.

Dear Lucy Silchester,
You have an appointment for Monday 30 May.
Yours sincerely,
Life

Life. Why of course.

My life needed me. It was going through a tough time and I hadn't been paying enough attention to it. I'd taken my eye off the ball, I'd busied myself with other things: friends' lives, work issues, my deteriorating and ever needy car, that kind of thing. I'd completely and utterly ignored my life. And now it had written to me, summoned me, and there was only one thing for it. I had to go and meet with it face to face.

CHAPTER TWO

I'd heard about this kind of thing happening which is why I wasn't making a great dramatic deal about it. I generally don't become overexcited about things anyway, I'm just not one of those people. I'm not easily surprised by things either. I think it's because I expect that anything can happen. That makes me sound like a believer and I'm not necessarily that either. I'll phrase it better: I just accept things that happen. All things. So my life writing to me, though unusual, wasn't surprising; it was more of an inconvenience. I knew that it would demand much of my attention for the foreseeable future and if that was an easy thing for me then I wouldn't have received the letters in the first place.

I beat the ice from the fridge-freezer with a knife and retrieved a cottage pie with my blue hand. While I waited for the microwave to ping I ate a slice of toast. Then a yoghurt. It still wasn't ready so I licked the lid. I decided that the arrival of the letter gave me permission to open a bottle of €3.99 Pinot Grigio. I stabbed the remainder of the ice from the fridge-freezer while Mr Pan ran to hide in a pink heart-decorated wellington boot still covered in dried muck from a summer music festival three years ago. I removed a wine bottle I'd forgotten to take from the freezer which was now a frozen solid block of alcohol and I replaced it with the new bottle. I wouldn't forget this one. I mustn't. It was the last bottle left in the wine-cellar-stroke-corner-cupboard-under-the-cookie-jar. Which reminded me of cookies. I also ate a double chocolate chip cookie while I waited. Then the microwaved pinged. I emptied the pie onto the plate, a big unappetising messy pile of mush, still cold in the middle but I hadn't the patience to put it back in and wait thirty seconds more. I stood at the counter to eat and poked at the warm parts around the edges.

I used to cook. I used to cook almost every night. The nights I didn't, my then boyfriend cooked. We enjoyed it. We owned a large apartment in a converted bread factory with floor-to-ceiling steel grid windows and original exposed brickwork on most walls. We had an open-plan kitchen-cum-dining-room and almost every weekend we had friends around for dinner. Blake loved cooking, he loved entertaining, he loved the idea of all of our friends, even family, joining us. He loved the sound of ten to fifteen people laughing, talking, eating, debating. He loved the smells, the steam, the oohs and aahs of delight. He'd stand at the kitchen island and tell a word-perfect story while dicing an onion, splashing the red wine into a beef bourguignon, or flambéing a baked alaska. He never measured anything, he always got the balance just right. He got the balance of everything just right. He was a food and travel writer, he loved going everywhere and tasting everything. He was adventurous. At weekends we never sat still, we climbed this mountain and that mountain, during summers we'd go to countries I'd never heard of. We jumped out of an airplane twice, we'd both bungee jumped three times. He was perfect.

And, he died.

Just joking, he's perfectly fine. Alive and well. Cruel joke I know but I laughed. No, he's not dead. He's still alive. Still perfect.

But I left him.

He has a television show now. He'd signed the deal when we were still together. It's on a travel channel we both used to watch all the time, and now and then I switch over and watch him walking the Great Wall of China or sitting in a boat in Thailand eating pad thai; and always, after his word-perfect review, in his perfect clothes – even after a week of climbing mountains, shitting in woods and not showering – he looks into the camera with his perfect face and he'll say, 'Wish you were here.' That's the name of the show. He told me in the weeks and months that followed our traumatic break-up, while he was crying down the phone, that he'd named it for me, that every time he said it he was talking to me and only me and never ever to anybody else. He wanted me back. He called me every day. Then every two days. Eventually it was once a week and I knew he'd been grappling with the phone for days trying to wait for that one moment to speak to me. Eventually he stopped calling and he'd send me emails. Long detailed emails about where he'd been, about how he felt without me, so depressing and so lonely I couldn't read them any more. I stopped replying to him. Then his emails got shorter. Less emotional, less detailed, always asking me to meet him though, always asking for us to get back together. I was tempted, don't get me wrong, he was a perfect man, and having a perfect, handsome man want you is sometimes enough to make you want him back, but that was in the weak moments of my own loneliness. I didn't want him. It wasn't that I'd met anybody else either, I told him that time and time again though perhaps it would have been easier if I'd pretended I had because then he could have moved on. I didn't want anybody else. I didn't really want anyone. I wanted to just stop for a while. I wanted to stop doing things and stop moving. I just wanted to be on my own.

I left my job, got a new one at an appliance company for half the salary. We sold the apartment. I rented this studio apartment, a quarter of the size of any other home I'd owned. I found a cat. Some would say I stole it but nevertheless, he/she is mine now. I visit my family when held at gunpoint, I go out with the same friends on nights that he's not there – my ex-boyfriend, not the cat – which is more often now that he's travelling so much. I don't miss him and when I do miss him, I switch on the TV and I get enough dosage of him to feel content again. I don't miss my job. I miss the money a little bit when I see something in the shops or in a magazine that I want, but then I leave the shop or I turn the page and I get over it. I don't miss the travelling. I don't miss the dinner parties.

And I'm not unhappy.

I'm not.

Okay, I lied.

He left me.

CHAPTER THREE

I was halfway through the bottle of wine by the time I built up the – not courage, I didn't need courage, I wasn't afraid – I needed to care. It took half a bottle of wine to care about returning a call to my life, and so I dialled the number listed on the letter. I took a bite of a chocolate bar while I waited for the phone to connect. It was answered on the first ring. It didn't give me time to chew, never mind swallow my chocolate.

'Oh, sorry,' I said with a stuffed mouth. 'I've chocolate in my mouth.'

'That's okay dear, take your time,' an upbeat older woman with a smooth American-pie Southern accent said perkily. I chewed quickly, swallowed and washed it down with some wine. Then I retched.

I cleared my throat. 'Finished.'

'What was it?'

'Galaxy.'

'Bubble or caramel?'

'Bubble.'

'Mmm, my favourite. How can I help you?'

'I received a letter about an appointment on Monday. My name is Lucy Silchester.'

'Yes, Ms Silchester, I have you in the system. How does nine a.m. suit?'

'Oh well, actually that's not why I'm calling. You see, I can't make the appointment, I'm working that day.'

I waited for her to say, *Oh silly us, asking you to come on a work day, let's cancel the entire thing,* but she didn't.

'Well, I guess we can work around you. What time do you finish?'

'Six.'

'How about seven p.m.?'

'I can't because it's my friend's birthday and we're going for dinner.'

'What about your lunch break? Would a lunch meeting suit you?'

'I've to bring my car to the garage.'

'So, just to summarise, you can't make the appointment because you've work in the day, you're bringing your car to the garage on your lunch break and you've dinner with friends in the evening.'

'Yes.' I frowned. 'Are you writing that down?' I heard tapping in the background. This bothered me; they had summoned me, not the other way around. They were going to have to find a time.

'You know, sweetheart,' she said in her long Southern drawl – I could almost see the apple pie slithering from her lips and landing on her keyboard, then her keyboard hissing and going alight, and my summons being forever wiped from the memory. 'You're obviously not familiar with this system.' She took a breath and I jumped in before the boiling apples had a chance to drip again.

'Are people usually?'

I'd knocked her off her train of thought.

'Pardon me?'

'When you contact people, when *life summons people to meet with it*,' I emphasised, 'are people usually familiar with the procedure?'

'Well,' the longest sing-song that sounded like *way-eell*, 'some are and some aren't, I suppose, but that's what I'm here for. How's about I make it easier for you by arranging for him to come to you? He'd do that if I asked.'

I thought about that, then suddenly, 'Him?'

She chuckled. 'That catches people out too.'

'Are they always *hims*?'

'No, not always, sometimes they're *hers*.'

'Under what circumstances are they men?'

'Oh, it's just hit or miss, sweetheart, there ain't no reason for it. Just like you and me being born what we are. Will that be a problem for you?'

I thought about it. Couldn't see why it would. 'No.'

'So what time would you like him to visit you?' She tapped some more.

'Visit me? No!' I shouted down the phone. Mr Pan jumped, opened his eyes, looked around and closed them again. 'Sorry for shouting,' I composed myself. 'He can't come here.'

'But I thought you said that wouldn't be a problem for you.'

'I meant it's not a problem that he's a man. I thought you were asking if *that* would be a problem.'

She laughed. 'But why would I ask you that?'

'I don't know. Sometimes health spas ask that too, you know, in case you don't want a male masseuse . . .'

She chuckled. 'Well, I can guarantee he won't be massaging any part of your anatomy.'

She made *anatomy* sound dirty. I shuddered.

'Well, tell him I'm very sorry but he can't come here.' I looked around at my dismal studio flat that I always felt quite cosy in. It was a place for me, my own personal hovel; it was not for entertaining guests, lovers, neighbours, family members or even emergency services when the rug caught fire, it was just for me. And Mr Pan.

I was huddled up by the arm of the couch and a few steps behind me was the end of my double bed. To my right was a kitchen countertop, to my left the windows and beside the bed was a bathroom. That was about the size of it. Not that the size bothered me, or embarrassed me. It was more the state of it. My floor had become the wardrobe. I liked to think of my scattered belongings as stepping stones, my yellow brick road . . . that kind of thing. The contents of my previous top-dollar penthouse wardrobe were bigger than the new studio apartment itself and so my too many pairs of shoes had found their home along the windowsill, my long coats and full-length dresses hung on hangers at the right- and left-hand ends of the curtain pole and I slid them open and closed as the sun and moon requested just like regular curtains. The carpet was as I have already described, the couch monopolised the small living area reaching from windowsill to kitchen counter, which meant you couldn't walk around it but had to climb over the back to sit on it. My life could not visit me in this mess. I was aware of the irony.

'My carpets are being cleaned,' I said, then I sighed as if it was just such a nuisance that I couldn't bear to think about it. It wasn't a lie. My carpets very much *needed* to be cleaned.

'Well, can I recommend Magic Carpet Cleaners,' she said brightly, as though suddenly jumping to commercial hour. 'My husband,' *ma husbaand*, 'is a devil for shining his boots in the living room and Magic Carpet Cleaners get that black polish right out, you wouldn't believe. He snores too. Unless I fall asleep before him I get none the rest of the night so I watch those infomercials and one night I saw a man shining his shoes on a white carpet, just like my husband and that's what caught my attention. Was like the company was made just for me. They took the stain right out, so I had to go out and get me some. Magic Carpet Cleaners, write it down.'

She was so intense I found myself wanting to invest in black shoe polish in order to test these magical cleaning infomercial people and I scrambled for a pen, which in accordance with the Pen Legislation Act of Since the Beginning of Time was not anywhere in sight when I needed it. With marker in hand I looked around for something to write on. I couldn't find any paper so I wrote on the carpet, which seemed appropriate.

'Why don't you just tell me when you can come see him, save us the back and forth.'

My mother had called a special meeting of the family to gather on Saturday.

'You know what, I know that this is so important, being summoned by my life and all, and despite having an important family gathering on Saturday, I'd really love to meet with him then.'

'Oh,' *ewwww,* 'sweetheart, I will make a special note that you were willing to miss that special day with your loved ones to meet with him but I think that you should take that time to be with your family. God only knows how long you've got 'em for and we'll see you the following day. Sunday. How does that grab you?'

I groaned. But not out loud, it was inside, deep within, a long agonised painful sound from a painful agonised place deep inside. And so the date was set. Sunday, we would meet, our paths would collide and everything I'd considered to be secure and anchored would suddenly slip and slide and change beyond belief. That's what I'd read would happen in a magazine interview with a woman who had met with her life. They provided before and after photos of her for the benefit of the uneducated reader who couldn't access picture images in their mind. Interestingly, before she'd met her life, her hair hadn't been blowdried, but it was after; she had no make-up or spray tan on before, but had after; she wore leggings and a Mickey Mouse T-shirt before and was photographed in harsh lighting, but wore a softly draped asymmetric dress afterwards in a perfectly lit studio kitchen where a tall vase of artistically placed lemons and limes showed how life had apparently made her more attracted to citric flavours. She wore glasses before meeting with life, she wore contacts afterwards. I wondered who had changed her more; the magazine or her life.

In just under a week's time I was going to meet my life. And my life was a man. But why me? I felt my life was going just fine. I felt fine. Everything in my life was absolutely fine.

Then I lay back on the couch and studied the curtain pole to decide what to wear.

CHAPTER FOUR

On the fateful Saturday that I'd been dreading ever since the day before I even heard about it, I pulled up to the electric gates of my parents' home in my 1984 Volkswagen Beetle that had backfired all the way up the exclusive estate, attracting a few unhealthy glares from the sensitive rich people. I didn't grow up in the house I was waiting outside and so it didn't feel like a return to home. It didn't even feel like my parents' home. It was a house that they lived in when they weren't in their holiday house, that they lived in when they weren't in their domestic house. The fact that I was waiting outside, pending permission to be granted, detached me from it even more. I had friends who drove straight up driveways, knew passwords and alarm codes, or used their own keys to visit their parents. I didn't even know where the coffee mugs were kept. The big gates had the desired effect, designed to keep out vagrants and deviants – and daughters

– though the deterrent for me was being trapped inside. A burglar would climb over them to get into the house, I would scale them to get out. As though picking up on my mood, my car, who I named Sebastian after my grandfather who was never without a cigar in his hand and as a result developed a hacking cough that eventually sent him to his grave, seemed to run out of steam as soon as it realised where we were going. The route to my parents' house was a tricky system of windy narrow roads in Glendalough that dipped and rose, twisted and turned around one giant mansion after another. Sebastian stopped and spluttered. I wound down my window and pressed the intercom.

'Hello, you've reached the Silchesters' Home for the sexually deviant, how can we fulfil your needs?' came a breathy male voice down the line.

'Father, stop messing about.'

There was an explosion of laughter through the speaker, causing two power-walking Botoxed blondes to end their secret nattering and whip their high pony-tails around to stare. I smiled at them but as soon as they saw me, a brown unimportant thing in a junk of metal, they looked away and shook their VPL-free tight little Lycra-covered raisin bottoms forward again.

The gates made a shuddering sound, unstuck themselves and then parted.

'Okay, Sebastian, let's go.' The car jerked forward, knowing what lay in its wake: a two-hour wait beside a bunch of pretentious automobiles he had nothing in common with. How similar our lives would be. The long gravelled driveway gave way to a car park with a water fountain of an open-mouthed lion spewing up murky water. I parked away from Father's bottle green Jaguar XJ and his 1960 Morgan +4 which he called his 'weekend car', and which he drove wearing his weekend attire of vintage leather gloves and goggles as though he were Dick Van Dyke in *Chitty Chitty Bang Bang*. He also wore clothes with these items, in case the image was more disturbing than intended. Beside Father's cars was my mum's black SUV. She had specifically asked for something that would require minimum driving effort on her part, and she had parking sensors covering so many angles that if a car drove by three lanes away on a motorway it beeped to signal its proximity. On the other side of the gravelled area was my eldest brother Riley's Aston Martin and my brother Philip's – the middle child's – family Range Rover that had been pimped up with all the upgrades including television screens in the backs of the headrests for the kids to watch on their ten-minute drive from ballet to basketball practice.

'Leave the engine running, I'll be out in two hours max,' I said, then patted Sebastian on the head.

I looked up at the house. I don't know what era it was, but it was not 'Georgewardian' as I had joked at the Schuberts' Christmas party much to my brothers' amusement, my father's disgust and my mother's pride. The house was striking, it was originally built as a manor by Lord Somebody who later gambled away his fortune and it was sold to somebody else who wrote a famous book and therefore we were required by law to place a brass plaque with his name outside the gates for literary geeks but mostly for passing power-walkers with raisin bottoms to look at and frown at because they didn't have a brass plaque outside their own houses. Famous Literary Writer had an illicit relationship with a male Depressed Poet who built an East Wing in order to get away on his own. The house had an impressive library containing communications from Lord Somebody to Lady Whatever, then more sweet talk from Lord Somebody to Lady Secret while he was married to Lady Whatever, and original writings from Famous Literary Writer which were framed and hanging on the walls. Depressed Poet's works stood unprotected on the shelf beside a world atlas and Coco Chanel's life story. He didn't sell well, not even after he died. After a well-documented tumultuous affair, Famous Literary Writer drank all his money away and the house was sold to a well-to-do German family who brewed beer in Bavaria and used it as their holiday home. While here, they also added on a very impressive west wing and a tennis court, which from the evidence of their faded black-and-white photographs their overweight and seemingly unhappy sailor-suited son Bernhard did not like to avail of. It was also possible to find an original bottle of the family beer in a walnut cabinet in the Silchester bar. The memories and traces of these other lives were palpable in the house and I often wondered what exactly it was Mum and Father would leave behind apart from Ralph Lauren's latest interiors.

Two animals which I still couldn't identify greeted me with scowls at the base of the stone steps leading to the front door. They looked like lions but they had horns and two legs twisted together in what could only be described as a debilitating stance that made me think that hundreds of years of staring at the fountain had left them desperate for the toilet. Unless Ralph Lauren was going through a dark phase, my money was on the drunk writer or the depressed poet to have chosen them.

The door opened and my brother Riley grinned out at me like a Cheshire cat.

'You're late.'

'And you're disgusting,' I referred to the intercom exchange.

He laughed.

I trudged up the steps and passed over the threshold into the black and white marble-floored hall with double-height ceiling where a chandelier the size of my flat dripped down.

'What, no gift?' he said, giving me a hug longer than I wanted just to annoy me.

I groaned. He was joking but I knew he meant it. My family belonged to a very serious religion called the Church of Social Etiquette. The heads of their church were People. As in, every action acted and word spoken was done on the basis of what would 'People' think? Part of that etiquette required you to bring a gift to a person's house even if that person was family and you were just calling by. But we didn't just do calling by. We did arranged visits, made appointments, spent weeks, months even, trying to rally the troops.

'What did you bring?' I asked him.

'A bottle of Father's favourite red wine.'

'Suck-up.'

'Only because I want to drink it.'

'He won't open it. He'd rather wait until everyone he loves is long dead and buried before he even thinks about sitting in a locked room to open it himself. Bet you ten, actually twenty,' I needed petrol money, 'he won't open it.'

'Your understanding of him is almost touching but I have faith in him. It's a deal.' He held out his hand.

'What did you get Mum?' I looked around the entrance hall to see what I could swipe for a gift.

'A candle and bath oil but before you make a thing about it, I found it in my apartment.'

'Because I bought it for what's-her-name, that girl you dumped who laughed like a dolphin.'

'You got Vanessa a gift?'

We were walking through the endless spaces of the house, room after room of seating areas and fireplaces. Couches we were never allowed to sit on, coffee tables we couldn't put our drinks on.

'As a consolation prize for going out with you.'

'She can't have appreciated it much.'

'Bitch.'

'Yeah, dolphin-laughing bitch,' he agreed, and we smiled.

We reached the final room in the back of the house. Once Lady Somebody's drawing room and then Depressed Poet's rhyming room, it was now Mr and Mrs Silchester's entertainment room: a walnut built-in bar with beer on tap and a smoky mirror on the back wall. In the glass case along the bar stood the original German beer from the 1800s with a black-and-white photo of the Altenhofen family posing on the front steps of the house. The room had plush salmon-toned carpets that your feet sank into, tall leather-upholstered chairs at a cocktail bar and smaller leather chairs dotted around walnut tables. Its main feature was a bay window which overlooked the valley below and the rolling hills beyond. The garden was three acres of rose gardens, a walled garden and an outside swimming pool with fresh water. The double doors from the bar were open and gigantic limestone slabs led down to a water feature in the centre of the lawn. To the side of the fountain and beside the rush of the babbling brook a table had been set up with white table linen, crystal and silverware. In my family there was no such thing as informality. It was such a wonderful picture. Shame I'd have to ruin it.

My mother was floating around the table in a white tweed Chanel to-the-knee number and monochrome flats, swatting away the wasps that threatened to invade her garden party. There wasn't a hair out of place on her blonde head, she held the same small smile on rose pink lips regardless of what was going on in the world or in her life or in the room. Pimped-up Range-Rover-owner-slash-reconstructive-plastic-surgeon-slash-closet-boob-job-surgeon and middle child Philip was already seated at the table talking to my grandmother who was sitting poised as usual in a floral garden-party dress, back poker straight, her hair scraped tightly in a bun, her cheeks and lips an appropriate rouge, pearls around her neck, her hands clasped in her lap and her legs joined at the ankles, no doubt as learned at finishing school. She sat quietly, not looking at Philip and probably not listening either while she surveyed my mother's work with her ever disapproving eye.

I looked down at my dress and smoothed it.

'You look great,' Riley said, looking away and trying to make me feel that he wasn't just attempting to fill me with confidence. 'I think she's got something to tell us.'

'That she's not our real mother.'

'Oh, you don't mean that,' I heard a voice behind me.

'Edith,' I said, before I'd turned around. Edith had been a housekeeper for Mum and Father for thirty years. She'd been there for as long as I could remember and brought us up more than any of the fourteen nannies who had been employed to take care of us throughout our lives. She had a vase in one hand and a gigantic bouquet of flowers in the other. She placed the vase down and held her arms out to embrace me. 'Oh Edith, they're lovely flowers.'

'Yes, they are, aren't they? I just bought them fresh today, I went to that new market down by . . .' she stopped, looked at me suspiciously. 'Oh, no. No, you don't.' She moved the flowers away from me. 'No, Lucy. You can't have them. Last time you took the cake I'd made for dessert.'

'I know, that was a mistake and I'll never do it again,' I said sombrely, then added, 'because she keeps asking me to make it again. Ah, come on Edith, just let me see them, they're beautiful, really beautiful.' I batted my eyelashes.

Edith resigned herself to fate and I lifted the flowers from her arms.

'Mum will love them. Thanks,' I smiled cheekily.

She fought a smile; even when we were kids she'd found it hard to give out to us. 'You deserve what's coming to you now, that's all I can say.' Then she returned in the direction of the kitchen, while dread filled inside me to the point of bursting. Riley led the way and I struggled to walk down the wide steps with the bouquet which took two of my strides next to Riley's one. He was down ahead of me and Mum almost lit up like a firework at the sight of her precious son making his way to her.

'Lucy, sweetheart, they're beautiful, you shouldn't have,' Mum said, taking the flowers from me and over-exaggerating her thanks as though she'd just been handed the Miss World title.

I kissed my grandmother on the cheek. She acknowledged it slightly with a small nod of her head but didn't move.

'Hi, Lucy,' Philip stood to kiss me on the cheek.

'We'll have to stop meeting like this,' I said to him quietly, and he laughed.

I wanted to ask Philip about the kids, I knew that I should, but Philip was one of those people who actually took the enquiry way too far and would go into the verbal diarrhoea of every single thing his children had said and done since I'd seen them last. I loved his children, I really did, but I just didn't care so much for what they'd eaten for breakfast that morning, though I'm pretty sure it was something to do with organic mangoes and dehydrated dates.

'I should put these in water,' Mum said, still admiring the flowers for my benefit though the moment had long since past.

'I'll do it for you,' I jumped at the chance. 'I saw the perfect vase for them inside.'

Riley shook his head incredulously behind her back.

'Thank you,' Mum said, as though I'd just offered to pay her bills for her lifetime. She looked at me adoringly. 'You look different, did you do something with your hair?'

My hand went immediately to my chestnut mane. 'Em. I slept with wet hair last night.'

Riley laughed.

'Oh. Well, it's lovely,' she said.

'That will give you a cold,' my grandmother said.

'It didn't.'

'It can.'

'But it didn't.'

Silence.

I left, and tottered over the grass in my heels to get to the stone steps. I gave up and kicked off my shoes; the stone under my feet was warm from the sun. Edith had moved the vase from the bar but I was happy about that; another errand to waste more time. I calculated in my head that from my late arrival to the flower/vase errand I had passed twenty minutes of the dreaded two-hour stay.

'Edith,' I called half-heartedly for nobody's benefit but my own, moving from room to room, moving further away from the kitchen where I knew she would be based. There were five large rooms facing the back garden. One from Drunken Literary Writer's time, two from the main original part of the house and then another two from the German beer family. Once I had walked through all of the rooms which were connected by oversized double doors, I stepped out in the hallway and looped my way back round. Across the hallway I could see the massive walnut double doors to my father's office were open. It was where Famous Literary Writer had penned his famous novel. It was where my father went through endless mounds of paperwork. Sometimes I even wondered if there was anything printed on the paper or if he just liked the feel of it, if it was some nervous disposition that meant he must look at and touch and turn paper.

Father and I have the best relationship. Sometimes our thoughts are so similar it's almost as if we're the same person. When people see us they are blown away by our bond, by the respect he holds for me, by the admiration I hold for him. Often he'd take days off work just to pick me up from my apartment and take me off on an adventure. It was the same when I was a child, the only daughter in the family, he spoiled me. Daddy's girl, everybody called me. He'd phone me during the day just to see how I was, send me flowers and Valentine's cards so I didn't feel lonely. He really was a special guy. We really did have a special bond. Sometimes he'd take me to a barley field on a windy day and I'd wear a floaty dress and we'd run around in slow motion and he'd become the tickle monster and try to catch me, chasing me around and around until I'd fall down on the barley which would be all around me, waving back and forth in the breeze. How we'd laugh.

Okay, I lied.

That was probably obvious from the slow-motion barley-field image. I pushed it too much there. In truth, he can barely stand me nor I him. But we do stand each other, just about enough, somewhere on the cusp of standing each other for the sake of world peace.

He must have known I was outside his office but he didn't look up, just turned another mysterious page. He'd kept those pages far from our grasp all of our lives, so much so that I'd become obsessed about discovering what was on them. When I was ten years old I finally managed to sneak into his office one night when he'd forgotten to lock the door, and when I saw the papers, with my heart pounding manically in my chest, I couldn't understand a word that was written on them. Law talk. He's a High Court judge and the older I got the more I came to understand how regarded he was as a leading expert on Irish criminal law. He'd presided over murder and rape trials since his appointment to the High Court twenty years ago. He was a real bag of laughs. His old-school views on many things had been nothing short of controversial; at times, if he hadn't been my father, I'd have taken to the streets in protest – or maybe that was because he was my father. His parents were academics, his father a university professor, his mother – the floral-dress-wearing old woman in the back garden – was a scientist. Though apart from creating tension in every room she walked into I don't know exactly what she got up to. Something to do with maggots in soil in certain climates. Father's a European Universities Debating Champion, graduate of Trinity College Dublin and the Honourable Society of King's Inns whose motto is 'Nolumus Mutari' meaning 'We Shall Not Be Changed' and that right there says a lot about him. All I know about my father is what the plaques on his office walls declare to the world. I used to think that everything else about him was a great big mystery that I would someday figure out, that I would unlock a secret and suddenly he would all make sense; and that in the end of his days – he an old man and me a responsible beautiful career woman with a stunning husband, longer legs than I'd ever had before and the world at my feet – we'd try to make up for lost time. Now I realise there is no mystery, he is the way he is, and we dislike each other because there isn't a part of either of us which can even begin to understand a minuscule part of the other.

I watched him from the doorway in his panelled office, head down, glasses low on his nose reading papers. Walls of books filled the room and the smell of dust, leather and cigar smoke was thick even though he'd stopped smoking ten years ago. I felt a tiny rush of warmth for him, because all of a sudden he looked old. Or at least older. And older people were like babies; something about their demeanour made you love them despite their ignorant selfish personalities. I'd been standing there for a while taking the place in and pondering this sudden feeling of warmth, and it seemed unnatural to just walk away without saying anything so I cleared my throat, then decided to do an awkward knuckle rap on his open door, a manoeuvre which caused the cellophane wrapped around the flowers to rustle loudly. He still didn't look up. I stepped inside.

I waited patiently. Then impatiently. Then I wanted to throw the flowers at his head. Then I wanted to pick each flower, petal by petal, and flick them in his face. What began as a mild innate happiness to see my father then turned to the usual feelings of frustration and anger. He just made things so difficult all of the time, always a barrier, always uncomfortable.

'Hi,' I said and I sounded like a seven-year-old again.

He didn't look up. Instead he finished reading the page, turned it and finished reading that one too. It may only have been one minute but it felt like five. He finally looked up, took his glasses off and looked down at my bare feet.

'I brought these flowers for you and Mum. I was looking for a vase.' It was probably the closest thing to *Dirty Dancing*'s 'I carried a watermelon' that I'd ever said.

Silence. 'There isn't one in here.' In my head I heard him say, *You fucking fool*, though he would never actually swear, he was one of those people who said "ruddy" which annoyed me to no end.

'I know that, I just thought I'd say hi while I was on my way.'

'Are you staying for lunch?'

I tried to figure out how to take that. He either wanted me to stay for lunch or he didn't. It must have meant something, all his sentences were coded and usually had undertones implicating me of being an imbecile. I searched for the meaning and then for what could be the possible follow-up. Couldn't figure it out. So I said, 'Yes.'

'I will see you at lunch.'

Which meant, Why would you disturb me in my office with a ridiculous 'hi' in your bare feet when I am due to see you at lunch any minute from now, *you ruddy fool*. He put his glasses back on and continued reading his papers. Again I wanted to fling the flowers at his head, one by one, just ping them off his forehead, but out of respect for Edith's bouquet I turned and walked out of there, my feet making a squeaky sound as they stuck to the floor. When I got to the kitchen I dumped the flowers in the sink, picked at some food, and went back outside. Father was there already greeting his sons. Firm handshakes, deep voices, a few renditions of 'We are men'; then they gorged on a couple of pheasant legs, clinked pewtered jugs, groped a boob or two, wiped their drooling mouths and burped – or at least I imagined them do that – and then they sat.

'You didn't greet Lucy, sweetheart, she was finding a vase for the beautiful flowers she gave us.' Mum smiled at me again as if I alone was all that was good in the world. She was good at doing that.

'I saw her in the house.'

'Oh, that's lovely,' Mum said studying me again. 'Did you find a vase?'

I looked at Edith who was placing bread rolls on the table. 'Yes, I did. The one in the kitchen beside the bin.' I smiled at her sweetly, knowing she would understand this to mean I had placed them in the bin, which I hadn't, but I liked teasing her.

'Where your dinner is,' Edith smiled back sweetly and mum looked confused. 'Wine?' Edith looked over my head, to everybody else but me.

'No, I can't, I'm driving,' I responded anyway, 'but Riley's going to have a glass of the red he brought for Father.'

'Riley is driving,' Father said, not addressing anyone in particular.

'He could have a small drop.'

'People who drink and drive should be locked up,' he snapped.

'You didn't mind him having a glass last week,' I tried not to be confrontational but it wasn't really working.

'Last week a young boy wasn't thrown through the windscreen of a car because the ruddy driver had too much to drink.'

'Riley,' I gasped, 'tell me you didn't?'

It was in poor taste, I know, but I think I kind of wanted it to be, for Father's sake, so he began a conversation with his mother as though I had never spoken. Riley shook his head incredulously, whether at my inappropriate humour, or because he'd failed to wet his lips with Father's precious wine, I wasn't sure but either way he lost the bet. Riley reached into his pocket and handed me a twenty-euro note. Father looked at the transaction disapprovingly.

'I owed her money,' Riley explained.

Nobody at the table believed I could possibly have loaned anybody any money so it all backfired on me. Again.

'So,' Mum began, as soon as Edith had finished setting up and we were all settled. She looked at me. 'Aoife McMorrow married Will Wilson last week.'

'Ah, I'm so delighted for her,' I said enthusiastically, stuffing a bread roll into my mouth. 'Who's Aoife McMorrow?'

Riley laughed.

'She was in your tap-dance class.' Mum looked at me, utterly surprised I'd forgotten my time-step acquaintance from when I was six years old. 'And Laura McDonald had a little girl.'

'Ee-I-ee-I-oh,' I said.

Riley and Philip laughed. No one else did. Mum tried to but didn't get it.

'I met her mother at the organic fair yesterday and she showed me a photo of the baby. Beeeauuuutiful baby. You'd eat her. Married and a mother all in one year, imagine that.'

I smiled tightly. I felt Riley's intense stare urging me to be calm.

'The baby was ten pounds, Lucy, ten pounds, can you believe it?'

'Jackson was nine pounds two ounces,' Philip said. 'Luke was eight pounds four and Jemima was eight pounds six.'

36

We all looked at him and pretended to be interested, then he went back to eating his bread.

'It's a lovely thing,' Mum said looking at me and scrunching her face up and hunching her shoulders. 'Motherhood.'

She was looking at me like that for too long.

'I was married by the time I was twenty,' my grandmother said as though it was some major feat. Then she stopped buttering her bread and looked me dead in the eye. 'I finished university when I was twenty-four and had three children by the time I was twenty-seven.'

I nodded as if in awe. I'd heard it all before. 'Hope they sent you a medal.'

'Medal?'

'It's just an expression. For doing something . . . amazing.' I tried to hold back on the bitter sarcastic tone that was just dying to get out. It was on the sidelines warming up, begging me to let it go on as a substitute for politeness and tolerance.

'Not amazing, just the right thing, Lucy.'

Mum came to my defence. 'Sometimes girls have babies in their late twenties now.'

'But she's thirty.'

'Not for a few weeks,' I replied, pasting on a smile. Sarcasm took its training top off, got ready to run on to the pitch.

'Well, if you think you can have a baby in a fortnight you've a lot to learn,' Grandmother said, biting into her bread.

'Sometimes they're older these days,' Mum said.

My grandmother tutted.

'They have careers now, you see,' Mum continued.

'She doesn't have one. And what precisely do you imagine I was doing in the laboratory? Baking bread?'

Mum was put out. She had baked the bread on the table. She always baked the bread, everyone knew that, especially my grandmother.

'Not breastfeeding anyway,' I mumbled, but it didn't matter, everybody heard me and they were all looking at me, and they weren't all happy looks. I couldn't help it, the substitutes were on the pitch. I felt the need to explain my comment. 'It's just that Father doesn't strike me as a breastfed man.' If Riley's eyes could have widened any more they would have popped out of his head. He couldn't help it, whatever laugh he'd been trying to keep in came out as a bizarre-sounding splurge of happy air. Father picked up his newspaper and cut himself off from the unfavourable conversation. He rustled it open in the same shuddering motion that I'm sure his spine was doing. We'd lost him, he was gone. Lost behind more paper.

'I'll check the starters,' Mum said quietly and gracefully slid from the table.

I didn't inherit Mum's gracefulness. In fact Riley did. Suave and sophisticated, he oozed charm and even though he's my brother I know he's a real catch at thirty-five. He'd followed Father into the legal profession and was apparently one of our finest criminal lawyers. I'd overheard that being said about him; I hadn't experienced his talents first-hand, not yet anyway but I wasn't ruling it out. It gave me a warm and tingly feeling thinking my brother held a get-out-of-jail-free card for me. He was often seen on the news going in and out of court with men with tracksuit tops over their heads and handcuffed to police officers, and many was an embarrassing time when I'd silenced public places to shout proudly at the TV, 'There's my brother!' and when I'd received glares of anger, I'd have to point out it wasn't the man with the tracksuit top over his head accused of doing inhumane things but the dashing one in the fancy suit beside him but by then nobody cared. I believed Riley had the world at his feet; he wasn't under any pressure to get married, partly because he's a man and there are bizarre double standards in my house and partly because my mother has an unusual crush on him which means no woman is good enough for him. She never nagged or moaned but had a very distinct way of pointing out a woman's flaws in the hope of planting the seed of doubt in Riley's mind forever. She would have had more success if she'd simply used a flash card of a vagina when he was a child and then shook her head and tutted. She's excited he's living it up in a swanky bachelor pad in the city and she visits him on the odd weekend when she gets the opportunity to fulfil some sort of odd thrill. I think if he was gay she'd love him even more, no women to be in competition with and homosexuals are so cool now. I heard her say that once.

Mum returned with a tray of lobster cocktails and after a shellfish episode at lunch in the Horgans' home in Kinsale, which involved me, a tiger prawn and a fire brigade, she also carried a melon cocktail for me.

I looked at my watch. Riley caught me.

'Don't leave us in any more suspense, Mum, what have you got to tell us?' he said, in his perfect way that brought everyone back from their heads to the table. He had that ability, to bring people together.

'I won't have one, I don't like lobster,' Grandmother said, pushing the plate away in mid-air before it had even reached the table.

Mum looked a little disheartened then remembered why we were all there and then looked at Father. Father kept reading his newspaper, unaware that his lobster had even been planted before him. Mum sat down, excited. 'Okay, I'll tell them,' she said, as if that was ever under dispute. 'Well, as you all know, it's our thirty-fifth wedding anniversary this July.' She gave us all a *where has the time gone by* look. 'And as a way of celebrating, your father and I . . .' she looked around us all, eyes twinkling, 'have decided to renew our vows!' Her excitement overtook her voice for the last three words and ended in a hysterical high-pitched shriek. Even Father lowered the paper to look at her, then noticed the lobster, folded away the paper and started eating it.

'Wow,' I said.

Many of my friends had gotten married in the last two years. There seemed to be an epidemic sweeping – as soon as one married, a whole load were engaged and sauntering down the aisle like puffed-up peacocks. I had seen reasonable, modern women be reduced to obsessive maniacs hell bent on traditions and stereotypes they'd spent all their working lives trying to fight – I had been a part of many of these rituals in unflattering, cheap off-coloured dresses, but this was different. This was my mother and this meant it would be monumentally, cataclysmically worse.

'Philip darling, Daddy would love it if you would be his best man.' Philip's face reddened and he seemed to grow a few feet in his chair. He bowed his head silently, the honour so great he couldn't speak. 'Riley darling, would you give me away?'

Riley beamed. 'I've been trying to get rid of you for years.'

Everybody laughed including my grandmother who loved a joke at my mother's expense. I swallowed, because I knew it was coming. I knew it. Then she looked at me and all I could see was a mouth, a big smiling mouth taking over her whole entire face as if her lips had eaten her eyes and her nose. 'Sweetheart, would you be my bridesmaid? Maybe we could do that with your hair again, it's so lovely.'

'She'll get a cold,' my grandmother said.

'But she didn't get one last night.'

'But do you want to run the risk of her having one?'

'We could get nice handkerchiefs made up in the same fabric as her dress, just in case.'

'Not if it's anything like the fabric of your first wedding dress.'

And there it was, the end of my life as I knew it.

I looked at my watch.

'It's such a pity you have to go soon, we have so much to plan. Do you think you could come back tomorrow and we could go through everything?' Mum asked, excited and desperate both at the same time.

And here came the dilemma. Life or my family. Both were as bad as each other.

'I can't,' I said, which was greeted by a long silence. Silchesters didn't say no to invitations, it was considered rude. You moved around appointments and went to hell and back in order to attend every single thing that you were invited to, you hired lookalikes and embarked on time travel to uphold every single promise that had been made by you and even by somebody else without your knowledge.

'Why not, dear?' Mum's eyes tried to look concerned, but screeched, *You have betrayed me.*

'Well, perhaps I can come over, but I have an appointment at noon and I don't know how long it will go on for.'

'An appointment with whom?' Mum asked.

Well, I was going to have to tell them sooner or later.

'I have an appointment with my life.' I said it matter-of-factly, expecting them not to have a clue what I was talking about. I waited for them to question and judge, and planned how to explain it was just a random thing that happened to people like jury duty, and that they didn't have to worry, that my life was fine, absolutely fine.

'Oh,' Mum said in a high-pitched yelp. 'Oh my goodness, well I cannot *believe* that.' She looked around the rest at the table. 'Well, it's such a surprise, isn't it? We are all so *surprised*. My goodness. What a *surprise*.'

I looked at Riley first. He was looking awkward, eyes down on the table, while he ran his finger over the prongs of a fork and softly spiked it with each one in a meditative state. Then I looked at Philip; his cheeks had slightly pinked. My grandmother was looking away as though there was a bad smell in the air and it was my mother's fault but there was nothing new about that. I couldn't look at my father.

'You already know.'

Mum's face went red. 'Do I?'

'You all know.'

Mum slouched in her chair, devastated.

'How do you all know?' My voice was raised. Silchesters didn't raise their voices.

Nobody would answer.

'Riley?'

Riley finally looked up and gave a small smile. 'We had to sign off on it, Lucy, that's all, just to give our personal approval to it going ahead.'

'You what?! You knew about this?'

'It's not his fault, sweetheart, he had nothing to do with it, I asked him to get involved. There had to be a minimum of two signatures.'

'Who else signed?' I asked looking around at them. 'Did you all sign?'

'Don't raise your voice, young lady,' my grand-mother said.

I wanted to throw Mum's bread at her head or mush lobster cocktail down her throat and perhaps that was obvious because Philip appealed to everybody for calm. I didn't hear how the conversation ended because I was racing up the garden – walking fast, not running, Silchesters didn't run away – and getting as far away from them as possible. Of course I hadn't left without excusing myself from the table, I can't remember exactly what I'd said, I'd mumbled something about being late for an appointment and politely abandoned them. It was only when I closed the front door behind me, raced down the steps, and landed on the gravel that I realised I had left my shoes on the back lawn. I hobbled over the stones, biting the inside of my mouth to stop my need to scream, and drove Sebastian at his top speed down the driveway and to the gate. Sebastian backfired along the way as a kind of *good riddance*, however that's when my great escape ended because I reached the electric gates and was trapped. I lowered my window and pressed the intercom.

'Lucy,' Riley said, 'come on, don't be angry.'

'Let me out,' I said, refusing to look the intercom in the eye.

'She did it for you.'

'Don't pretend you had nothing to do with this.'

'Okay fine. We. We did it for you.'

'Why? I'm fine. Everything is fine.'

'That's what you keep saying.'

'Because that's what I keep meaning,' I snapped back. 'Now open the gate.'

CHAPTER FIVE

Sunday. It had loomed over me all weekend like that giant gorilla over that building in that film and finally it had plucked me into its evil clutches. I'd had a night full of various 'me meeting life' scenarios. Some had gone well, others not so well, one was entirely in song and dance. I had every conversation imaginable with life – in that weird dream way that made absolutely no sense when you woke – and now that I was awake, I was exhausted. I pressed my eyelids together again, squeezed them tight and forced myself to have a dirty dream about the cute guy on the train. It didn't happen, Life kept bursting in on us like a judgemental parent catching a naughty teen. Sleep wouldn't come, my head had already woken up and was planning things; smart things to say, quick retorts, witty comebacks, intelligent insights, ways to cancel the meeting without seeming insulting, but mostly it was planning my wardrobe. On that note, I opened my eyes and sat up. Mr Pan stirred in his bed and watched me.

'Morning, Hilary,' I said and he purred.

What did I want to say to my life about myself? That I was an intelligent, witty, charming, desirable, smart woman with a great sense of style. I wanted my life to know that I had it all together, that everything was under control. I surveyed my dresses on the curtain pole. I had pulled them all across to block out the sunlight. I looked at my shoes below them on the windowsill. Then I looked out the window to check the weather, back to the shoes, back to the dresses. I wasn't feeling any of it; this was a job for the wardrobe. I leaned over and opened the wardrobe door and before it had fully opened, it hit the edge of the bed. It didn't matter, I could see in just enough. The bulb inside the wardrobe had blown about a year ago and so I reached for the torch beside my bed and shone it inside. I was thinking, trouser suit, skinny fit, black tuxedo jacket, a touch of eighties revival shoulder pad; black vest; heels, 85mm. It said to me, Jennifer Aniston recent *Grazia* cover but it would hopefully say to Life, easy-going, relaxed but that I took my life seriously, suit-wearing-serious. It also said, someone has died and I'm going to their funeral, but I was hoping Life wouldn't be thinking about death. I left Mr Pan sitting in a peep-toe double platform watching Gene Kelly in a sailor suit in *On the Town* with promises I'd take him outside in a few days. From the elevator I heard my next-door neighbour's front door close. I pounded on the button to close the door, but I was caught. A trainer appeared through the crack in the closing doors and there she was.

'Almost got away,' she smiled. The doors slid open and the buggy was revealed. She manoeuvred it into the confined space and I was almost knocked back out into the corridor by the overloaded baby bag over her shoulder. 'I swear it just takes me longer and longer to get out of the apartment every day,' she said, wiping her shiny forehead.

I smiled at her, confused as to why she was talking to me – we never talked – then looked above her to watch the numbers light up as we moved down.

'Did he disturb you last night?'

I looked into her buggy. 'No.'

She looked shocked. 'I was up half the night with him screaming the place down. I was sure I'd have the building banging on my door. He's teething, the poor thing, his cheeks are flaming red.'

I looked down again. Didn't say anything.

She yawned. 'Still, at least the weather is nice this summer, nothing worse than being cooped up inside with a baby.'

'Yeah,' I said when the doors finally opened. 'Have a good day,' and I ran out ahead of her before she took the conversation outside.

I probably could have walked to the offices where I was due to meet Life but I got a taxi because the cute guy wouldn't be on the train at this hour and I couldn't rely on Sebastian to get me anywhere after yesterday's trip up the mountains. Apart from that I wasn't too sure where I was going and there was nothing worse than meeting your life with blistered feet and sweaty armpits. The building was visible from a mile away, it was a horrendous construction, a brown oppressive square high-rise block on stilts with steel windows, a giveaway to the age of the building when Lego architecture in the sixties was acceptable. As it was Sunday the building was deserted and the car park beneath the block was empty apart from one lonely car with a punctured wheel. The one that couldn't get away. The security booth was unoccupied, the barrier was up. No one cared if the entire thing was airlifted and brought to another planet, it was so ugly and desolate. Once inside, the building smelled of damp and vanilla air freshener. A reception desk dominated the small lobby with a desk so high I could just make out the tip of a back-combed bouffant hair-sprayed head. As I neared I discovered that what I'd thought was air freshener was actually perfume. She sat painting thick nails with blood-red varnish, layering it so thickly it was gloopy. She was watching *Columbo* on a small TV monitor on the desk.

'Just one more thing,' I could hear Columbo say.

'Here we go,' she chuckled, not looking at me but acknowledging me. 'He knows he did it already, you can tell.' It was the American-pie woman I'd spoken to on the phone. While Columbo asked the murderer for his autograph for his wife she finally turned to me. 'So what can I do you for?'

'We spoke on the phone this week, my name is Lucy Silchester and I have an appointment with Life.' I gave a high-pitched laugh.

'Oh yes, I remember now. Lucy Silchester. Did you call that carpet-cleaning company yet?'

'Oh . . . no, not yet.'

'Well, here you go, I can't recommend it no more than I already did.' She placed the business card on the desk and slid it toward me. I wasn't sure if she had brought it especially for me or if she was so enthusiastic about the company that she carried a suitcase of cards around with her to hand out to passers-by. 'You promise me you'll call now, won't you?'

Amused by her persistence, I agreed.

'I'll just let him know you're here.' She picked up the phone. 'Lucy's here to see you.' I strained my ear to hear his voice but I couldn't make anything out. 'Yes indeedy, I'll send her on up.' Then to me, 'Take the elevator and go up to the tenth floor. Take a right, then a left, you'll see him then.'

I made to leave then paused. 'What's he like?'

'Oh, don't you worry – you're not scared, are you?'

'No,' I waved my hand dismissively. 'Why would I be scared?' Then I gave that same laugh that told everyone within a five-mile radius that I was scared, and made my way to the elevator.

I had ten floors to prepare myself for my grand entrance. I fixed my hair, my posture, my lips all pursed in a sexy but I-didn't-know-it way; my stance was perfect, a few fingers of one hand tucked into my pocket. It all said exactly what I wanted to say about me but then the doors parted and I was faced with a ripped leather chair with a tattered women's magazine missing its cover and a wooden door in a wall of glass with uneven Roman blinds. When I went through the door I was faced with a room the size of a football pitch filled with a maze of cubicles separated by grey partition walls. Tiny desks, old computers, tattered chairs, photos of people's kids, dogs and cats pinned around the desks, personalised mouse pads, pens with pink furry things stuck on top, holiday photos as screen savers, birthday cards, random cuddly toys and multicoloured mugs that said things that weren't funny. All those things people do to make their squalid little square foot feel like home. It looked exactly like my own office and it immediately made me want to pretend to photocopy something to waste some time.

I made my way down the maze of desks, looking left and right wondering what on earth I'd find, trying to keep the same cool friendly look while inside I was frustrated that my big meeting with Life was in this shithole. And suddenly there he was. My life. Tucked behind a grotty desk, head down scribbling on a ratty notepad with a pen that by the looks of his constant scribbles on a pad, wouldn't work. He wore a wrinkled grey suit, a grey shirt and a grey tie with the triple spirals of life embossed on it. His hair was black and peppered with a little grey and was dishevelled, his face had a few days of stubble. He looked up, saw me, put down the pen, stood up, then wiped his hands on his suit leaving damp wrinkled marks. He had black rings around his eyes, his eyes were bloodshot, he sniffled and he looked like he hadn't slept for years.

'Are you . . .?' I did a little playful smiley thing.

'Yeah,' he said blandly. 'You're Lucy,' he held out his hand. 'Hi.'

I bounced over to him, long strides, pretending to be oh so excited by the moment. I reached out and shook his hand, gave him the biggest smile I could possibly muster, wanting to please him so much, wanting to prove to him that I was fine, that every-thing was absolutely fine. His handshake was limp. His skin was clammy. His hand quickly slid away from mine like a snake slithering out of my grasp.

'So,' I said, overenthusiastically, sitting down. 'We finally meet,' I said mysteriously, trying to catch his eye. 'How are you?' I could tell I sounded over the top. The room was too big, too empty, too bland, too depressing for my tone but I couldn't stop.

He looked at me. 'How do you think I am?'

He said it rudely. Very rudely, in fact. I was taken by surprise. I didn't know what to say. This wasn't how people spoke to each other. Where was the pretence that we liked each other, that we were both happy to be there, that we'd meet again? I looked around hoping that nobody was listening.

'There's no one here,' he said. 'No one works on Sundays. They have lives.'

I fought my instinct to snap back. 'But don't other people's lives work in this building too?'

'No.' He looked at me as though I were stupid. 'I just rent this space. I don't know what they do,' he referred to the empty desks.

Again, I was taken aback. This was not how it was supposed to go.

He rubbed his face tiredly. 'I didn't mean to come across as rude.'

'Well you did.'

'Well I'm sorry.' He said it without any amount of sincerity.

'No you're not.'

Silence.

'Look . . .' He leaned forward and I really didn't mean to, but I leaned back. He had bad breath. It was a bit of an awkward moment. He sighed, then continued, 'Imagine you had a friend who was there for you all the time and you were there for them, but they stopped being there for you as much as they used to which you can understand a little because people have things to do, but then they're around less and less no matter how much you try to reach out to them. Then suddenly one day – nothing – they're gone. Just like that. Then you write to them, and you're ignored and then you write to them again and you're ignored and finally you write to them again for a third time and they barely even want to make the appointment, they're so busy with their job, their friends and their car. How would you feel?'

'Look, I assume you're referring to me in that little hypothesis but it's ridiculous.' I laughed. 'Clearly it's not the same thing. I would never treat a friend that way.'

He gave a wry smile. 'But you would do that to your life.'

I opened my mouth but nothing came out.

'So let's just get started,' he said, pressing the power button on the computer.

Nothing happened. We sat in an awkward awful tense atmosphere while he became frustrated with the computer. He pressed the power button over and over again, tested the socket, unplugged it, plugged it in again.

'Just check the—'

'I don't need your help, thank you. Please take your hands off the—'

'Let me just—'

'Get your hands off the—'

'. . . twiddle the connection here—'

'I'd appreciate it if you'd just—'

'There.'

I sat back. The computer made a whirring noise.

He took a slow breath. 'Thank you.'

He didn't mean it.

'Where did you get that computer – 1980?'

'Yeah, about the same time as you got that jacket,' he said, eyes on the monitor.

'That's just childish.' I pulled my jacket in tighter around me. I folded my arms, crossed my legs, looked away. This was a nightmare, this was worse than I ever could have imagined. My life was an absolute bastard with a chip on his shoulder.

'What did you imagine this would be?' he asked, finally breaking the silence.

'I didn't know what this would be,' I said, still in a huff.

'But you must have imagined something.'

I shrugged, then thought of one of the images I'd had of me and Life in a canoe somewhere picturesque, him rowing, me reading from a book of poetry in a pretty sun hat and a Cavali dress I'd seen in a magazine that I couldn't afford – the magazine as well as the dress. I thought of me in a magazine doing my interview about Life with blow-dried hair, a full face of make-up, contact lenses, a draped asymmetric dress, good lighting. Maybe even a vase of lemons and limes beside me. I sighed and finally looked at him again. 'I thought it would be like a therapy session. You'd ask me about my job, my family, if I'm happy, that kind of thing.'

'Have you ever been to a therapy session?'

'No.'

He looked at me intensely.

I sighed. 'Yes. Once. When I quit my job. It was around the time I dumped my boyfriend and bought a new apartment.'

He didn't blink. 'You were fired. Your boyfriend left you and you're renting a studio flat.'

I gave him a weak smile. 'Just testing you.'

'It would help the whole process if you didn't lie to me.'

'They're not lies if the end result is the same.'

He lit up a little, if that was possible for him. He undimmed anyway.

'Tell me how that works.'

'Okay, so if I was to say that I won the lottery then that would be a barefaced lie because I'd clearly have no money but I would have to live my life as if I was a millionaire which would be complicated to say the least, but if I say I quit my job it doesn't matter because I no longer work there so I don't have to keep up the pretence of going there every day. If I say I bought a new apartment, it's not a lie because the fact is I don't live in the old one any more and I'm living in a new one.'

'And the last thing you said.'

'What thing?'

'About your boyfriend.'

'It's the same thing.' To my surprise, I struggled saying it because I knew he wanted me to say it. 'Saying that . . . I dumped him is the same thing as saying . . . you know . . . the other way around . . .'

'That he left you.'

'Well, yeah.'

'Because . . .'

'Because the outcome is still the same.'

'Which is . . .'

'That we're not together.' And on that note, my eyes filled up. I hated my eyes, the deceiving bastards. Mortified is not the word. I can't remember the last time I cried over Blake, I was so over him I couldn't even begin to explain it but it was like when someone asks you if there's something wrong over and over again, and usually after a while something is wrong – you're angry and you want to physically hurt them. The same thing was happening now, because he was making me say all those words, making me say them out loud in a method of trying to fool me into admitting something he thought I hadn't dealt with; it was as though it was working and I was feeling sad for that person that he thought I was. But I wasn't that person. I was fine. Everything was fine.

I wiped my eyes roughly before any tears fell. 'I'm not sad,' I said angrily.

'Okay.'

'I'm not.'

'Okay,' he shrugged. 'So tell me about your job.'

'I love my job,' I began. 'It gives me an enormous sense of satisfaction. I love working with people, the communication with the public, the innovative business environment. I feel like I'm doing something worthwhile, helping people, connecting with people, that I can direct them onto the right path, make sure that they are guided. Of course the enormous plus—'

'Sorry to interrupt you. Can we just clarify what it is that you do?'

'Yes.'

He looked down and read, 'You translate instruction manuals for your company?'

'Yes.'

'And this company makes fridges, cookers, ovens, that kind of thing.'

'Yes, they are the largest appliance-manufacturing firm in Europe.'

'Okay, carry on.'

'Thank you. Where was I? Of course, the enormous plus side to my work is the people I work with. They are the kind of people who inspire and motivate me to reach further and higher not just in my field of employment but in my life.'

'Okay.' He rubbed his forehead. It was flaky. 'These people that you work with are the people you refer to, in private, as Graham the Cock, Quentin aka Twitch, Louise the Nosy Bitch, Mary the Mouse, Steve the Sausage and Edna Fish Face.'

I kept a straight face. I was quite impressed by my imaginative nicknames. 'Yes.'

He sighed. 'Lucy, you're lying again, aren't you.'

'Not really. They do make me want to be a better person – better than *them*. They do make me want to reach further and higher in my office so that I can get *away from them*. See? Not a lie. Same outcome.'

He sat back and studied me, ran his hand across his stubble and I could hear the scratching sound.

'Okay you want to hear the absolute truth about that job or about any job?' I offered. 'Fine. Here it is. I'm not one of those people who lives and breathes their job, I don't take it so seriously that I want to stay longer than I'm paid for or want to socialise with the people I spend most of my waking hours with and would never choose to say more than two words to in the real world. I've stayed in that job for two and a half years because I like that gym membership is included, even if the gym equipment is crap and the room stinks to high heaven of smelly jockstraps, it saves me money on going elsewhere. I like that I get to use the languages I spent years finessing. I don't have many friends who speak German, Italian, French, Dutch and Spanish with me.' I tried to impress him with that.

'You don't speak Spanish.'

'Yes, I know that, killjoy, but my employers don't,' I snapped.

'What happens when they find out? Will you get fired – again – in a similar spectacular style?'

I ignored him and continued my spiel. 'I don't use the vomit word "passion" that I hear so many people use these days when they talk about their work, as if that alone will get you through the day. I do the job I'm paid to do. I'm not a workaholic.'

'You don't have the dedication.'

'Are you advocating workaholicism?'

'I'm just saying it takes a certain amount of consistency, you know, the ability to throw yourself wholly into something.'

'What about alcoholics? Do you admire them too? How about I become one of them and you can be proud of my consistency?'

'We've moved away from that analogy now,' he said, irritated. 'How about we just say straight out that you lack focus, consistency and dedication?'

That hurt. 'Give me an example.' I folded my arms.

He tapped a few keys on the keyboard, read for a while.

'Someone at work suffered a heart attack so you pretended to the paramedics that you were his next of kin so that you could go in the ambulance and leave work early.'

'It was a suspected heart attack and I was worried about him.'

'You told the ambulance driver to let you off at the end of your block.'

'The man had an anxiety attack, he was fine five minutes later.'

'You're half-assed, you waste time, you never finish anything that's not a bottle of wine or a bar of chocolate. You change your mind all of the time. You can't commit.'

Okay so that finally got to me. Partly because it was just rude but mostly because he was completely correct. 'I was in a relationship for five years, how is that a problem with commitment?'

'He left you three years ago.'

'So I'm taking time to be with myself. Get to know myself and all that crap.'

'Do you know yourself yet?'

'Of course. I like myself so much I'm planning to spend the rest of my life with me.'

He smiled. 'Or at least fifteen minutes more.'

I looked at the clock. 'We have forty-five minutes left.'

'You'll leave early. You always do.'

I swallowed. 'So?'

'So nothing. I was just pointing it out. Would you like some examples?' He tapped the keyboard before I had time to answer. 'Christmas dinner in your parents' house. You left before dessert. Didn't even make main course the year before, a new record.'

'I'd a party to go to.'

'Which you left early.'

My mouth fell open. 'Nobody even noticed.'

'Well, that's where you're wrong. Again. It was noted.'

'Noted by who?'

'By whom,' he corrected and pressed the down button over and over. I wanted to move to the edge of my seat but I didn't want to give him the satisfaction. I sat quietly looking around the office, pretending I didn't care. And because I was pretending I didn't care, I realised that meant I did.

Finally he stopped tapping.

My head whipped around to face him.

He smiled. Then he pressed the down button again.

'This is ridiculous.'

'I'm sorry, am I boring you?'

'Actually, yes.'

'Well, now you know how I feel.' He stopped tapping. 'Melanie.'

My best friend. 'What about her?'

'She was the girl who was peeved about your leaving early.'

'Nobody says "peeved".'

'Quote, "I wish for once she could just stay until the end." Unquote.'

I was a bit annoyed about that, I'm sure I could think of plenty of times I had stayed till the end.

'Her twenty-first,' he said.

'What about it?'

'The last time you stayed until the end of one of her parties. In fact, they couldn't get rid of you, could they? You slept overnight.'

Tap, tap, tap.

'With her cousin.'

Tap.

'Bobby.'

I groaned. 'She didn't care about that.'

Tap tap tap.

'Quote, "How could she do this to me on my birthday? My grandparents are here, everybody knows. I'm mortified." Unquote.'

'She didn't tell me that.'

He just shrugged.

'Why is this a big deal? Why are we talking about this?'

'Because they are.'

Tap tap tap.

'"I'm sorry she left, Mum, want me to go talk to her?" That's Riley, your brother.'

'Yeah, I get it.'

'"No, sweetheart, I'm sure she's got somewhere

62

more important to be." Unquote. You left your family lunch yesterday thirty-two minutes ahead of time in a rather dramatic fashion.'

'Yesterday was different.'

'Why was it different?'

'Because they betrayed me.'

'How did they do that?'

'By signing off on my life audit.'

He smiled, 'Now that's a good analogy. But if they hadn't, you wouldn't be here, with me.'

'Yes, and look how swell it's all going.'

Silence.

'So let's cut to the chase. This meeting is about me leaving dinners and parties early.' That wasn't so bad, I could deal with that, I would just explain why I left each event, where I was going afterwards. This whole thing could be over sooner than I thought.

He started laughing. 'Hell, no. I just got side-tracked.' He looked at his watch. 'We don't have much time to cover anything. Shall we arrange to meet again?'

'We've got thirty minutes left.'

'No more than five going by your usual exit strategy.'

'Get on with it,' I said.

'Okay.' He leaned forward. 'So what are you doing?'

'What do you mean, what am I doing? I'm sitting here, wasting my time talking to you, is what I'm doing.'

For the next part he didn't need notes, he just stared straight into me. 'You get up at seven a.m.

every morning except Saturdays and Sundays when you arise at one p.m.'

'So?'

'You have a nutrition bar from your corner cupboard, a cappuccino from Starbucks at the end of your block, you buy the newspaper, sometimes you drive, sometimes you take the train to work, you do the crossword. You arrive at work between nine and nine thirty, you don't get started on anything until ten. You take a cigarette and coffee break at eleven, even though you don't smoke but think it's unfair that smokers receive extra breaks. You take an hour lunch break at one p.m. You sit alone, you do the crossword. You are always late back to your desk. It takes you until two thirty to begin work again but for the afternoon you are diligent and complete your work. You finish at six p.m.'

'Why are you telling me things that I already know?' I spoke like I didn't care but in truth it was disturbing to listen to. It was disturbing to know that all the little things I did in secret were being noted by somebody, and being logged in a computer for some stressed-out office nerd to read like I was some sort of solitaire game.

'You go to the gym every day after work. You're supposed to jog for twenty minutes but always stop at seventeen, you work out for thirty minutes more. You sometimes meet friends for dinner, you would always rather be at home, you always leave early. You go to bed, you do the crossword. You get up at seven a.m.'

He left a silence.

'You see a theme emerging?'

'I'm prone to solving crosswords? So what? What's your point?'

He sat back then, studied me again with his tired unblinking eyes.

'No. What's yours?'

I swallowed a large dry lump that had formed in my throat. 'Well, that's very profound.'

'Not really. It's just a question. Okay, why don't I speak in a way that you understand. Here's what's going to happen. You're going to leave here in thirty minutes, exactly on time at the end of our meeting, then you're going to try to forget everything we've talked about. You will succeed. I will be reduced to an annoying frustrating little man who made you waste a few hours of your Sunday and you'll go back to living your life exactly the way you were.'

He stopped. I waited for more, but there wasn't anything. I was confused. He couldn't possibly believe that. Then I got it. 'That's a lie.'

'It's not a lie if the outcome is exactly the same.'

I didn't want to ask but I had to. 'And what's the outcome?'

'You'll be as alone and as bored and as unhappy as you were before you met me, but this time it will be worse because this time you'll know it. You'll know it every second of every day.'

And on that note, I grabbed my bag and left. With exactly thirty minutes to go, just like he'd said.

CHAPTER SIX

Silchesters don't cry. It was what my father had told me when I was five years old and I'd fallen off my bike after taking the stabilisers off for the first time. He had been beside me, guiding me along the driveway of our home, though he was further away than I'd have liked but I didn't want to tell him that because I knew he would be disappointed. Even at five I knew that. I didn't hurt myself, I was more in shock over the feel of the hard tarmac as my knee slammed down on it and as the bicycle got crushed between my legs. I'd held out my arms to him for help but in the end I got to my feet by myself under his instructions. I still remember his voice. *Move the bike away from your leg. Now stand up, don't make that noise, Lucy, stand up.* I'd stood up, hunched as though my leg needed amputation, until I was told to stand up straight. I'd wanted a hug but I didn't say so, knew that asking for and wanting one would be wrong in his eyes, but knowing in my heart that it wasn't. It was just the way he was and that's what I always understood. Even at five years old. Apart from the time Blake left me and when Life reminded me about it, I rarely cried and rarely felt the need to.

In the end it had all ended so quickly. We were together for five years, we had a sociable, fun, busy life together. We had talked about marriage and all of those things and while we weren't remotely ready to do any of them yet, the understanding was that we would eventually. To each other. When we grew up. But in the process of growing up, I lost him. Somewhere along the way. Not over one day, it happened gradually, he disappeared a little more and more every day. Not his presence, we were always together but I felt like *he* was going somewhere, even when we were in the same room. Then he sat me down and we had the chat. And that was it. Well, the chat came after an important conversation.

He'd just signed the deal to do his new travel show at that time so he'd started travelling on his own, I suppose it was kind of practice, or that's what I thought it had been at the time but maybe it was something more. Maybe he was searching for something he just couldn't find in our converted bread-factory apartment. Sometimes now I think he was seeing somebody else but I have absolutely no reason other than paranoia to back that up. He had been on a trip to Finland and when he returned you'd swear he'd just walked on the moon or had a religious experience. He wouldn't stop talking about the calm, the quiet, the peace, how much he was at one with whatever the hell else could survive in minus forty degrees. He kept telling me how I had no idea, I couldn't possibly understand what he was talking about. I told him I could understand. I understood the calmness, the clarity, the contentment in life when you have that perfect moment. Yes I did, I understood. I didn't use the same words when he was describing it, my eyes didn't light up to a pure icy blue as if I was seeing the gates of heaven, but yes I understood those feelings.

'Lucy, you don't understand, believe me *you* do not understand.'

'What do you mean, "*you*" do not understand? What's so different about me to other people that I couldn't possibly understand what it's like to have a moment of fucking contentment? You don't have to go to Kathmandu to find inner peace, you know, some of us have it right here in the city. In a bubble bath. With a book. And a glass of wine.'

And then followed the chat. Not immediately after, it may have been a few days, it may have been a few weeks. But whatever it was, it was afterwards. It had given me enough time to digest that he felt I was a different type of person from him, one who didn't understand the depths of him. I had never felt that before. I had always known we were different, but I didn't know that he knew that. It sounds like a small detail but actually when really thought about, it became everything.

When I travelled, I travelled to see new places; when he travelled, he travelled to find new parts of himself. I guess when you're trying to find all the parts of yourself, it's difficult to be with someone who's already fully intact.

Then here's where we did a stupid thing, and he walked me into a scenario that I wish I could change every day of my life. Obviously, I was upset. I was very upset, I was so upset I turned to religion – the Silchester religion of worrying about what *People* would think. He told me that if it made me feel any better we could tell people that I left him. Now, in my current reasonable-ish state I don't know why I would have agreed to that. But I did. It helped me after the break-up, it gave me a strength that I needed while having those conversations with friends and family so I could say, 'It just wasn't working, I had to leave him.' Because when I said that, there were fewer questions. If I'd told them he left me, there would be endless amounts of pity, of trying to figure it all out on my behalf, what I did wrong, how was it my fault, then them being afraid to talk about it when they met him or saw him with a new girlfriend. My dumping him was to make everything easier. Only it wasn't easier because he had left me and I had to listen to every little thing about him and pretend it didn't hurt, and then see him on his TV show and pretend it didn't hurt and whenever I got angry at him I had to listen to how I had no reason to be angry and how hurt he might be, the poor thing, and I was trapped in this big fat lie.

Because I ended up carrying around this big secret that nobody knew about, this big ball of hurt that had turned to anger, which often turned to pity, then loneliness because I never had those necessary conversations to help me get over it properly, I felt alone in my secret reality. So in the initial stages I carried that hurt and anger and pity around with me and due to circumstances I may reveal at a later date, got fired from my respectable job that paid well, but to be able to tell people why I got fired I'd have to tell them *why* I got fired and I couldn't do that because after so much time it would just frankly be weird to admit a lie of that magnitude, so I told everyone I quit and then the rest of my life fell into its own new place following a bunch of big fat lies. And they were big fat lies no matter how much the outcome was still the same.

That is all that I will admit to because, as it turned out, I felt happy with how my life had settled. If Life had tried to meet with me two years ago, I would have understood, because I felt like I was falling but not now, not any more. I'd fallen from a great height and was wedged into what some may assume was a rather precarious place that could easily snap and break and send me falling again, but I was very happy, cosy even, and everything was fine, absolutely fine.

When I reached the lobby of the depressing Lego building, American Pie was gone. I left the chocolate bar I'd brought for her on the counter, the one she said she liked when we spoke on the phone, and exited the building and tried to forget about the frustrating little man who wasted a few hours of my Sunday. But I couldn't. That frustrating little man represented my life and for once I just couldn't forget it. Right in that moment I had no distractions to take my mind off it – no car to fix, no email to send, no paperwork to fax, no family member to call, no friend's problem to delve into – and I was experiencing a mild feeling of anxiety. My life had just told me that I was going to be alone and miserable. I don't know what you're supposed to do with that information, I really don't. He didn't tell me how I could not be alone and miserable and all I wanted to do was fight the reality, like patients who have received news of an illness and feel in denial about it, because you might be diagnosed but you still don't feel the symptoms. I saw a café at the next corner and found the solution. I like coffee, it makes me happy in the small way that things you like can lift you, so I figured a café would mean I was in company, and the coffee would mean I was with something that made me happy. No more alone and miserable. Inside was full, with the exception of one small table. I squeezed by the tables, chatter loud in the air. I was happy about that, other voices would take my mind off my own. I ordered a coffee and sat back, satisfied that I could eavesdrop on other people's conversations. I needed to stop thinking about it. My life was fine, absolutely fine. I was a single woman with a job who was happy, I needed a distraction. Any kind of distraction. The café door opened, the bell rang and half the café automatically looked up. Then the straight males went back to their conversations and the remainder continued gawking because in walked the most beautiful man I had ever seen in the flesh. He scanned the café and then headed in my direction.

'Hi,' gorgeous man smiled, resting his hands on the chair opposite me. 'Are you alone?'

'Excuse me?'

'Is anybody sitting here? The café's full, do you mind if I join you?'

There was actually a free seat behind me but I wasn't going to point that out. The man had a beautiful face, perfectly proportioned nose and lips and eyes and a jawline you could grate cheese on. I thought about my family signing off on Life's intervention, I just couldn't figure it out; why on earth Life had come to me, there were plenty of people who were unhappy after relationships ended, surely this wasn't an emergency case. I had moved on, I was living my life. I wasn't afraid to meet new people. I wasn't stuck in the past. What did they think was wrong with me?

'No problem,' I said, then drained my cup as he sat down. 'In fact, you can have the table to yourself, I'm just leaving to see my boyfriend.'

He looked disappointed but nodded his thanks.

Okay, I lied.

But in only a few hours from then, the outcome would be the same.

CHAPTER SEVEN

'We were up at four thirty this morning,' he panted, beads of sweat trickling down the sides of his face and getting lost in his suntanned stubble-lined jaw. 'The trail from the hostel to Machu Picchu has taken about one and a half hours. We were told to wake up that early so that we could leave Wiñay Wayna by five thirty to get to Machu Picchu before sunrise.' He was wearing a navy blue T-shirt, the sleeves were tight around his biceps, sweat marks were on his chest, on his back, under his arms. He wore beige combat shorts and walking boots, his legs were tanned and muscular like the rest of his body. There was a long shot of him walking the trail and I paused the TV.

Mr Pan jumped onto the couch beside me. 'Hi, Mary.'

He purred.

'He's doing the Inca Trail today. We were supposed to do that one together. Let's see who else he's doing it with now . . .' I studied the girls in the long shot. She wasn't there. I pressed play again.

'As you can see the trail contours around this mountainside and drops into cloud forest before coming to an almost vertical flight of fifty steps leading up to the final pass at Intipunku, which means Sun Gate.' Lots of shots of him panting, shots of scenery, close-ups on him, his walking shoes, his rucksack, the back of his head and the view before him, the reflection in his sunglasses. All of them were new, nothing I'd bought him. 'And here we are,' he smiled at the camera, big white perfect teeth. He looked off into the distance, took off his glasses to reveal his beautiful eyes and his face changed. 'Wow.'

I paused it on his face. Studied him and smiled. Knew that it was for real, that it hadn't been filmed twenty times already for his best look, knew that he was in heaven right there, right then and in a funny way I felt like I was experiencing it with him. Just like we used to do together, years ago. The camera panned and then I could see what he could see, the whole of Machu Picchu spread out before us.

'There it is, Machu Picchu in all its glory. A fantastic sight. Beautiful,' he said, taking it all in. There was a wider shot of him assessing the view. I paused the TV again and studied the girls around him. She wasn't there. I pressed play again. It cut to later, he had wiped the sweat from his face, had changed his T-shirt to a fresher version of the same one, was sitting down and looked rested, had caught his breath for the final wrap-up scene. He gave his little summary of his journey and then, 'Remember that happiness is a way of travel, it's not a destination.' Then he smiled, those teeth, those eyes, that hair, those arms and hands – I remember them all around me, sleeping beside me, showering with me, cooking for me, touching me, kissing me. Dumping me. 'Wish you were here,' he said with a wink, and he was gone and the credits took the place of his face.

'Me too,' I whispered. I swallowed a hard dry lump of nothing that had stuck in my throat. Had that awful sick feeling in my stomach, and the pain in my heart that came when the credits finished and it hit me that he was gone. I waited for the initial pain to go and then I paused the credits and searched. Her name was still there. I used my laptop to go on Facebook and check her status. Single.

I was psychotic and I knew it but I also knew that most of the time my paranoia was correct, and that most of the time it wasn't paranoia, it was gut instinct and most of the time that was correct. But it had been almost three years and they hadn't, by the looks of it, gotten together. I didn't even know how present she'd be in his life as a production assistant; I didn't know how TV shows worked, but when he'd first signed the deal to do the show we went to meet with the team. I'd met her and I got a feeling about her. That was all, one of those girlfriend feelings that you get about other girls. Then when we broke up I got a huge feeling about her, and those feelings had manifested into something so massive it was bordering on obsessive. But I couldn't help it. Her name was Jenna. Jenna was a bitch. And every time I heard the name Jenna I thought of her and immediately hated the poor unrelated person named Jenna. She was from Australia and I hated everyone from Australia. It was a very weird thing that had taken over me, I didn't even know her and I'd previously liked Australia, but I'd created this persona around her, this dislike for her and her country and anything, however minuscule, that I knew about her.

Just to taunt myself I imagined them having sex on the top of the mountain as soon as the camera was turned off and I wondered who he'd camped out with all those nights in that tiny little tent, in those close overcrowded little hostels. All of the environments he was in were too close for him to share with another woman, especially Jenna, especially the character that had grown in my mind. She would crawl into his tent in the dead of night and reveal her naked self to him, he would try to fight his urges but he wouldn't be able to because he was a man and he was all pumped up from the walk up the mountain, and being in touch with nature made him even hornier. Every time I watched an episode, I pictured them together. I didn't even know what a production assistant did but I Googled it to find out. I didn't know if she was a set PA or an office PA; a big difference because it either meant she was with him all the time or their paths rarely crossed. Occasionally I looked through the other names on the credits to make sure someone else hadn't slipped in that could also be sleeping with him on location, but I had investigated them through the power of Google and surmised that Jenna, the bitch from Australia, was the only woman he would go for.

My mobile rang, and took me out of my latest daydream. It was Riley again. Since lunch the previous day I had had nine missed calls from Riley and two from Mum. Silchesters didn't ignore people, make a drama or cause a fuss, so I had texted them both that I was unavailable to speak and that I'd call them back as soon as I could. It wasn't a lie. I just didn't know how to be with them. I couldn't be angry with them because as concerned family members they were only trying to help, but I couldn't entertain mindless chit-chat because I was genuinely hurt, flabbergasted even, that they felt I was in such dire need of help that they couldn't come directly to me to tell me. I had always done my best not to reveal anything about myself to my family, even to Riley. Despite him being my accomplice during family gatherings, he was not my best friend; he was my brother and there were things that brothers didn't need or want to know.

I ignored the call and as soon as it stopped I immediately sent a polite text about how I was currently out with friends. He texted back straight away.

—Then u left ur tv on cos I'm outside ur door.

I leaped up, Mr Pan did too but he didn't follow me. His courage always gave out when we got to the bathroom door. He nipped in there to defend me from behind the wash basket.

'Riley?' I called through the door.

'Yes.'

I sighed. 'You can't come in.'

'Okay. Can you come out?'

I unlocked the door, barely opened it so he couldn't see inside and slid out to him. He tried to look in. I closed the door.

'Have you got company?'

'Yes. A hot naked man with a large erection is lying on my bed waiting for me, if you want to come in.'

'Lucy.' He had a pained expression.

'I'm only joking.'

'So there's no one there?'

'No, there is.' It wasn't a lie. Mr Pan was waiting for me.

'Sorry. Is it . . . you know?'

'Life? No. I met him in his office earlier today.'

'Him?'

'Yeah.'

'Weird.'

'Yeah.'

'How did it go?'

'Yeah, good. He was nice, just wanted to check in and have a chat, that kind of thing, I probably won't have to meet him again.'

'Really?'

'Don't sound so surprised,' I snapped.

78

'Okay.' He shifted his weight to his other foot. 'So everything's okay?'

'Yeah, he was a bit confused as to why he had to meet me at all really.'

'Really?'

'Yeah, it's just like one of those random breath tests only it's a random life test. They picked me completely at random, unfortunately for me.'

'Oh. Okay . . .'

I let the silence hang.

'Well, I'm here because I found these.' He took a pair of shoes out from behind his back. 'I'm checking around the kingdom to see who they fit.'

I smiled.

'May I?' He got down on bended knee, lifted my foot, saw I had odd socks on and visibly tried hard not to comment. He removed my sock and slid my foot into the shoe. He looked at me in mock surprise.

'Now do we live incestuously ever after?' I asked.

He frowned, then leaned against the door frame and stared at me.

'What?'

'Nothing.'

'What, Riley? You didn't just come here to give me my shoes.'

'Nothing,' he repeated. 'Just . . .' He looked like he was going to say something serious. 'It's just that I met someone who used to work with you a few years ago in Quinn and Downing and he just said a few things to me . . .' He studied me. I tried to look confused, not fearful as I felt, and he changed tack. 'Anyway, he was probably wrong.' He cleared his throat.

'Who was it?' I asked coolly.

'Gavin Lisadel.' He studied me intensely some more.

I rolled my eyes. 'The biggest drama queen I've ever worked for.' In truth a perfectly reputable guy. 'I've heard he's coming out with all kinds of weird stories about me. Don't worry, whatever it is, it's a lie. I heard he's been cheating on his wife with a man for years, so you know . . .' He was a happily married family man as far as I knew. I had just destroyed Gavin's perfect image in less than one minute but I didn't care, he had destroyed mine too, not that it had ever been perfect and even if he had, he probably wasn't lying. Then I felt bad about what I'd said so I added quickly, 'But everyone really likes him and he's really good at his job.'

Riley nodded, still not convinced but he changed the mood. 'I still can't believe you said Father wasn't the breastfed kind.' He started laughing, then threw his head back and laughed even louder.

Eventually I joined in. 'Well? Do you think she'd have bothered? Old wrinkly tits?'

He shook his head, disgusted by the thought.

The door opposite me opened and a friendly apologetic face popped out. 'Hi, Lucy, I'm really sorry, do you mind keeping it down a little? I've just— oh hi,' she said, noticing Riley.

'Sorry,' Riley apologised. 'I'm just leaving.'

'No, it's rude of me to ask, it's just that I've

got . . .' She pointed her thumb back into the apartment but didn't say anything. 'You look so alike. Are you Lucy's brother?' she asked, studying him.

'I am. Riley.' He reached out his hand and they shook, which was weird because I couldn't even remember my neighbour's name; I'd forgotten it the moment we met and it seemed rude as the time went by to ask so I just never addressed her, there was a lot of *hey* and *hi* and *hello you* and I had a strong suspicion it was Ruth but I'd never had the full confidence to go for it.

'I'm Claire.'

And it was just as well.

'Hi, Claire.'

Riley was giving her one of his best cute but sweet but strong and masculine, you-can-trust-me, flirtatious looks, which freaked me out but Claire wasn't completely delusional, she untangled herself from his web of silent promises, and quickly said her goodbyes.

'Must be losing your touch, Riley.'

He looked at me, serious again.

'Don't worry, it happens to us all.'

'No, not that . . .'

'What, Riley?'

'Nothing.' He aborted the thought, and made his way to the elevator.

'Thanks for the shoes,' I said more gently.

He didn't turn around, just lifted his arm up in a salute and disappeared into the elevator. Just before I closed my door I heard my neighbour – whose name I'd already forgotten – open her door and quickly say, 'If you ever want to come in for a coffee or anything, just come straight over. No notice needed, I'm always here.'

'Oh. Okay.' It felt awkward. It had been at least a year since I'd met her and apart from the chat in the elevator it was the longest sentence either of us had ever said to one another. She used to never speak when I saw her. Probably spending all that time cooped up inside had made her desperate to talk to anyone, including me.

'Thanks. Eh . . . likewise.' Then I couldn't think of anything to say so I closed the door.

Only I never wanted her to call over for a coffee and I never wanted Riley to come into the apartment. He'd never been in before, none of my family had. None of my friends had either. It was my space. But it was becoming an eyesore even to me. The carpet had to be cleaned. I would clean it myself without telling the landlord because I didn't want him checking it and seeing the burns and then charging me for the damage. I searched for where I'd written the company name on the carpet and grabbed the phone and quickly dialled directory enquiries before I changed my mind. I knew something monumental was happening. I was doing something that needed to be done and I felt the burden of it every step of the way. As they connected me and the phone rang, I began to think of hanging up. It wasn't just the phone call; it was having to follow through that bothered me. I'd have to stay in from work one day,

I'd have to wait for some stranger to arrive hours after he'd promised and then I'd have to show him all the personal private stains that I wanted removed. How humiliating. It rang and rang, and then it sounded like it was about to be answered or go to an answer phone when it went through another bout of ringing. I was about to hang up and abort the situation when a man answered.

'Hello?'

It was noisy. Pub noisy. I had to move the phone away from my ear.

'Sorry, just be a minute,' the voice shouted and I wanted to shout back that it was okay, that I'd got the wrong number, partly because I'd changed my mind – I didn't want the hassle of a stranger in my home – and partly because I was beginning to think I had genuinely been connected to the wrong number. I searched for the business card I'd been given by American Pie to see if it matched the number on my screen. But the phone wasn't by his ear to hear me explain, it was being rubbed against his body or dozens of other bodies as he made his way to somewhere quieter.

'Just a minute,' he shouted again.

'Actually it's okay,' I yelled despite being in a silent room. But he was gone again.

Finally there was silence, I could hear footsteps, then laughter in the distance, then, 'Hello? Are you still there?'

I fell back on the couch. 'Yes, hi.'

'Sorry about that, who's this?'

'Em, actually this is going to annoy you seeing all you had to do to get outside but I think I've got the wrong number.'

'After all that,' he laughed.

'Yep, sorry.' I climbed over the back of the couch and was in the kitchen. I looked in the fridge. Nothing to eat as usual.

He went quiet, then I heard a match and he inhaled. 'Sorry, bad habit. My sister said if I took up smoking I'd meet someone.'

'I pretend I'm a smoker at work to get more breaks.' I was surprised I'd said it out loud.

'What if they find you not smoking?'

'If someone's there, then I smoke.'

He laughed. 'That's a long way to go for a break.'

'I'll do anything for a break.'

'Like talk to wrong numbers?'

'Something like that.'

'Want to tell me your name or does that break the wrong-number code of ethics?'

'I've no problem at all telling a complete stranger my name. It's Gertrude.'

'That's a lovely name, Gertrude.' I could hear the smile in his voice.

'Why, thank you.'

'I'm Giuseppe.'

'Nice to meet you, Giuseppe. How's Pinocchio doing?'

'Ah, you know, telling fibs and bragging about being unattached.'

'He's always at it.' Then I realised that despite it being more comfortable than a phone conversation with my own father, this was weird. 'Well, I'd better let you get back to the pub.'

'Actually I'm at an Aslan gig.'

'I love Aslan.'

'We're in Vicar Street, you should come.'

'Who's "we"?'

'Me and Tom.'

'Well, I would go but Tom and I had a falling-out and it would just be awkward if I showed up.'

'Even if he apologised?'

'Believe me, he'll never apologise.'

'Tom's always putting his foot in his mouth, just ignore him. I have a spare ticket, I can leave it for you at the ticket desk.'

His familiarity intrigued me. 'I could be a toothless married woman with ten kids and an eye patch.'

'Christ, are you a woman?'

I laughed.

'So are you coming?'

'Do you always ask wrong numbers out?'

'Sometimes.'

'Do they ever say yes?'

'Once, and I got a toothless married woman with ten kids and an eye patch.'

'Have they sung "Down on Me"?'

'They haven't started yet. Is that your favourite?'

'Yep.' I opened the freezer. Chicken curry or cottage pie. The chicken curry was a week out of date; the cottage pie would be out of date tomorrow.

I reached for the chicken curry and stabbed the film with a fork.

'Have you ever heard them live?'

'No, but it's on my list of things to do.'

'What else is on your list?'

'Eat dinner.'

'You aim high, I like it. Want to tell me your real name now?'

'Nope. Want to tell me yours?'

'Don.'

'Don what?'

'Lockwood.'

My heart did a funny thing. I froze. Mr Pan noticed my mood change and jumped up and looked around for what he needed to defend me against, or hide from.

'Hello?' he said. 'Are you still there?'

'Did you say Don Lockwood?' I asked slowly.

'Yes, why?'

I gasped. 'Are you joking?'

'Nope. Born and bred. Actually that's a lie, they called me Jacinta, then they found out I was a boy. It's much easier to tell the difference now, I assure you. Why, is this not a wrong number after all?'

I was pacing the kitchen, no longer interested in my chicken curry. I didn't believe in signs because I couldn't sign read but it was just an unbelievably exciting coincidence. 'Don Lockwood . . . wait for it . . . is the name of Gene Kelly's character in *Singin' in the Rain*.'

'I see.'

'Yes.'

'And you are a fan of either Gene Kelly and/or of this movie so this is very exciting news to you.'

'Only the biggest.' I laughed. 'Don't tell me no one's ever said that to you before.'

'I can safely say, no one under the age of eighty-five has ever said it to me before.'

'Not even any of your wrong numbers?'

'Not even them.'

'How old are you?' I asked, suddenly afraid I was having a conversation with a fifteen-year-old and that the police were on their way.

'I'm thirty-five and three-quarters.'

'I can't believe in all of your thirty-five and three-quarters years no one has ever said that to you before.'

'Because most of the people I meet aren't one hundred years old like you.'

'I'm not going to be one hundred for at least two weeks.'

'Ah. I see. Thirty? Forty? Fifty?'

'Thirty.'

'It's all downhill from there, believe me.'

And he went silent, and I went silent and then it wasn't natural any more and we were just two strangers on a wrong number who both wanted to hang up.

I got in there first. 'It was nice talking to you, Don. Thanks for the offer of the ticket.'

'Bye, toothless married woman,' he said and we both laughed. I hung up and caught a glimpse of myself in the bathroom mirror and I looked like my mother, just a face full of a smile. It faded fast at the realisation that I'd just spoken to an absolute stranger on the phone. Maybe they were right, maybe I was losing it. I went to bed early and at twelve thirty my phone rang, waking me in fright. I looked at the number flashing and didn't recognise it, so I ignored it and waited for it to stop so I could go back to sleep. A few seconds later the phone rang again. I answered it, hoping it wasn't bad news. All I could hear was noise, screams and shouts. I moved it away from my ear, then heard the music, then heard the singing, then recognised the song. He was calling me, Don Lockwood was calling me, so I could hear my favourite song.

'*If you think your life's a waste of time, if you think your time's a waste of life, come over to this land, take a look around. Is this a tragic situation, or a massive demonstration, where do we hide?*'

I lay back on the bed and listened to the song, then when it was finished, I stayed on the line to speak to him. As soon as the next song started, he hung up.

I smiled. Then texted him.

—*Thanks.*

He texted back straight away.

—*One less thing on your list. Nite.*

I stared at those words for a long time then added his number into my phone. Don Lockwood. Just seeing it there made me smile.

CHAPTER EIGHT

A week later I awoke at seven a.m. in a stinker of a mood. I do believe that's the technical term for it. I hadn't been asleep for a week; it's just the amount of time that passed until anything of note happened in my life. I knew I was in a bad mood as soon as I opened my eyes and realised that the apartment reeked of the prawn cocktail that I'd left out on the counter. I felt irritation to the very core of me; like that damp cold that goes right to the bone and is impossible to shake off. I also think that my body had sensed that a new envelope had arrived on the burned carpet even before I'd found it. I could tell it had recently been left there because it hadn't been peed on and it had landed on top of the little pink marie-rose paw prints from when Mr Pan had knocked over the prawn cocktail and walked it around the carpet.

I had received a letter every day since I'd met Life the previous Sunday. I had ignored all of them and nothing was going to change this Monday. I stepped over the envelope like a child whose only power is to exercise authority on a dolly. Mr Pan must have known what he'd done and sensed my mood because he stayed clear of me. I showered, pulled a dress down from the curtain pole and was ready in minutes. I gave Mr Pan his breakfast, ignored the letter for the second week running and left the apartment.

'Morning, Lucy,' my neighbour said, opening the door as I stepped outside. I was suspicious of her timing; if I didn't know any better I'd have guessed she had been standing at her door waiting for me.

'Morning,' I said and searched my irritated brain for her name but there was no room for information, only frustration. I turned my back on her and locked the door.

'Do you mind if I ask a favour?' Her voice sounded shaky and I immediately turned around. Her eyes were red and swollen as if she'd been crying all night. I felt myself soften as my bad mood took time out. 'Would you mind leaving this at security for me? I've organised a courier to collect it but they said they wouldn't come upstairs. He's sleeping so I couldn't leave him . . .'

'Of course, no problem.' I took the sports bag from her.

She wiped her eyes, and said thanks but her voice had given up on her and it came out as a whisper.

90

'Are you okay?'

'Yes, thanks, I just . . . em . . .' That shaky voice again while she tried to compose herself. She straightened her back and cleared her throat, tried to maintain some kind of dignity but her eyes kept filling up and she fought hard to control them. 'My mother was taken to hospital yesterday. It's not looking very good.'

'I'm so sorry to hear that.'

She waved a hand dismissively to hide her embarrassment, tried to compose herself. 'There are just a few things that I thought she'd need in there. I mean, what do you give a person who . . .' She finished the sentence in her head.

'They won't let you visit?'

'Oh, they will. I just can't get in to her because . . .' She looked back into the apartment to her baby.

'Oh.' I knew what I was supposed to say next but I wasn't sure if I wanted to, wasn't sure if it was right. I spoke reluctantly, 'I could babysit for you, if you want. For . . .' I didn't know whether to say him or her, 'the baby.'

'Yes. Conor.' She cleared her throat again. 'It's very kind of you to offer but I don't really like leaving him . . .'

'I completely understand,' I jumped in, relieved. 'I'll leave these at the desk for you.'

She whispered her thanks again. I was at the elevator when she raised her voice down the hall. 'Lucy, if I change my mind, and do need you, if

91

it's, you know, an emergency, how will I contact you?'

'Oh. Well. You could wait till I get back at around sevenish or . . .' I didn't want to do it, I didn't want to give her my mobile. I knew it would lead to general annoyance down the line. 'You could email me . . .' I looked at her face, so distraught but hopeful. Her mother was possibly dying and I was telling her to email me. 'Or you could call me.' Her shoulders seemed to relax. I gave her my number and got out of there. I got a cappuccino from Starbucks at the end of my block; I bought a newspaper and had to miss seeing cute guy on the train in order to drive Sebastian to work. I had to bring him to the garage again that day and I was already dreading the bill. I used my ID card to get in through the turnstiles at the entrance to my office building. Mantic was outside the city in a new commercial outlet with architecture that looked like an extraterrestrial spaceship landing. Ten years ago they had moved the factory to Ireland and merged the offices together in a clever manoeuvre to increase productivity, and since moving here and paying extortionate rents, their profits had decreased and they'd had to lose one hundred employees from the twelve-hundred-strong company. Mantic was Greek for having prophetic and divine powers, which was ironic really, seeing all the trouble they were in, but no one was laughing at the joke. It seemed that, for the time being anyway, things had settled and we were assured that we were safe but most felt delicate after the shock of losing so many before. We were still surrounded by the empty desks and chairs of those who had already gone and though we held sympathy for the people who had lost their jobs, we had also enjoyed finding better-positioned desks and more comfortable seats.

I had been surprised I wasn't one of the first to go. I worked as a translator in the instruction-manual section, which was now a team of six people. Translating instruction manuals for the company's appliances into German, French, Spanish, Dutch and Italian may seem like an easy enough task and it was, only I didn't speak Spanish, or I did, but not very well and so I outsourced that part of the job to a contact I had who spoke very good Spanish, in fact perfect Spanish because she was in fact from Madrid. She didn't mind doing it and it was nothing that the gift of a bottle of poitín at Christmas didn't sort. It had worked for me so far; however my contact was often lazy and slow and left me on tenterhooks by delivering the translations at the eleventh hour. I had received a first degree in business and languages and a masters in international business. I'd spent a year working in Milan, a year in Germany and I'd done my masters in a Paris business school; I'd taken night classes to learn Dutch as a kind of a personal project but it was on a friend's hen night in Madrid where I'd met the woman who would become my Spanish alibi. Despite my not having studied law like my father and Riley or medicine like Philip I think my father was marginally proud of my university accomplishments and my knowledge of languages, until I moved to this job and whatever little delight he had for me went out the window.

The first person in the office I met every morning was Nosy Bitch, but who was christened Louise by her parents. I shall name her Nosy in the interest of taste. She was the administrator, was getting married in twelve months' time and had been planning her big day ever since Day One in the womb. When Fish Face, the boss, wasn't around, she flicked through magazines and ripped out pictures to create mood boards of her perfect day. Not that I was a woman of absolute substance but I liked to think I possessed at least some and I was tired of her incessant chat about all things cosmetic, which would have been the same choices regardless of the man she married. Her inquiry into other people's "special day" was endless. She wasn't so much a magpie for information as a piranha because she devoured every word as soon as it was spoken. Conversations with her were interviews and I knew every question was designed to suit her making a decision about her own life but never out of courtesy to ask about mine. She would turn her nose up at things she didn't like, and when she heard something that she found pleasing she would barely listen to the end of the sentence before scurrying back to her desk to document her new findings. I disliked her quite intensely and the fact that she wore tight T-shirts, with ridiculous logos, that failed to cover her love handles continued to annoy me more and more every day. It was the minutiae of any person that watered the seeds of dislike, though on the contrary the things I hated most about Blake, like his teeth grinding in his sleep, ended up being the very things I missed most about him. I wondered if Jenna the bitch minded his teeth grinding.

Today Nosy wore a blazer over a black T-shirt, which had a picture of Shakespeare and beneath read *Prose before Hos*. Sometimes I wondered if she even understood what they meant.

'Good morning, Lucy.'

'Morning, Louise.' I smiled at her and waited for random question number one of the day.

'Have you ever been to Egypt?'

I'd been there with Blake. We'd done the whole shebang: ridden camels in the Sahara, sat with the pharaohs, dived in the Red Sea, cruised the Nile. However, Nosy was asking for purely selfish purposes, not so she could float with me in my wonderful memory bubbles. 'No, sorry,' I said, and the hope on her face diminished. I went straight to my desk, threw my cappuccino cup in the bin, hung my coat up and headed off to make a fresh coffee. The rest of the team was squished inside the galley kitchen.

'What's this? A secret meeting?'

'Good morning, princess,' Graham the Cock greeted me. 'Coffee?'

'It's okay, I'll make it.' I squeezed past him to get to the kettle. He leaned out from the counter a little so I had to rub against his crotch. I considered kneeing him. Graham was the office cock who had watched one too many episodes of *Mad Men* and was on the lookout for an office affair. Married with children, of course, he slicked back his hair in a greasy quiff in an effort to emulate his Madison Avenue advertising allies and wore so much aftershave you could tell that he'd arrived by the sweet stench that lingered in the air. I didn't feel one bit complimented by his smarmy advances; I might have, if I'd wanted to spend a night with Pepé Le Pew and if his advances weren't directed at every woman who so much as walked within a mile of his pong. To give him some credit, he might once upon a time have been attractive if his venture into a lifetime of commitment with the same human being who wanted to share everything with him including his soul, yet who would never understand the real him, hadn't killed his internal spark.

I filled the kettle with water.

'Did you hear?' Mary the Mouse said in her voice that always seemed to be a decibel under a normal speaking tone. Mary's eyes were almost twice the size of her head, an amazing miracle of nature. Her nose and lips were dots on her face, hence the nickname Mouse.

'Hear what?'

'Now, now, we don't want to scare Lucy, she's

just walked in the door.' That was Quentin, named Twitch because of his habit of blinking both eyes twice in twenty-second intervals which increased in meetings or when he was addressing a crowd. He was a nice man, if not a little boring, and I had no problems with him. He did the graphics for the manuals so he and I worked closely together.

'We're having a meeting in Edna's office this morning,' Mouse said, her little face still and her big eyes moving around like a frightened rodent.

'Who told you that?'

'Louise heard it from Brian in Marketing. Everybody's section is having a meeting.'

'Brian Murphy or Bryan Kelly?' Steve the Sausage asked.

Explaining Steve's nickname was simple. Steve, bless him, looked like a sausage.

'What's the difference?' Mouse asked, eyes wide.

'Brian Murphy spells Brian with an *i* and Bryan Kelly spells Bryan with a *y*,' I said, knowing full well that's not what she meant. I felt Cock's breath on my neck as he laughed to himself and I was pleased. I was a laughter whore, I'd take it from anyone.

'No, I mean why does it matter who told us?' she asked timidly.

'Because Brian Murphy is full of shit, and Bryan Kelly isn't,' Cock explained.

'I've always found both of them to be reputable men,' Twitch said respectfully.

Mouse pulled open the door. 'Louise?'

Nosy joined us in the already crammed kitchen. 'What's going on?'

'Was it Brian Murphy or Bryan Kelly who told you about the meeting?'

'What does it matter?'

'Because Bryan Kelly is full of shit,' I said, deliberately mixing it up. Cock smiled again, the only one who noticed.

'And apparently Brian Murphy isn't,' Mouse said. 'So who said it?'

'Which guy is Brian Murphy?' Nosy asked. 'Is he the redhead or the one with the bald patch?'

I rolled my eyes, made my coffee as quickly as possible and pushed my way through the group. 'Either way it means more cuts, doesn't it,' I said to no one in particular. And no one in particular answered. Everyone just stared into the distance and retreated to their minds, thinking about the personal dangers ahead.

'I'm sure everything is going to be fine,' Twitch said. 'Let's not all worry.'

But they already were, so I returned to my desk to do my crossword and left them all at it.

Commonplace, lacking originality or wit.

I looked around.

Banal.

When I heard the office door open, I hid the crossword under some paperwork and pretended to concentrate on new manuals as Fish Face tottered by, the smell of leather and perfume following after her. Edna Larson was the boss of our section and looked very much like a fish. Her forehead was high, her hairline started far back on her head, her eyes popped, and her cheekbones were sucked in, emphasised even more by the bronzer she applied to show off their already quite evident height. Fish Face went into her office, and I waited for the Venetian blinds to open. They didn't. I looked around and noticed that everybody was doing the same. After a while of waiting for the meeting to be called we realised it was business as usual and the rumour had been merely that – which sparked off a small debate about the strength of Bryan Kelly's word versus that of Brian Murphy.

We went about our morning. I took a cigarette break on the fire escape so I wouldn't have to go all the way downstairs to get outside, but even though I didn't smoke I had to actually smoke because Graham came with me. I turned down both his offers of lunch and dinner, and as though understanding that those two things were far too much commitment for me he came back with a counter-offer, so I then turned down his suggestion of no-strings-attached sex. Then I sat with Twitch for an hour over the new super-duper steam-oven manual that neither of us could afford even if we sent all our own home appliances to a pawnshop. Edna still hadn't opened her office blinds and Louise hadn't once taken her eyes off the windows, even when she was on the phone.

'It must be personal,' Louise said to no one in particular.

'What must be?'

'Edna. She must be having a personal issue.'

'Or else she's dancing around naked and lip-syncing to "Footloose" on her iPod,' I suggested, and Graham stared at the windows with hope, planning new offers in his head.

Louise's phone rang and her perky phone voice replaced her dull tones but she quickly lost her enthusiasm and we could tell there was something wrong immediately. We all stopped working and stared at her. She hung up slowly, eyes wide and looked at us. 'Every other department has just finished their meetings. Bryan Kelly is gone.'

There was a long hushed silence.

'That's what you get for being full of shit,' I said quietly.

Graham was the only one who got the joke. Even though I wouldn't sleep with him, I appreciated that he still took time to laugh at my jokes and for that, he commanded my respect.

'It's Brian Murphy that's full of shit,' Louise said, frustrated.

I pursed my lips.

'Who was that on the phone?' Sausage asked.

'Brian Murphy,' Louise said.

That was it, we all couldn't help but laugh and we were joined together for the first time ever in a moment's laughter during a horrible awkward time in their lives. I say 'their' because I didn't feel it, I didn't feel worried or anxious or afraid because I didn't feel like I had anything to lose. A redundancy package would have been quite nice, and quite the bonus after my last job dismissal. Then Edna's door finally opened and she looked out with red-rimmed bloodshot eyes. She looked around at all of us in what could only be described as a lost apologetic way and for a moment I searched myself to see what I was feeling but the only thing I felt was completely indifferent. She cleared her throat. Then:

'Steve. Can I see you, please?'

We all looked on in horror as Steve made his way in. There was no more laughter. Watching Steve leave the office afterwards was like watching an ex-boyfriend move out. He packed away his things quietly with tears in his eyes: his photograph of his family, his mini basketball and basketball hoop, his mug that said *Steve likes his coffee black with one sugar,* and his Tupperware of lasagne that his wife had made him for his lunch. And then after handshakes from Twitch and me, a back pat from Graham, a hug from Mary and a kiss on the cheek from Louise, he was gone. An empty desk just like he had never been there. We worked in silence after that. Edna didn't open her blinds for the rest of the day and I didn't take any more cigarette breaks, partly out of respect for Steve but mostly because they were his cigarettes that I used to smoke. Though I wondered how long it would take any of them to think about Steve's desk and how the lighting was so much better there.

I left them at lunchtime as I always did, this time to bring my car back to the garage for the second week running. Once there I was handed another letter from Life and I returned to the office in an even worse mood.

I cursed to high heaven as I sat down and then sprang back up again.

'What's wrong?' Graham asked, looking amused.

'Who put this here?' I lifted the envelope and waved it around the room. 'Who put this on my desk?'

There was silence. I looked at Louise at reception, she shrugged. 'We were all in the canteen for lunch, nobody saw, but I got one too. It's addressed to you.' She came towards me with the envelope.

'I got one too,' Mary said, handing it to Louise to pass to me.

'There was one on my desk too,' Twitch said.

'I was going to give it to you later,' Graham said suggestively, taking an envelope out of his inside pocket.

'What do they say?' Louise asked, collecting the envelopes and bringing them to me.

'It's private.'

'What kind of paper is that? It looks nice.'

'They're too expensive for invitations,' I snapped. She backed off, uninterested.

Including the letter I'd found in my apartment this morning, and the letter he'd sent to the garage, he had written to me seven times in one day. I waited until the usual busy work hum had started up before I rang the number on the letter. I expected American Pie to answer. She didn't. Instead it was Him.

He didn't even wait for me to say hello before saying, 'Have I finally got your attention?

'Yes, you have,' I said, trying to hold my temper.

'It's been a week,' he said. 'I haven't heard from you.'

'I've been busy.'

'Busy with what?'

'Just doing things, my God, do I have to explain every little detail?'

He was silent.

'Fine.' I planned to kill him with my monotony. 'On Monday I got up and went to work. I brought my car to the garage. I went for dinner with a friend. I went to bed. On Tuesday I went to work, I collected my car, I went home, and I went to bed. On Wednesday I went to work, I went home, I went to bed. On Thursday I went to work, I went to the supermarket, I went home, I went to a funeral and then I went to bed. On Friday I went to work, then I went to my brother's house and babysat the kids for the weekend. On Sunday I went home. I watched *An American in Paris* and wondered for the hundredth time if I'm the only person who wants Milo Roberts and Jerry Mulligan to get together? That little French girl just played him like a fool. This morning I woke up and then I came to work. Happy now?'

'How very exciting. Do you think that continuing to live like a robot is actually going to make me go away?'

'I don't think that I've been living like a robot but regardless of what I do, quite obviously you're not going away. I brought my car to the garage today and Keith the mechanic handed me a letter from you, which he had *already opened* and in no uncertain terms suggested that sex with him would sort me out. Thank you for that.'

'At least I'm helping you meet men.'

'I don't need help meeting men.'

'Perhaps in keeping them then.' That was low and I think even he knew that. 'So when can we meet again?'

I sighed. 'Look, I just don't think this whole thing is going to work out with you and me. It might be good for other people but not for me. I really like my space, I like to do things without someone breathing down my neck all the time so I think the mature adult thing to do here is for you to go your way and I'll go mine.' I was impressed by my tone, by my firmness. Hearing my words, *I* wanted to separate from me, which weird as that is, was essentially what I was trying to do. I was trying to break up with myself.

He was silent again.

'It's not as if every moment together is a bag of laughs either. We don't even enjoy each other's company. I mean, really, we should just walk away.'

He still didn't speak.

'Hello, are you still there?'

'Just about.'

'I'm not allowed personal calls while at work so I should go now.'

'Do you like baseball, Lucy?'

I rolled my eyes. 'I don't know anything about it.'

'Have you ever heard of a curveball?'

'Yeah, it's what the guys with the ball throw at the guys with the bats.'

'Succinct as always. More specifically, it's a type of pitch thrown in a way that imparts forward spin to the ball causing it to dive in a downward path.'

'Sounds tricky,' I humoured him.

'It is. That's why they do it. It catches the batsman out.'

'That's okay, Robin always rescues him. I think they've a thing going on.'

'You don't take me seriously.'

'Because you're talking about an American sport of which I know nothing of and I'm in the middle of my work and I'm seriously concerned about your mental health.'

'I'm going to throw you one,' he said simply, his voice playful now.

'You're going to . . .' I looked around the room. 'Are you in here? You're not allowed play with a ball indoors, you should know that.'

Silence.

'Hello? Hello?'

My life had hung up on me.

Mere moments later Edna's door opened again. Her eyes were back to normal but she looked tired. 'Ah Lucy, there you are, could I see you for a moment, please?'

Mouse's eyes widened even more. Cock gave me a sad look; nobody left for him to pester.

'Yes, sure.'

I felt all eyes on me as I went into her office.

'Sit down, there's nothing to worry about.'

'Thank you.' I sat in front of her, perched on the edge of the desk.

'Before I start, this came for you.' She handed me another envelope.

I rolled my eyes and took it from her.

'My sister got one of those before,' she said, studying me.

'Really?'

'Yes. She left her husband, and she's living in New York now.' Her face changed as she talked about her family but she still looked like a fish. 'He was a bastard. She's really happy.'

'Good for her. Did she do an interview with a magazine, by any chance?'

Edna frowned. 'I don't think so, why?'

'Never mind.'

'If there's anything I can do to make you . . . happier here, then you'll let me know, won't you?'

I frowned. 'Yes, of course. I'm really fine, Edna, thank you. I think this was just a computer error or something.'

'Right.' She changed the subject. 'Well, the reason I called you in is because Augusto Fernández, head honcho from the German office, is visiting us tomorrow and I was wondering if you would be able to take the lead and introduce him to the gang in here. Maybe we can do our best to make him feel welcome and let him know how hard we're all working in here.'

I was confused.

'He doesn't speak very good English,' she said.

'Oh. For a minute there I thought you wanted me to sleep with him.'

It could have gone either way. Instead she threw her head back and laughed heartily. 'Oh Lucy, you're the perfect medicine; I needed that, thank you. Now I know you like to do your own thing at lunchtime but I'll have to ask you to stay in here just in case he drops by. Michael O'Connor is showing him around the building, of course, but when he gets here it would be nice to welcome him to our little group. Tell him what everybody does and how hard we're all working. You know?' She was giving me the eye. *Please don't let any of us get fired*. I liked that she cared.

'No problem. I get it.'

'How's everyone doing out there?'

'Like they've just lost a friend.'

Edna sighed and I heard and felt the stress she must have been under. I left the office and they were all gathered around Mouse's desk, like penguins huddled together for warmth afraid to drop their eggs, all looking at me in anticipation, pale faces worried that I'd been fired.

'Does anyone have a spare cardboard box?'

There was a chorus of distressed tones.

'Just joking, but nice to know you care,' I smiled and they relaxed but were a little annoyed. But then something Edna had said hit me and I suddenly tensed up. I knocked on the door, went back inside. 'Edna,' I said rather urgently.

She looked up from her paperwork.

'Augusto, he's from . . .'

'Head office, in Germany. Don't tell the others, I don't want them to worry any more than they already are.'

Relief. 'Of course. It's just not a typical German name,' I smiled. I went to close the door.

'Sorry, Lucy, I understand what you mean now,' she called out to me. 'He's Spanish.'

I smiled but inside I wept. I was worried, I was very worried, because apart from having only just enough Spanish to order a round of Slippery Nipples and to ask for a limbo bar, I had very little other vocabulary in my head, and though they didn't know it yet the team were relying on my schmoozing to get them through the next elimination process. It was only then when I sat down and saw the letters still lying on my desk that the conversation made sense.

Him and his analogies; Life had thrown me a curveball.

CHAPTER NINE

'He did the Inca Trail last week, did you see that?' my friend Jamie said to the table.

We were in The Wine Bistro in the city, our usual haunt for catching up, and being served by the usual gay waiter with the fake French accent. There were seven of the usual suspects gathered around for Lisa's birthday. There used to be eight before Blake had started all his travelling but he might as well have been sitting at the head of the table that night, exactly opposite from me, from the way they were all going on. They'd been talking about Blake for the past twenty minutes, ever since main course had arrived, and I sensed it could go on for another twenty so I had stuffed my mouth with as much salad as I could. Silchesters didn't talk while eating so apart from the occasional nod of interest and raised eyebrow I didn't need to take part. They talked about last night's episode where he'd travelled around India; I'd watched it and hoped Jenna had gotten Delhi belly. They talked about things he'd said, things he'd seen, things he'd worn and then they lovingly ripped him apart about his smarmy final comments and that cheesy look down the camera lens followed by the wink – that was personally my favourite part, but I didn't tell them that.

'What did you think of it, Lucy?' Adam asked, killing their discussion and directing it all at me.

I took a while to chew then swallowed some lettuce leaves. 'I didn't see it.' I shoved more into my mouth.

'Oooh,' Chantelle joked, 'she's so cold.'

I shrugged.

'Have you ever seen it?' Lisa asked.

I shook my head. 'I'm not sure if I have the station. I haven't checked.'

'Everyone has the station,' Adam said.

'Oh. Whoops.' I smiled.

'You were supposed to go on that trip together, weren't you?' Adam asked again, leaning on the table, pushing all his energy towards me.

Adam pretended to joke but even if it was almost three years ago, his best friend being dumped still seriously aggrieved him. If I hadn't been the target of his aggression my admiration for his loyalty would have been far greater. I'm not quite sure how Blake had managed to create such steadfast devotion in Adam but whatever he said, or whatever crocodile tears he'd spilled with him, it had worked and I was public enemy number one. I knew it and Adam secretly wanted me to know it, but it seemed that nobody else knew it. Again paranoia was taking over but I followed it like it was my guide.

I nodded at Adam. 'Yeah, we planned to go for his thirtieth.'

'And you made him go on his own, you cruel bitch,' Lisa said, and they laughed.

'With a film crew,' Melanie added, kind of in my defence.

'And a spray tanner, by the looks of it,' Jamie added and they laughed.

And Jenna. The bitch. From Australia.

I just shrugged again. 'That's what you get when you give me fried eggs instead of poached. A girl can't be dealing with shoddy breakfast in bed.'

They laughed, but Adam didn't. He glared at me in defence of his friend. I shovelled more salad into my mouth and looked at Melanie's plate to see what I could steal. As usual it was full of food. I speared a baby tomato, that'd give me at least twenty seconds of chewing. The tomato burst in my mouth and the seeds fired down my throat and made me choke. Not a cool reaction. Melanie handed me a glass of water.

'Well, he didn't do too badly, we did end up in Vegas for his thirtieth,' Adam said and gave me a long knowing look that just killed me. The lads looked at each other with cheeky expressions, instantly sharing a weekend of craziness that would never be revealed. My heart twisted as I pictured

Blake on a bar with a stripper licking Pernod off his abs and popping olives from his belly button. It wasn't a party trick of his, just a mind trick of my own.

My phone beeped. Don Lockwood's name flashed up onto my screen. Since our phone conversation over a week ago I'd tried to think of some kind of comeback for the Aslan song but failed. As soon as I opened the text a photo popped up. It was a porcelain figure of a haggard old woman with an eye patch and beneath it his text read:

–Saw this and thought of you.

I zoned out of the conversation and immediately texted back.

–It's rude to take my photo without permission. Would have given you my winning smile.

–You have no teeth, remember?

I smiled cheesily, and took a photo of my teeth. I pressed send.

Melanie gave me a curious smile.

'Who are you texting?'

'No one, I was just seeing if I've lettuce stuck in my teeth,' I said, easily. Too easily. I was getting good at this.

'You could have asked me. Seriously, who is it?'

'Just a wrong number.' It wasn't a lie. I reached into my bag and put twenty euro on the table. 'Guys, it was swell but I have to go now.'

Melanie groaned. 'But we hardly got to talk.'

'We've done nothing but talk,' I laughed, standing up.

'But not about you.'

'What do you want to know?' I took my coat from the gay waiter with the fake French accent who'd pointed at the coat rack and said, '*Zees one?*'

Melanie was a bit taken aback by being put on the spot. 'Well, I just wanted to hear what's going on with you but you're halfway out the door so we don't have time for that.'

I allowed gay waiter with fake accent to help me put my coat on, then said, '*Il y a eu une grande explosion. Téléphonez les pompiers et sortez du batiment, s'il vous plaît,*' which meant there has been a big explosion, telephone the emergency services and evacuate the building immediately. He looked a bit frazzled, smiled, then hotfooted it away before I could rip off his mask *Scooby Doo* style. 'Well, we don't need much time to talk about me because there's nothing interesting happening. Trust me. We'll catch up on our own sometime, next week I'll go to one of your gigs and we can have a bop in the booth?' Melanie was a much-in-demand DJ hot on the party circuit who went by the name DJ Darkness, more after the fact that she never saw daylight as opposed to being a tribute to her stunning Armenian looks.

She smiled and gave me a hug and rubbed my back affectionately. 'That sounds great, even though we'll have to lip-read. Ooh,' she squeezed me tighter, 'I just worry about you, Lucy.'

I froze. She must have sensed it because she let

go very quickly. 'What do you mean you worry about me?'

She looked like she'd put her foot in it. 'I didn't mean for it to be insulting, are you insulted?'

'Well, I don't know yet, I don't know what that means, when your friend tells you they're worried about you.' They were all listening now. I was trying to keep it light-hearted but I wanted to get to the bottom of it. She'd never said that before, why was she saying it now? What was it about me that was making people suddenly worry about me? The comment she'd made about my leaving a party of hers played on my mind; maybe there were lots of things she felt about me that I didn't know. Suddenly I wondered if they were all in on it, if they'd all signed the same paperwork as my family had. I looked at them all. They looked worried.

'What?' I beamed at everyone. 'Why are you all looking at me like that?'

'I don't know about them but I was hoping for a fight,' David piped up. 'Cat fight, pinch her, scratch her, poke out her eyes.'

'Rip off her clothes, tweak her nipples,' Jamie joked, and they all laughed.

'I'm not going to rip off her clothes,' I smiled, wrapping my arm around Melanie. 'She's hardly wearing any.'

They laughed.

'I just wanted to know why she was worried about me, that's all,' I said playfully. 'Is anybody else at this table worried about me?'

They took turns and I'd never felt so loved.

'Every day you get behind the wheel of that car,' Lisa said.

'Only that you can drink me under the table,' David added.

'I've concerns about your mental health,' Jamie said.

'I'm worrying about that dress with that coat,' Chantelle said.

'Great, anyone else want to take a pop at me?' I laughed.

'No, I'm not worried about you at all,' Adam offered.

No one heard his meaning like I heard it.

'And so on that joyous note, I'm leaving you all. I've to be up early in the morning. Happy birthday, Lisa. Bye bye, bump,' I kissed her belly.

And I was gone.

I got the bus home. Sebastian was on a drip and was heavily medicated and so was having to sleep over in the garage.

My phone beeped.

–*Impressive canines. Maybe send me more photos and I can piece you together. If your boyfriend doesn't mind?!*

–*Slick.*

–*That's not an answer.*

–*It is. It's just not the answer you were looking for.*

–*What are you doing tomorrow?*

–*Busy. Going to be fired.*

—Boyfriend . . . job . . . You're not having a good week. I'd like to help with one of them!

—You speak Spanish?

—A requirement for boyfriends?

—Again . . . slick. However. A requirement to keep my job. About to be revealed as a non-Spanish-speaking Spanish translator.

—Hate it when that happens. Estoy buscando a Tom. Means I'm looking for Tom. Came in handy in Spain. That's all I'll ever be allowed to say.

Later that night as I lay in bed listening to a Spanish language tape, I received a text.

—Am slowly but surely breaking down your alias. Certainly not toothless, not married, perhaps an eye patch and ten kids. Tomorrow, will investigate.

I turned the flash off my camera phone, raised it to my face. I took a picture of my eyes. It took me a few tries to get them right. Sent it. I waited with my phone in my hand for him to respond. There was nothing. Maybe I'd gone too far. Later that night my phone beeped and I dived on it.

—You showed me yours . . .

I scrolled down and I was staring at a perfectly formed, unpierced ear.

I smiled. Then closed my eyes and slept.

CHAPTER TEN

I took a forkful of my three-bean salad, in which I could only find two bean types, and which I was eating at my desk for the first time in two and a half years. Louise had stolen a large leather executive chair from somewhere – after the redundancies, random chairs were a regular feature – and they were currently re-enacting an office version of *Mastermind*. Twitch was in the hot seat and his specialist subject was '*Coronation Street*: Major Events 1960–2010'. Mouse was the quizmaster, firing questions at him from the Internet, Louise was timing him and so far he was doing well with three passes and a score of fifteen. Graham had his head in his hands and was staring down at his opened baguette and occasionally moving a hand from his head to pick out a gherkin.

'I don't know why you just don't tell them not to put gherkins in. You do this every day,' Louise said, watching him.

'Concentrate on the time,' Mouse said, panicked, then spoke even more quickly. 'In 1971 how did Valerie Barlow leave the show?'

And in equally rapid speech Twitch fired back, 'Electrocuted herself with a faulty hairdryer.'

Any moment from now Mr Fernández was going to walk through the door and after two and a half years in the job, I was going to have to reveal to the office my complete inability to speak Spanish. I was cringing with the embarrassment it was causing me already and what was surprising me was the horrible feeling that I knew I was going to let them down, a concern I had never previously possessed. The smaller the numbers got in our office, the more it felt like a dysfunctional family and although I was always on the outside looking in, I realised that though we weren't quite a tight group we were certainly a less loose one. We didn't all particularly like one another but we were protective of our unit, and in a way, I had betrayed them all. I had thought about pretending to be sick that day and also about confronting Fish Face about my lack of Spanish which would avoid the public embarrassment in front of the team but would be privately humiliating. In the end I'd decided against both routes because a part of me said that perhaps I could play my life at his own little game and there was a chance that I could learn an entire language overnight, and so after admiring Don Lockwood's perfectly formed ear last night I had hit the Spanish language books. I had discovered at three in the morning that it was impossible to learn a language overnight.

Graham finally finished picking out his gherkins and took a bite of his baguette. He watched the game of *Mastermind* unfold with a weary look. It was at times like that I found him attractive; when he wasn't pretending to be somebody he wasn't. He looked at me and we shared a look of fond annoyance at the game. Then he winked and I detested him again.

'Okay my turn.' Louise practically lifted Twitch from the chair to jump into it herself.

Flustered, Twitch stood up and fixed his glasses.

'Well done, Twitch,' I said.

'Thank you.' He pulled up his trousers, so that his belly showed above and below his belt-line, and looked proud.

'What is your specialised subject?' Mouse asked Louise.

'"Shakespeare's Plays",' Louise said very seriously.

Graham was midway into taking a bite of his baguette. He froze. We all looked at her.

'Only joking. "The Life and Times of Kim Kardashian".'

We laughed.

'You have two minutes, let's begin. For whom was Kim Kardashian's father, Robert Kardashian, attorney during a controversial case in the nineties?'

'O. J. Simpson,' she said, so fast the words were barely audible.

Twitch sat beside me and we watched.

'What are you eating?' he asked.

'Three-bean salad but look, I can only find two beans in it.'

Twitch leaned over to study it. 'Kidney beans, chick peas . . . did you eat the other one?'

'No, definitely not, I'd have noticed.'

'I'd bring that back if I were you.'

'But it's half gone, they'll think I've eaten them.'

'It's worth a try. How much did that cost you?'

'Three-fifty.'

He shook his head in disbelief and sucked in air. 'Yeah, I'd take that back.'

I stopped eating and we returned our gaze to the Mastermind game.

'In which spin-off show did Kim Kardashian move city to set up a new clothing store with her sister?'

'*Kourtney and Kim Take New York*,' she yelped. 'The clothing store is Dash.'

'You don't get extra points for extra information,' Graham complained.

'Ssh,' she silenced him, keeping an eye on the clock.

I heard Michael O'Connor's voice in the corridor: loud, confident and informative as he pointed out the mediocre facts of the floor I lived on every day. Edna must have heard them too because she opened the door to her office and gave me the nod. I stood up and smoothed my dress down, hoping that crease-free humming-bird-patterned material would help my ability to speak Spanish. Michael O'Connor greeted Edna at the door and it was up to me to bring Augusto into the office.

I cleared my throat, held out my hand as I walked towards him.

'*Sr Fernández, bienvenido.*'

We shook hands. He was extremely handsome and I became even more flustered. We looked at one another in a long silence.

'Em. Em.' My mind went completely blank. All the phrases I'd learned quickly flew out of my head in an obvious act of sabotage.

'*¿Hablas español?*' he asked.

'Uh-huh.'

He smiled.

Finally I remembered something. '*¿Cómo está usted?*' How are you?

'*¿Bien, gracias, y usted?*' The words were fast and didn't quite sound like the voice on the tape but I recognised some of them so just went with it, trying to speak faster like him.

'Uhhh. *Me llamo* . . . Lucy Silchester. *Mucho gusto encantado.*' It's a great pleasure to meet you.

He said something long and fast and detailed. Smiling sometimes, then looking serious, using his hands in a presidential way. I nodded in turn, smiling when he did and looking serious when he did. Then he went silent and waited for a response.

121

'Okay. *¿Quisiera bailar conmigo?*' Would you like to dance with me?

His forehead wrinkled. Behind Mr Fernández's head I could see Graham trying to stuff his baguette into a drawer in a panic as if eating at his desk at lunchtime would rob him of his job. Gherkins were flying everywhere so I went to Twitch's desk instead. This knocked me off course; in my head I had planned to begin my spiel with Graham and now I had to move down to the second paragraph of the piece I'd learned in my head. Twitch stood up, fixed his glasses, proud as a peacock.

'I'm Quentin Wright, pleasure to meet you.' Twitch, twitch, blink, blink.

Quentin looked at me. I looked at Augusto. My mind went blank.

'Quentin Wright,' I said in a kind of Spanish accent, and they shook hands.

Augusto said something. I looked at Twitch and I swallowed hard. 'He'd like to know what you do here.'

Twitch frowned. 'Are you sure that's what he said?'

'Eh, yes.'

He looked confused but then went on a rant, talking about his past experience and what an honour it was for him to work for the company. It would have been touching if I hadn't wanted to stop him after every single sentence. I looked at Augusto. Smiled. 'Um, he said, *un momento por favor*.' One moment please. '*España es un país maravilloso.*' Spain is a marvellous country. '*Me gusta el español.*' I like Spanish.

Augusto looked at Twitch, Twitch looked at me.

'Lucy,' Twitch said accusingly.

I was sweating; I could feel a hot rush flow through my body. I don't ever remember feeling so very . . . embarrassed. 'Em . . .' I looked around the room trying to think of an excuse to leave and then Gene Kelly rescued me again and it came to me: Don Lockwood's text. '*Estoy buscando a Tom.*' I'm looking for Tom.

They both frowned.

'Lucy,' Quentin asked rather nervously, twitching far more times than I'd ever seen before, 'who's Tom?'

'You know Tom,' I smiled at him. 'I have to go find him, it's very important that I introduce Mr Fernández to him.' Then I looked at Augusto and repeated, '*Estoy buscando a Tom.*'

The room was spinning as I started to walk away. Some shouting from the corridor stopped me in my tracks. It was such a relief to hear a distraction that I wasn't sure if I was imagining it. Then the others in the office reacted and I knew I wasn't. Michael O'Connor and Edna stopped talking, he popped his head out the door to take a look. Then there were more voices shouting, loud male angry voices. Then there was scuffling, then breathing and panting as if people were getting physical. And then a couple of things happened all at the same time. Edna said something to

Michael O'Connor and he quickly closed the door to protect us all from whatever it was; Mouse and Nosy instantly huddled together; Cock quickly moved closer to them to protect them. Edna looked as if she had seen a ghost, and seeing her face made me think it was the end. Michael O'Connor very smoothly made his way to Augusto, took him firmly by the elbow and led him into Edna's office where he closed the door behind them, leaving us sitting ducks for whatever it was that was going on outside our door.

'Edna, what's going on?'

Her face was white and she was confused and clearly didn't know what to do. The shouts got louder outside as they made their way closer, there was a bang as it sounded like a body hurtled at the wall beside us, followed by a shout of pain, and we jumped. Suddenly Edna kicked into boss mode and her voice was firm.

'Everybody, I want you all to get down under your desks. Now.'

'Edna what's—'

'Now, Lucy,' she shouted and everybody got down on the ground and crawled under their desks.

From under mine I could see Mary huddled up under hers, rocking back and forth and crying. Graham, who was close by, was trying to reach out to her from under his desk to comfort her and also silence her. I couldn't see Louise, she was on the far side of the room and Twitch was as still as could be, sitting on the floor staring at a photograph of his wife and children, the one of them all having a picnic, with his son on his shoulders and his wife carrying their daughter, the photo where he had most hair and I wondered if he was happier then, and because of it. I peeked outside to see where Edna was and I saw her standing up, taking deep breaths, pulling down the end of her suit jacket, then taking more deep breaths, then pulling down the end of her suit jacket some more. Every few moments she would look up at the door and have a determined look in her eye, as if she could take on anything, and then it would waver and she would take her deep breaths and pull down on her jacket again. And what did I do? All I could do was stare at the three-bean salad that I had knocked on the floor in the craziness, and piece by piece go through the beans looking for a third type. Kidney bean, tomato, sweetcorn, pepper, chickpea, kidney bean, red onion, lettuce, chickpea, tomato. It was all I could manage to stop myself from doing what my body and mind wanted to do, which was freak out.

The shouting and bangs got louder and louder. We could see people running past our window at top speed, women with their shoes in their hands, men without their jackets, just running. Everybody was running, why couldn't we? My question was answered very quickly. I saw someone running in the opposite direction to the fleeing men and women, a familiar shape. He was running straight to our door. Then I saw a team of security men chasing him. Our door burst open.

It was Steve. Sausage.

He had his briefcase in his hand, his suit jacket was ripped at the sleeve and there was blood gushing from a gash in his forehead. I was so shocked I couldn't speak. I looked at Twitch to see if he could see what I could, but his hands were in front of his face, his shoulders were shaking, he was quietly crying. At first I was relieved, it was only Steve. I was about to jump out from under my desk and run to him when he threw down his briefcase and dragged a nearby desk across the floor to block the door. Despite his physical shape he moved quickly, and then piled chair after chair on top of the desk to block the door. Once he was satisfied, he picked up his briefcase again and with his breathing way out of whack, made his way to his desk.

He started shouting, 'My name is Steve Roberts and I work here. My name is Steve Roberts and I work here. You cannot remove me from these premises.'

When the others realised who it was, they began to slowly creep out from under the desks.

Graham was first up. 'Steve, man, what are you—'

'Stay away from me, Graham,' Steve shouted, his breathing all over the place; the blood was dripping from his nose and his chin down onto his shirt. 'They can't take this job away from me. All I want to do is sit down and go to work. That's all. Now back off. Seriously, you too, Mary, you too, Louise.'

Quentin was still under the desk. I stood up.

'Steve, please don't do this,' I said, my voice shaking. 'You'll get into so much trouble. Think of your wife and your kids.'

'Think of Teresa,' Graham said, adding the personal touch. 'Come on.' His voice was gentle. 'You don't want to let her down.'

Steve was softening, his shoulders were relaxing, his eyes becoming a little less hardened but they were so black, so dark and wild. He was looking around as though he was wired, as though he was on something, not able to focus on one thing.

'Steve, please don't make this any worse,' Edna said. 'We can end this now.'

But it was as though a switch was flicked and he turned again. He glared at her and almost threw his briefcase at her and my heart quickened. 'It can't get any worse, Edna, you have no idea how bad things are already. You have no idea. I am fifty years old and today a twenty-year-old girl told me that I am unemployable. Unemployable? Apart from the day my baby girl was born, I've never missed a day's work in my life.' His voice was full of venom and he directed his anger at Edna. 'I've always done my best for you, always.'

'I know that. Believe me—'

'You are a liar!' he shouted, voice thick with rage. His face was bright red, the veins in his neck protruded. 'My name is Steve Roberts and I work here.'

He put his briefcase down, pulled out his chair and sat down. His hands were shaking as he tried to open his briefcase. When he couldn't do it he yelled so loudly we all jumped and he thumped his fist down on the desk. 'Graham, open it!' he shouted. Graham hopped to it and opened the brown battered briefcase that Steve had carried with him every day that I'd been here, and then he wisely took several strides backward, away from Steve. Steve calmed a little then placed his mug back down, the one that said *Steve likes his coffee black with one sugar*, but he banged it down so hard that the bottom chipped. He replaced his basketball and hoop and the photograph of his children. There was no packed lunch. His wife hadn't planned on him coming in today. They were messily placed, not as he had them before. Nothing was like he had it before.

'Where's my computer?' he said quietly.

Nobody answered.

'Where's my computer?' he screamed.

'I don't know,' Edna said, her voice trembling a little. 'They came and they took it this morning.'

'Took it? Who took it?'

Banging began on the door to the office as security tried to get in. The door wouldn't budge, he had cleverly – though I think accidentally – placed one of the chairs below the door handle and it was firmly lodged. I could hear voices outside talking at top speed, trying to figure out what to do. They were worried, not so much about us I imagined but about the two heads of the company inside,

128

and I was hoping Steve wasn't going to find out any time soon either. The action at the door wasn't doing anything to help Steve's temper. The constant rattle of the chairs and desk at the door was like a slow simmer and we were all waiting for the big explosion. Steve was starting to panic.

'Well then, get me your computer,' he said.

'What?' Edna was taken aback.

'Go into your office and get me your computer. Or better yet, how about I take your desk, how do you like that?' he shouted. 'Then I'll be the boss around here and they won't be able to get rid of me. Maybe I'll fire you,' he shouted. 'Edna! You're fucking fired! How do you like that?'

It was beyond disturbing watching a colleague fall apart like this. Edna just looked at him, gulped hard, didn't know what to do. Her two bosses who held her life in their hands were hiding out in her office.

'You can't go in,' she stuttered. 'I locked it at lunchtime and I can't find the key.' She struggled saying it and we all knew, even Steve in his demented state knew, that it wasn't true.

'Why are you lying to me?'

'I'm not, Steve,' she said a little stronger. 'You really can't go in there.

'But it's my office,' he shouted, moving closer to her. He shouted in her face and she blinked with each word. 'It's my office and you have to let me in. It will be the last thing you do before you pack up your things and leave!' His demeanour was intimidating, there were six of us in there, two more in Edna's office, and together we could have taken him down but he had us all captivated, frozen in our spots in fear of a man we thought we knew.

'Steve, don't go in there,' Graham said.

Steve looked at him, confused. 'Why, who's in there?'

'Just don't, okay?'

'Someone's in there, aren't they? Who is it?'

Graham shook his head.

'Quentin, who is it?'

It was only then I'd noticed Quentin had risen from below the desk.

'Tell them to come out,' he said to Edna.

She was wringing her hands.

'I can't do that,' she said, giving up, her confidence dying.

'Quentin, open the door for me.'

Quentin looked at me; I didn't know what to do.

'Open the damn door,' Steve screamed and Quentin scurried over. He opened the door slowly, didn't look inside and immediately returned to his desk to be away from the action.

Steve moved a little closer to the office, peeked inside. Then he started laughing. But not happy laughter, it was demented, disturbing.

'Get out,' he said to the men inside.

'Look, Mr . . .' Michael O'Connor looked at Edna for help.

'Roberts,' she whispered, but not deliberately.

'You don't even know my name,' Steve screeched and his face was bright red, his nose was covered in blood, the bloodstain on his shirt was spreading. 'He doesn't even know my name,' he shouted to the rest of us. 'Just yesterday you ruined my life and you don't even know my bloody name,' he yelled. 'My name is Steve Roberts and I work here!'

'We all need to calm down here, maybe open the door and tell everybody outside that we're okay, then we can discuss what's happened.'

'Who's he?' Steve said, looking at Augusto.

'This is . . . he doesn't speak English, Mr Roberts.'

'My name is Steve,' he shouted. 'Lucy,' he screamed and my heart went from a mile a minute to stopping. 'Get over here. You speak languages, ask him who he is.'

I didn't move. Quentin looked at me with concern and I knew that he knew.

'He's Augusto Fernández from the German office and he's here to visit us today,' I said, my voice cracking along the way.

'Augusto . . . I've heard of you. You're the guy who fired me,' Steve said, getting worked up again. 'You're the fucker who fired me. Well, I know what to do with you.'

Steve rushed towards him and it looked as though he was going to punch him.

Michael O'Connor grabbed Steve to pull him back but Steve was quick, he punched him in the stomach and Michael went flying back into Edna's office and landed on the ground. I heard the bang as his head hit the desk. I don't think Steve noticed. He had stopped inches before Augusto's face. We waited for a head butt, a punch, something awful to happen to his perfect sun-snogged Spanish face but it didn't happen.

'Please give me back my job,' Steve said in a gentle voice that broke my heart. Blood had rolled down to his mouth and it spattered as he spoke. 'Please.'

'He can't do that, Mr Roberts,' Michael said from inside, clearly in pain.

'Yes, he can, give me back my job, Augusto. Lucy, tell him I want my job back.'

I swallowed. 'Em . . .' I tried to think of words, I tried to think of all I'd learned but the knowledge just wasn't there.

'Lucy!' he roared and he reached into his pocket. I thought he was going for a handkerchief. It would be normal for him to reach for that, blood was pouring from his head, covered his nose and was on his hand from where he'd wiped his mouth. I waited for the handkerchief to come out of his pocket but instead I saw a gun. Everybody screamed and dived to the ground, apart from me because it was pointed at me and I had frozen.

'Tell him to give me my job back.' He moved closer to me, all I could see was a black thing pointing at me. It was shaking in Steve's trembling hand. I could see his finger on the trigger and he was trembling so hard I was afraid it would go off any minute. My legs were shaking; I could feel my knees about to go. 'If he gives me my job back, I will let him go safely. Tell him.'

I couldn't answer him. He rushed at me again, the gun only inches away from my face. 'Tell him!' he screamed.

'For fuck's sake put the gun down,' I heard Graham yell, terror in his voice.

Then the others started shouting and it was too much, it was too much for me to bear. I was afraid it would be too much for Steve to take too, all those voices, all those terrified voices confusing our thoughts.

My lips were trembling, my eyes filling. 'Please, Steve, don't do this. Please don't do this.'

He toughened up, 'Don't cry, Lucy, just do what you're paid to do and tell the man I want my job back.'

My lips trembled so much I could barely make out the words. 'I can't.'

'Yes, you can.'

'I can't, Steve.'

'Just do it, Lucy,' Graham said encouragingly. 'Just say what he wants you to say.'

The banging on the door stopped and I felt lost. More lost than I'd ever been. I thought they'd left us. They'd left us on our own.

'I can't.'

'Do it!' Steve shouted. 'Do it, Lucy!' He waved the gun closer to my face.

'Jesus, Steve, I can't do it, okay? I can't speak Spanish. Okay?' I shouted back.

There was a silence, everyone looked at me in shock as if that revelation was more surprising than the brandished gun, then they remembered, and quickly returned their gaze to Steve.

Steve was looking at me as shocked as everybody else, then his eyes darkened again and the trembling in his hand stopped and his arm firmed up. 'But they fired me.'

'I know. I'm sorry, Steve. I'm really sorry.'

'I didn't deserve it.'

'I know,' I whispered.

In the middle of the thick silence, while Michael was slowly rolling onto his side to get to his feet and the others were cowering together, Quentin stood up. Steve whipped around with the gun to face him.

'Jesus, Quentin, get down,' Graham shouted.

But Quentin didn't move. Instead he faced Mr Fernández, who was in a terrified state on the floor, and in a firm voice with what sounded like word-perfect Spanish he began to speak to him. Augusto rose to his feet and also remained cool and responded, his voice authoritative and believable even though none of us had a clue what he was saying. In the middle of this madness they carried out a conversation of complete calm. Suddenly there was the sound of a drill from outside. Movement, at last, and the door handle began to rattle. Steve looked at the door and it seemed that a little part of him gave up.

'What did he say?' he asked Quentin. His voice

was quiet and we could barely hear him over the noise of the drill.

Quentin, full of twitches, recited Augusto's response. 'He said that he is very sorry about the error which led to you losing your job. He is sure there was a mistake in the system and as soon as he is able he will make a phone call to head office to have you reinstated. He is very sorry for the distress this has caused you and your family and he will very quickly make plans to have you back in the job as quickly as possible. It is obvious from your actions today that you are a fine dedicated worker that he and the company should be extremely proud of.'

Steve's chin lifted higher with pride. He nodded then. 'Thank you.' Swapping the gun to his other hand, he moved towards Augusto and reached out with his free bloodied hand. They shook hands. 'Thank you very much,' he said. 'It's an honour to work for your company.'

Augusto nodded, warily and wearily both at the same time.

Then the door handle fell off, the door burst open, the desk was thrown across the room and three men dived on Steve.

As soon as I had the opportunity that day I made my call.

He answered.

'Okay,' I said, my voice still trembling from the shock. 'I'll meet you again.'

CHAPTER ELEVEN

We had arranged to meet the following day in Starbucks at the end of my block. I couldn't meet him on the day of the office incident, I would rather not have seen anybody or anything, apart from Mr Pan and my bed, that day, but word had reached my mother, via on-the-hour-every-hour news bulletins, and she was frantic with worry. Father was up the walls. Mum had sent a messenger into the court with word that her daughter's office had been held at gunpoint and Father had demanded a recess in a controversial high-profile case. He had broken every speed limit for the first time in his life to make it home to Mum and they'd sat around the kitchen table together eating apple pie and drinking tea, crying and hugging and reminiscing on the little Lucy stories they loved to regale so much, bringing my soul to life as if I had been shot in the office that day.

Okay, I lied.

I'm not sure how Father felt about it – the underlying feeling was probably that I deserved it for landing such a lowly job with standard people – but I was in no mood to learn his thoughts on the matter. I'd refused to visit, insisting I was fine, but even I knew this time that I was lying and so Riley had landed on my doorstep unscheduled.

'Your chariot awaits,' he said as soon as I'd answered the door.

'Riley, I'm fine,' I said but it didn't sound credible and I knew it.

'You're not fine,' he said. 'You look like crap.'

'Thanks.'

'Just get your things and come with me. We're going to my place. Mum's meeting us there.'

I groaned. 'Please, I've had a rough day as it is.'

'Don't speak about her like that,' he said, serious for a change, which made me feel bad. 'She's worried about you. It's been on the news all day.'

'Fine,' I said. 'Wait here.'

I closed the door and tried to gather my things but I couldn't think, my mind was numb, it wouldn't work. In the end I gathered myself and grabbed my coat. When I stepped out into the corridor my neighbour whose name I'd forgotten was talking with Riley. He was leaning in towards her, oblivious to my presence, so I cleared my throat, a long loud, phlegmy sound that echoed in the corridor. That got his attention. He looked at me, annoyed by my interruption.

'Hi, Lucy,' she said.

'How's your mother?'

'Not good,' she said, deep frown lines appearing between her eyebrows.

'Have you been in to see her?'

'No.'

'Oh. Well, if you decide to, remember I'm here to . . . you know.'

She nodded her thanks.

'Your neighbour seems nice,' Riley said once we were in his car.

'She's not your type.'

'What's that supposed to mean? I don't have a type.'

'Yes, you do. The blonde vacuous type.'

'That's not true,' he said. 'I go for brunettes too.'

We laughed.

'Did she mention her baby to you?'

'No.'

'That's interesting.'

'Are you trying to put me off her? Because if you are, telling me that she has a baby won't work. I once dated a woman with two kids.'

'Ha. So you are interested in her.'

'Maybe a little.'

I found that weird. We sat in silence and I started thinking about Steve pointing a gun at my face. I didn't want to know what Riley was thinking about.

'Where's her mother?'

'In hospital. I don't know which one and I don't know what's wrong with her. But it's serious.'

'Why hasn't she seen her?'

'Because she says she won't leave her baby behind.'

'Have you offered to babysit?'

'Yes.'

'That's nice of you.'

'I'm not all bad.'

'I don't think any part of you is bad,' he said, looking at me. I wouldn't meet his eye so he looked back at the road. 'Why doesn't she bring the baby to the hospital with her? I don't understand.'

I shrugged.

'You do know, come on, tell me.'

'I don't.' I looked out the window.

'How old is the baby?'

'I don't know.'

'Come on, Lucy.'

'I honestly don't know. She puts it in a buggy.'

He looked at me. 'It.'

'Little boys and girls look the same to me. Until they're ten I haven't a clue what sex they are.'

Riley laughed. 'Does her mother not approve of her being a single mother? Is that what it is?'

'Something like that,' I said and concentrated on the world passing by and not on the gun I kept seeing in my face.

Riley lived two kilometres from the city centre in Ringsend, an inner suburb in Dublin, where he occupied a penthouse that overlooked Boland's Mills on Grand Canal Dock.

'Lucy,' my mum said, with eyes big and worried, as soon as I walked in the door. I kept my arms behind my back as she squeezed me tight.

'Don't worry, Mum, I wasn't even in the office,' I said out of nowhere. 'I had to run an errand and missed all the fun.'

'Really?' she asked, her face filling with relief.

Riley was staring at me, which was making me uncomfortable; he'd been acting very strangely the past few days, less like the brother I knew and loved and more like a person who knew I was lying.

'Anyway, I brought you this.' I removed my hands from behind my back and gave her a doormat that I'd swiped from outside the door of Riley's neighbour. It said *Hi, I'm Mat* and looked good as new.

Mum laughed. 'Oh Lucy, you're so funny, thank you so much.'

'Lucy,' Riley said angrily.

'Oh, don't be silly, Riley, it was no trouble at all. It wasn't expensive.' I patted him on the back and moved into the rest of the apartment. 'Is Ray here?' Ray was Riley's flatmate and was a doctor; they were never at home at the same time as they both worked opposite hours. Whenever he was home Mum flirted unashamedly with him, though she did ask me once before if Ray was Riley's boyfriend. It was wishful thinking on her part for a trendy homosexual son who would never replace her with another woman.

'He's working,' Riley explained.

'Honestly, do you two never get to spend any quality time together?' I asked, trying not to laugh, and Riley actually looked like he wanted to do a double-leg takedown and send me to the ground just like he did when we were younger. I quickly changed the subject, 'What's the smell?'

'Pakistani food,' mum said giddily. 'We didn't know what you wanted so we ordered half the menu.' Mum got excited about being in her handsome bachelor son's apartment where she got to do exotic things like eat Pakistani food, watch *Top Gear* and operate a remote-control fire that changed colour. It was a long way to a Pakistani restaurant from their house and Father wouldn't be remotely interested in making the journey with her or watching anything other than CNN. We opened a bottle of wine and sat down at a glass table, by floor-to-ceiling windows that overlooked the river. Everything was reflective and shiny, shimmering in the moonlight.

'So,' Mum said and I could tell from her tone that she meant a serious probing conversation was about to begin.

'How are the wedding-vow renewal plans going?' I asked first.

'Oh . . .' She forgot what she was going to ask me and perked up. 'There's so much I have to talk to you about. I'm trying to choose a venue.' And I listened to her for the next twenty minutes talking about things that I never knew a person ever

141

needed to consider when it came to four walls and a ceiling because the alternatives of no ceiling and/or three walls or less were apparently too overwhelmingly enticing.

'How many people are going?' I asked when I heard some of the venues she was thinking of.

'So far there's four hundred and twenty.'

'What?' I almost choked on my wine.

'Oh, it's mostly your father's colleagues,' she said. 'Given his position it's difficult to invite some and not others. People get very offended.' And feeling as if she'd spoken out of turn, she corrected herself. 'And rightly so.'

'So don't invite any of them,' I said.

'Oh, Lucy,' she smiled at me, 'I can't do that.'

My phone started ringing, and Don Lockwood's name flashed on the screen. Before I had a chance to control my facial muscles, I took on the characteristics of a giddy child.

Mum raised her eyebrows at Riley.

'Excuse me, I'll just take this outside.'

I stepped out onto the balcony. It was a wraparound so I moved away from their eyeline and earshot.

'Hello?'

'So, did you get fired today?'

'Not quite. Not yet anyway. But it turned out the guy didn't know who Tom was. Thanks for the tip all the same.'

He laughed lightly. 'Same thing happened in Spain. Tom's a mystery. Don't worry. It could have been worse. You could have been in the office where that poor guy went ballistic.'

I paused. I immediately thought it was a trap but then my better judgement overrode it – how on earth could he have known, he didn't even know my real name, couldn't possibly have known that I even worked there.

'Hello?' he asked, worried. 'Are you still there?'

'Yes,' I said quietly.

'Oh, good. I thought I'd said something wrong.'

'No, you didn't, it's just that . . . well, that was my office.'

'Are you serious?'

'Yes. Unfortunately.'

'Jesus. Are you okay?'

'Better than he is, anyway.'

'Did you see the guy?'

'Sausage,' I said, staring across the river at Boland's Mills.

'Excuse me?'

'I nicknamed him Sausage. He was the softest man in the building and he pointed a gun right at my head.'

'Shit,' he said. 'Are you okay, did he hurt you?'

'I'm fine.' But I wasn't fine and he knew it but I couldn't see him and I didn't know him so it didn't matter and I kept talking. 'It was only a water pistol, you know, we found out afterwards when they'd . . . got him down on the ground. It was his son's. He'd taken it that morning and told his wife he was going to get his job back.

Jesus, a fucking water pistol made me question my whole life.'

'Of course it would. I mean, you didn't know, did you?' he said gently. 'And had he pulled the trigger you could have had very frizzy hair.'

I laughed, threw my head back and laughed.

'Oh God. There was me hoping I'd get fired, and he gave up his life to get his job back.'

'I wouldn't say his life, it was hardly a deadly weapon, though I haven't seen you with frizzy hair. I haven't seen you at all. Have you got hair?'

I laughed. 'Brown hair.'

'Hmm, another piece of the puzzle.'

'So tell me about your day, Don.'

'I can't beat yours, that's for sure. Let me take you for a drink, I bet you could do with one,' he said gently. 'Then I can tell you all about my day face to face.'

I was quiet.

'We'll meet somewhere crowded, somewhere familiar, you choose where, bring ten friends with you if you want, ten men, big men with muscles. I'm not into big men by the way, or any men, I'd rather you not bring them at all but if I said that first you'd think I was planning to kidnap you. Which I'm not.' He sighed. 'Smooth, aren't I?'

I smiled. 'Thank you, but I can't. My brother and my mother are holding me hostage.'

'You've had a day of it. Another time then. This weekend? You'll see there's more to me than just a beautiful left ear.'

I started laughing. 'Don, you sound like a really nice guy—'

'Uh-oh.'

'But frankly, I'm a mess.'

'Of course you are, anyone would be after the day you've had.'

'No, not just because of today, I mean generally, I'm a mess.' I rubbed my face tiredly, realising contrary to my own popular opinion that I genuinely was a mess. 'I spend more time telling a wrong number things I don't even tell my family.'

He laughed lightly and it felt like his breath whistled down the phone to my ear. I shuddered. I felt as though he was standing right beside me.

'That's got to be a good sign, hasn't it?' He livened up. 'Come on, if it turns out I'm a big fat ugly thing that you never want to see again then you can leave and I'll never bother you again. Or if it turns out that you're a big fat ugly thing, you'll have nothing to worry about because I'll never want to see you again. Or maybe you're looking for a big fat ugly thing and in that case there's no point in meeting me because I'm not.'

'I can't, Don, I'm sorry.'

'I can't believe you're breaking up with me and I don't even know your name.'

'I told you, it's Gertrude.'

'Gertrude,' he said, a little defeated. 'Right, well, just remember you called me first.'

'It was a wrong number,' I laughed.

145

'Okay then,' he said finally. 'I'll leave you alone. I'm glad you're okay.'

'Thanks, Don. Goodbye.'

We ended the call and I leaned on the rail and looked out as the reflection from all the apartments' lights shimmered in the black water. My phone beeped.

—A parting gift.

I scrolled down.

A pair of beautiful blue eyes stared back at me. I studied them until I almost imagined them blink.

When I went back in to Mum and Riley they were kind enough not to ask any questions about the phone call but while Riley went to get the car keys to drop me home, Mum took a moment and I sensed a special chat.

'Lucy, I didn't get the opportunity to talk with you after you left lunch last week.'

'I know, I'm sorry I left so hastily,' I said. 'The food was lovely, I just remembered I had to meet somebody.'

She frowned. 'Really? Because I felt that it was because I signed the documents for the appointment with your life.'

'No, it wasn't,' I interrupted. 'It really wasn't. I can't remember what it was but it was, you know, important. I'd stupidly double-booked, you know how forgetful I am sometimes.'

'Oh. I was sure you were angry with me.' She studied me. 'It's okay if you tell me you were angry at me.'

What was she talking about? Silchesters didn't reveal such things.

'Of course not. You were just looking out for me.'

'Yes,' she said relieved. 'I was. But I didn't know what to do for a very long time. I didn't sign the paperwork for weeks, I thought if there was something wrong you could maybe come to me and talk about it. Even though I know Edith is so good at helping you with things that maybe you don't want to tell your mummy.' She smiled shyly and cleared her throat.

Awkward, awkward, horrible moment. I think she was waiting for me to disagree but I wasn't sure, so I didn't say anything. Where was my ability to lie when I needed it?

'Eventually I talked it over with your father and I decided to sign it.'

'He told you to sign it?' I asked as gently as I could but felt the anger building inside me. What would he know about my life? He'd never asked me one question about myself, never shown the slightest bit of interest in—

'No, actually,' Mum broke in on my thoughts. 'He said it was all a load of nonsense but that made me realise that I didn't agree with him. I don't think it's all a load of nonsense. I think, what harm could it do? You know? If my life wanted to meet with me, I think I'd be rather excited,' she smiled. 'Something exciting like that happening, it must be wonderful.'

I was impressed by her acting against Father's instructions and intrigued and surprised by her desire to meet with her life. I would have thought it would be the last thing she'd want to do. What would *People* say?

'But mostly I was worried, that it was my fault too. I'm your mother and if there is something wrong with you well then—'

'There's nothing *wrong* with me, Mum.'

'Of course there isn't, I phrased it wrongly, I'm sorry. I meant—'

'I know what you meant,' I said quietly, 'and it's not your fault. If there *was* anything wrong with me, that is, it wouldn't be your fault. You haven't done anything wrong.'

'Thank you, Lucy.' She looked a decade younger then and it had never occurred to me until that moment that she would be feeling guilty about the state of my life. I thought that was solely my job.

'So,' she perked up again. 'Did you meet with her?'

'It's a him actually, and I met him last week.'

'Him?'

'I was surprised too.'

'Is he handsome?' Mum giggled.

'Mum, that's disgusting, he's my life.'

'Of course.' She tried to hide her smile but I could see her secretly hoping for wedding bells. Any man would do as a son-in-law, or perhaps she was hoping for a match for Riley.

'He's not handsome at all, he's ugly actually.' I

pictured him with his clammy skin, bad breath and snivelling in his creased suit. 'But anyway it's fine, we're fine. I don't think he wants to meet again.'

Mum frowned again. 'Are you sure?' Then she left me for a moment and came back with a bag filled with envelopes with the life spirals imprinted on the front, all in my name and addressed to her home. 'We received one in the post every day last week. And again yesterday morning.'

'Oh,' I said. 'He must have forgotten my address. No wonder I didn't receive them.' I shook my head and laughed. 'Maybe Life's one big problem is disorganisation.'

Mum smiled at me, rather sadly.

Riley came out of his bedroom, car keys at the ready, and saw the envelope in my hand. 'Oh, are we doing that now?' He reached into a drawer in the hall table and came over to the dining table with a pile of envelopes in his hand. He threw them down on the table, grabbed a poppadom and crushed it in his mouth. 'Do me a favour, will you, sis? Stop ignoring your life. These were blocking my postbox up.'

At first I had been indifferent towards my life, now, after the day I'd had, I was angry at it, but then these letters being sent to my family made me even angrier. I was due to meet him the following day in Starbucks. I had insisted he didn't visit my apartment. Edna had called to tell me we'd been given the day off work and I was glad of it this time, not just for the break from the job but because I was genuinely embarrassed about the spectacular style in which my lack of Spanish was discovered. To deliberately put me in a situation just to get me to meet him was beyond despicable. He hadn't just jeopardised my safety but the safety of everybody in that room. Because of this anger, I was looking forward to my second appointment with Life.

The following day as I worked through intelligent nasty things to say to my life, my mobile rang. It was a number I didn't recognise so I ignored it. But it rang again. And again. Then there was banging on the door. I rushed to open it. It was my neighbour, whose name I couldn't remember, in a panicked state.

'I'm so sorry to disturb you. It's my mother. My brother called me. They told me to go to the hospital immediately.'

'No problem.' I grabbed my keys and closed my door behind me. She was trembling.

'It's okay, you need to go to her,' I said gently.

She nodded. 'It's just that I've never left him before . . .'

'It's okay. Trust me, it'll be fine.'

She led me into the apartment and in a jittery state brought me around it, shooting orders at me. 'I've made his bottle; warm it up before you feed him. He'll only drink it if it's warm. He feeds at seven thirty, he likes to watch *In the Night Garden* before going to bed. Just press play on the DVD. Then he goes straight down. He won't sleep without Ben. Ben is the pirate teddy over there. If he wakes up and is distressed, singing "Twinkle Twinkle" will calm him down.' She brought me around showing me everything, teething rings, cuddly toys, the steriliser in case I dropped the bottle and needed to make a fresh one. She looked at her watch. 'I'd really better go.' She stalled. 'Maybe I shouldn't, maybe I should stay.'

'Go. Everything is fine here.'

'Yes, you're right.' She threw on her coat and opened the door. 'Okay. I'm not expecting anybody to call around, and you won't have friends over or anything, will you?'

'Of course not.'

'And you've got my mobile number, haven't you?

'In here,' I waved my phone in the air.

'Okay. Thank you.' She bent over the playpen. 'Bye, baby. Mummy will be home soon,' she said, tears in her eyes. And she was gone.

Which left me in trouble. I called Life's office but there was no answer, and his secretary didn't answer either which meant she had finished for the day and he was already en route to Starbucks. I waited until it was time for us to meet before calling Starbucks.

'Hello,' a stressed-out guy sounding under pressure answered.

'Hi, I'm supposed to be meeting someone there right now and I need to tell them—'

151

'What's their name?' he interrupted.

'Oh, em, actually I don't know his name but he's wearing a suit, probably looks a little stressed and tired and—'

'Hey, someone on the phone for you,' he shouted down my ear and he was gone. I heard the phone being passed over.

'Hello?'

'Hi,' I said in my friendliest voice. 'You'll never believe what just happened.'

'You'd better not be calling to cancel,' he said immediately. 'I seriously hope you're just running late, which is insulting enough to be perfectly honest, but anything but cancelling.'

'I am, but not for the reason you think.'

'What reason do you think I think?'

'That I'm not interested in you and that's not true, well it kind of is true and I'm learning I have to change that, but it's not the reason I'm cancelling. A neighbour of mine asked me to babysit. Her mother is really sick and she had to rush to the hospital.'

He was silent as he considered it. 'That's right up there with "my dog ate my homework".'

'No, it's not, it's not even close.'

'What's your neighbour's name?'

'I can't remember.'

'That's the worst lie you've ever come up with.'

'Because it's not a lie. If I was lying I would have made up a name like . . . Claire. Actually, I think that is her name. Claire,' I said. 'Her name's Claire.'

'Are you drunk?'

'No. I'm babysitting.'

'Where?'

'In her apartment. Across the hall from mine. But you can't come here in case that's what you're thinking. She specifically said no strangers allowed in.'

'I wouldn't be a stranger if you'd keep our appointments.'

'Well, let's not punish her for my mistakes, shall we.'

He ended the call in less of a rage than he began it and, I hoped, believing every word I'd said. However, I was settled on the rocking chair watching Makka Pakka on the Pinky Ponk drinking pinky ponk juice in *In the Night Garden* but really thinking about the events of the day before when I heard knocking on my door for the second time that night. I opened the door and saw him, standing at the door to my apartment, his back turned to me.

'Are you checking up on me?' I asked.

He turned.

'You shaved,' I said, surprised. 'You don't look nearly as miserable as you were.'

He look past me in into the apartment. 'So, where's the baby?'

'You can't come in. This is not my home, I can't just let you in.'

'Fine, but at least you can show me the baby. For all I know you could have just broken into this apartment in order to get away from me. And don't look at me like that, that's exactly the kind of thing you'd do.'

I sighed. 'I can't show you the baby.'

'Just bring it to the door. I won't touch it or anything.'

'I can't show you the baby.'

'Show me the baby,' he repeated in turn. 'Show me the baby, show me the baby.'

'Shut up,' I hissed. 'There is no baby.'

'I knew it.'

'No, you don't know anything.' Then I whispered, 'She *thinks* there's a baby, but there is no baby. There *was* a baby but he died, and she thinks or she pretends, or I don't know what she does, but she acts like there's a baby. There is no baby.'

He looked uncertain, looked past me in the hall. 'I see a lot of baby things lying around.'

'There are. She takes the buggy out for a walk but it's always empty, she thinks he's teething and crying all night but I don't hear anything. There's no baby here. I've been looking at the photos and he's the oldest in this. I think he was at least one when he died. Here.'

I took a photo from the hall table and passed it to him.

'Who's the man?'

'I think he's her husband but I haven't seen him for at least a year. I don't think he could cope with her like this.'

'Well, that's depressing.' He handed the photo

back to me and we sat in silence for a moment, both sobered by the situation. Life broke the minute's silence. 'So you have to stay in there even though there's no baby?'

'If I leave and she comes back, I can't tell her that it's because she has no baby, that would be cruel.'

'So you can't come out and I can't go in,' he said. 'Oh, the irony.' He smiled and for the briefest moment he was attractive. 'We can talk here,' he said.

'We already are.'

He slithered down the door and sat on the ground in the hallway. I followed him and sat across from him in the hallway of the apartment. A neighbour got out of the elevator, took a look at us and walked through the middle. We stared at one another in silence.

'People can see you, can't they?' I asked.

'What do you think I am, a ghost?' He rolled his eyes. 'I may be completely invisible to you but other people in this world pay plenty of attention to me. Other people actually want to know about me.'

'Okay, okay, touchy,' I said.

'Are you ready to talk?'

'I'm angry at you,' I said almost immediately, suddenly remembering all that I'd rehearsed in my head.

'Why?'

'Because of what you did to all those people yesterday.'

155

'What *I* did?'

'Yes, they didn't deserve to get involved in your . . . your curveball or whatever you called it.'

'Hold on, you think I manipulated those people into doing what happened yesterday?'

'Well . . . didn't you?'

'No!' he said emphatically. 'What do you think I am? Actually, don't answer that. All I did was synchronise the Augusto Fernández thing, I had nothing to do with whatever his name is.'

'Steve,' I said firmly. 'Steve Roberts.'

He looked amused. 'Ah, now there's a loyalty I didn't see last week. What was it you called him? Sausage?'

I looked away.

'I didn't organise that. You are responsible for your own life and what happens in it, so are the other people. Your life had nothing to do with what happened there. You were feeling guilty,' he said, and because it wasn't a question I didn't answer.

I put my head in my hands. 'I have a headache.'

'Thinking about things will do that, you haven't done it for a while.'

'But you said you planned the Fernández thing. You meddled with his life.'

'I didn't meddle. I synchronised your lives. Made your paths cross in order to help both of you.'

'How did that help him? The poor man had a gun to his head and it didn't need to happen.'

'The poor man had a water pistol to his head and I think you'll find he'll be better off after all this.'

'How?'

'I don't know. We'll have to watch this space.'

'Didn't matter at the time that it was a water pistol,' I grumbled.

'I'm sure it didn't. Are you okay?'

I was silent.

'Hey.' He stretched out his leg and tapped my foot with his, playfully.

'Yes. No. I don't know.'

'Ah, Lucy,' he sighed. He came across the hall and hugged me. I pushed away at first but he held on tighter and eventually I gave in and hugged him back, my cheek against the fabric of his cheap suit, breathing in his musty smell. We pulled away and he tenderly wiped imaginary tears away with this fingers. His kindness made him look moderately more attractive. He handed me a tissue and I gave my nose a loud, wet blow.

'Be careful,' he said. 'You'll wake the baby.'

We both laughed, guiltily.

'I'm pathetic, aren't I?'

'I'm leaning towards saying yes but I should ask you first, in what way?'

'Here I am after being held at gunpoint with a water pistol, babysitting a baby that doesn't exist.'

'Sitting with your life,' he added.

'Good point. Sitting with my life, that is a person. It doesn't get any weirder than this.'

'It might. We haven't even started yet.'

'Why doesn't she have her life following her around? How sad is this?' I referred to the toy-littered floor behind me.

He shrugged, 'I don't get involved in other people's lives. You are my sole concern.'

'Her life must be in denial,' I said. 'You should take a leaf out of her life's book.'

'Or out of yours.'

I sighed. 'You really are that unhappy?'

He nodded, and he looked away from me. He worked his jaw as he took a moment to compose himself.

'But I don't understand how things are so bad for you. I feel fine.'

'You don't feel fine.' He shook his head.

'I don't wake up every day singing "Good Morning", but I'm not,' I lowered my voice, 'pretending that things are there when they're not.'

'Aren't you?' He looked amused. 'It's like this. If you fall and break a leg you feel pain and you go to the doctor, they take an X-ray and you hold it up to the light and everybody can see the broken bone. Yeah?'

I nodded.

'You have a sore tooth, you can feel the pain, so you go to the dentist and he sticks a camera in your mouth, sees the problem, you need a root canal or something, yeah?'

I nodded again.

'These are all very acceptable things in modern

158

society. You're sick; you go to the doctor, you get antibiotics. You're depressed; you talk to a therapist, they might give you anti-depressants. Your greys show; you get your colour done. But with your life you make a few bad decisions, get unlucky a few times, whatever, but you have to keep going, right? Nobody can see the underneath part of who you are, and if you can't see it – if an X-ray and a camera can't take a picture of it for you – in this day and age the belief is, it's not there. But I am here. I'm the other part of you. The X-ray to your life. A mirror is held up to your face and I'm the reflection, I show how you're hurting, how you're unhappy. It's all reflected on me. Make sense?'

Which made sense about the bad breath, the clammy skin and the bad haircut. I mulled it over. 'Yes, but that's rather unfair to you.'

'That's the card I was dealt. Now it's up to me to make myself happy. So you see, this is as much about me as it is about you. The more you live your life, the happier I feel, the more satisfied you are, the healthier I am.'

'So your happiness depends on me.'

'I prefer to see us as a team. You're the Lois Lane to my Superman. The Pinky to my Brain.'

'The X-ray to my broken leg,' I said and we smiled and I felt a kind of a truce being called.

'Did you talk to your family about what happened? I bet they were worried about you.'

'You know I did.'

'I think it's better that we both treat our conversations as if I don't know anything.'

'Don't worry, I do. I saw my mum and Riley yesterday. I went to Riley's. We had Pakistani takeaway and Mum insisted on making me hot chocolate like she did after I'd fallen when I was little,' I laughed.

'That sounds nice.'

'It was.'

'Did you talk about yesterday?'

'I told them I was in another office, running an errand, and that I missed the entire thing.'

'Why did you do that?'

'I don't know. So I wouldn't worry them.'

'Well, aren't you the thoughtful one,' he said sarcastically. 'It wasn't to protect them; it was to protect you. So you wouldn't have to talk about it, so you wouldn't have to admit *feeling* anything. That weird word you don't like.'

'I don't know. Maybe. All the things you say sound very complicated and I don't think in that way.'

'Want to know my theory?'

'Go on.' I rested my chin on my hand.

'A couple of years ago when Blake . . .' he stalled, 'was dumped by you.'

I smiled.

'You started lying to other people, and because you lied to them you made it a lot easier to lie to yourself.'

'That's an interesting theory but I have no idea if it's true or not.'

'Well, we'll put it to the test. Soon you'll have to stop lying to others – which will be harder than you think, by the way – and then you'll start learning the truth about yourself, which will also be harder than you think.'

I rubbed my aching head, wishing I hadn't got myself into this mess. 'So how does it happen?'

'You let me spend time with you.'

'Sure, weekly appointments?'

'No, I mean, I come to work with you, meet your friends, that kind of thing.'

'I can't do that.'

'Why not?'

'I can't just bring you to the dinner table at my parents' house or out with friends. They'll think I'm a freak.'

'You're afraid they'll know things about you.'

'If my life – you – sits down at the table they'll pretty much know everything.'

'Why is that so terrifying?'

'Because it's private. You're private. No one brings along their life to a dinner party.'

'I think you'll find that most people that you love do exactly that. But it's not the point, the point is we need to start doing more things together.'

'That's fine with me, just let's not you and me do things with friends and family. Let's keep it separate.'

'But you're doing that already. None of them know anything about you.'

'It's not going to happen,' I said.

He was silent.

'You're going to turn up anyway, aren't you?' I asked.

He nodded.

I sighed. 'I don't lie to everyone, you know.'

'I know. The wrong number.'

'See? Another weird thing.'

'Not really. Sometimes wrong numbers are the right numbers,' he smiled.

CHAPTER TWELVE

He wanted to begin our journey together by seeing where I lived. I think he felt seeing it would unlock all the great mysteries about me to him. I didn't agree, I felt it would merely unlock a door to an unkempt studio flat and send putrid fish smell blasting in his face. Metaphor understanding was merely the beginning of our differences. We were debating it when Claire returned from the hospital and looked anxiously at the stranger and me sitting on the floor outside her apartment. I stood immediately.

'I didn't let him in,' I said.

Her face softened, and she looked at him. 'You must think I'm rude.'

'No, you're perfectly right,' Life said. 'Though I'm surprised you let her in.'

She smiled. 'I appreciate Lucy's help.'

'How's your mother?' he asked.

I knew he was still testing my alibi and I'd

passed the test, because her face said it all. Nobody could pretend to be so distraught.

'She's stable . . . for now,' she said. 'How's Conor?'

'Em. He's asleep.'

'Did he drink his bottle?'

'Yes.' I'd poured it down the sink.

She seemed happy and fumbled in her bag for her purse and produced some cash. 'This is for your time, thank you so much,' she said, thrusting it at me. I really wanted to take it. Really. Sebastian needed so much repair work, the carpet still needed to be cleaned, my hair could do with a professional blowdry, I could do with buying something other than microwave dinners but no, Life was watching me so I did the right thing.

'I couldn't possibly take that.' I pushed the words out, though they were dying to stay inside. 'It was my pleasure, really.'

Then came the moment. I put the key in the lock and turned it. I held out my hand for him to enter before me. He looked excited. I felt anything but. I followed him and closed the door, painfully aware of the smell and hoping he would be polite enough not to mention it. Mr Pan stirred and stretched, and then came slinking forward to meet our new guest, his hips slowly and lazily going from side to side in a hypnotic state like the campest cat in the world. He looked at my life and then ran himself along his legs, tail high in the air.

'You have a cat,' he said and went to his knees and stroked him. Mr Pan bathed in the glory of his attention.

'This is Mr Pan, Mr Pan this is . . . what do I call you?'

'Life.'

'I can't introduce you to people as that, we'll have to think of a name.'

He shrugged, 'I don't care.'

'Okay Engelbert.'

'I don't want to be called Engelbert.' He looked around the room at my numerous Gene Kelly photographs in frames, and at the poster for *Singin' in the Rain* on the bathroom door. 'Call me Gene.'

'No, you can't be called that.' There were only so many Genes I could have in my life. One, and a Don Lockwood whom I'd told never to call me again.

'Who's the other guy?' he asked.

'Donald O'Connor, he plays Cosmo Brown.'

He put on an American fifties accent. 'Well then, call me Cosmo Brown.'

'I'm not introducing you to people as Cosmo.'

'It's Cosmo or Life, doll.'

'Okay, fine. Let me show you around.' I stood at the front door like an air steward and held out my arms as if going through the emergency procedures. 'To my left is the bathroom. If you want to use it you must put on the kitchen extractor fan light as the bulb is gone in there. To my right is the kitchen. Further to my left is the bedroom and

further to the right is the living room. Tour over.'
I bowed. He could see everything from where he
stood, all he had to do was move his eyes.

He surveyed the space.

'So what do you think?'

'It stinks of fish. And what is that on the carpet?'

I sighed. He couldn't even do a minute of politeness, the very foundations which my life was built
on. 'It's prawn cocktail, Mr Pan spilled it and
walked it into the floor. Okay?'

'Okay, but I meant that.' He pointed at the
writing on the carpet.

'Oh, that's the name of a carpet-cleaning
company.'

'Of course it is.' He looked at me and his eyes
were smiling. 'I'm not going to ask why it's written
on the floor. Call them,' he said and went straight
to my corner cupboard and rummaged through
my treats. Mr Pan followed at his heel, the traitor.
Life sat up on the counter and munched on some
cookies, which annoyed me, I was planning on
eating them for dinner. 'The carpet is disgusting;
you have to call them.'

'I don't have time to stay home from work to
let them in. Things like that are always a bother.'

'Ask them to come at the weekend and if they
can't, there's always the strong possibility that
you'll be fired tomorrow.'

'I thought you were supposed to make me feel
better.'

'I thought you wanted to get fired.'

'I did. But I wanted a redundancy package, not to get fired just because I don't speak Spanish.'

'It's hardly a small detail, you are supposed to be their languages expert.'

'I speak five other languages,' I snapped.

'Ooh, but you don't speaketh the truth,' he laughed before putting an entire cookie in his mouth.

I looked him up and down, disgusted. 'You have moobs.'

'What's that?'

'Check it in your little computer, why don't you.'

'I will.' He took out his iPhone. 'Now call them, the carpet is disgusting. It hasn't been properly cleaned since you moved in and I suspect even longer so it's got yours and some stranger's skin and hair and toenails, and cat hairs and whatever bugs and bacteria are living on him engrained in it and every time you breathe in, you are inhaling it into your lungs.'

Disgusted, I immediately grabbed his phone from his hand but he held on tight. 'That's my phone, use your own. I'm Googling "moobs".'

I blocked my nose and dialled directory enquiries to connect me. A second before it was answered I hoped Don would answer again. But he didn't. It was an older man named Roger and in two minutes I'd arranged for him to call by on Sunday. I ended the call feeling quite proud of myself. I had done something. But Life wasn't about to congratulate me, he was glaring at me angrily.

'What?'

'Man boobs.'

I laughed. 'Well, you've let yourself go a little, haven't you?'

'Through no fault of my own.'

'I work out five days a week,' I defended myself.

'Which is probably the only reason why we're both still standing,' he said, hopping off the counter, climbing over the back of the couch and sitting down.

'I can't help commenting on your appearance. You look so . . . dirty. You need a make-over. Do you have anything else in your wardrobe?' I paused. 'Do you have a wardrobe?'

'This isn't *Clueless*, Lucy, I'm not a project. You don't get to spend a day polishing my nails and perming my hair and everything is okay again.'

'What about a back, sack and crack?'

'You're disgusting and I'm ashamed to be your life.' He bit into another cookie and nodded in the direction of my bed. 'Any visitors over there?'

'I don't feel comfortable talking to you about that.'

'Because I'm a man?'

'Because . . . I don't think it's important. And yes. Because you're a man. But I'm not prudish.' I raised my chin, and then climbed over the back of the couch to join him. 'The answer is no, nobody has ever been in here but that's not to say there hasn't been any activity.'

'That's disgusting.' He rolled up his nose.

'I don't mean in that bed.' I rolled my eyes. 'I mean in my life.'

'Hold on.' He smiled and reached into his rucksack and took out an iPad. 'That'd be Alex Buckley,' he read. 'Stockbroker, you met him in a bar, you liked his tie, he liked your tits but he didn't say that out loud. Not to you anyway, he did say it to his colleague Tony who replied, "Why the fuck not." Charming. But he did say to you and I quote, "There must be something wrong with my eyes, I can't seem to take them off you." Unquote.' He howled laughing. '*That* works for you?'

'No.' I picked at a feather in the cushion, pulled it out. Mr Pan watched me, moved closer to play with the feather. 'But the drinks he bought for me did. Anyway, he was nice.'

'You went back to his place,' he read, then he looked disgusted. 'I don't think I need to read all of this. Bla bla bla, then you left before breakfast. That was ten months ago.'

'That wasn't ten months ago, that was . . .' I counted back in my head. 'Well, it wasn't ten months ago anyway.'

'Last time you saw any action,' he said, mock-disapprovingly. 'Outside of this apartment anyway.'

'Shut up about that. So I'm fussy when it comes to men. I can't just sleep with any guy.'

'Yes, because Alex Buckley the stockbroker who liked your tits was so special.'

I laughed. 'You know what I mean.'

169

'Fussy is an understatement.' He became serious. 'You're just not remotely ready for men. You're not over Blake.'

'I'm so over Blake, it's ridiculous,' I exaggerated, sounding like a petulant teen.

'You're not. If you were over him, every man you've met since would not have involved a large intake of alcohol. If you were over him, you'd be able to move on and meet someone new.'

'May I remind you that feeling complete is not about meeting a man. It's about being content within yourself.' I tried not to laugh when I said it.

'To thine own self be true,' he said and nodded. 'I believe that. But if you're unable to meet somebody else because you're stuck in the past then that's a problem.'

'Who says it's my problem? I'm always open to meeting someone new.' I grabbed the cookies from him.

'What about the guy in the café, the Sunday we met? I practically threw him at you and you didn't give him half a look. Quote, "I have to go see my boyfriend,"' he mimicked me. 'Unquote.'

I gasped. 'You set me up?'

'I had to see how bad you were.'

'I knew it. I knew he was too attractive to be a normal person, he was an actor.'

'He wasn't an actor. You're not getting this. I synchronised your lives. Made your paths cross in order for something to happen.'

'But nothing happened so you failed,' I snapped.

'Something did happen. You turned him down and he went back to his girlfriend whom he was missing dearly and was regretting breaking up with. Your response to him made him realise.'

'How dare you use me like that.'

'How am I using you? How else do you think life happens? A series of coincidences and occurrences have to happen somehow. Our lives all crash and collide and you think there's no reason or rhyme to it? If there wasn't any reason for it all, what would be the point? Why do you think anything happens at all? There is an outcome, repercussions and occurrences to everybody you meet and everything you say. Honestly, Lucy.' He shook his head and bit into another cookie.

'But that's the point, I didn't think there *was* one.'

'Was a what?'

'A point!'

He frowned, confused. Then he got it. 'Lucy, there's always a point.'

I wasn't sure I believed that. 'Who else have you *synchronised* my life with?'

'Lately? Not many that would stand out to you. Just that nice American lady at reception. I can tell by your face you're shocked by that one, and by the way, you can thank her I'm here today because it was her that made me want to give you another chance after our last meeting.'

'Like you weren't desperate to meet me again anyway.'

'Believe me, I wasn't. But when you left her the chocolate bar I had a Willy Wonka moment.'

'Is that secret code for something private?'

'No. You know the part where Slugworth tells Charlie to steal the everlasting gobstopper and he'll take care of his family forever but Charlie doesn't and leaves the gobstopper on Wonka's office desk at the end of the film which shows Wonka Charlie's true worth as a person?'

'You've just given the whole thing away.'

'Shut up, you've seen it twenty-six times. You left the bar of chocolate for Mrs Morgan and that was a very thoughtful thing to do.'

'Yeah, well, she said she liked them.'

'It reminded me that you do have a heart, you do care about people, that's never been the problem. I just have to try to make you care about me.'

That just simply broke my heart. Nobody had ever uttered words like that to me before and there he was, this young exhausted desperate-looking man with bad breath and a crumpled suit just wanting to be liked.

'So that was the point to you hiring her? So that I could get another chance with you?'

He looked surprised. 'I never thought about it like that.' Then suddenly he yawned. 'Where am I sleeping?'

'Wherever you usually sleep.'

'I think I should stay here, Lucy.'

'Okay, that's no problem,' I said calmly. 'I'll just be at my friend Melanie's house if you need me.'

'Ah yes, Melanie, who's annoyed at you leaving everything so early all of the time.' He messed around on his iPad again. 'The same Melanie who said straight after you left the restaurant the other day, quote, "There's something up with her, I can't wait to get her on her own to find out what," unquote.' He looked pleased as punch. I was horrified. Time alone was not what I needed with Melanie right now and I wasn't going to go back to Riley's to stay with him and Mum.

'You can sleep on the couch,' I said, defeated, then climbed over the back of the couch to get to my bed.

He slept on the couch with Mr Pan, covered by a spare dusty blanket that I dug out from the top of the wardrobe while he shone the torch inside for me, all the time tutting. Not out loud, but I could hear it in my head, a constant rhythmic tut-tut-tut-tut like the grandfather clock we had in the echoey hall when I was a child that used to scare me and keep me awake at night until I stuffed a pillow in its pendulum and then blamed it on Riley. He snored so loudly that for the first time in a long time, my life kept me awake all night. Remembering the grandfather clock trick, I threw a pillow at him somewhere around two a.m. but I missed and ended up sending Mr Pan into a fit. Four minutes past eleven was the last time I saw on the clock before I fell asleep and was woken at six by him taking a shower, then he sneaked out and arrived back shortly afterwards, clattering

173

the keys down on the counter and banging around and making enough noise to wake the building. I knew he was trying to disturb me so I deliberately kept my eyes closed at least ten minutes longer than I actually wanted. Finally the smell stirred me. He was sitting at the counter eating an omelette. His shirt sleeves were rolled up to his elbows, his hair was wet and slicked back. He looked different. He looked clean.

'Good morning,' he said.

'Wow. Your breath doesn't smell bad any more.'

He looked insulted. 'Whatever,' he said, going back to reading the paper. 'Your words can't hurt me. I got you coffee and the crossword.'

I was taken aback, genuinely touched. 'Thanks.'

'And I bought a bulb for your bathroom light. You can put it in yourself though.'

'Thank you.'

'And that omelette is still hot.'

On the counter was a ham, cheese and red pepper omelette.

'Thanks so much,' I smiled. 'That's really thoughtful of you.'

'No problem.'

We sat in silence together, eating, listening to a man and a woman on breakfast television hop from soap gossip to current affairs and then to a recent study into teenage acne. I didn't replace the bulb; it would have taken too much effort and too much time in a morning that was already rushed after sitting down and eating a normal breakfast. I left the door ajar and took a shower, all the time watching the door to make sure my life wasn't a perv. I got dressed in the bathroom. When I came out, he was ready with his rucksack and his crinkled suit. I had been surprisingly comfortable with him but all of a sudden I smelled a rat. There was always a catch.

'Well, I guess this is goodbye for today,' I said hopefully.

'I'm coming to work with you,' he said.

I was nervous going into the office, obviously because I had to face everybody after Tuesday's incident but mostly because I had Life with me. I was just hoping that security would rid me of at least one problem. I swiped my ID card and the barrier moved for me to pass. Life walked into the bar directly behind me and I heard him make a sound as if he'd been winded. I tried not to smile but failed miserably.

'Hey,' security called. They were vigilant at the best of times but after the episode with Steve they were on high alert.

I turned around and tried to look as apologetic as possible at Life. 'Look, I'm going to be late, I have to run. I'll catch up with you at lunchtime, okay?'

His mouth fell open and I turned around and hurried to the elevator, trying to blend in with the crowd as if I was being chased. As I was waiting I watched the security guard twice Life's width make his way over to him as if he was going to bash him. Life reached into his rucksack and pulled out some paperwork. The security guard took it as though it were a piece of rotten fish and read through it. Then he looked at me, looked back to the paper, looked at my life, then gave the paper back to him and walked back to his desk. He pressed the button behind it and the barrier opened.

'Thanks,' Life called. The security guard waved him on. Life smiled smugly at me and we rode the stuffed elevator together in silence. The usual suspects were in the office before I got there, huddled together and quite obviously talking about me because as soon as I entered they hushed and looked up. All eyes immediately went to Life. Then back to me.

'Hi, Lucy,' Nosy said. 'Is that your lawyer?'

'Why, are you looking for one for the wedding?' I answered cattily.

Graham didn't laugh and that put me off a bit, he always laughed at my crap jokes. I wondered if that meant he wasn't going to be a sex pest any more and that bothered me too. My response to Louise had been a cheap comeback, but in reality it was disguising the fact that I didn't know what to say. I'd had a lot of time to think about how to introduce my life to people but beyond calling him Cosmo – which I guessed would create more questions than answers – I still couldn't think of a story. I could think of a perfectly good lie. I could think of many perfectly good lies; he was a terminally ill patient whose final wish was to spend time with me, he was an out-of-town cousin, he was a college boy looking for some experience, he was a mentally ill friend on day release, he was a journalist writing an article on modern-day working women and chose me as his subject. All of these things I'm sure everybody would believe but Life would not approve of. I was trying to come up with the perfect lie that he would approve of, which was ironic because in the history of the entire world, I guessed there probably hadn't been one of those yet and probably never ever would be. Edna saved me from the siege of looks, stares, and pending questions and accusations by calling me into the office for a session of the same, but at least with her it was one-on-one and I could take her on. As I made my way to her office, I smiled at the others, sweet and apologetic for having to part company with them. I turned to Life before I went in and under my breath said, 'Are you going to wait out here?'

'No, I'll go in with you,' he said, keeping his voice at a normal level, which stopped me from speaking any further.

I went into Edna's office and sat down at the circular table she had by her window. She had a fake white rose in a tall slim vase, and a copy of *Ulysses* on the shelf behind her desk; two of the things on my list that always annoyed me about her because I despised fake flowers and guessed she had probably never read Ulysses in her life but liked how having it on her shelf made her look. She looked at my life.

'Hello,' she said in a *who are you* kind of way.

'Ms Larson, my name is . . .' he looked at me and I saw his lips twitch as he fought a smile, 'Cosmo Brown. I have some paperwork here for you which details how I'm allowed to be with Lucy Silchester at all times, and includes confidentiality agreements which have been signed by me and have been stamped and notarised by a recognised notary. You can trust that anything I learn about the company in this conversation will not go any further but anything that is discussed with Lucy regarding her personal life will be well within my rights to discuss as I so wish.'

She took the paperwork and as she read, I saw the realisation pass over her face. 'Okay Mr Brown, please have a seat.'

'Please, call me Cosmo,' he smiled and I knew it was a dig at me.

She looked at him when she spoke. 'This meeting is about the events which took place on Tuesday. I'm sure you're aware of the incident regarding Steven Roberts.'

Life nodded.

'Excuse me, do you have to address him when you speak about me?' I looked at Life. 'Does she have to address you?'

'She can look at whoever she likes, Lucy.'

'But it doesn't *have* to be you.'

'No, it doesn't have to be me.'

178

'Okay.' I looked back at Edna. 'You don't have to address him.'

'Thank you, Lucy. Now, where was I?' She returned her gaze to Life. 'So what we are going to discuss is not what happened to Steve, though if there are any personal worries that Lucy has about what happened and frankly I wouldn't be surprised if there were, then as her immediate superior I am the person she can speak to about any issue that arises from what happened—'

'Eh, excuse me, but I'm here. You don't have to speak as though I'm not here.'

She looked at me then, fixed me with a steely stare and I wished she'd continued looking at Life. 'This meeting is to do with the revelation that surfaced from those events in which we discovered that you can't actually speak any Spanish.'

'I can speak Spanish. I was just under so much pressure. There was a gun in my face and I couldn't think.'

Edna looked relieved and she finally softened. 'Lucy, that is what *I* assumed, I mean, my goodness, I could barely remember my own name under the circumstances and I was just hoping to hear confirmation of that. As you can understand I have to officially go about—'

'Excuse me, can I interrupt here?' Life said.

I looked at him with wide eyes. 'I don't think you're allowed to.' I looked at Edna. 'Is he allowed to? I think he's just supposed to witness my life and not actually partake in any—'

'No, no, I'm allowed to partake,' he said to me. Then he looked at Edna. 'I'd like to confirm that Lucy cannot speak Spanish.'

My mouth dropped. Edna's eyes widened even more than her fish eyes.

'I'm sorry, did you say "can" or "cannot"?'

'I will verify that I said "cannot".' He said the word slowly and accentuated the t. 'She,' he pointed at me to make sure we were all totally clear it was not the fake rose on the table that we were talking about, 'is unable to speak Spanish. I think there is a danger here of you being deceived again and it's only appropriate that I jump in and keep you wise to the situation.' He looked at me as if to say, *That okay? Did I handle that well?*

I was speechless. My life had stabbed me in the back. Edna was momentarily speechless too but then she found her voice again. She continued to talk to him instead of me.

'Cosmo, I'm sure you understand that this is a very serious situation.'

I felt beads of sweat break out on my forehead.

'Of course,' he agreed.

'And so as Lucy is employed as our language specialist for the manual and has been for the past two and a half years, I am concerned that her lack of knowledge of Spanish has put the customers who buy the products in grave danger and the company in jeopardy. I mean, who on earth was writing the Spanish translations? Were they even accurate? Were they from a dictionary?'

'They were from a very reputable national Spanish speaker whose translations of the appliance directions have been second to none,' I said quickly.

'Well, you don't actually know that,' Life said.

'There have never been any complaints,' I said, tired of being stabbed in the back.

'That we know of,' Edna said and Life agreed.

'Who is this person who was translating the work for you?' Edna asked, unable to hide the shock from her voice.

'From a reputable—'

'You said that,' he interrupted.

'—Spanish business person,' I continued anyway. 'It was actually more of a sub-contract than *cheating* though I know nobody has brought up that word but that is what I've been made to feel like I'm doing.' I took the high ground. 'Look, I speak every other language perfectly, that is definitely not a lie, tell her.'

I looked at Life to back me up but he put up his hands. 'I don't think that's my role here.'

I gulped and lowered my voice. 'Look, if you could just allow me to keep my job, please, then maybe let Quentin do the Spanish translations and it's all kept in-house and it's all perfectly legal and there's nothing to worry about. I apologise profusely for not telling the complete truth—'

'For lying,' Life said.

'For not telling the complete truth,' I continued.

'For lying.' He looked at me. 'You lied.'

181

'Look, who doesn't lie on their resumé?' I finally snapped. 'Everybody does. Ask any of those guys out there if they've ever lied and they'll all tell you they exaggerated the truth a little. I bet you have too.' I looked at Edna. 'You've said you worked at Global Maximum for four years and everyone knows it was only two years, and half of that was in junior management and not senior like you said you were.'

Edna's eyes widened. Then realising what I'd said, mine did too.

'But that's not to say you *lied*, I just mean we all exaggerate the truth, that's not to take away from any accomplishments that you or I may or may not have—'

'Okay, I think I may have heard enough here,' Edna said, massaging her temples. 'I'm going to have to bring this up on a higher level.'

'No, please don't do that.' I reached across and held her arm. 'Please don't. Look, there's nothing to worry about. You know legal wouldn't have cleared any manual we did if it all wasn't one hundred per cent accurate. Things get checked all the time, I'm not the person with the last say here. So nothing can backfire on you and if it ever *ever* did, then you've nothing to worry about because you didn't know. Nobody knew.'

'Did Quentin know?' she asked, her eyes narrowed.

'Why do you ask?' I frowned.

'Just tell me the truth, Lucy. Quentin knew, didn't he?'

I was taken aback. 'Nobody knew.'

'But he knew on Tuesday, when Steve was asking you to translate. He knew then, he was straight up from under the table.'

'I think everyone knew then, it was obvious I hadn't a word in my head.'

'I think you're lying again,' she said.

'No, I'm not. Okay, I'm not exactly lying, I think Quentin found out a little earlier when—'

Edna shook her head. 'How much else do I have to pull out of you, Lucy? I mean—'

'No no, listen,' I interrupted. 'He only knew a couple of minutes earlier when I was trying to speak to Augusto Fernández.'

She wasn't really listening to me. She had given up. 'I don't know.' She was tidying her paperwork away and she stood. 'I don't know what to believe any more. Frankly, I'm surprised at you, Lucy, I really thought that you of all people had it all together, out of everyone in this . . .' She looked out at the desks outside. 'Well anyway, I'm surprised at you. But then,' she looked at Life, 'I thought the same about my sister and she found herself in the same,' she searched for a word to describe my current situation, '*predicament* as this.'

Life nodded as if they'd shared a secret.

She sighed. 'Quentin did know, he didn't know, you don't seem to be very clear or convincing on that fact.'

'No, no, I'm sure about this, please—'

'I think we've taken enough time here,' she said.

'Why don't you go back and join the others and I'll have a think about what we've discussed. Thank you, Lucy. Thank you, Cosmo.'

She shook both our hands and I was quickly ushered out of her office. I went back to my desk in shock at what had occurred. Life followed me. Sat down at the empty desk that looked directly opposite. He drummed his fingers on the table.

'So what do you do now?' he said. 'Want me to photocopy anything?'

'I can't believe you did that,' I said. 'I just can't believe you had the nerve to do that to me. What happened to the *we're a team* talk? You were just sweet-talking me so you could make a fucking fool out of me.' I raised my voice by accident and the others looked over at me. 'I'm going for a cigarette,' I said, then stood up and left the room, my chin high and mighty as I made my way under everybody's watchful gaze.

The last thing I heard before I left the room was his voice loud and clear saying, 'She doesn't smoke. She pretends to, to get extra breaks.'

I slammed the door behind me.

CHAPTER THIRTEEN

I was standing on the fire escape, secret smoking location number three of the year after the disabled toilet on the second floor and the cleaning staff service room. Two other people were there too; a man and a woman but they weren't there together and none of us spoke. It wasn't like the smoking section outside a club or pub where everybody spoke to everybody, united by the happiness of being out on a social occasion. This was work and the only reason we were all here, apart from needing to feed the nicotine fix, was to get away from talking to people. We had come here to have a break from thoughts and the hard work that came with the constant interaction with idiots. Or at least people we considered idiots because they were not mind readers and we had to, patiently, use polite words to explain things that we were thinking when really inside we were fighting the urge to take their heads in our hands and softly and repeatedly thud their foreheads off the wall. But there was no such politeness here; we were shutting off our brains, deliberately ignoring each other and satisfied by our right to do so, concentrating only on breathing in and blowing out smoke. Only I wasn't. I hadn't stopped thinking, and I wasn't smoking.

I heard the door open behind me. I didn't bother turning around, I didn't care if location number three had been found and we had all been caught. What was another misdemeanour on my current rap sheet? But the other two did care and they hid their cigarettes in their closed and quickly yellowing palms, forgetting the rising smoke would give the game away, and they both quickly turned to see who had stumbled upon their lair. They didn't appear too concerned by who they saw but they didn't relax either which meant it wasn't the boss but it wasn't someone they knew. The man took a final long drag of his cigarette and quickly left, the scare of the close call enough to ruin his nicotine thrill. The woman stayed where she was, but eyed the new guest up and down as she had done with me when I joined them. I still didn't turn around to see who it was, partly because I didn't care who it was, but mostly because I knew who it was.

'Hi,' he said, standing so close to me our shoulders rubbed.

'I'm not talking to you,' I said, staring straight ahead. The woman sensed something juicy and settled down to suck on the remainder of her cigarette.

'I told you it was going to be harder than you thought,' he said gently. 'But don't worry, we'll get there.'

'Will we now,' I said. 'Excuse me,' I turned to the lady, 'would you mind if I borrowed a cigarette, please?'

'I think she means can she *take* it. She can't give it back once it's smoked,' Life added for me.

She looked at me as though she'd rather sell her favourite grandmother but she gave me one anyway because that's what people do, they're mostly polite, even when they're feeling rude inside.

I inhaled. Then I coughed.

'You don't smoke,' he said.

I inhaled again in his face, then tried to stifle the cough that immediately came after.

'Why don't you just tell me why you're so angry?'

'Why?' I finally turned to him. 'Are you demented? You know bloody well why. You made a fool of me in there. You made me look like a . . . like a . . .'

'Liar, by any chance?'

'Look, I had a plan. I had it all under control. You were just supposed to sit there and observe, that's what you said.'

'I never said that.'

'Somebody said that.'

'No, you assumed.'

187

I silently fumed.

'So tell me, what was the great plan? You were going to lie again and all of a sudden like the great genius you are, learn Spanish overnight?'

'I have a great aptitude for learning, that's what my French teacher said,' I huffed.

'And your civics teacher said "could do better".' He looked away. 'I did the right thing.'

Silence. The smoker sniffed.

'Okay, so I should have told the truth, but there has to be another way of doing this. You can't just bulldoze your way into my life and try to fix every little lie that I've ever told. What are you going to do when you meet my parents? Come out with every little fib and give them a heart attack? Are you going to tell them that instead of a study group, I had a house party the night they went to my Aunt Julie's fortieth and that their darling nephew Colin shagged a girl in their bed and Fiona streaked across the lawn for the last bit of hash and that no, I'm sorry, it wasn't vegetable soup on the floor like I said it was, it was Melanie's vomit and I shouldn't have let the dog eat it? And by the way, Lucy can't speak Spanish.' I gasped for air.

He was taken aback. 'Even your parents think you can speak Spanish?'

'They paid for a summer there, what else was I meant to tell them?' I snapped.

'The truth? Does that ever occur to you?'

'That I was a podium dancer in a night club

188

instead of doing the job they set up for me at a hotel reception?'

'Maybe not, then.'

'I mean, where does the big reveal begin and end? One minute you're buying light bulbs and the next minute you're telling my father I think he needs to get off his high horse and stop being a pretentious little shit. You need to have a little sensitivity about this, you're supposed to be helping me make things better, not putting me in the unemployment line and ending what little relationship I already have with my family. We need to have a plan.'

He was silent for a while, I could see he was mulling it over and I waited for one of his analogies but none came. Instead he said, 'You're right. I'm sorry.'

I pretended to keel over the banister but he and the smoker pulled me back, thinking I was serious.

'Thanks,' I said to her, a little embarrassed, and she quite wisely found that an appropriate time to leave.

'But I'm not sorry for what I did, just the way that I went about it. We'll work on another strategy for the future.'

I respected his fairness, his ability to admit when he was wrong. So I took another drag of the cigarette and then put it out, as a mark of respect. But he wasn't finished and I examined the crushed smouldering cigarette to see if I could pick it up again and continue smoking.

'I couldn't just sit there and listen to you lie again, Lucy, and I'm never going to be able to do that so whatever strategy we work out, it has to involve you not lying again. It gives me heartburn.'

'My lying gives you heartburn?'

'Right there.' He rubbed the centre of his chest.

'Oh. Well, I'm sorry about that.'

He winced and rubbed it again. 'Your nose just grew, Pinocchio.'

I shoved him playfully. 'Why don't you just let *me* tell people the truth? In my own time, that is.'

'I don't think there's enough time in the world to allow that to happen.'

'Well, I'm not going to gather the troops and admit everything all at once but I'll do it. I'll do it when the time is right. How about we agree that I just won't tell any more lies from now on, and you do your little accompanying, observing thing if you have to.'

'How will you stop yourself from lying?'

'I think I know how not to lie if I don't want to,' I said, insulted. 'It's not as if I have a problem.'

'What is it about the wrong-number guy that makes you tell the truth?'

'Who?'

'You know who. See, you've just done it again,' he said, amused. 'Your first reaction is to deny any knowledge of anything.'

I ignored his insight. 'I told him not to call me any more.'

'Why? Did you call and he was engaged?'

Though he was pleased with his joke, I ignored it. 'Nah. It was just too weird.'

'That's a pity.'

'Yeah,' I said vaguely, not sure if it was pitiful. I held out my hand. 'So have we got a deal? I don't lie, you observe?'

He thought about it. 'I want to add to it.'

I dropped my hand. 'Of course you do.'

'Every time you lie, I reveal a truth.' He held out his hand. 'Deal?'

I thought about it; I didn't like it. I couldn't truthfully promise that I would never lie again, all I could do was try, and I couldn't trust him to reveal any amount of truth in my life, but if I agreed to the deal then at least it put the ball in my court and he wouldn't be charging around my life like a bull in a china shop. 'Fine. It's a deal.' We shook on it.

It was tense when I got back to the office. The others couldn't figure out whether to be angry with me or not, just as they couldn't figure out whether to be angry with Steve or not so we just worked in silence, no doubt putting aside any issues that needed discussion with one another in the newly created *when everything gets back to normal tray* beside the inbox and the outbox. Life faced me from the opposite desk, which was acceptable because I bet there wasn't a soul in the room, apart from Edna, who could remember the name of the guy who worked there. He'd been knocked out in round one early last year when I had nothing to do with him from where I sat in the corner right beneath the air-conditioning vent and my sole task every day was to try keep warm and do everything to stop Graham from staring at my nipples. Needless to say, Augusto Fernández's quite earnest promise that he would do all in his power to give Steve his job back was nonsense, and so Steve's desk stood empty. If Life had chosen to sit at that desk, however, that would have caused a stir. It would have been too raw, too painful. Life looked through his computer all day, tap-tap-tapping and making notes, watching me, observing how I spoke to the others which was at an all-time low seeing as nobody was willing to communicate.

Then I started to think about what he'd said. About the wrong number, about Don Lockwood, about why I didn't lie to him. I don't know why I didn't lie to him but the most obvious answer was because I didn't know him, he was a complete stranger to me and the truth didn't matter with him.

The truth didn't matter. Why did it with everybody else?

I picked up my phone and went through my photos; I stopped at the one of his eyes, studied them, zoomed in and out of them one by one like an obsessive stalker, saw the flecks of aqua, almost green, in the blue, then I set it as my screen saver. It looked pretty impressive when I placed my phone on the desk and they were staring up at me.

'What are you smiling at?' Life asked me, and his sudden voice made me jump.

'What? Jesus, you scared me. Don't creep up on me like that.'

'I was sitting right here, what were you doing?'

'Oh,' I was about to say *nothing*, when I looked down at the screen saver. I didn't want to lie. 'Just looking at photographs.'

Satisfied I was telling the truth, Life decided to take a break and headed off to the kitchen. Graham's eyes followed him across the room; then he looked around at everyone else to make sure they were staying put at their desks, stood up and followed Life into the kitchen. I watched the door, waiting for one of them to come out but when five minutes had passed I began to worry. Life had been in the kitchen too long with Graham the Cock, I hoped he hadn't fallen prey to one of his offers of a dalliance, a thought which I knew couldn't be true but made me queasy. I stood at the filing cabinet which Louise had strategically placed by the kitchen door, opened a drawer and pretended to look for a file while eavesdropping.

'So she lied about the Spanish,' Graham said.

'Yep,' Life said, sounding like he was eating, and he was scraping something. A yoghurt pot, I deducted. That was Louise's, she was on WeightWatchers and snacked all day on yoghurts which had more sugar in them than a doughnut.

'Well, well, well. And she lied about smoking.'

'Yep,' he said again. Scrape, scrape, scrape.

'You know that I smoke,' Graham said.

'No, I didn't know that.' And it sounded like he didn't care much either.

'We sometimes go out there together, me and Lucy, to the private place,' Graham said, keeping his voice low, not because he was talking about the private smoking place but in that way that men did when they were talking about sexual things they had done, or more usually wished they'd done.

'The fire escape,' Life said, keeping his voice at normal level, which told anyone who wasn't Graham that he didn't want to lower his tone of voice or subject of conversation.

'I was thinking that she might have a thing for me. That pretending to be a smoker was just a way to get close to me.' Graham gave a naughty little chuckle, forgetting about the fact that it was always he who followed me.

'You think?' Scrape, scrape.

'Well, it's hard to get close in here, with this lot. What do you think? Has she ever mentioned anything to you about me? Or she wouldn't have to say it, you'd just know, wouldn't you? Go on, you can tell me.'

'Yeah, I pretty much know everything,' Life said and I was annoyed that Cock knew he was my life. It was enough that he tried to come on to me, never mind trying to sweet-talk my life as well.

'So what do you think? Does she want some?'

'Want some?' The scraping stopped. The yoghurt had been demolished, the integrity insulted.

'She's turned me down a few times, I won't lie to you, but the thing is I'm married and for a girl like Lucy, that's not her thing. But I still feel there's something . . . Has she told you anything about me?'

I heard a squeak – the bin lid rising; heard the plastic bag rustle as something was dumped – the yoghurt pot; heard a clink in the sink – the spoon. Then heard a long sigh – my life.

'Graham, I can safely say that Lucy wants to like you and occasionally sees glimpses of a nice guy but deep down, deep, deep down she thinks you're an absolute asshole.'

I smiled, closed the file drawer and swiftly returned to my desk. I knew then that though he'd stabbed me in the back just that morning, by the afternoon, he had my back. The office, namely Graham, was even quieter that afternoon and I wasn't fired that day. Lying in bed that night I knew Life was awake because he wasn't snoring. I was running through everything that had happened that day and all that had been said; between me, Life and everybody else stuck in between. I eventually came to one conclusion.

'You planned all that, didn't you?' I asked to the dark empty room.

'Planned what?'

'You deliberately went in and told Edna the truth in a way that would make me come up with the idea to tell the truth myself.'

'Sounds like you're analysing everything too much, Lucy.'

'Am I right?'

Silence.

'Yes.'

'What else are you planning?'

He never answered me. It was just as well.

CHAPTER FOURTEEN

I regretted arranging with Melanie to meet the following night. Not just because Life had kept me awake all night with his snoring but because the night out with her was one giant bullet that I had been trying to dodge for a long time. In order to make up for leaving dinner early the previous week I'd promised I'd go to Melanie's next set in Dublin. It happened to be Friday in the coolest club in the city, for that month at least. It was so cool it didn't even have a name, which meant that everybody called it the Club on Henrietta Street with No Name, which was ironic. It was a private club, or at least it had been renovated and marketed with the intention of being a private club, but with its extortionate charges – most likely stemming from the bill for the hundreds of gas heaters placed outside to fool Irish people into thinking and feeling like they were not in inner-city Dublin but in fact West Hollywood – mixed with the times we were living in it meant that it was letting anybody in. Anybody they considered pretty and fabulous during the weekend, that was, and then mid-week just any ugly person at all to cover paying staff wages. Tonight was Friday, which meant they were going for pretty and fabulous which didn't hold much luck for my life. I'd heard the grumbles that it wasn't as busy as it used to be – one hundred fewer people on a Friday – which the grumblers surmised was a sign of the times. I thought that was ironic because it was more a sign of the times that a club with no name, situated in what used to be one of the worst slums in Europe – where people were housed in tenements in Georgian buildings that the rich had moved out of to live in the suburbs, where up to fifteen people shared one room, with up to one hundred people with all kinds of diseases living in one building with one toilet in the back garden where livestock lived – was more accurately the sign of the times.

I rang the buzzer on the large red door and waited for a small section of it to open and a dwarf to step outside. That didn't happen. The entire door was opened by a bald man dressed in black who resembled a bowling ball, and treated entries as though he were Prince Charming and the female arrivals were simply for him alone to pluck his princess before his evil father married him off to an ogre. He might have been happy with my appearance but unfortunately he didn't like the look of my life, which was ironic because that was the nature of club life; you weren't supposed to bring your lives with you. You were supposed to leave them at home in the cluttered bathroom beside the hairspray and the fake tan and all the other condiments that went into making you feel like someone else.

The bowling ball stared at my life with a face like he'd just eaten shit. Life reached for his inside pocket again for the piece of paper that gave him access to all areas in my life.

'Don't,' I said, holding my hand up to stop him.

'Why not?'

'Not here.' I looked at the security guy. 'Could you please get Melanie Sahakyan for us?'

'Who?'

'DJ Darkness. We're guests of hers.'

'What's your name?'

'Lucy Silchester.'

'And what's his name?'

'Cosmo Brown,' Life said loudly and I didn't need to turn around to know that he felt this was hilarious.

'His name isn't on the list. It should be a plus-one.'

'It's not a plus-one here.' He spoke as if the clipboard alone revealed the mysteries of the world. I wondered what the clipboard would say about the Mayan 2012 beliefs, or if it wasn't on the list it didn't count. He studied my life. Life didn't much care, he leaned on the glossy black railings where impoverished children with dirty faces had once climbed, and seemed to enjoy the spectacle that was taking place.

'There must be a misunderstanding. Could you please get Melanie?'

'I have to close the door. You can wait in here, he has to wait outside.'

I sighed. 'I'll wait here.'

On looks, I could get into the club. With my life, I couldn't. It was a cruel, cruel world. As groups passed us by and I heard snippets of their conversations before they entered the club I wondered whether, if everyone was to be judged in that way, the club would be completely empty. And *that* would be a sign of the times. Five minutes later the door swung open and Melanie stood there in a black handkerchief dress with bangles all the way up her tanned arms to her elbows; her hair was swept back in a high pony-tail and her cheekbones were ebony and shiny as though she were an Egyptian princess.

'Lucy!' She held her arms open to hug me. I turned so that when we hugged she was facing sideways and not over my shoulder and staring at my life. 'Who else is with you?' I pushed past her into the entrance, revealing my life to her. Life followed me inside. Melanie gave him the quick once-over, so quick only I would notice her thick lashes move up and down. Life didn't notice, he was busy taking off his crumpled suit jacket to hand to the woman at the cloakroom, which was a line of golden muscular arms sticking out of a wall. She hooked his coat over the protruding middle finger of the arm. What a statement. He rolled his sleeves up to his elbows and he looked much better but nothing like the golden muscular arms.

'You're a secretive little thing,' Melanie said to me.

'It's not like that, really, at all,' I shuddered.

'Oh,' she said, disappointed. 'Hello, I'm Melanie,' and she held out her bangled arm.

Life gave her a megawatt smile. 'Hi, Melanie, nice to meet you in the flesh, I've heard so much about you. I'm Cosmo Brown.'

'Cool name,' she laughed. 'Isn't that . . .?'

'Yes, from the film. He's never been here before and he's really excited so come on already, show us around!' I pretended to be excited and Melanie got excited by my excitement and hotfooted it out of there. Everywhere we went all the men stopped and stared at Melanie, which was a shame for them because they were barking up the wrong tree. This had been a blessing for me because ever since she had come out at the age of sixteen and men discovered she wasn't only not interested but not even open to negotiation, they turned to me, which I didn't mind as I had a minimal amount of pride, and even less as a teen.

The club so far had been designed in the theme of the four elements of life; finally we reached a closed door, which had the number five on it. Life looked at me questioningly.

'The fifth element,' I explained.

'Which is . . . love?'

'Romantic,' Melanie said. 'But no.' She pushed open the door and gave him a cheeky wink. 'It's alcohol.' And in a giant champagne glass posed a burlesque dancer with nipple tassles and no other clothes that I could see, unless the fabric in question had disappeared into the cracks. I expected Melanie to start DJing immediately so that no more questions could be asked, or if they were it could be the usual mouthing and lip-read one-word answers to shoot-the-breeze questions, but it was early yet and her set didn't begin until after twelve so we sat around a table and Melanie examined my life.

'So how do you two know each other?'

'We work together,' I answered.

He looked at me and I could hear him say, *Remember our deal.*

'Well, we kind of do.'

'You work at Mantic?' Melanie asked him.

'Nope.' He stared at me. *You lie, I tell a truth.*

'No,' I laughed. 'He doesn't work there. He . . . he's eh, he's . . . from out of town,' I said, looking to Life for approval. Not technically a lie. I could see him mulling it over.

He gave me a nod of approval, but a *you're skating on thin ice* look.

'Groovy,' Melanie said, looking at him for the answer. 'But how do you two know each other?'

'He's my cousin,' I blurted out. 'He's sick.

Terminally ill. He's spending the day with me to write an article on modern women. It's his dying wish.' I couldn't help it.

'You're cousins?' she said, surprised.

Life started laughing. 'Of all of those things, the fact that we're *cousins* surprises you?'

'Well, I thought I'd met them all.' Then she softened her tone. 'So that's sad news. You're a journalist. Are you okay?'

Life and Melanie laughed.

'Come on, I've been friends with Lucy all of my life, I know her well enough to know when she's lying.'

If only she knew.

'You just can't help yourself, can you?' Life said to me. 'Okay, now it's my turn.' He leaned in towards Melanie and I braced myself. She smiled and leaned in flirtatiously. 'Lucy doesn't like your music,' he said and sat back.

Melanie's smile faded, she sat back too. I buried my head in my hands.

Life looked at me. 'I think I'll get some drinks now. Lucy?'

'Mojito,' I said from behind my hands.

'The same.'

'Great.'

'Tell them to put it on my tab,' Melanie said, not looking at him.

'It's okay, I'll claim it back on expenses,' he said and wandered off.

'Who is that horrible little man?' she asked.

I cringed. I just simply couldn't tell her now. 'Melanie, I never said that I didn't like your music. I said that I didn't *get* your music, which is not the same as saying I don't like it. It has beats, rhythmic kind of things that I just don't recognise.'

She looked at me, blinked once and said as if I had never spoken at all, 'Lucy, who is that man?'

I buried my face in my hands again. It was my new thing. If I couldn't see them, they couldn't see me. I came back up for air. Then I put my phone on the table and looked at Don's eyes for back-up. 'Okay fine, here's the truth. That man is my life.'

Her eyes widened. 'That is so romantic.'

'No, I mean, he *is* my actual life. I received a letter to meet with him from the actual Life Agency a while ago and this is it. This is him.'

Melanie's mouth hung open. 'You are shitting me. That's your life?'

We both turned to watch him. He was standing at the bar on tiptoe, trying to get served. I cringed again.

'He's . . . wow, well, he's . . .'

'Miserable,' I finished for her. 'You called my life a horrible little man.'

Her Bambi eyes were full of concern. 'Are you miserable, Lucy?' she asked.

'Me? No. I'm not miserable.' It wasn't a lie. I didn't *feel* miserable, just slightly unhappy ever since Life had made himself and my flaws known to me. '*He* is bloody miserable.'

'Tell me how it works.'

'He's like the Pinky and I'm the Brain,' I said. 'Or I'm the X-ray and he's the broken foot.' I tried to explain but got confused. 'He's the nose and I'm the Pinocchio. Yes,' I smiled, 'I got the last one right.'

'What are you talking about?'

I sighed. 'He just accompanies me. Like this.'

'Why?'

'To observe and then to try to make things better.'

'For who? For you?'

'And for him.'

'What kinds of things, what's wrong?'

I searched my brain for an answer that wasn't a lie. There were very few thoughts in my head. Melanie *never* read the papers or listened to the news so she wouldn't know about the office incident. 'For example. There was a thing at work the other day. A man I work with was fired then came back to the office with a gun – don't worry, it was a water pistol though we didn't know it at the time, but he shook everybody up and a couple of things happened so now Life is here for a while.' It was as vague as I could possibly make it.

I thought a fire alarm went off and was momentarily thankful that we'd have to evacuate and the conversation could be dropped, but then realised it was the sound of an American police car going *whoop whoop*. I looked around for the action and saw a waitress walking towards us with a police-car light flashing on the tray along with our drinks.

'Well, that's subtle,' I said.

'Hi, guys,' the waitress sang. 'The man says he'll have his at the bar.'

'Thanks.' Melanie looked her up and down, gave her the biggest flirtiest smile she could. When the girl walked away Melanie leaned in. 'She's new. She's cute.'

I checked her out. 'Nice legs.'

When Melanie told me she was gay when we were teenagers I was immediately unnerved though I tried not to show it. It wasn't because I was homophobic, it was more because we had spent all our lives being extremely close, sharing a lot of things together such as changing rooms, showers, toilets on nights out, that kind of thing. I didn't know how to move forward with continuing those habits after she'd informed me she liked women. I didn't do a good job of trying to hide it so one night while I'd run to barricade myself into a toilet cubicle by myself, she firmly informed me – and the rest of the queue behind her – that she was under no circumstances, nor would she ever *ever* be, remotely interested in me. This resulted in my feeling worse, particularly by the use of the double 'ever', I mean, would she ever even *consider* giving me a chance? It was quite possible that I could change in the future, and her close-mindedness bothered me. We sipped our drinks. I was hoping we could now change the subject though I knew there wasn't a chance of that happening.

'So what kinds of things happened?' She picked up where we left off.

'Oh, nothing, I just got into a bit of trouble, that's all.'

Her eyes widened. 'What kind of trouble?'

'I told a little fib on my resumé.' I waved a hand dismissively.

Melanie threw her head back and laughed. 'What did you say?' She was enjoying this but I knew she wouldn't for much longer, it was leading to somewhere I didn't want to go. I was planning on telling a juicy big lie when Life must have sensed it and rejoined us at the table.

Melanie looked at him with new admiration. 'Lucy was just telling me that you're her life.'

Life looked at me, happy I'd told a truth. 'That's great, Lucy.'

'This is so cool, can I give you a hug?' She didn't wait for an answer, and went straight for the kill, wrapping her long limbs around him and squeezing. Life seemed to melt at the attention. He closed his eyes. 'Wait a minute.' She pulled away. 'I have to get a photo.' She rooted in her bag for her phone and held it up to herself and Life. He smiled, his teeth a mustard colour next to Melanie's white gnashers. 'That's one for Facebook. So, Lucy was telling me she fibbed on her CV.' She smiled and hunkered down for the gossip, her big glossy lips permanently planted on the straw in her drink, like the man in the tank sucking on oxygen.

'Really?' Life looked at me, impressed again. I was getting Brownie points.

'Yeah.' I scratched my head. 'I just said I could speak a language, but I can't.' I threw it away, hoped that we could laugh over it and it would be gone but I knew I couldn't be so lucky.

Melanie threw her head back and laughed again. 'What was it? Swahili or something?'

'No,' I laughed awkwardly.

'Why, what language did you say? Honestly, Cosmo, I have to squeeze information about herself out from her all the time.'

'Spanish.'

Her dark eyes darkened a little but she smiled, though not as ecstatically. 'You're even worse at Spanish than me.'

'Yeah,' I smiled. I wanted to change the subject, but I couldn't think of anything to say that wasn't forced and unnatural.

'But what if they'd asked you to use it?' she said, and I was sure she was testing me.

'They did.' I took a sip of my drink. 'They did all the time. Our main manual languages are English, French, Dutch and Italian.'

'And Spanish,' she said, studying me.

'And Spanish,' I confirmed.

She sucked on her straw, her eyes not moving from mine. 'So what did you do?' She was slowly getting it, or she'd already got it. Or I was paranoid but I already knew my paranoia was instinct so either way I was in trouble.

208

'I got a little help.'

Life was looking from her to me and me to her, sensing something was up but not knowing exactly what. I waited for him to take his computer out to search for the answer but he didn't. He politely sat it out.

'From who?' she asked. She was still now. Tense. Expectant. Waiting for confirmation.

'Melanie, I'm sorry.'

'Don't be sorry, just answer the question,' she said coldly.

'The answer is yes and I'm sorry.'

'You went to Mariza.'

'Yes.'

She stared at me, shocked. Even knowing it was coming, she couldn't believe it. I thought she was going to throw her drink over me but the anger subsided and she just looked hurt. 'You've been in contact with Mariza?'

Mariza was the love of her life who'd broken her heart very badly and we were all destined to hate her for the rest of our lives. And I did, until she emailed me one day asking after Melanie's well-being. I'd done the proper friend thing at first, being coldly distant and distantly cold, telling lies about how Melanie was doing great, but then it changed and I needed her.

'Only a little contact. It was just for translations, nothing personal.'

'Nothing personal?'

'Okay maybe a little. She was always asking

about you, I told her you were travelling the world, really successful, meeting other people, I never ever told her anything about you that you wouldn't have wanted me to say. I promise. She was worried about you.'

'Sure she was.' Then another thought. 'You've been in that job for how long?'

'Two and a half years,' I mumbled. I was so embarrassed, partly because it was happening in front of my life but mostly because it was happening at all.

'So for two and a half years you've been contacting her. Lucy, I can't believe this.' She stood up, took a few random steps in different directions but ultimately didn't want to go anywhere. She returned to the table but remained standing. 'How would you feel if I had spent the last two and a half years contacting an ex of yours without your knowledge, while you haven't heard a thing directly from them since the moment they broke up with you? The amount of times I wondered what she was doing, or where she was, and *you knew* all that time and didn't say anything. How would you feel if I did that to you?'

Life looked at me. I felt he was urging me to say something, something about Blake. I couldn't risk him telling a truth at this time. Not now, it was the wrong time, but I couldn't lie.

'I understand. I'd be incredibly hurt too.' I swallowed. 'But you do speak to Blake all the time,' I said in my defence.

She looked at me as though I were stupid. 'Blake is different. Blake didn't just decide one day for no clear reason to step on your heart and crush it into a million little pieces. You left Blake. You have no idea how I feel.'

Life's eyes were bearing into me. Speak now or forever hold your peace. I held my peace.

She stopped herself before she said too much, though she already had. 'I need to take a minute, I just need to get some air.' She grabbed her cigarettes from the table and went outside.

I looked at my life. 'Happy now?'

'I'm feeling a little better.'

'The better I do for you, the more I alienate other people. What good is that for me?'

'Right now, not much, but down the line it'll pay off. They just need to get to know you.'

'They know me.'

'You don't even know you, how can you expect them to?'

'Very philosophical.' I grabbed my bag.

'Where are you going?'

'Home.'

'But we just got here.'

'She doesn't want me here.'

'She never said that.'

'She didn't have to.'

'So make it up to her.'

'How?'

'By staying. You've never done that before.'

'And do what?'

He raised his eyebrows. 'Dance.'

'I am not dancing with you.'

'Come on.' He stood up and grabbed my hands and pulled me up. I fought him but he was strong.

'I don't dance,' I said, trying to pull myself away from him.

'You used to. You and Blake were Dirty Dancing competition winners two years in a row.'

'Well, I don't dance any more. There's no one even on the dance floor, we'll look like tools. And I'm not dirty dancing with you.'

'Dance like they're not watching.'

Which they were, including Melanie who had come back inside and was currently watching us from the darkness, even though she was mad at me. I felt a weight I didn't even know was there lift from my shoulders at having revealed a truth. Life was like a drunken uncle at a bad wedding, attempting to dance like John Travolta in a bizarre mix between *Pulp Fiction* and *Stayin' Alive*, but he was happy and he made me smile. So I did a little Uma Thurman and danced with Life like no one was watching until we were the last on the floor and last out the door. He was persuasive; life has a way of getting what it wants when it really knows what it wants.

CHAPTER FIFTEEN

'So tell me about your dad,' Life asked the following morning. We were sitting on a park bench drinking coffee from take-out cups and watching Mr Pan chasing a butterfly and leaping around with such joy I tried not to think about the fact the last time he'd felt grass under his feet was when I'd walked it into the flat.

'First of all, it's not Dad,' I corrected him. 'It's Father. He made that very clear as soon as our lips could form actual words. And secondly, there's not much to tell.'

'Really?'

'Yes, really.'

Life turned to the old woman beside him. 'Excuse me, this lady's boyfriend left her but they concocted a lie to make people think it was the other way around.'

'Oh,' the lady said, confused, thinking she should

have known what he was talking about but couldn't quite figure it out.

'I can't believe you did that,' I grumbled.

'You lie, I tell a truth,' he repeated his mantra.

'I didn't lie, there's really not much to tell about my father.'

'Lucy, has it ever occurred to you that I might be here for a specific reason? And as soon as I investigate all areas and find the thing that's wrong with you, I'm gone, out of your life. You won't have to see me again and imagine how happy your days will be then? So it's in your best interest to cooperate, even if you think the thing I'm asking you about is a non-issue.'

'What are you here to fix?'

'I don't know, it's exploratory surgery. I examine all areas, see what the problem is.'

'So you are the endoscope to my anus.'

He winced. 'Again we're having metaphor issues.'

We smiled.

'I recall you saying that your father was a pretentious little man who needed to get off his high horse. That implies there's something to talk about.'

'I didn't say that, I called him a pretentious little *shit*.'

'I was paraphrasing.'

'We've just never gotten along. We used to, to a certain extent, when we were polite enough to tolerate one another but there's no room for politeness any more.' I looked at him. 'Are you here to sort out daddy issues? Because if so, we might as well call the whole thing off now because if I really had daddy issues I would spend my days trying to endlessly please him which would result in my becoming a high achiever, and right now I'm not even close to that. He can't even piss me off enough to make me successful. Our issues are just a waste of time.'

'You're right. You're a failure, you don't have daddy issues.'

We laughed.

'He doesn't like me,' I said simply. 'There's nothing deeper to it than that, nothing to fix, nothing to explore. He's just never liked me.'

'What makes you say that?'

'He told me.'

'He didn't tell you that.'

'You know that he did. When I got fired from my last job it was the final straw for him, which was ridiculous because up to that point I had actually been doing well so it should technically have been the first straw. Actually, it shouldn't have been a straw at all because I didn't tell him I was fired, I told them I left the job because I didn't agree with the company's take on their environmental responsibility. We had an argument and I told him I knew he hated me and he said quote, "Lucy, I don't hate you, I just don't like you very much." Unquote.' I looked at him. 'So there, it's not just my paranoia. Take out your little computer and see for yourself.'

'I'm sure he just meant in that moment.'

'Yes, he absolutely meant in that moment, thing is, the moment hasn't ended, we're still stuck right in it.'

'Why did you get fired?'

We had finally arrived at it.

I sighed. 'Do you know what CSR is?'

He frowned and shook his head.

'CSR, or Corporate Social Responsibility to you, is a form of corporate self-regulation integrated into a business modal. CSR policy honours the triple bottom line: people, planet, profit. It's like a corporate conscience, integrating the public interest in corporate decision-making by encouraging community growth and development and voluntarily eliminating practices that harm the public, regardless of legality. The idea is that the company makes more profit by operating with perspective though some argue that it distracts from the economic role of business.' I took a sip of coffee. 'I agree with the former, by the way. I worked in a large multinational who should have taken their policy more seriously, and I didn't agree with the decisions they were making.'

'So what happened? You found paper in the plastic bin?'

'No.' I rolled my eyes. 'I won't get into the exact ins and outs but I basically shared my opinions with the CEO and I was swiftly fired.'

Life nodded his head to himself and pondered what I'd said. Then he threw his head back and laughed, laughed so loudly the old lady beside him jumped with fright, laughed on behalf of the entire country. He was breathless by the time he'd finished.

'Man, that was a good one,' he said. 'Thanks.'

'You're welcome.' I took a slug of my coffee, gearing myself up for the payback.

'I think you'll find it was worth it though.' He turned to the old lady, 'Sometimes she doesn't wash her bras for weeks at a time.'

I gasped. The lady finally stood up and left.

'So where did you get that lie from?' he asked.

'Wikipedia. Couldn't sleep one night and so I surfed around for a good story.'

'Nice. Is that what you told everybody?'

'Yep. No one ever asked what exactly the company practices were that I didn't agree with. I was going to go with something like illegal dumping but it seemed too obvious and too eighties.'

He laughed again. Then stopped. 'You didn't tell your dad that, did you?'

'Yes, I did.' I cringed, recalling the moment. 'It turned out he already knew the truth but he still let me say my little spiel first before revealing it. He's the only one who knows the truth behind that particular lie. Hence the argument.'

'How did he know?'

'He's a judge, and I have learned the judging world is a small one.'

'Ah. Care to kindly share the truth with me?'

I drained my cup and fired it into the nearest basket. It missed and hit the ground. I sighed wearily, the world heavy on my shoulders just because of that one incident, then got up and put it back in the bin and returned to the bench.

'I was drunk while collecting a client from the airport. I got lost, so we drove around for an hour, he missed a meeting and then I dropped him at the wrong hotel and left him there.' I looked at him. 'They fired me and I lost my driver's licence for a year, so I sold the car and rented a flat in the city where I could cycle everywhere.'

'Which tied in with the environmentally responsible thing.'

I nodded.

'Clever.'

'Thanks.'

'So technically you lied to your father and he caught you out and you're angry with him for being angry with you?'

I thought about that; wanted to protest, justify myself, and explain the years I'd endured his patronising comments and his pushiness, which had played a large part in our relationship breakdown because of course it was so much more complicated than just one argument, but it was too much to explain and I didn't know where to start, hadn't the time, energy or inclination to delve into its infinitesimal detail so eventually I took the lazy way out and nodded.

'Problem is, your lies are built on top of other

lies, aren't they? You tell one, you have to tell another, you reveal a tiny truth and the whole thing falls apart, so you keep building on them, like the lying at work about speaking Spanish being linked to Melanie and her ex-girlfriend.'

I nodded.

He continued. 'You tell people you got fired at work, they'll ask *why* – because you were drunk – because *why* – because that was the day Blake left you and you were upset and you had a day off and you weren't thinking straight so you opened a bottle of wine and drank it, and then the company called you even though you were on a day off and told you there was a problem, you needed to collect Robert Smyth from the airport for an important meeting; and there was a lot at stake, you'd already lost your boyfriend, you didn't want to lose your job too, so you hopped in your car, drunk but not as drunk as you eventually became because it hadn't hit you yet, and you got worse as the hour wore on, you had a disastrous day and as a result lost your job, your licence and your car.'

It sounded so sad, my whole life tangled up in a string of ridiculous lies that went from bad to worse.

'If you already know all of this stuff, then why do you ask?'

'I want to hear something the computer files aren't telling me.'

'And do you?'

'Yes.'

I looked at him for more.

'That you're not reckless. You're just sad.'

Silchesters didn't cry but it didn't mean Silchesters didn't ever *want* to cry. I wanted to then but I didn't do it. We sat together in a long but not uncomfortable silence; at least five minutes passed when we didn't utter a word. It was a beautiful day, the park was full, there wasn't a breeze in the air, everything was still, everyone was lazy, lying on the freshly cut grass, reading or eating or gossiping or doing what we were doing, which was taking it all in. Finally he broke the silence.

'But I do think you spend your days trying to endlessly *dis*please him. Which is something,' he said.

It came out of nowhere, a random comment and I pretended not to know what he was talking about. But I did.

That night was Chantelle's birthday, which meant we were all summoned to the Wine Bistro. We never bought each other presents, instead agreeing on covering the birthday girl or boy's share of the meal. We used to meet weekly in Blake's and my apartment but when we split up we all moved to this restaurant where the food was cheap but good. Life met me down the block and to my absolute surprise and delight was wearing jeans, and beneath the crusty crumpled suit jacket was a fresh white linen shirt. Good teeth and better clothes, surely it meant I was on the up. I couldn't stop yawning – he still hadn't bothered to get any nose plugs, but the yawning wasn't just down to being tired, I was incredibly anxious, which he picked up on.

'Don't worry, it's going to be okay.'

'Of course I'm worried, I've absolutely no idea what you're going to say to them.'

'I'm not going to say anything, I'll just observe. But if you lie, I'll tell a truth.'

Which made me anxious; my friendships were built on lies. I yawned again. 'Just watch out for Adam. He's Blake's best friend and he hates me.'

'I'm sure he doesn't hate you.'

'Just watch out.'

'Okay.'

I started power-walking up the street which was difficult in double platforms; I felt like I was trying to run in a dream but wasn't getting anywhere. Breathlessly, I started giving him the rundown. 'Lisa is pregnant, she's got about a month to go and she's got all this fluid stuff in her face and hands so don't stare too much, and please bear with her. David is her husband, he's the guy bearing with her. Lisa used to go out with Jamie years ago and David and Jamie are friends and sometimes it gets a bit weird but generally it's fine. They didn't cheat or anything, they got together years later so don't worry about that.'

'Okay, I'll try not to worry about Jamie and David. If at any stage you think I'm getting too interested in their exciting lives you just jump right in there and stop me.'

'You know, sarcasm is the lowest form of wit.'

'And yet it is still extremely funny.'

'Chantelle will probably try to come on to you – she gets very flirty after drink – so if you feel a hand under the table, it's her. Adam's girlfriend Mary is a photographer and wears black all the time and I don't trust her.'

'Because she wears black?'

'Don't be ridiculous, because she's a photographer.'

'Well, I'm so glad it was just me being ridiculous.'

'She's always trying to see things in different angles. Everything. Even simple things like me saying, "I went to the shop today." She'll be like,' I took on a deep and slow voice, '"Why? Which shop? Are you afraid of shops? Is it because of your childhood? How was the light there?"' Life laughed at me and I returned to normal, panting and striding, striding and panting. 'She complicates things. Which leaves . . .' I went through them all in my head. 'Me. And I'm in so much trouble right now.' I stopped walking outside the restaurant and faced him, 'Please don't make my friends hate me.'

'Lucy, give me your hand.' I wouldn't, so his hand chased mine in the air.

'No, they're clammy.' I looked into the restaurant, saw them all sitting there. I was last, as usual. 'Great, we're late.'

'If it's any consolation you'll be the first out of there.'

'Are you psychic too?'

'No, but you never stay till the end. And my hands are not clammy,' he said, more to himself than to me, feeling them. He grabbed my hands. 'See?'

They were actually dry; I was most definitely on the up, only I didn't feel like that right then.

'Lucy, look at me. Calm down. I won't make your friends hate you any more than they already do. That's a joke, don't look so scared. Seriously, I won't make your friends hate you. I promise. Now breathe.' We resumed walking and he was still holding my hand. I momentarily calmed and then I saw Adam watching us from inside the restaurant and I quickly let go of Life and then I panicked again. As soon as we entered, the waiter with the fake French accent saw me, and he didn't even attempt to hide the dread in his eyes.

'*Bonjour,*' I said to him as I took off my jacket. '*D'accord, tu peux rester près de moi tant que tu ne parles pas de la chaleur qu'il fait ici.*' Okay, you can stand beside me as long as you don't talk about how hot it is here.

He gave me a big smile that showed he had just about had enough of me, and picked up the menus. 'Zis way,' he mumbled.

'What was that about?' Life asked.

I didn't answer, I was too busy following the fake French waiter and pasting on a big fake smile

223

to my friends who weren't looking at me but who had all eyes on Life. Everyone was sitting in their favourite places apart from Melanie; her seat was empty because she had flown to Ibiza that morning to work at a P Diddy party. I sat at the head of the table and stared down to where Blake should be. It was always a reminder. Life sat beside me in Melanie's place. They were all staring at us.

'Everybody, this is—' I stalled slightly but not long enough for anybody to notice, I hoped.

'Cosmo Brown,' he finished for me. 'I'm a friend of Lucy's, I'm in town for a few weeks.'

I looked at him in surprise, then at everybody else to see if they'd swallowed it. Why wouldn't they? They were nodding, making friendly happy sounds, and one by one they introduced themselves, the men shaking hands across the table. Adam eyed him warily, Mary no doubt checked the lighting on his face for signs of childhood trauma.

'Cosmo,' Lisa said, looking at her husband David. 'I like that name.' She rubbed her swollen belly.

'Yeah,' David said, trying to be polite to both Lisa and my life but clearly hating the name.

'So it's a boy,' Chantelle said, catching them out.

'No,' Lisa said.

The others jeered while Lisa tried to speak over them.

'I told you that we don't know, but *if* it was a boy, Cosmo would be nice. My God, I've to be so specific with you.' She buried her head in the menu.

'So how long do you two know each other?' Adam asked.

Interesting first question. I translated it as, *So how long have you been sleeping with Lucy behind Blake's back?*

I looked at Life feeling nervous that he would blurt it all out, but he kept his promise.

'Oh . . .' Life looked at me and laughed. 'Forever.'

'Forever?' Adam asked, eyebrows raised. 'How long are you in Dublin for?'

'I'm not sure yet,' Life said, taking off his awful suit jacket and turning up his new linen shirt sleeves. 'I'm going to see how things go.'

'Are you here working?'

'Generally? Or now?'

'Here, in Dublin,' Adam said.

'It's business and pleasure,' Life said with a big smile so that the lack of information didn't seem at all rude. I needed to learn from him. Little pieces of information were better than lies. Though it didn't seem to be working with Adam as he wanted to know everything about my life.

'What line of work are you in?' he asked.

'Don't worry, it's nothing to be threatened by.' Life held his hands up defensively, making a point of Adam's interrogation. Everyone laughed, apart from Adam who seemed annoyed. Mary put her hand in his lap and gave his hand a little squeeze. It said, *Calm down.* She hated me too. When Blake and I broke up I hadn't heard from her again – a clear sign that we were only friends because our

225

boyfriends were – and while it was insulting I was quite happy about never having to go to bizarre photograph exhibitions again such as 'Moments in Thyme: a unique and distinct look at nature'.

'I'm joking with you,' Life said directly to Adam. 'I'm an auditor.'

I pursed my lips and tried not to smile; I knew it was a direct reference to the first time we'd met and I'd told him I felt my life was being audited. I think it was a subconscious move but Life put his arm around the back of my chair in a protective way – but it could have been read differently, which is how I think Adam took it, because he was looking at me as if I was the most disgusting piece of shit he'd ever seen.

'That's what we needed to do,' Lisa said suddenly, hand on belly again. 'Paperwork. Did you sign those forms?' She looked at David.

'No, I forgot.'

'I left them on the kitchen counter beside the phone so that you wouldn't miss them.'

'And I didn't miss them, I saw them, I just forgot to sign them.'

Lisa's face reddened.

'We'll do it when we get home,' David said calmly. 'It's Saturday anyway, not much we can do.'

'It was fucking Friday yesterday when I told you to sign them,' she snapped.

David looked at Jamie wearily.

'So Blake is home,' Jamie said, lifting the mood.

My ears perked up but as usual I was

self-conscious about my reactions to anything that concerned him so I put my head into my menu and pretended to read. I read *Soup of the day* thirteen times again.

'Cosmo, do you know Blake?' he asked.

'Blake.' Life looked at me and my heart was thudding.

'Yes, Blake, the poor innocent man she cruelly dumped like the femme fatale she is,' Chantelle joked. 'And we'll never let her forget about it.'

I shrugged, nonchalantly.

'Honestly, I think all women should deal with break-ups like you, Lucy,' Lisa said. 'My God, remember what I was like?'

Everybody groaned as they collectively remembered the drama of Lisa's late-night tearful phone calls, the *never* wanting to be alone, the endless battles to convince her that she was *not* having a heart attack – that while painful, it was just her heart hurting. Jamie smiled fondly, presumably at the memory of them being together and not the bitter break up which ensued. He and Lisa shared a look. David shifted uncomfortably in his seat.

'Well, you have to be positive about it, don't you,' I said, trying to give them a confident smile but feeling like my lips were trembling inside. 'At least we split before the property market collapsed and made a good profit.' Which I'd spent. 'We'd never sell that apartment now.'

They looked at me.

'I loved that apartment,' Chantelle said sadly.

I did too. 'It was always too hot,' I said dismissively. I thought of Blake walking around the rooms with no clothes on after I'd pumped up all the heat deliberately. He was always too hot, and like a furnace in bed. I looked at the menu. *Hot soup of the day. Hot, hot, hot.*

'I've never met him,' Life said to Adam, who was still waiting for a response.

'He's a cool guy,' Adam said.

'Of course he is. You're his best friend.'

'What do you mean by that?'

'May I take your orders, please?' The waiter arrived in the nick of time. It sounded like '*ordairs plez*', as though all his training had been taken from an episode of *'Allo, 'Allo.*

I learned a lot about Blake during that dinner, such as that his last show was going to be airing this week and he was home for the remainder of the summer; he had opened an outdoor sports activity and adventure centre in, wait for it, Bastardstown, Co. Wexford, something we'd talked about doing together. He was doing everything we'd talked about doing together, only without me. I looked into the menu again and blinked a dozen times. *Soup of the day, soup of the day, soup of the day.*

'You guys talked about opening that together, didn't you,' Adam said.

'Eh, yeah,' I said, blasé, eyes scanning the menu. 'Maybe I should sue him for stealing my idea.' The others smiled, apart from Adam of course,

228

and then Lisa started ordering, in her new bossy tone, changing all the dishes to suit her dietary needs. The waiter, slightly nervously, had to excuse himself from the table to see if the chef would do as she wished. Moments later the chef himself came out to join us at the table. He really was French and very politely informed her that he couldn't do the goat's cheese pastry without the goat's cheese because then it would just be pastry and he already had the goat's cheese wrapped in it.

'Fine,' Lisa snapped, her face heating up again. 'I'll have bread.' She clapped the menu shut. 'Just a plate of bread, please, because that's all I can eat here, only I can't because there are nuts in it and I can't eat nuts.'

'I'm sorry,' David said, red-faced, 'She's very tired.'

'Don't apologise on my behalf, thank you very much.' She moved awkwardly in her seat. 'It has less to do with being tired and more to do with these fucking chairs which are so uncomfortable.' Then she started crying. 'Shit,' she squeaked. 'I'm sorry. I've something in my eye.' Her voice finished at an octave higher than a chipmunk.

'Lees,' Jamie said softly, pointing at the menu, 'look, they've got roasted peppers on the side. You love them. Why don't you order them?'

David looked at Jamie, a little bit annoyed.

'Oh my God,' Lisa smiled at Jamie, 'remember them?'

'Yeah,' Jamie laughed, 'that's why I mentioned them.'

I'm sure David was picturing them having sex on a bed of roasted red peppers when the reality was probably that they had both gone to a restaurant and eaten a lot of peppers one day like the naughty divils they were.

'Okay,' Lisa sighed and opened the menu again.

We all turned away from the conversation while the chef lowered himself to his knees and patiently went through the menu with Lisa to see what he could and couldn't do for her.

'So where are you staying?' Chantelle asked Life. She hadn't started coming on to him yet, partly because she was only on her second glass of red wine and partly because she wasn't yet sure if we were together.

'I'm staying with Lucy,' he replied and I tried really hard not to look at Adam's face.

'Wow,' she said. 'We're never allowed in Lucy's place, it's like a big secret or something. You've seen the inside, tell us, what are we missing?'

I laughed. 'Ah, come on, I'm not hiding anything.'

'Porn?' Jamie asked once the chef had left, 'It's porn, isn't it? Because I'm thinking she has a penchant for magazines and she leaves them lying around.'

'No, it has to be more exciting than that.' Chantelle moved in closer. 'Tell me there's someone chained up inside because that's what I've been imagining for the past three years.'

230

I laughed at them. Jamie winked.

'She was hiding someone anyway,' Adam said, reaching for a piece of bread. Again nobody noticed his comment. I know that they all heard it, I just didn't understand why they didn't hear it the same way as I did. But maybe Life did.

'What was that?' he asked, and then I wished he hadn't noticed because I didn't like his tone. It was the same tone Blake would use before we ended up getting into a ridiculous fight with some guy at a bar who was looking at me the wrong way. And Adam was rising to it because Adam had been looking for me to take that tone ever since Blake and I split up.

'Ah, come on, how long have you guys known each other? Forever? I'm guessing that's a couple of years at least, isn't it? And as far as I can remember Lucy was with Blake a couple of years back.' He was keeping his tone light, a small smile on his face, but you could see the anger beneath, steaming from his flared nostrils.

'Adam,' Lisa said, shocked.

'Come on, I'm sick of this, always skirting around the subject like she's high almighty.'

'Because it's none of our business,' Chantelle said, eyes wide and warning at Adam.

'Blake's our friend,' Adam said.

'And so is Lucy.' Lisa gave him a look.

'Yes, but he's not here because of her and that makes it our business.'

'He's not here because he got a job he always

wanted that required him to leave the country. Get over it,' Jamie backed me up, veins throbbing in his neck. I could tell he was angry. I wanted to give him a big kiss but I was more concerned with finding an excuse to leave the table immediately, as everything had been lowered to a level that made me deeply, deeply uncomfortable.

'I think we should all just change the subject,' David said.

The waiter moved around the table and stood beside me. He could sense it was an awkward moment for me and he was loving it. They were all looking at me to speak, to say something that would clear this tension.

'Soup of the day,' I said. 'Please.'

Adam rolled his eyes. 'There she goes again, not answering anything about anything, all fucking mysterious.'

'I just don't know what soup it is,' I joked, weakly.

'Butternut squash and corn,' the waiter said.

Adam mumbled something under his breath that I didn't catch, and I was quite pleased as my knees were already trembling from the long line of personal insults from a supposed friend. I was used to that from Adam, but he wasn't hiding them now; everybody could hear his tone and not just my paranoid ear.

'Hey, man, don't speak about her like that,' Jamie said, suddenly serious. Suddenly it was all very serious.

'I don't even know why we're all talking about this, it was what, three years ago?' David asked.

'Two,' I said quietly. 'Two years and eleven months.'

And eighteen days.

Jamie looked at me.

'Yeah, so it was ages ago, they went out, they broke up, they moved on, they'll meet someone else. Just because two people were together once doesn't mean we all have to dwell on it forever,' David ranted. This made everybody stare at him knowing he was referring to his own personal life, namely Jamie and Lisa. David took a gulp of water. Jamie studied his plate. Lisa reached for more bread and picked the nuts out.

'I'm just saying what all of us were thinking,' Adam said.

I swallowed. 'You *all* think I cheated on Blake?' Now that was news to me. I looked around the table.

Chantelle looked awkward. 'It just all seemed a bit sudden and then you became so secretive . . .'

'I'm staying out of this,' said David. He wouldn't meet my eye, which said it all.

'I raised the issue *once*,' Lisa said. 'I'm not going to lie, but I'm not like Cagney and Lacey over there, trying to figure it out every second of my day.'

'Cagney and Lacey were two people,' David said without thinking and Lisa looked at him with demon eyes.

Jamie ignored them and looked me straight in the eye. 'I absolutely do not think that you cheated on Blake. You are perfectly entitled to break up with whoever you want, whenever you want – no offence, man,' he added to Life, 'without us having to know anything about it. It's none of our business. Adam has had too much to drink and he's full of shit.'

'Hey,' Mary said, insulted, 'he's not drunk.'

'Fine, he's just full of shit,' Jamie joked, but no one laughed, not even him, because it wasn't really a joke.

'Mary?' I looked at her. 'Do you feel the same?'

'Your behaviour seemed to change drastically, Lucy. As far as Blake was concerned everything between you was *fine* and then, as Chantelle said, you just left him and became, well, very secretive.' She looked at my life. 'I mean, no offence, this is the first we've heard of you. I'm surprised she even invited you.'

'We're just friends,' I said, feeling extremely uncomfortable.

'So now we're supposed to believe that this guy is just her friend?' Adam said to Jamie.

'Who *gives* a shit? Why do you care so much?' Jamie asked.

'He cares because Blake is his best friend, and Adam is loyal, and poor Blake doesn't know what he did wrong—' Mary began, but I interrupted her. I didn't need to hear any more. I couldn't or I would break all of the Silchester rules in less than a minute.

'Yeah, poor Blake,' I interrupted, and stood up. I heard the shake in my voice. Silchesters didn't cry and they certainly didn't get angry, but I was close to blowing it. 'Poor little Blake, living such a sorry little life travelling the world, while here's me livin' it up with my fabulous job, in my fabulous mysterious apartment, with my secret lover.' I grabbed my bag. Life followed my lead and stood. 'And you're right, Adam, he's not just my friend. He's a lot more than that because a friend is what you were supposed to be, and he's been there for me a lot more than you ever have.'

And then I left. Early. When I got outside I kept walking until I was too far away for them to see or hear me. Then when I found the right place, in a doorway, away from everyone, I took out a tissue from my pocket and thought about breaking all the rules. I waited, and waited, knowing that there must be tears, *years'* worth of them all built up and ready to fall. But nothing came so I crumpled the tissue and stuffed it back in my pocket. Not now, not over them; my tears had pride.

Life appeared beside me with a concerned look on his face. When he saw that I was all right he said, 'Okay, maybe you're right.'

'He hates me.'

'No.' He looked confused. 'Jamie and David are totally okay with each other after the whole Lisa thing.' He said it in such a deliberate mock-gossip way that it made me smile. 'Though technically I

don't know if that's true,' he added, 'but they are
the least of my worries. Are you cold?'

I shivered as the night breeze picked up.

'Come on,' Life said gently, then he took off his
jacket and wrapped it around my shoulders,
keeping his arm draped protectively around me,
and under the orange glow of the streetlights, we
walked home together.

CHAPTER SIXTEEN

'What do you want to do today?' I asked.

We were enjoying a lazy morning on the couch; the Sunday papers were strewn around the place, used and abused, as we'd searched for our favourite sections and discarded the remainder and then fell in and out of silence as we commented on, laughed at and shared stories we were reading. I was perfectly content in his company and it seemed he was in mine too. My clothes curtains were open to allow the sun to shine through and the windows were wide open, bringing in the fresh air and the sound of Sunday silence. The flat smelled of pancakes and maple syrup, which he'd made, and fresh coffee, which stood on the counter, still piping. Mr Pan had settled in, on and all around Life's shoe, looking like he was the cat who got the cream, which ironically he had, along with fresh blueberries which I had planted and grown myself in the organic roof garden I'd cultivated since Life had come into my world. I'd freshly plucked them that morning while wearing a straw sunhat wrapped with a white ribbon and a white see-through linen dress that blew in a hypnotic way in the gentle breeze on the rooftop to the delight of the male neighbours, who were chilled out on deckchairs, oiled up with sun lotion like cars in a showroom.

Okay, I lied.

Life bought the blueberries. We don't have a rooftop garden. I saw the dress in a magazine and miraculously, I had become a blonde in that daydream.

'Today,' I continued, closing my eyes, 'I just want to stay in bed.'

'You should call your mother.'

They swiftly opened. 'Why?'

'Because she's trying to plan a wedding and you're not helping.'

'It's the most ridiculous thing I've ever heard; they're already married, it's just an excuse to give her something to do. She needs to take up pottery. Besides, neither are Riley or Philip helping. And I can't meet her today because the carpet people are coming. They'll probably be late. Those kinds of people are always late. I think I'll cancel them.' I reached for my phone.

'You will not. I found a grey hair on my sock today and I know it wasn't from a head and I know it wasn't mine.'

I put the phone back down.

'And you should call Jamie back.'

'Why?'

'When has he ever called you before?'

'Never.'

'So it must be important.'

'Or he was drunk and he hit against his phone and dialled my number by mistake.'

Life looked displeased.

'So he was going to say sorry for what happened last night at dinner, and he doesn't need to apologise, he didn't do anything wrong. He was on my side.'

'So call him back and tell him that.'

'I don't want to talk about it with anyone.'

'Fine, you just sweep more crap under the rug, because that rug's going to get so bumpy it'll trip you up.'

'You think any of these phone calls are more important than spending time with my *life*?' I thought I'd win him on that.

He rolled his eyes. 'Lucy, you are in danger of going in entirely the wrong direction. I didn't want you to become a selfish woman who sits around all day talking about herself with her life. You need to find a balance. Take care of you but take care of the people who care about you too.'

'But it's hard,' I whinged, covering my head with a pillow.

'And that's Life. Why did I want to meet you?'

'Because I was ignoring you.' I spoke the words I was trained to speak. 'Because I wasn't dealing with my life.'

'And now what are you doing?'

'Dealing with my life. Spending every little second with my life, so much so that I can barely pee on my own.'

'You'd be able to pee in private if you fixed the light bulb in the bathroom.'

'It's so much hassle,' I sighed.

'How is it?'

'Firstly, I can't reach it.'

'Get a stepladder.'

'I don't have one.'

'So stand on the toilet.'

'It's a cheap plastic cover and I'll fall through.'

'So stand on the edge of the bath.'

'It's dangerous.'

'Right.' Life stood up. 'Stand up.'

I groaned.

'Stand up,' he repeated.

I pulled myself up like a grumpy teen.

'Now go across to your neighbour and ask her if you can have a loan of a stepladder.'

I collapsed back on the couch again.

'Do it,' he said sternly.

I stood up again, huffily, and made my way to the door. I went across to Claire's apartment and knocked and returned moments later with a stepladder.

'See, that wasn't so bad, was it?'

'We talked about the weather, so yes, it was bad. I hate mindless talk.'

He snorted. 'Now put the ladder in the bathroom.'

I did as I was told.

'Now climb up.'

I followed his instructions.

'Now unscrew the light bulb.'

He shone the torch up so that I could see what I was doing. I unscrewed the old bulb, whimpering like a child who'd been forced to eat vegetables. It finally came loose so I stopped my complaining to concentrate. I handed him the old bulb.

'Act like I'm not here.'

I tutted, then sang, 'I hate my life, I hate my life,' over and over while climbing back down the stepladder, put the bulb in the sink, threw him a nasty look, took the new bulb out of the box, climbed back up the ladder and began to screw it in. Then it was in. I climbed back down the ladder, flicked the switch and the room was flooded with light.

'Yay, me!' I said, lifting my hand to high-five Life.

He looked at me as if I was the saddest specimen he had ever seen.

'I'm not high-fiving you for changing a light bulb.'

I lowered my hand, cringing slightly, then perked up. 'What now, more pancakes?'

'Now that the room is lit up, you could do with giving this place a good clean.'

'Nooo,' I groaned. 'You see, that's why I don't do things, it leads to having to do *other* things.' I folded up the stepladder and left it in the

241

hallway beneath the coat rack, beside the mucky boots from the summer festival, the last festival I went to with Blake, when I'd been informed I'd flashed Iggy Pop from my perch on Blake's shoulders.

'You're not going to leave that there.'

'Why not?'

'Because it's going to gather dust and stay there for the next twenty years just like those boots covered in muck. Give it back to Claire.'

I did what I was told and dragged it back across the hall. 'Come on.' I took him by the hand. 'Let's snuggle on the couch again.'

'No.' He let go of me and laughed. 'I'm not lying around here all day, I'm going to take the rest of the day off.'

'What do you mean? Where are you going?'

He smiled. 'Even I need a rest.'

'But where will you go? Where do you live?' I looked up towards the sky and jerked my head. 'Is it up there?'

'The next floor?'

'No! The . . . you know.' I jerked my head again.

'The sky?' He opened his mouth wider than I've ever seen a person open it and he laughed. 'Ah Lucy, you really make me laugh.'

I laughed along with him as if I'd made a joke, though I hadn't at all.

'I can give you some homework before I leave, if you want, just so you don't miss me.'

I scrunched up my nose. He made for the door.

'Okay, fine, sit back down.' I patted the sofa. All of a sudden I just didn't want to be alone.

'What do you dream about, Lucy?'

'Cool, I love dream conversations.' I got cosy. 'Last night was a sex-with-the-cute-guy-on-the-train dream.'

'I'm pretty sure that's illegal.'

'We didn't do it *on* the train.'

'No, I meant because he's so young and you're going to be thirty any minute now,' he teased. 'Anyway, that's not what I meant. I mean, what do you dream about as in your hopes and ambitions?'

'Oh,' I said, bored. I thought about it. Then, 'I don't get the question.'

He sighed and spoke to me as if I was a child. 'What things would you really, really like to do if you could? Something you'd like to accomplish, like a dream job for example.'

I thought about it. 'An *X Factor* judge so I can throw stuff at the contestants if they're crap. Or pull a trapdoor and they go flying down into a bath of beans or something, that'd be cool. And I'd win the fashion contest every week, Cheryl and Dannii would be like, "Oh, Lucy, where did you get your dress?" and I'd be like, "Oh, this? It's just a little something I found on my curtain pole." And Simon would be like, "Hey, you two girls should take some tips from Lucy, she's—"'

'Okay, okay, okay,' Life said, putting his fingers

to his temples and lightly massaging his head. 'Any other *better* dreams?'

I thought about it some more, feeling under pressure. 'I'd really, really like to win the lottery so that I never have to work again and can buy all the stuff I want.'

'That's not a real dream,' he said.

'Why not? It happens to people. That woman in Limerick? She won thirty million and now lives on a desert island, or something.'

'So your dream is to live on a desert island.'

'No.' I waved my hand dismissively. 'That'd be boring and I hate coconut. I'd take the money though.'

'That's a lazy dream, Lucy. If you have a dream, you want to at least be able to *try* to achieve it in some way. Something that is seemingly beyond your grasp but that you know that with a bit of hard work you could possibly achieve. Walking to your local newsagent to buy a lottery ticket is not inspiring. Dreams should make you think, *If I had the guts to do it and I didn't care what anybody thought, this is what I'd really do.*' He looked at me hopefully, expectantly.

'I'm a normal person, what do you want me to say? I really want to see the Sistine Chapel? I don't give a crap about a painting that I have to dislocate my neck to see. That is not a dream to me, that is a *requirement* whilst on holiday in Rome, which by the way I already carried out when Blake brought me there on our very first weekend away.'

I was aware that I was standing up and raising my voice but I couldn't help it, I felt strongly that this was a ridiculous issue he had raised. 'Or what else do people dream about? Jumping out of airplanes? I've done it, even did an instructor's course so I could pull you out of an airplane any day of the week if I wanted. See the Great Pyramids? Done it. On my twenty-fifth birthday with Blake. It was hot and they are as big and majestic as you think they are but would I ever go again? No, a weird man tried to get me in his car when Blake went to the toilet in the nearby McDonald's. Swim with dolphins? Did it. Would I do it again? No. Nobody tells you they stink up close. Bungee jump? Did it, when Blake and I were in Sydney. I even did shark-cage diving in Capetown, not to mention a hot-air balloon trip with Blake for Valentine's Day one year. I've done most things that people dream about and they weren't even my dreams. They were just things that I did. What were they talking about in the paper today?' I picked up one of the pages I'd been reading and stabbed an article. 'A seventy-year-old wants to go up in one of those space aeroplanes so that he can see the earth from space. Well, I'm living on earth right now and it's pretty shitty from here, why would I want to see it from another angle? What could that possibly *do* for me? Those dreams are a waste of time, and that was the most ridiculous question you've ever asked me. I used to do stuff all the time, so how dare you make me feel like I'm nothing without a dream.

Is it not enough that my life is insufficient enough for you that my dreams have to be too?'

I took a deep breath after my rant.

'Okay.' He stood up and grabbed his coat. 'It was a stupid question.'

I narrowed my eyes. 'Then why did you ask it?'

'Lucy, if you're not interested in this conversation then we won't have it.'

'I'm not interested, but I want to know why you asked it,' I said defensively.

'You're right, you've clearly lived your life to the fullest and there's nothing left to do and now it's time for you to stop. You might as well die.'

I gasped.

'I'm not saying you're going to die, Lucy,' he said, frustrated with me. 'Not now, anyway. You will eventually.'

I gasped again.

'We all are.'

'Oh. Yes.'

He opened the door and looked back at me. 'The reason I asked you, is because regardless of what you say, or how much you lie, you are not happy with where you are right now, and when I ask you about what you want, anything in the whole entire world, no holds barred, you say *winning money and buying stuff*.' He spoke sharply and I was embarrassed.

'I still think most people would say the lottery.'

He threw me a look and made for the door again.

'You're angry with me. I don't understand why

you're angry with me, just because you don't like my dream. I mean, this is ridiculous.'

He spoke gently which unnerved me more. 'I'm angry because not only are you not happy where you are, but you can't even think of where you'd rather be. Which I think is . . .' He searched for the word. 'Sad. No wonder you're stuck in a rut.'

I thought about it some more, thought about my dreams, my wishes, my ambitions, where I wanted to be that would make me feel better than being here. I couldn't come up with anything.

'Thought so,' he finally said. 'See you tomorrow.' He took his coat and rucksack and left the apartment, which was the worst possible end to the most beautiful beginning of a day.

His comments niggled at me. They always did, it was as though he spoke in a certain tone that only managed to speak to the brain like a whistle for a dog inaudible to the human ear. I tried to think about my dreams, where I wanted to be, what I really wanted but I think to know what you want, you have to know what you don't want and all I could figure out was that I really wished Life hadn't contacted me so I could have continued on the path I was going on. Life had complicated things, Life had tried to make things move on when I was perfectly content. He called it a rut, but he'd moved me from that place already, by merely pointing out that I was there, and I would never be able to go back. I liked my rut, I missed my rut, I would mourn my rut forever.

By midday, I had a headache but a tidy flat, and unsurprisingly, the cleaning company hadn't arrived. Nor had they by twelve fifteen. By twelve thirty I was beginning to celebrate the fact that they'd forgotten and was making arrangements in my head on how best to spend my freedom, but I wasn't successful with coming to any conclusions. Melanie was away but even still, we hadn't had any contact since our last meeting and I know I wasn't top of her list of people to talk to right now. After dinner the night before, my friends who thought I was a cheat weren't on my own list of people to talk to. And though the demise of Blake and me was swiftly followed by my personality transplant – which at the time I thought nobody noticed but now, with the benefit of Life's teaching, I could now see that everybody had noticed – I understood their thinking but it still hurt.

A knock at the door disturbed my thoughts. It was Claire, with a wet and wrinkly face, crying again.

'Lucy,' she sniffed. 'I'm so sorry to disturb you on a Sunday, I heard the television on and . . . well, I was wondering if you could mind Conor again. I wouldn't ask, only the hospital have called me again and said it's an emergency and . . .' She broke down.

'Of course. Do you mind if I keep him in here with me? I have people coming to clean the carpet and I need to be here.'

She thought about it; she didn't look too certain but then she didn't have much choice. She went back into her apartment and closed the door. I wondered if she sat down and slowly counted to ten before returning to me or if she actually went through the motions of picking him up and strapping him in. I felt a deep sadness for her. The door opened and the empty buggy was pushed out and into my apartment, the straps tied.

'He's been asleep for five minutes,' she whispered. 'He usually sleeps for two hours in the day so I should be home by the time he wakes. He hasn't been well lately, I don't know what's wrong with him.' She frowned and examined the empty buggy. 'So he may sleep a little longer than usual.'

'Okay.'

'Thank you.' She took one last look at the pushchair and turned to go. When she looked out into the hallway there was a man standing outside her apartment.

'Nigel,' she said, shocked.

He turned around. 'Claire.' I recognised him as the man in Claire's photographs: her husband, Conor's father. He looked at the number on her door and then at the number on mine. 'Am I at the wrong apartment?'

'No, this is Lucy, our . . . my neighbour. She's going to babysit.'

He looked at me in such a way that I wanted to curl up and die. I knew he was thinking that I was taking advantage of her but what could I do, tell her that there was no child? Surely she knew that, deep down in her heart.

'For free,' I blurted out just so that he would at least forgive me for that. 'And she wouldn't go otherwise.'

He nodded once, understanding, then his eyes moved back to her. His voice was gentle. 'I'll drive you there. Okay?'

I closed the door behind them.

'Hi again,' I said, to the empty space in the buggy. 'Mummy and Daddy won't be long.'

Then I put my head in my hands and sat slumped across the counter. Mr Pan leaped up and I felt his cold nose near my ear. I Googled people's dreams and ambitions, and instantly bored, I closed the laptop. Twelve forty-five came and went and then I had an idea. I took a photograph of Gene Kelly's face on the poster on my bathroom door and sent it to Don Lockwood with a text:

–*Saw this and thought of you.*

Then I waited. And waited. Anxiously. Then hopefully. Then with deep disappointment. Then with a hurt so deep it cut me like a knife. I didn't blame him. I'd told him never to call me again but still I hoped. Then the hope faded and I was depressed. And alone, and empty, and lost. And not even one minute had passed by.

I opened the fridge-freezer and stared at the empty shelves. The longer I stared, the more the food didn't appear. Then my phone beeped. I slammed the door and dived on the phone.

Typically, simultaneously, the door buzzed too. I decided to savour the text and answered the door first. A red Magic Carpet stared back at me. It was emblazoned on the chest of the man who faced me. I looked up; he was wearing a blue cap with another picture of a carpet on it, low over his face. I looked behind him: nobody else, no tools or equipment.

'Roger?' I asked, stepping aside for him to come in.

'Roger is my dad,' he said, entering the flat. 'He doesn't work weekends.'

'Okay.'

He looked around. Then at me.

'Do I know you?' he asked.

'Eh. I don't know. My name is Lucy Silchester.'

'Yeah, I have it on the . . .' He lifted his clipboard in the air but didn't finish his sentence. But he kept staring at me, right into my eyes. Searching and curious. It made me nervous. I looked away and took a few steps to the kitchen so that the counter would separate us. He realised this and took a few steps back, which I appreciated.

'So where are the others?' I asked.

'The others?'

'The cleaning people,' I said. 'Isn't there a team?'

'No, just me and my dad. But he doesn't work weekends as I said, so . . .' He looked around. 'Is it okay if it's just me?'

His asking made it easier.

'Yes, sure.'

'My stuff is in the van. I just wanted to come up and take a look before I brought it all the way up.'

'Oh. Okay. Should I help you carry something?'

'No, thanks. I'm sure you can't leave the little one.' He smiled and tiny dimples appeared and he was suddenly the most beautiful man I'd ever seen. Then I thought of Blake, and then he wasn't any more. It always happened like that.

I looked at the buggy. 'Oh, that. It's not mine. I mean, he. It's a neighbour's. I mean *he* is a neighbour's. I'm minding him.'

'How old is he?' He smiled fondly, lifting his chin so he could see into the buggy.

I pushed the cover down further so he couldn't. 'Oh, one-ish. He's asleep.' As if that explained anything.

'I'll try to work as quietly as possible. Are there any areas in particular you want me to concentrate on?'

'Just the floor.' I meant it seriously but it came out funny. He laughed.

'The entire floor?'

'Just the dirty bits.'

We both smiled. He was still cute, even when placed on the Blake barometer.

'So that's probably the entire thing,' I said.

He looked around at the floor and I was suddenly aware of a handsome man standing in my little private hovel. I was embarrassed. Suddenly he got down on his knees and examined an area on the floor. He rubbed it with his hand.

'Is that—?'

'Oh yes, I just wrote it down so I wouldn't forget. I couldn't find any paper.'

He looked at me with a big grin. 'Did you use permanent marker?'

'Eh . . .' I rooted in the drawer in the kitchen for the marker. 'Here.'

He studied it. 'This is permanent, you know.'

'Oh. Can you get it out? Because if you can't, my landlord will roll me up in it and throw me out.'

'I'll try.' He looked at me, amused. 'I'll get my equipment from the van.'

I sat back on the stool and intended to make the time pass by stalking Don Lockwood. I read his text.

—She rears her pretty head. So how has your week been?

—Haven't been held at water-pistol point since Tuesday. How's Tom?

I heard a phone beep in the corridor and sensed the cleaning guy was back. But he didn't appear. I peeped my head around the corner and saw him reading his phone. 'Sorry,' he said, popping it into his pocket. He picked up a machine that looked like an oversized vacuum cleaner and carried it inside. The muscles in his arms puffed out to three times the size of my head. I tried not to stare but I failed.

'I'm just going to sit here. If you need anything, if you get lost or anything, I'm here.'

He laughed, then studied the oversized couch.

'It came from a bigger apartment,' I explained.

'It's nice.' He had his hands on his hips, inspecting it. 'It might be a problem to move.'

'It comes apart.' Like everything else in here.

He looked around. 'Do you mind if I put some of it on the bed and some in the bathroom?'

'Of course, but if you find any money underneath, it's mine. Anything else is yours.'

He lifted the couch and I stared at his muscles, which were so large they pushed out all thoughts from my head. 'I won't have much use for this,' he laughed, looking at a dusty cerise pink bra on the floor. I tried to think of a funny response but instead I ran to pick it up, stubbed my toe on the corner of the kitchen counter and went flying onto the couch.

'Sshhit.'

'Are you okay?'

'Yes,' I squeaked. I grabbed my bra and tried to crumple it into a ball, then I held my toe until the pain went away. 'I'm sure you've never seen a bra before, I'm glad I dramatically dived onto the floor to get it,' I said through gritted teeth.

He laughed. 'What is it with this guy?' he asked, passing Gene Kelly on the bathroom door and placing another part of the couch inside. 'Girls love him.'

'He was the working man's dancer,' I explained,

254

rubbing my toe. 'None of that pretentious top-'n'-tails stuff that Fred Astaire did. Gene was, you know, a real man.'

He seemed interested, then went back to his work and didn't say another word. Finally I sensed no movement so I looked up. He was standing in the middle of the room with a piece of the couch in his arms, looking around, lost. I could see his dilemma: the bed was piled high, the bathroom including the bath was jam packed and there was nowhere else to place the couch.

'We could put it out in the corridor,' I said.

'It will block the way.'

'What about the kitchen?'

There was a small space on the floor, which was where the buggy was. I moved the buggy and he came towards me, but I don't know what happened, his toe hit something, I heard his boot bang, maybe against the counter, and the couch went flying out of his arms and on to the buggy.

'Oh, my God,' he shouted. 'Oh, my God.'

'It's OK,' I said quickly, trying to explain. 'It's okay, there's nothing—'

'Oh, fuck. Oh, my God,' he repeated over and over as he tried to lift the couch off the buggy.

'Relax, it's okay. There's no baby in there,' I said loudly. He paused and looked at me like I was the oddest person on the planet.

'There isn't?'

'No, look.' I helped him lift the couch and place it on top of the counter. 'See, it's empty.'

'But you said . . .'

'Yeah, I know. It's a long story.'

He closed his eyes and swallowed, sweat on his brow. 'Jesus.'

'I know, I'm sorry, but it's okay.'

'Why do you—'

'Please don't ask.'

'But you—'

'Honestly, it's really best you don't ask.'

He looked at me once more for an answer but I shook my head.

'Fuck,' he whispered, taking a deep breath. He gave the buggy one more look to make sure he hadn't imagined it and then took another deep breath and went about setting up his giant vacuum-cleaning equipment. Then took his phone out of his pocket and texted. Tap, tap, tap. I rolled my eyes at Mr Pan. We were going to be here all day if he kept up with that phone.

'So.' He finally turned to me. 'What I'm going to do first is use hot-water extraction to clean the carpet. Then I'll protect it and deodorise it.'

'Okay. Were you in an infomercial, by any chance?'

'No,' he groaned. 'That was my dad. Fancies himself as a bit of an actor. He wants me to do one but I think I'd rather . . .' He thought about it. 'Yep, I'd rather die.'

I laughed. 'It could be fun.'

He looked at me, widened his eyes. 'Really? Would you do it?'

'If you paid me I would pretty much do anything.' I frowned. 'Except what I just made it sound like I'd do. I wouldn't do *that*.'

'I wouldn't ask you to. Not for money, I mean.' His face pinked. 'Can we change the subject?'

'Yes, please.'

My phone beeped and we both took it as a good sign to stop talking immediately.

—Bloody Tom. He met a girl and decided to grow up, he's moving in with her next week. I'm a flat-mate down so . . . thirty-five-and-three-quarter-year-old tall dark handsome man seeking anybody who can pay the rent.

I texted back.

—Are you looking for someone too?! I'll send the word out. Personal question: what's your dream? Something that you really want.

The carpet cleaner's phone beeped. I tutted, but my disapproval couldn't be heard over the sound of the cleaner. He turned it off and took his phone from his pocket.

'You're popular today.'

'Yeah, sorry.' He stopped to read it. Then he texted back.

My phone beeped.

—A coffee. Want one now really badly.

I looked up at the cleaning guy; he was cleaning away, deep in thought. I hopped off the stool.

'Would you like a coffee?'

He didn't respond.

'Excuse me, would you like a coffee?' I said louder.

He looked up. 'You must have read my mind. Would love one, thanks.'

He took a slug, placed it on the counter and went back to work. I sat down and read back over my texts, reading between the lines for more answers while I waited for another response. The carpet cleaner took out his phone again. I really wanted to say something but I held my tongue because I began to study him then, the small secret smile that was on his lips as he texted, and it immediately made me hate the person at the other end of that phone. He was texting a girl and I hated her.

'Is this going to take long?' I finally said, without the niceness in my voice.

'Sorry?' He looked up from the text.

'The carpet. Will it take long?'

'About two hours.'

'I'm going to take the baby for a walk.'

He looked confused. He should be. I was. I received Don's response when I was in the elevator.

–*My dream is to win the lottery so I can quit my job and never have to work again. But what I really really want? Is to meet you.*

I stared at the text, open-mouthed. The elevator had reached the ground floor and the doors had— opened but I was taken aback and forgot to step out, partly because we had the same lazy dream but mostly because he had said such a beautiful borderline-cheesy thing that was actually quite adorable but terrifying. The doors to the elevator closed and before I'd a chance to press the buttons, it went up again. I sighed and leaned against the wall. We stopped on my floor. It was the cleaning guy.

'Hello.'

'I forgot to get out.'

He laughed and looked in the buggy. 'So what's his name?'

'Conor.'

'He's cute.'

We laughed.

'Are you sure we don't know one another?' he asked.

I studied him again. 'Did you used to be a stockbroker?'

'No,' he laughed.

'Did you ever pretend to be one?'

'No.'

'Well then, no.' I really think I'd have remembered if I'd met him before – he was the highest up on the Blake barometer of any other human being living or dead. He was vaguely familiar but that may have been because I'd been staring at him all morning like a dirty old man. I frowned and shook my head. 'I'm sorry, I don't even know your name.'

He pointed at his chest where there was a stitched-in label. It said, *Donal*. 'My mother did it, insisted it would make the company more modern. It was her idea to do the infomercial. She read one marketing book about Starbucks and now she thinks she's Donald Trump.'

'Without the comb-over, I hope.'

He laughed. The doors opened and he let me walk out first. 'Whoa,' I said when we got outside. The van was bright yellow with a red magic flying carpet emblazoned on the side. On the roof rack was a larger-than-life rolled-up plastic red carpet.

'You see? This is what they force me to drive. The carpet turns around when the engine's on.'

'That's some book your mother read. It's just for work though, isn't it? It's not as though it's your everyday van.' From the way he was looking at me I could tell I was wrong. New thought. 'Wouldn't it be cool if this was your everyday van?'

He laughed. 'Yep. It's a real babe-magnet, isn't it?'

'It's like a superhero car,' I said, circling it, and he looked at it again with new eyes.

'I never thought of it like that.' Then he studied me again. It was like he was trying to say something but couldn't. I got goose bumps. 'I'll be finished in about an hour,' he said instead. 'The floor will be wet so I advise you not to walk on it for a few hours. I'll come back this evening to put your furniture back if that's okay and make sure you're happy with the service.'

I was going to tell him not to bother coming

back to replace the furniture, that I could do it, but I stopped myself, partly because there was no way in the world I could lift all the furniture, but mostly it was because I actually wanted him to come back. 'Don't worry about locking up, you can just close the door behind you.'

'Okay, great. Nice meeting you, Lucy.'

'Nice meeting you too, Donal. See you later.'

'It's a date,' he said, and we laughed.

Conor and I sat on the bench in the park and when no one was looking I put him in the swing. I knew he wasn't there, but for Claire, and for the memory of him, I stayed there until the sun went down behind the park trees, pushing him back and forth and hoping his little soul somewhere out there was saying *Wheeee*, just like mine suddenly was.

That evening, when the buggy was safely back with Claire, I took my shoes off, brought a high stool to the centre of the floor and sat down to watch Blake's travel show. Just as it began I heard a key in the door. It opened and Life entered, wearing a new blazer.

'How did you get a key?'

'I made a copy of yours when you were asleep,' he said, taking off his blazer and tossing the keys onto the counter like he lived here.

'Thanks for asking for my permission.'

'Didn't need to, your family already signed the paperwork.'

'Ah-ah-ah,' I said as he took a step onto the carpet. 'Shoes off, it's just been cleaned.'

'What are you watching?' he asked, doing as he was told and looking at the paused image of a snake rising from a basket.

'Blake's travel show.'

He raised his eyebrows and studied me. 'Really? I thought you never watched the show.'

'I do sometimes.'

'How often?'

'Only on Sundays.'

'I believe his show is only on on Sundays.' He brought a stool beside me. 'The carpet doesn't look any different.'

'That's because it's wet. It'll brighten up when it dries.'

'What were they like?'

'Who?'

'The carpet people.'

'It was just one man.'

'And?'

'And he was very nice and he cleaned the carpet. Can you stop talking? I want to watch this.'

'Touchy.'

Mr Pan leaped into his lap and we sat uncomfortably on our stools and watched Blake. He was climbing across some rocky mountains, wearing a navy vest that was covered in sweat stains and revealed rippling back muscles. It made me think of the carpet-cleaning guy. It struck me as unusual that Blake, the most perfect man in the universe, would cause me to think positively of another man, and once I was comfortable with that thought, I compared their muscle sizes.

'Does he wear fake tan?'

'Shut up.'

'Does he do his own stunts?'

'Shut up.'

I paused the TV, searched for her. She wasn't there.

'What are you doing?'

'Shut up.'

'So what is the obsession with Blake anyway?'

'I'm not obsessed.'

'I mean last night. I know you said you didn't want to talk about it but I think we should. I mean, you broke up three years ago. What's the deal with your friends? Why are they so involved in what happened with you and him?'

'Blake is their centre of gravity,' I said, watching him climb across the cliff barehanded. 'We both used to be, believe it or not. We were the ones who arranged everything, who brought everyone together. We held dinner parties every week, had parties, organised holidays, nights out, trips away, that kind of thing.' I pressed pause, studied the scene, unpaused it again. 'Blake is a lively guy, he's addictive, everyone likes him.'

'I don't.'

'Really?' I looked at him surprised, then turned back to the TV quickly so I wouldn't miss anything. 'Well, you're biased, it doesn't count.'

I paused the TV again, then unpaused.

'What exactly are you doing?'

'Shut up.'

'Please stop telling me to shut up.'

'Please stop giving me cause to.'

He watched the rest of it mostly in silence with the occasional snide remark. Then finally as Blake was finished bargaining in the *souks* and trying to charm snakes – to which Life maturely commented that he was a charming snake – he sat down in a café in Djemaa el Fna, the large central square in the old city and gave his final thought to camera.

'Someone once said, the world is a book and those who do not travel, read only a page.'

Life groaned and pretended to vomit. 'What a crock of shit.'

I was surprised; I rather liked that one.

Then Blake winked. I savoured the moment, my eyes glued to the final seconds of my time with him for this season; after this, all that I would learn about him would be propaganda from the Blake Party – if I ever heard from them again.

'Do you think that maybe he left you because he's gay?' Life asked.

I ground my teeth together, fighting the urge to push my life off the stool. It would be pointless, it would be like cutting my nose off to spite my face and I was thinking about that when my life changed forever. The next shot was quick, so quick that any untrained eye could have missed it, but not my eye, not even my bad eye could miss it which had worse vision after Riley had blown a pen bomb – a ball of paper blown from the outer plastic shell of a pen – in my eye when I was eight years old. I hoped and prayed and wished on every lucky thing that due to my as yet undiagnosed but ever present psychotic tendencies, that I'd merely imagined what came next. The camera zoomed out and I paused and searched. It was her. There she was. Jenna. The bitch. From Australia. Or at least I thought it was her. They were in a busy noisy café, at a table piled high with mounds of food with at least a dozen other people. It looked like the Last Supper. I hopped off the stool and moved closer, stood right up at the screen. If it was her, it would be her last supper.

'Hey, the carpet,' Life said.

'Fuck the carpet,' I said, venom in my voice.

'Whoa.'

'The little . . .' I paced up and down before the screen, watching their frozen toast, their glasses pushed up against each other suggestively, both looking into each other's eyes, or at least her at him and him at something over her shoulder, but still in the general direction. 'Bitch,' I finally said. I played it again, watching their toast, rewound it and watched it once more. I examined their shared look: yes, they definitely looked at one another as their glasses clinked, did that mean something? Was it code? Were they secretly silently saying to one another, *Let's you and me clink tonight just*

265

like we did on the top of Everest? The thought made my stomach heave. Then I analysed their body language, and then even looked at the food on their plates; they had shared a few dishes and they disgusted me. My heart was pounding, thudding in my chest, I felt like the blood wanted to jump out of my veins. I needed to climb through the television and into their world so I could break them up and ram the Moroccan meatballs down her throat.

'What on earth is wrong with you?' Life asked. 'You look possessed, and you're ruining the carpet.'

I turned around and fixed him with the most determined look I could muster. It wasn't difficult, I felt it inside. 'I know why you're here.'

'Why?' He looked worried.

'Because I'm still in love with Blake. And I know what my dream is, the thing that I really, really want, the thing that I'd do if I had the guts and didn't care what anybody thought. It's him, I want him. And I have to get him back.'

CHAPTER SEVENTEEN

'I have to go to him,' I said, pacing.

'No, you don't.'

'*We* have to go to him.'

'No, we certainly do not.'

'This is why you're here.'

'No . . .' He spoke slowly. 'I'm here because you're delusional.'

'I'm in love with him,' I said, still pacing, my mind working overtime while I tried to plan winning him back.

'You're ruining the carpet is what you are.'

'I knew she was out to get him. I'd known it ever since I met her and she asked him if he'd like ice and lemon in his drink. The way she said it, I just knew. '"*Ice*",' I imitated her. '"Do you want *ice* with that?"'

'Whoa, hold on, who are we talking about now?'

'Her.' I finally stopped pacing and pointed at the paused TV screen with the remote control in my hand as though it was a weapon. 'Jenna. Jenna Anderson.' I spat the name out.

'And she is?'

'The PA. I couldn't figure out whether she was an office PA or a set PA but now I know. Now I know for sure.' I started pacing again.

'What do you know for sure?'

'That she's the set PA, would you keep up?' I snapped. 'Wait a minute, where's my laptop?' I trampled over the damp carpet and opened the corner cupboard. I reached for my laptop, and a cookie which I demolished while the computer started up. Life watched me, from the high stool. I went to her Facebook page and viewed her status. I gasped.

'What now?' he asked, bored.

'Her status has been updated.'

'To what? Herdswoman?' he said, looking at the paused screen where she sat surrounded by cloaked men.

'No.' My mind was racing. I knew it, I knew my paranoia was a guide.

'Does it say to whom her status belongs?'

'No.' I stared at her Facebook page intensely as I tried to read beyond the entry page. 'I bet she's got photographs of the two of them in there, all kinds of comments and inside information. If I could just get in, then I could see it all and I'd know for sure.'

'Don't you ask people to be your friends on those things?'

'Don't you think I thought of that years ago? She said no, the bitch.'

Life sucked air in. 'You should have changed your name.'

'I did.'

'Then you should have used your own name.'

'Are you crazy? Why would any spy use their own identity?'

'Oh, you're a spy now. Okay, Double D, I think you should calm down now.'

'I can't calm down. They'll still be a relatively new couple, when was that show filmed? I can still break them up,' I said, filled with hope. I ran across from the kitchen to my bed that was piled high with the couch.

'Aye, aye, aye, watch the carpet!' he called.

'Screw the carpet,' I said rather dramatically. 'This is my life.' Then I grabbed a suitcase from the top of the wardrobe and started throwing things in, random things, nothing that would actually ever come to being one complete outfit, but the motion of packing was helpful.

'*I'm* your life and I'm telling you to just stop for a moment and think.'

I obeyed him but only because I needed him. A plot was formulating in my head and he was central to it.

'You can't just pack a bag and chase him to . . .' He looked at the TV. 'Morocco.'

'I'm not going to Morocco. I'm going to Wexford.'

'Well, isn't that glamorous. Thelma and Louise would have been a whole lot different if they'd decided to go there.'

'His adventure school is there. If I leave now with Sebastian, I can be there by the morning.'

'It's unlikely that you'll get there at all with Sebastian. Anyway, you've got work in the morning.'

'I hate my job.'

'I thought you said you liked it.'

'I lied. I love Blake.'

'I thought you said you were over him.'

'I lied. I hate my job and I love Blake.' I punched the air. Saying it felt right.

He sighed. 'It's like one step forward and two steps back with you.'

'I have to go,' I said more calmly. 'It's why you're here. I know it. When you left I Googled people's dreams. Because you were right, I didn't have one, which is rather pathetic, I *should* have one.'

'I don't know which is more pathetic, not having a dream or *Googling* other people's.'

'It was for inspiration – and you know what one person online said?' I was quite breathless about it now that it applied to me. 'They said they want to someday, someway, somehow be reunited with the one true love that they lost.' My voice ended in a squeak. 'How romantic is that?'

'Not very if the true love in question is a fake-tan-wearing selfish snake.'

'Come on,' I begged, 'when you meet him you'll

realise that you actually like him. *Everybody* likes him.'

'He doesn't like you,' Life said bluntly. 'He left you. Three years ago. What makes you think anything will change?'

I swallowed. 'Because I've changed. You've changed me. He might like me now.'

Life rolled his eyes, not wanting to fall for it but he couldn't help it, he gave in. 'Fine, I'll go with you.'

I celebrated and gave him a hug. He didn't reciprocate.

'But you have to promise me that you'll go to work tomorrow. You're in a lot of trouble, it won't do you any good not to show up. And you have to visit your mother. You can go to see Blake after work on Tuesday. Drive up and down in one night so that you're back in work by Wednesday.'

'I thought you wanted me to take care of my life,' I whinged. 'I thought that work was a distraction from taking care of the things that count.'

'It is sometimes, but it's not now. It's the opposite now.'

'What's that supposed to mean?'

'It means that now Blake has become a distraction from taking care of the things that count.'

'You make me sound so clever, as if I'm deliberately doing all this emotional distraction stuff.'

'Not clever, just stupid. You have such blinkers on with Blake that you wouldn't even recognise the perfect man of your dreams if he was standing right next to you.'

I narrowed my eyes, uncertain of whether he was trying to tell me something.

'No, not me.'

'Phew.'

'He could even be right outside that very door,' Life said, mysteriously.

The doorbell rang. I froze. Then I gathered myself, I didn't believe in signs, I didn't even trust sat nav. I looked at Life.

He smiled and shrugged, 'I heard footsteps in the corridor, just thought I'd chance it.'

I rolled my eyes and pulled the door open. It was the carpet guy. I'd forgotten about him.

'Sorry I'm late, I was delayed on another job and I would have called but my battery went dead, which means I'm late for my next appointment and my dad will have a fit. Do you mind if I borrow a charger or use your phone to call—' He stepped into the apartment and saw Life. He seemed a bit put out, ended his story and respectfully nodded. 'Hello.'

'Hi, I'm just a friend of Lucy's,' my life said, swinging his legs back and forth from his perch on the high stool. 'There's nothing at all romantic going on between us.'

Donal laughed. 'Okay.'

'Now that you're here to supervise the crazy lady, I'm leaving.' He hopped off the stool. 'All those track marks in the carpet are hers. She's a pacing, raving uncontrollable lunatic.'

Donal studied the ground. 'What were you doing in here, wrestling?'

'Metaphorically speaking, yes,' Life responded.

'You can't leave, we have so much to discuss,' I said to Life, panicking.

'About what?'

'About the *trip*.' I made big eyes at him.

Donal lifted the suitcase from the furniture.

'Wexford,' Life said to Donal, bored.

'To an outdoor adventure centre,' I said in defence of our trip.

'In Bastardstown, no less,' Life said, raising an eyebrow.

'Ah yeah, that's the man off the TV's place,' Donal said. 'I've seen it advertised. Blake somebody.'

'Blake Jones,' I said, feeling proud.

'Yeah, that's him.' Donal made a face and not a nice one, which led me to believe he didn't like Blake. 'And remember,' Donal said, putting on a posh accent, 'the only true wisdom is in knowing you know nothing.'

Life laughed loudly and clapped his hands. 'That's a good impression. Isn't it, Lucy?'

I scowled.

'He's her ex-boyfriend,' Life explained to Donal, who immediately stopped smiling and looked worried.

'I'm really sorry, I wouldn't have said anything.'

'Don't worry,' Life said, waving a hand dismissively. 'Or as Blake would say, "Nothing that is worth knowing can be taught."'

Donal laughed but turned it into a cough instead for my benefit.

'We can talk about the big trip tomorrow. In the mean time, give the man your phone, he needs to call his father.'

'My battery's low,' I said.

Life gave me a look and spoke in a warning tone. 'Lucy, give the man your phone.'

'The battery is low,' I said slowly, so that he'd understand.

'Fine, you made me do this.' Life turned to Donal. 'Donal, I am not Lucy's friend. I am Lucy's life, I have contacted her in an effort to fix the mess she has made of herself. So far you have done a wonderful job with her carpet. I'm spending time with her because right now she needs me, though at the moment I'm strongly considering medication as the best course of action.'

I gasped.

'You lied about the battery on your mobile.' He justified his truth.

I opened and closed my mouth but nothing would come out. I reached into my pocket and grudgingly handed Donal the phone.

'Let me walk you to the door,' I said, taking one step to get there. I held it open for him. While Donal was out of earshot I added in a hushed voice, 'I thought you could claim it on expenses. I can't afford my own bill, never mind other people making calls.'

'I'll give you the fifty cent,' Life said and threw me a cheeky smile, revealing new sparkling white

274

teeth, before disappearing down the hallway. When I turned around, Donal was looking at me with a shocked expression as though he'd seen a ghost.

'What?' I asked, worried. 'What happened?'

'Where did you get this photo?' He lifted up the phone, showing me the pair of Don Lockwood's eyes on my screen saver.

'The guy who owns the eyes sent it to me,' I replied, confused. 'Why?'

Realisation passed over his face. 'Because they're mine.'

CHAPTER EIGHTEEN

'What are you talking about?' I stayed at the door, back pressed up against the metal while my mind ran through the various possibilities. The enduring emotion throughout all of the scenarios was anger. OK, I didn't know Don Lockwood, he was a wrong number, but I had been honest with him when I had never been honest with anybody – myself included – definitely for the past two years, quite possibly in my entire life, and it doubly hurt that he had conned me. 'Why would he take a photo of your eyes and send them to me?'

He was grinning broadly, laughing at a joke that I didn't get. 'No, *I* took the photo. *I* sent it to you. Lucy, I'm Don.'

'No, you're not, you're Donal, your shirt says Donal.' And a shirt wouldn't lie. It couldn't; it was a shirt.

'My mother stitched this. She's the only person in the world who calls me Donal. Lucy . . .' He emphasised my name and smiled. '*Of course,* you're such a Lucy.'

I stared at him, like that gaping fish again trying to figure it all out, then he took his cap off, ruffled his hair a bit self-consciously and looked at me. Then Bam! His eyes hit me, it was almost like a physical reaction, my head jerked back on my neck as if I'd been punched. They were the eyes I'd been staring at all week and there they were in the same room as me, moving, blinking, with a perfect nose and cute dimples beneath them. I don't know if it's possible for a human being to do this, but I melted.

'You have me on your screen saver,' he grinned proudly, waving my phone in the air.

'I thought they were nice eyes. Not as nice as the ear, but nice.'

He turned his head to the side and proudly modelled his left ear.

I wolf-whistled and he laughed.

'I knew it,' he said, shaking his head. 'I kept looking at you and I knew that I knew you. So it wasn't a wrong number after all,' he said.

'Sometimes wrong numbers are the right numbers,' I said mainly to myself, echoing Life's earlier sentiments. I had thought he was being philosophical but for once he was being literal. I was still trying to figure it out. 'But directory enquiries connected me to the company number, not your mobile.'

'You called on a weekend. My dad doesn't work weekends, so the office number gets diverted to my mobile phone.'

'I'm so stupid. I heard pub noises and just assumed . . .'

'You're not stupid,' he said softly. 'You're just an idiot.'

I laughed.

'So we were texting each other right beside one another all day.'

I had to think about it. All that time I had hated the person at the other end of his phone and all that time that person had been me. The irony.

'Which, by the way, was extremely unprofessional of you,' I said.

'Couldn't help it. But you didn't respond to my last text which, by the way, was extremely rude of you.' He handed me back the phone.

I scrolled through and read the end of his last text:

—But what I really really want? Is to meet you.

I thought about it, he was looking at me for an answer but instead of giving him one straight away, I texted him back:

—OK. Meet you for a coffee in five minutes?

I put the phone down, ignored him and headed straight for the cupboard from which I removed two mugs, and the coffee granules.

'What are you doing?' he asked, watching me.

I ignored him and continued. Then his phone beeped. I watched him from the corner of my eye. He read it. Texted. Sent. Then he didn't look at me and just got straight back to work, removing the furniture from my bed and lining it up back in front of the TV. I watched him as I waited for the kettle to boil.

My phone beeped.

–Just finishing work. See you in five.

I smiled. We went about our business in silence, me making the coffee, him putting the couch back together. Then when he was finished, he made his way over to the kitchen.

'Hi,' he said. 'Don Lockwood.' He held his hand out to greet me.

'I know,' I said, placing the coffee into it instead. 'How was work?'

He looked down into his mug as though deciding whether to drink it or not and then he placed it down on the counter. Then he took my mug from my hands and placed it down beside his. And then he stepped closer, put his hand to my face – his fingers touched my face so tenderly – and he leaned in and kissed me. Not since I was twelve years old at the six-thirty-to-eight-thirty disco in my local leisure centre when Gerard Looney and I had slobbered all over each other for three consecutive slow songs without coming up for air, had I kissed someone for that length of time. But I couldn't stop and I didn't want to stop, so just for a change of scenery we automatically started working our way from the linoleum, to the brand spanking newly cleaned and slightly damp carpet, then our feet left the floor completely as we collapsed on the bed.

* * *

'I have an idea for your infomercial,' I said later that evening, lying on my side and leaning on my elbow to look at him. I continued in an advertiser's voice. 'We'll take the dirt from your carpet and bring the filth to your bed. We'll clean your carpets and seduce your wives while you're at work.'

He laughed and joined in, 'Want us to know if your curtains *really* match your rug?'

'Uugh,' I laughed, slapping him playfully. 'Besides, I've no curtains.'

'No,' he said, looking at the curtain pole with amusement. 'You haven't much of a rug either.'

'True,' I smiled, and we laughed.

'So,' he said in a more serious tone, turning on to his side so that we were facing one another. 'Tell me about life.'

I groaned. 'This is very serious pillow talk.'

'No, I don't mean *your* life, I mean the guy who was in the apartment. Jesus, what do you think I am, *interested* in you?'

'I should hope not,' I laughed. 'I was hoping you were just using me for my body.'

'I am.' He moved closer.

'What do you know about this kind of thing?'

'That Life contacts you and you have to meet them and make some changes. I read an interview with a woman in a magazine while I was at the dentist.'

'Did she have an over-the-top blowdry and was standing beside a vase full of lemons and limes?'

He laughed. 'I can't remember the details. But

she was happy afterwards, that's what I remember.' He studied me and I waited for him to ask me if I was unhappy the way everybody else did, but he didn't, probably because I'd tensed up and was as stiff as an ironing board beside him. 'I've never met anyone who's actually met with their lives before. You're the first.'

'How proud I feel.'

'Well, whatever about pride, you shouldn't be embarrassed.'

I went quiet.

'Are you embarrassed?'

'Tell me a fart joke or something. This subject is too serious.'

'I'll go one better than that.' I felt him move beside me, then a disgusting smell.

I couldn't help but giggle. 'Thank you.'

'Anything for you.' He kissed my forehead.

'That's very thoughtful of you. We're practically married now.'

'Nah, if we were married, I'd have wafted it.'

It was disgusting but I laughed, loved the closeness and the level of comfort with him, but I was worried. It had been a long time since I'd bedded a stunning man. It had been a long time since I'd slept with any man – a stockbroker who liked my tits ten months ago, but a longer time since a man like him who I'd truly felt at home with – and *never* had I brought a man back to my flat. Don had seen my world, he had entered my bubble that I'd created for nobody else but myself and though I'd enjoyed every second of it and hadn't thought of Blake once, now as he was looking at me with the eyes that I felt belonged more on my phone screen saver and less in my bed, all I wanted was for him to leave. I thought I'd made a mistake. The adrenaline I'd felt when I'd discovered my true feelings for Blake mere hours earlier had returned. I was thinking of Jenna, Jenna the slut from Australia, and wondering if they lay like this together, naked and contorted, and it made my heart twist.

'Are you okay?' he asked cautiously.

'Yeah.' I snapped out of it. I suddenly wanted to be alone again but it was dark, it was ten o'clock on a Sunday night, I wasn't sure if he intended on staying over or if he was going to leap out of bed any second thanking me for my time.

'Didn't you say that you were late for an appointment earlier?' I asked.

'No, it's okay, it's not important now.'

'I won't take it personally,' I said, perking up. 'If there's somewhere you have to be then please feel free to leave.'

'I was supposed to have dinner with my parents but really you've done me a favour. Sex with a stranger is far more important.'

I tried to figure out another way to make him leave; wanting them to stay was usually enough.

'What were you thinking about a few minutes ago?'

'When?'

'You know when.'

I didn't say anything.

'It's just that, I lost you,' he said tenderly, stroking my hair in a hypnotically relaxing rhythm. I battled to keep my eyes open. 'You were right there, and then you were gone.' He was speaking so gently, so melodically, that I was present again. He moved closer and kissed me.

'Ah. There you are,' he murmured, then kissed me more intensely.

And despite my inner emotional protestations and despite feeling torn inside about my love for Blake, my body couldn't help but respond to him and I got lost all over again.

He didn't snore. He slept so silently I barely knew he was there. His skin was warm, not blazing hot like Blake's. He kept to his side of the bed, not a foot or a knee or an arm across the line. His skin smelled of marshmallows, tasted salty from sweat. And despite the fact that I lay there planning what to bring in my half-packed suitcase beside our strewn clothes on the floor, and working out what I would do and say when I met Blake, I reached out to the warm sheets and felt for his hand. The silent sweet-smelling sleeper opened his closed palm and wrapped it around mine. We held hands and I slept. Then Life came knocking, or in my case, let himself into my flat with his own set of keys.

CHAPTER NINETEEN

I was woken by the clatter of keys on the kitchen counter. Don jumped beside me, startled, probably disoriented, and immediately sat up in bed, ready to defend.

'It's okay,' I said groggily. 'It's just him.'

'Who?' he said, alarmed, as though there were a secret love I hadn't told him about, which technically there was but that certain secret love would not be bursting into my flat with his own set of keys and singing 'Earthsong' by Michael Jackson.

'My life,' I said, trying to speak with my mouth closed to avoid travelling morning breath. I offered him an apologetic smile. For my life interrupting him, not for my breath.

'At six a.m.?' He looked at his watch.

'He's a twenty-four-seven kind of man.'

'Right.' He smiled. 'Of course. Will he approve of this?'

Life had suddenly stopped singing and the rustles of plastic bags had stopped.

'Do I hear talking?' Life asked in a sing-song voice. 'Do I hear the voice of a *man* in little Lucy's bed?'

I rolled my eyes and ducked under the covers. Don chuckled and protected his modesty by pulling the sheet to above his waist.

'Oh, Loo-ccee,' my life sang, his voice getting louder as he got closer. 'Have you been a naughty girl? Hey, it's you,' Life said, standing at the end of my bed. 'Yes!'

I had to laugh as Life whooped with delight.

'I take it you approve,' Don said.

'Approve? Of course I do. Does this mean she doesn't have to pay for the carpets because if so, your plan worked, Lucy. You should have seen what she did to the window cleaner.'

I crawled up to the surface. 'I didn't sleep with him to pay for the carpets,' I said, insulted, then turned to Don. 'Though that would be a really lovely gesture, thank you so much, Don.'

Don laughed. Life sat at the edge of the bed. I kicked him off and he wandered away without a fight and then made his way back with a tray, which he placed on Don's lap. 'I didn't know if you liked marmalade or jam or honey so I brought all three.'

'What about me?'

'Make your own.'

Don chuckled. 'This is great. Do you do this for all of Lucy's men?'

Life lay down on the end of the bed. 'Don, there

isn't enough bread in the world for me to feed Lucy's lovers.'

Don laughed.

'This doesn't bother you? Having him around?' I asked, surprised.

'He's a part of you, isn't he?' Don responded, then handed me half of his toast.

Life raised his eyebrows at me. I wanted my life to go away, and as sweet and wonderful as he was, I wanted Don to go too. I had to go see a man about our love.

'You look really rough right now,' Life said to me, munching on some toast. He looked at Don understandingly. 'You must be thinking *shit* right now, are you? It's okay if you are, we both understand. She's just not a morning person. She's a little dodgy after one p.m. too.'

Don laughed. 'I think she's beautiful.' He handed me more toast.

I was embarrassed. Life didn't offer a comeback; instead he studied me.

'Thanks,' I said quietly, taking the toast, but my appetite was gone. He was all the right things at exactly the wrong time. The nicer he was, the more uncomfortable I felt.

'So does this mean our little trip is cancelled?' Life asked, picking up on my mood and putting me on the spot.

'No,' I replied awkwardly, angry he'd mentioned it in Don's presence. 'Can you please leave us alone now?' I asked.

'No,' he said defiantly.

'If you don't leave us alone now, you'll regret it.'

'Are you threatening me?'

'Yes.'

He took another bite of his toast, didn't budge from the bed.

'Fine,' I said. I threw off the covers and walked butt naked to the bathroom leaving Life choking on his toast and Don whooping like a college boy.

I showered in the new light of my bathroom, feeling uncomfortable about my life and my one-night stand sitting outside together. I didn't want the water to ever stop falling. My fingers were close to shrivelling and the bathroom was so full of steam I could barely see the door, but I couldn't move. I couldn't face Don. I wanted the water to wash away the guilt, the confusion over my feelings for Blake, which – whatever they were – were making whatever feelings I'd had for Don the night before suddenly insignificant. As I was shampooing for the third time, I had a thought: what was making me so sure that Don wanted more from me? He might have been perfectly content with a one-night stand, so feeling hopeful, I perked up and turned off the water. They were quiet outside. I climbed out of the bath. The voices started again, low murmurs in which I couldn't make out their words. I wiped the condensation from the mirror and stared at a red blotchy heat-rashed face.

I sighed.

'Come on, Lucy,' I whispered. 'Just get this over with so you can get to Blake.'

But even at that idea I felt a slight dread. Again, I didn't like what I had but I didn't know what I wanted, so I was once again aimless. When I stepped out into the kitchen – fully dressed – they went quiet. They were sitting beside each other at the counter, drinking coffee and eating omelettes. They looked at me. Don's eyes fluttered over me with a softness; Life gave me the once-over but didn't seem overly impressed. Mr Pan looked up from the bed of shoes at the window and monitored me just as I would him if he'd pissed on the mail – as though he knew the bad thing that I had done.

'Well, it was obvious you were talking about me,' I said, making my way to the kettle.

'I'm your life and he just slept with you, what else were we going to talk about? He gave you four out of ten, by the way.'

'Don't listen to him.'

'I never do.'

'There's coffee in the pot,' Life said.

'You leave me some coffee but you don't make me breakfast?' I said to Life.

'I didn't make breakfast.'

'Oh.' I looked at Don.

'It's in the oven,' he said. 'Warming.'

'Oh. Thanks.' Very unusual behaviour for a man who never wanted to see me again, but still, I had hope. Rather self-consciously I opened the oven door.

'Be careful, the plate's hot,' Don warned but my brain took a while to compute the meaning of his words and it was too late. My hand was stuck to the plate. I screeched. Don jumped off the stool and grabbed my hand.

'Let me see,' he said, his voice and face all concerned. Even through my excruciating pain I took a moment to take in his face, all dark and concerned and beautiful. But the pain, the pain overtook all cuteness. Don held my hand in his and guided me around the kitchen like he was Ratatouille. I ended up with my hand underneath the cold tap and Don wouldn't let go of me, even when the water became too cold and I wanted to take it away. 'You have to leave it there for at least five minutes, Lucy,' he said sternly.

I opened my mouth but I decided not to object.

'How did you do that?' Life asked, impressed.

'What?'

'Make her not answer back.'

Don smiled briefly, then concentrated on my hand with that concerned look.

'I think you'll have to amputate,' Life said, still sitting down and shovelling another forkful of egg into his mouth.

'Thanks for your concern. This,' I nodded at Don, 'this is proper concern.'

'He just slept with you, he has to pretend to respect you.'

He joked but I knew that my life was impressed and I could tell that he was happy. He was wearing a new suit, navy blue, which brought out the colour of his eyes, which had once been nondescript and were now strikingly blue. His cold had cleared up, leaving his nose less large looking, his teeth had been brushed, his breath was better and he looked good. He sounded happy; he teased me but with love. It should have made me happy too, but it concerned me. I was unsure. Something was wrong.

'Why are you so dressed up?' I asked him.

'Because I'm meeting your parents this evening,' he said.

Don looked at me, with sympathy I think, which I appreciated.

'Actually, not just me. *We* are meeting your parents. I called your house yesterday and spoke to a lovely woman named Edith. She was very sweet and very excited that we were both coming to visit, she said she'd inform your parents immediately and prepare a special dinner.'

I think I had a mini panic attack. 'Do you have any idea what you've just done?'

'Yes. I returned your many calls from your mother for you, which you need to thank me for. Your mother needs you and you haven't been there. She also needs you.' He looked at Don. 'There's coffee on the carpet on the Persian rug in the drawing room.' Life made a mock shock-horror face. 'So I gave her your number.'

I was more angry over him giving my mum Don's number than arranging a dinner. There I was trying to find ways to get rid of Don and already he was going to infiltrate my parents' home. He would be the only man in the world apart from my life to be in both my home and theirs.

'You don't understand how unnecessary this is. You have no idea how much she doesn't need me. She is perfectly capable of organising her own funeral without any help from anyone. As for my dad . . . Jesus, what have you done? He's going to meet you? He will have nothing to say to you, absolutely nothing.' I put my head in my only free hand and then realised Don was listening to everything so I removed my hand and acted as if I hadn't said any of those things. 'It looks nice out today, doesn't it?'

Life shook his head at Don. Don, who was still holding my hand under the freezing cold water, did something with his entire *being*, without moving an inch or saying a word, but which let me know that he was there for me.

We stepped out into the chilly morning, colder because we stood in the shadow cast by my apartment building. Across the road in the park we could see sunlight, but no sun could reach where we were standing and my wrap-around dress whipped up around my thighs as the wind blew. My hands tried desperately to keep it down and though it was nothing he hadn't seen before, it was different now.

'Would you like a lift in my superhero car?' Don asked casually but I could tell he was feeling uncomfortable. Not only was he embarrassed about his mode of transport but it was the morning after the night before, night had become day and he was still in the same clothes, and I was detached, and had been for the past half–hour. I wasn't giving him very much to cling onto.

'No thanks, I have to drive to my parents straight after work.'

Now for the awkward moment: did we shake hands, high-five or kiss goodbye? Mr Don Lockwood, thank you ever so much for the hot random spontaneous sex, it was truly a pleasure being acquainted with you and your private parts but really I must dash and tell my ex-boyfriend I still love him. Toodle-pips.

'I have a day off tomorrow, if you'd like to meet up. Go for lunch. Or have coffee, or dinner or drinks.'

'That's a lot of options,' I said awkwardly, trying to figure out how to say *none of the above* in a polite way. 'I have to take a trip after work and I won't be back until . . .' I was going to say 'late' but maybe Blake would take me back then and there and I'd have to hire a removal van to pack up my flat and relocate to Bastardstown, Co. Wexford. That should have felt exciting, but it didn't, because I loved my little flat and I didn't want to ever leave it. Would Blake come and live with me in it? The Blake I once knew wouldn't have been seen dead in a flat like that, there wasn't enough surface in the kitchen for him to roll out the dough for his pizza base, and if he tossed it in the air it would get stuck in the strip lighting. We'd be battling for space on the curtain beam – he had as many clothes as I did – and he probably wouldn't fit in the narrow bath, never mind the two of us like we used to do on Sunday evenings with a bottle of wine. I pictured Jenna wrapping her legs around his waist in the tub and my heart began pumping at top speed again. I got lost in my mind trying to figure out the logistics of my future with Blake in my new life while Don was looking at me.

'Of course,' he said, studying me a little too intensely for my liking. 'You're going to see your ex.'

I didn't know what to say, so I didn't say anything.

He cleared his throat. 'It's not much of my business but . . .' And then he decided not to go there, maybe because I had looked away. His new tone surprised me; it was immediately distanced, a little bit hardened. 'Okay, well, thanks for last night.' I looked at him and he nodded and walked away. He waved at Life, Life waved back, and he got into his car, started up the engine. I didn't want it to end like this, even though it had been me who had led it in this direction, but I couldn't bring myself to say anything. I didn't want the outcome reversed, just how it came about, so I watched him drive away feeling like the biggest bitch in the world and then I headed to my car.

'Hey.' Life chased after me. 'What happened?'

'Nothing happened.'

'He just walked off, did you have a fight?'

'No.'

'Did he ask you out again?'

'Yes.'

'And?'

'I can't. We're going away tomorrow.'

I put the key in the car door but it wouldn't budge. I battled with it under Life's stare.

'We're going there and back for the *evening*. You'll be back again late tomorrow night.'

'Yeah, maybe.'

'What do you mean, maybe?'

I was frustrated with the key, I was frustrated with my life and I snapped.

'Tomorrow I am going to tell the love of my life that I am still in love with him. Do you think for one minute that I'm hoping I'll be back by tomorrow night in order to go on a date with a man who drives a yellow van with a magic carpet on it?'

Life was momentarily stunned, then he took the key from my hand, turned it gently and the door opened. 'Let's go,' he said.

'That's it?' I watched him walk around the car to the passenger side, cool, calm and collected.

He shrugged.

'No lectures, no weird psychology, no meta-phors, that's it?'

'Don't worry, nothing speaks louder than a

294

lifetime of regret and self-loathing.' He got into the car and turned on the radio.

Adele's 'Someone Like You' was playing. He turned it up.

I turned it down. He turned it back up. I listened for a short while about how her love had moved on and found somebody else but eventually I had to change it to NewsTalk.

He looked at me and frowned. 'You don't like music?'

'I love music, I just don't listen to it any more.'

He twisted around in his seat to look at me. 'Since when?'

I pretended to think about it. 'About two years.'

'Two years, eleven months and twenty days, by any chance?'

'That's a bit specific, I don't know.'

'Yes, you do.'

'OK, fine.'

'You can't listen to music.'

'I didn't say I *can't*.'

He switched over to Adele again. I quickly switched it off.

'Ha!' he said and pointed a finger at me. 'You *can't* listen to music.'

'Fine! It makes me sad. Why are you so happy about that?'

'I'm not,' he snapped. 'I'm just happy I'm right.'

We looked away from each other, both in a huff now. I felt that today was one of those days that I did not love my life.

I lost him in the queues to get through security and into Mantic, and after searching around for him in every place I could think of I eventually gave up and went to the office by myself; but he'd got there before me and was sitting in the black leather chair being questioned by a rapidly speaking Mouse who was reading from a sheet of paper. Nosy had Graham's watch in her hand, set to stopwatch mode, Twitch was standing by with the largest beam on his face drinking from his *Best Dad in the World* mug. I joined him and watched my life.

'In what year did Lucy get so drunk she went to a tattoo parlour and got a heart tattoo?'

'2000,' Life responded instantly.

My eyes widened. *I* was his specialist subject.

'And where is said tattoo?'

'On her arse.'

'Be more specific.'

Life flapped at the air trying to think. 'I saw it this morning. Eh . . . eh . . . eh, her left buttock.'

'Correct.'

Graham looked at me with hungry eyes and everyone cheered.

'At the tender age of five, Lucy got her first stage role as what in *The Wizard of Oz*?'

'A Munchkin.'

'What did she do on the opening night?'

'Peed her pants and had to be taken off stage.'

'Correct!' Mary laughed.

'Ah Lucy, there you are,' Twitch said, finally

noticing me. 'I had a word with the cafeteria this morning about your three-bean salad.'

I had to take a moment to remember.

'I told them that a colleague of mine had purchased the salad and that as far as we could see there were only two bean types in the three-bean salad. She asked me if I'd seen my colleague eat the beans to which I took enormous offence and asked to see the manager. Anyway, to make a long story short because I was in there a very long time assuring them of your word . . .'

The others cheered at another correct response from Life but I was so touched that Twitch still believed in me despite the Spanish incident that I didn't want to tune into them.

'. . . while I was in there they checked the remaining containers and indeed you're right, the entire stock of three-bean salads consisted of only two beans. It was missing the cannellini beans which to be perfectly honest isn't a bean that I'm familiar with.' He was clearly in awe of this discovery. 'So I said to the manager, "How do you intend on compensating my colleague who did not receive what was promised, it's like a shepherd's pie without the lamb, a sherry trifle without the sherry. It's simply *unacceptable*."'

'Oh, Quentin.' I covered my mouth and tried not to laugh at his deathly serious face. 'Thank you.'

'No need to thank me . . .' He reached into his bottom drawer and retrieved a brown paper bag.

'Here it is, a complimentary two-bean salad and a voucher for lunch.'

'Quentin.' I threw my arms around him. 'Thank you.'

He was a little flustered.

'Thank you for defending my honour.'

Fish Face entered the office and eyed everyone up, took in Quentin and me standing away from the others.

'I always have your back, Lucy, don't you worry,' Twitch said, just as Edna walked by.

Edna eyed me warily and I knew instantly that she thought we were talking about how Quentin was protecting me over the Spanish inquisition.

'I'm sorry, could you please repeat the question,' Life said loudly for my benefit only.

'What language,' Mary asked timidly but with the greatest smile, 'does Lucy's CV say she can speak but in truth has no knowledge of?'

'Well, you all know this one,' Life said. 'On three. One, two . . .'

'Spanish!' they all shouted simultaneously, including Twitch, and they all looked at me and laughed.

I couldn't help but join in. I think I had just been forgiven.

CHAPTER TWENTY

'So you're Lucy's life.' Nosy was sitting on the edge of Life's new desk, which he'd assigned for himself further away from me. Louise had positioned herself there for the last few minutes and was heavily monitoring him.

'Yep,' he replied, tapping away on his laptop, not looking at her.

'And that's your job?' she asked.

'Yep.'

'Are you anyone else's life as well?'

'Nope.'

'So it's just one person at a time.'

'Yep.'

'When she dies, do you die?'

He stopped tapping and raised his head slowly. He glared at her, she didn't take the hint.

'Do you?' she asked again. 'And I don't mean, if you're both in the same car accident. I mean, if she dies and you're in a different place do you drop dead too?'

He began typing again.

She chewed her bubble gum, blew a small bubble that popped and stuck to her lips. She scraped it off with her false nails. 'Do you have family?'

'Nope.'

I stopped working and looked up at him.

'Do you live alone?'

'Yes.'

'Do you have a girlfriend?'

'No.'

'Are you allowed to have one?'

'Yes.'

'I mean, are you able to have one? Like, as in, does your, you know—'

'Yes,' he interrupted her. 'It works.'

'But you don't have one.'

He sighed. 'A girlfriend or a—'

'A girlfriend,' she interrupted, horrified.

'No.'

'So you live alone.'

'Yep.'

'And your life revolves around Lucy.'

'Yes.'

Suddenly I felt sad for him, guilty even. I was all he had and I wasn't giving him much. He looked up suddenly and I quickly looked away and back at my paperwork.

'Do you want to come to my wedding?'

'Nope.'

Louise finally dragged herself away from his desk, to annoy somebody else, but as soon as she was gone, I heard the keys of his laptop stop tapping. I looked at him from the corner of my eye. He was staring at his screen, chewing the inside of his mouth, lost. I mistimed it and he caught my eye.

'Did he call?'

'Who?'

'Who do you think? Mr Shake 'n' Vac.'

I rolled my eyes. 'No.'

'Did he text?'

'No.'

'Bastard,' he said, seeming insulted.

'I don't mind,' I said, amused by his reaction.

'Lucy.' He swung his chair around to face me. 'Believe me, if I care, then you care. Look.' He pointed at his chin.

'Eeww.'

'Is it big?'

He had a great big spot on his chin.

'Massive,' I said. 'It looks sore. You got that because he hasn't called?'

'No, I got this because you did something to make him not call.'

'Of course, it's my fault.'

Graham had stopped working and was watching the exchange with amusement. Then Edna's door opened and we all looked up. She stared at me, then at Twitch. 'Quentin, could I see you, please?'

'Of course.' He stood up, pulled his brown

trousers up past his belly as usual, pushed his glasses onto the bridge of his nose, smoothed down his tie and made his way to Edna. He didn't look at any of us, which made it worse. As soon as the door closed I jumped up and gasped.

'Oh my God, I can't believe it,' I said to the others.

'What?' Mary looked concerned.

'She's called him in.' I made big eyes at her and for some unknown reason pointed repeatedly at the door.

'Yes, so?' Louise asked.

'What? None of you think this is a big deal?' I asked, astonished. Usually it was me who wasn't concerned.

They shrugged and looked at each other.

'What about you?' I looked at my life.

He was examining his phone. 'Do you remember if I gave him my number? Maybe he'll call me. Or even a text. A text would be nice after last night.'

'Quentin is going to get fired and it's all my fault,' I exclaimed.

They all jumped up from their chairs wanting to know more, apart from Life who rolled his eyes at my dramatics and then turned his attention back to his phone for a call from Don.

'I can't tell you.' I paced up and down, wringing my hands. 'We don't have time for that. I have to think of a way to prevent him from getting fired.' I looked at them all, they stared back at me with dull tired faces. If they could think of a way of stopping him from being fired they would have either used it already to help the others we lost or they were saving it for themselves. I paced some more, going through everything in my head.

I looked at Life, looking through his phone, searching for a text. 'Maybe the signal is out,' he said to himself, raising his phone in the air and moving it around. 'I'm going to try out in the hall.' He opened the door and left the room.

'I know what I have to do,' I said firmly.

'What?' Nosy asked but I couldn't answer, I was already charging towards the office, my mind made up, the words forming in my mouth.

I pushed open the door and burst into the room. Edna and Quentin looked up.

'Fire me,' I said firmly, standing in the middle of her office, my legs apart ready to take on the world.

'Excuse me?' Edna asked.

'Fire me,' I repeated. 'I do not deserve to be in this job.' I looked at Quentin and hoped that he would understand this, 'I am a two-bean salad. I didn't deliver on what I promised, I don't deserve to be here, I only truly appreciated being here in the past two weeks. Before that, I took this job and everybody in this building for granted.' I studied Edna's face and she just looked shocked. I needed her to be angry, I needed her to fire me so that Quentin could stay. I gulped. 'I gave everybody nicknames, I'd rather not tell you what they are but if you want me to I will.' I closed my eyes

303

tight. 'Yours was something to do with a fish.' I opened them again, embarrassed. 'I wasted a lot of time. I smoke indoors. I am a fire hazard, I could have killed us all.'

I heard Mary gasp behind me and realised that I hadn't closed the door and they were all listening. I turned around. Life had come back into the office and was staring at me with an open mouth. I hoped that he was proud; I wasn't lying, I was sacrificing myself, I was doing the right thing to protect an innocent man.

'Up until last week, I didn't even like this job,' I continued, spurred on by the sight of Life. 'I wanted to be fired. But I realise now that was unfair because all of these good people were being fired all around me and it should have been me. I'm sorry, Edna, and I'm sorry to all the people who were fired and I'm sorry to Louise and Graham and Mary and Quentin. Please don't fire Quentin, he has done nothing wrong. He didn't know about my Spanish lie until that morning, he honestly didn't know. Please do not punish him for my mistakes. Fire me.' I finished and bowed my head.

There was a silence. It's fair to say it was a shocked silence.

Edna cleared her throat. 'Lucy, I wasn't firing Quentin.'

'What?' I quickly looked up and then at their table; there were papers strewn about, diagrams, instructions.

'We were discussing the new heating-drawer

manual. I was asking Quentin to translate the Spanish section.'

I made an O shape with my mouth.

Quentin was sweating. 'But Lucy, thank you very much for defending me.' He twitched more than ever.

'Eh . . . You're welcome.' I wasn't sure what to do so I started to back away. 'Shall I just . . .' I threw my thumb back towards the open door.

'I think,' Edna raised her voice, 'bearing in mind all that you said and all that has occurred in the past while that you should . . .'

She left it for me to answer. 'Leave?'

She nodded. 'Do you think that's wise?'

I thought about it. Felt so embarrassed it was beyond belief. I nodded and whispered, 'Yes. Em, perhaps it is. I'll go get my things.' I halted. 'Do you mean now?'

'I think that's a good idea,' she said gently, clearly embarrassed for me but probably happy that I'd solved her problem.

'Okay,' I whispered. 'Em . . . Bye, Quentin. It was lovely working with you.' I shuffled over and held out my hand. He took it, looking rather confused, looking from Edna to me. 'Eh, thank you, Edna. I enjoyed working with you,' I lied, having just revealed that I thought she was something close to a fish. 'Maybe I can call you another time for a reference or something.'

She looked unsure but shook my hand anyway. 'Good luck, Lucy.'

I turned then and finally faced everybody in the office. They were lined up on the walkway to the door. Life wasn't in the office.

'He's outside,' Mouse told me.

I shook everybody's hands. Once again, for the third time in a fortnight, they weren't sure whether to love me or loathe me. I packed away my things – I didn't have much, I had never personalised my desk – and I awkwardly backed out of the room, waving and thanking them and apologising all at the same time. Then I closed the door, and took a deep breath.

Life was looking at me. Fuming is not the word. 'What the hell was that about?'

'Not here.' I lowered my voice.

'Yes, here. What the hell did you do that for? You were keeping your job, I can't believe it but for some reason, you got away with it. And what did you do? Threw it all away. Marched in there and deliberately threw it all away. What is it with you? Why do you deliberately sabotage every good thing that happens in your life?' He was shouting now and I wasn't just embarrassed, I was also scared. 'Do you want to be miserable?'

'No.'

'I don't believe you.'

'Of course I don't.'

'Would you just ignore everybody else for one moment and concentrate on me?' he shouted. 'For once!'

I looked at him immediately. He had one

hundred per cent of my attention and everybody else's.

'I thought you'd be proud of me. I defended Twitch, even though it turned out I didn't actually *need* to, but I did. I put other people first instead of myself, and now we have enough time to go to see Blake so that I can tell him I love him. Everything works out just . . . em, perfectly.'

He lowered his voice but the anger bubbled beneath his words as he battled to keep them under control. 'The problem, Lucy, has never been your ability to put other people first, it has been your complete inability to put yourself first. But however much you try to dress this one up as a selfless act of kindness, it doesn't cut it. You did not go in there to defend Quentin, you went in there to give up *again* and I wouldn't put it past you to have concocted this entire thing just to get to Blake quicker than tomorrow.'

I can't say it hadn't passed through my mind.

'But I love him,' I said weakly.

'You love him. Will your newly discovered unrequited love pay the bills?'

'You sound like my father.'

'No, I sound *responsible*. Know what that means?'

'Yes,' I said firmly, standing up for myself. 'It means I live unhappily ever after. Whereas I am now taking back control of my life.'

'Taking it back? Who had it?'

I opened my mouth and then closed it again.

307

'Please don't put the guilt trip on me. I'll get another job.'

'Where?'

'I don't know where,' I said. 'I'll have to look around, I'm sure there's something really great for me. Something that I'm *passionate* about.'

He groaned at the use of that word. 'Lucy, you're not passionate about anything.'

'I am about Blake.'

'Blake won't pay the bills.'

'He might if we get married and I have babies and I give up work,' I said, joking of course. I think.

'Lucy, you had a good job and you threw it away. Congratulations. I am so fed up with you, when are you going to grow up?' He looked at me with such disappointment, then he walked away.

'Hey, where are you going?' I started to follow but he sped up. I ran after him and joined him in the elevator. There was somebody else in there so we didn't speak. He looked straight ahead while I stared at him and willed him to look at me. The elevator doors opened and he darted outside at top speed. Finally we were outside in the chilly air.

'Where are you going?' I called. 'We have to go to Wexford! Woo-hoo!' I whooped. 'To follow a *dream*. See? Life? I have dreams.' I ran along behind him like a small dog.

'No, Lucy, you have to go for dinner with your family.'

'You mean, *we* have to go for dinner with my family.'

He shook his head. 'I'm done.'

He rushed towards the bus stop. A bus swiftly came along and stopped and he got on and was lost from sight, leaving me standing alone in the car park.

When I got back to the apartment I tried to ignore the tousled bed while I packed my bag for Wexford. There was no point waiting till tomorrow to go and see Blake if I didn't have a job any more; I officially no longer had anything here to hold me back, apart from dinner at my parents this evening . . . and a cat. I knocked on Claire's door and waited, hearing the music to *In the Night Garden* in the background. Finally Claire answered. She looked exhausted.

'Hi, Lucy.'

'Are you okay?'

She nodded but her eyes filled.

'Is it your mother?'

'No.' A tear ran down her cheek and she didn't bother wiping it. I wasn't sure if she even noticed it was there. 'She's actually getting better, it's just Conor, he's, you know, not well.'

'Right.'

'And I haven't been getting much sleep. Anyway.' She wiped her face roughly. 'What can I do for you?'

'Oh, you know what, you have enough on your plate, it's okay.' I backed away.

'No, please, I need a distraction, what is it?'

'I have to go away for a few days and I was wondering if you would be able to take care of my cat? I don't expect him to stay in your place or anything, just check on him every now and then and maybe bring him to the park when you're going, and feed him?'

She was looking at me angrily.

'What? What have I said?'

'You don't have a cat,' she said, her eyes dark.

'Oh! I forgot you didn't know.' I lowered my voice. 'I've had him for years but if anyone finds out I'll be evicted and it just doesn't seem worth it,' I joked then turned serious. 'You don't mind that I have a cat, do you?'

'I've never seen him.'

'He's right behind me.'

'No, he's not. Lucy, whatever you're doing, it's not funny.'

'I'm not doing anything. What are you talking about?'

'Were you talking to Nigel?'

'Nigel? Who's Nigel? Should I have been?'

'My husband,' she said angrily.

'No! I've no idea what you're talking about. What . . .' But I didn't get a chance to finish my sentence because the door slammed in my face. 'What the . . .?' When I turned around to interrogate Mr Pan on what on earth he'd done to poor Claire, I finally understood. Mr Pan wasn't there, he'd run off down the corridor leaving her to think I was asking her to mind an invisible cat. Feeling cruel, even though that hadn't been my intention, I ran after him and found him, right at the feet of a grumpy neighbour who never spoke to me.

'Oh, my goodness,' I said in shock. 'Is that a stray cat? How on earth did he get in here? Or maybe it's a she? Who's to know? Let me just get rid of him for you.' I scooped Mr Pan up in my arms and hurried back to my apartment, mumbling, 'Dirty, yucky, horrible stray cat,' for anyone and everyone to hear.

CHAPTER TWENTY-ONE

I sat at the dining table in my parents' home and fought the urge to fidget with everything. I clasped my hands on the table and contained the anxiety that I felt within. I hadn't yet found the courage to tell them that once again I was lifeless, not because I had brushed it under the carpet as I used to do, but because Life disagreed with my decisions and had left me. I had stalked him with phone calls all afternoon in a pretend effort to apologise but really it was to see if we could cancel the family dinner. He hadn't answered the phone and then after six tries his phone was switched off. I didn't leave a message; I couldn't find the words because I wasn't near sorry enough to beg for his forgiveness and he would sense I wasn't genuine. It wasn't a good situation to be in; it was neither funny nor clever. It was one thing to ignore your life yourself, it was quite another for your own life to ignore – then abandon

– you. If Life had given up on me, what chance did I have?

The evening was too chilly to eat outside and so Edith had decided to set up the dining room, my parents' most formal room and used only for special occasions. Initially I had thought she was trying to get me back for stealing her cake and presenting it to Mum as my own home-baked gift, just like the bouquet of flowers last time, but on observing her that evening, I felt she was genuinely excited to meet the extra special guest and wanted him to receive the grandest of Silchester welcomes. Mum hadn't held back on preparations either as every room leading off the entrance hall had a Waterford Crystal vase filled with fresh flowers, the dining table was cloaked in white linen, the finest silverware was laid out, her hair was freshly blowdried, and she was wearing a pink and turquoise tweed Chanel shift dress and jacket with one of her dozens of pairs of flat pumps. Most people called their dining rooms *the dining room*, or in some households *the kitchen table*; we, however, called our dining room *the Oak Room*. Thanks to our great Literary Writer who came before us, the walls of the dining room were panelled floor to ceiling in oak, and crystal wall lights shone over the expensive eclectic collection of paintings – some abstract, some of men with tweed caps dipped low as they worked the bogs in Mayo.

'Can I help?' I asked Mum as she floated into the room for the third time, carrying a sterling silver tray to add to the table of condiments which totalled more than any human being would ever need in a lifetime let alone in one meal. There were tiny silver bowls of mint sauce, mustard – wholegrain and French – olive oil, mayonnaise and ketchup, all with tiny silver spoons displayed beside them.

'No, dear, you are our guest.' She surveyed the table. 'Balsamic?'

'Mum, it's fine, really, I think there's plenty on the table.'

'He might like some balsamic for that lovely two-bean salad you brought for Mum, Lucy,' Riley said, stirring it – the tension not the condiments.

'Yes.' Mum looked at Riley. 'You're right. I'll get it.'

'She likes salad,' I defended my gift to her.

'And that it came in a plastic container from your work canteen makes it all the more special,' he smiled.

I hadn't told them my life wasn't coming for dinner partly because I didn't know whether he would show or not but mostly because I rather stupidly thought it wouldn't make much difference whether or not he turned up. I thought that when the time came I could think of a polite excuse for why he couldn't make it, but I misjudged it. I hadn't anticipated such eagerness on their part to be acquainted with my life. There was a buzz in the air, an excitement and surprisingly, almost a nervousness. That was it. My mum was nervous.

She was rushing around trying to make sure everything was perfect in an effort to please my life. Edith was too, which astonished me. Technically it was me they were trying to please and I couldn't help but feel flattered, but mostly I knew I was in trouble. The news wasn't going to go down well and the later I left it the worse it was going to get.

The gate intercom buzzed and Mum looked at me like a deer caught in headlights. 'Is my hair okay?' I was so surprised by her behaviour – Silchesters didn't get flustered – that I couldn't answer so she rushed to the gilded mirror above the gigantic marble fireplace and stood on tiptoe to see the top of her head. She licked her finger and stuck a hair down in place. I looked around at the table settings for eight people, and suddenly I was nervous.

'It may be the carpet man,' Edith said, trying to calm Mum down.

'Carpet man? What carpet man?' I asked, my heartbeat beginning to quicken.

'Your life friend kindly gave me the number of a carpet company whom he said did wonders in your apartment, though I wish he could have come after the dinner,' she frowned as she examined the time again. 'I must say, it was so pleasant speaking to him on the phone, I'm really looking forward to meeting him in person. I know I'm going to love him' Mum scrunched up her face again and hunched her shoulders at me, lovingly.

'The carpet man?'

'No, your life,' she laughed.

'What happened to the carpet, Sheila?' my grandmother asked.

'Coffee on the Persian rug in the drawing room. Long story but I desperately need it cleaned by tomorrow because Florrie Flanagan is visiting.' She looked at me. 'Remember Florrie?' I shook my head. 'You do, her daughter Elizabeth just had a baby boy. They called him Oscar. Isn't that nice?'

I wondered why she never asked Riley whether the birth of any child was ever nice. We heard footsteps coming towards the door. I watched as Mum took a deep breath and smiled in preparation, and I tried to think quickly what to do if either Don or my life walked in the door. I didn't need to worry as Philip popped his head in the door. Mum exhaled.

'Oh, it's you.'

'Well, thank you for the warm welcome,' Philip said and as he stepped inside his seven-year-old daughter, Jemima, followed him. She was as serene as always, her face didn't change, no expression but a calm look around the room and her eyes slightly widened and lit when she saw Riley and me.

'Jemima,' Mum said, rushing towards her for a hug. 'What a lovely surprise.'

'Mum couldn't come today so Daddy told me I could visit,' she said in her soft voice.

Riley cupped his breasts and I tried not to laugh.

316

Philip's wife Majella had transformed herself over the past ten years so much that there wasn't a part of her skin that could move voluntarily. Philip was a plastic surgeon and though he claimed it was only ever reconstructive surgery, Riley and I did wonder if it had become cosmetic 'on the side' for his wife, something my father would be appalled at. I always felt that as a result of Majella's surgery, her daughter Jemima, following her lead, was completely without expression. When she was happy, she appeared serene; when she was angry, she was serene. She didn't frown, didn't smile too largely, her forehead rarely crumpled, just like her Botoxed mother. Jemima high-fived Riley on the way around the table to me. My grandmother tutted.

'Hello, Puddle Duck,' I said, giving her a big hug.

'Can I sit beside you?' she asked.

I glanced at my mother who looked confused and started to pick up place names and think aloud in that way that mothers do. Finally she said yes and Jemima sat beside me and Mum returned to adjusting the knives and forks, which were already perfectly laid out. She seemed distracted. Silchesters weren't distracted.

'Did the carpet company say who they would be sending out?'

'I spoke to a man named Roger. He said he didn't work late in the evenings but his son would come around.'

My heart lifted, then sank, then lifted, bobbing

up and down as though it were a buoy in the high seas. Oddly I felt excited to see him, but didn't want it to be here.

Mum continued to move perfectly placed knives and forks around the table. 'How are the wedding plans going, Mum?' Philip asked.

When Mum looked up she had a slightly pained expression but it vanished so quickly I had to question whether it had been there at all.

'Everything is going very well, thank you. I ordered both your and Riley's suits. They are sublime. And Lucy, I received your dress measurements from Edith, thank you. I chose a wonderful fabric and I really didn't want to order it without showing you first.'

I hadn't sent my dress measurements, that must have been Life, which annoyed me – and it made sense as to why I'd woken up with a measuring tape wrapped around my chest – but I was relieved I could give approval before it was ordered. 'Thank you.'

'But the dressmaker told me if I didn't order it by Monday it wouldn't be ready on time so I had to tell them to go ahead.' She looked a little worried. 'Is that okay? I did call and call but you were busy, probably with . . . what do we call him, dear?'

'You don't have to call him anything,' I said dismissively, then, gritting my teeth, 'I'm sure the dress will be lovely.'

Riley chuckled.

'It will stain,' my grandmother said, coming

alive. 'Mark my words, that fabric will stain.' She turned to me, 'Lucy, we can't be seated with a guest without knowing his name.'

'You can call him Cosmo.'

'What can I call him?' Riley asked.

Jemima laughed without moving her forehead. An astonishing feat of nature, as she hadn't a drop of rat poison under her skin.

'What kind of a name is that?' my grandmother asked, disgusted.

'It's a first name. Cosmo Brown is his full name.'

'Oh, that's the man from the film . . .' Mum started clicking her fingers as she tried to remember. My grandmother looked at her with further disgust. 'Donald O'Connor played him in . . .' She clicked, clicked, clicked. '*Singin' in the Rain*!' she finally said and laughed. Then, full of concern again, 'He doesn't have a nut allergy, does he?'

'Donald O'Connor?' I asked. 'I don't know, I think he passed away some years ago.'

'From nuts?' Riley asked.

'I think it was congestive heart failure,' Philip said.

'No, I mean your friend, Cosmo,' Mum said.

'Oh no, he's alive.'

Riley and Philip laughed.

'I wouldn't worry about him,' I said. 'Isn't it just nice that we're all gathered here together, regardless of whether he's here or not.'

Riley caught the tone and leaned forward to catch my eye. I wouldn't do it.

On that note Edith rushed into the dining room, her cheeks flushed. 'Lucy,' she said gently. 'I wonder when your friend will arrive. It's just that the lamb is now ready as Mr Silchester likes it and he has an important phone call at eight p.m.' I looked at the clock. Life was ten minutes late and father had only allocated thirty minutes for dinner in his schedule.

'Tell Mr Silchester that he can delay his phone call,' Mum said sharply which surprised us all, 'and he can eat his meat a little more well done than usual.'

We were all silent, including my grandmother, which was unheard of.

'Some things are more important,' Mum said, straightening her back and the silverware again.

'Maybe Father can join us now and my friend can catch up with us later. There's no point in waiting if he's going to be much later,' I said to Edith, giving her my emergency-eyes look, which I hoped she would interpret as *He's not coming, heeeelp!*

On that note the intercom at the gate buzzed.

'That's him,' Mum said with excitement.

I looked out the window and saw Don's bright yellow van with the slowly turning flaming red magic carpet that looked like it was on a spit at the gate. I jumped up and pulled the curtains to the three grand windows closed dramatically. 'I'll greet him. You all stay here.'

Riley studied me.

320

'I want it to be a complete surprise,' I said, then I ran from the room and closed the door. I was pacing in the entrance hall when Edith came out of the kitchen to join me.

'What are you up to?'

'Nothing,' I said, biting my nails.

'Lucy Silchester, I have known you all of your life and I know you're up to no good. I have one minute to fetch your father so I need to know if I should be prepared.'

'Fine,' I hissed. 'My life and I had a fight and he's not coming today.'

'Merciful hour.' Edith held her hands to her head. 'Why don't you just tell them?'

'Why do you think?' I hissed.

'So who's this here?' We heard the car stop in the drive, the engine cut out.

'The carpet man,' I hissed.

'And why is that bad?'

'Because I slept with him last night.'

Edith groaned.

'But I'm in love with someone else.'

She moaned.

'I think.'

She whined.

'Oh, God, what am I going to do? Think, think, think, Lucy.'

Then I instantly had a plan. She must have seen it in my face.

'Lucy,' she said in a warning tone.

'Don't worry.' I grabbed her hands and held on

to them tight. I looked her dead in the eyes. 'You don't know anything, nobody told you anything, you are not responsible, it has nothing to do with you, it is all my decision.'

'How many times in my life have I heard those words?'

'And isn't it always okay?'

Edith's eyes widened. 'Lucy Silchester, of all the things you have ever done, this is the worst.'

'They'll never know. I promise,' I said in an attempt to calm her.

She whimpered and shuffled off to get my father.

I stepped outside and pulled the front door closed behind me. Don was getting out of his car and he looked up at me in surprise.

'Hi, welcome to my country retreat,' I said.

He smiled, but not as widely as he used to. He came up the steps towards me, and suddenly I had an overwhelming desire to kiss him again. I didn't know what to say but from inside the house I could hear my father's study door open and his footsteps across the hallway.

'Lucy is outside greeting him now, sir,' I could hear Edith saying breathlessly as she tried to catch up with him.

'Fine. Let's just get this nonsense over and done with, shall we,' he said.

We both heard him.

'I'm sorry about this morning,' I said, genuinely meaning every word of it.

Don studied me, to see if I genuinely meant every word of it.

'I told you I was messed up. Not that that makes it any better, but I am. I don't know what I want. I thought I did. But Life has shown me that I don't. I don't have a clue what I'm doing and I need to figure it out. I'm trying to figure it out.'

He nodded, studied me some more. 'Are you still in love with your ex?'

'I think so. But I don't *know.*'

He was quiet for a moment. 'Your life told me he might have a new girlfriend.'

'My life has one?'

'No, Blake. He told me when you were in the shower.'

'That's a very strong possibility.'

He looked around the estate, then back at me. 'I don't love you, Lucy.' He paused. 'But I do know that I like you. A lot.'

I put my hand on my heart. 'That's the nicest thing anyone's ever said to me.'

'I don't want to be used in some experiment in your life.'

'You're not being used.'

'And I don't want to be second best.'

'You'd never be. I just feel like I need to tie up a few loose ends in my life, that's all.'

He seemed satisfied with that. There was nothing more I could think of to say.

He looked around at the house. 'Are you nervous about this?'

'Completely. I haven't been in a relationship for three years, I'm making every single mistake I could possibly make.'

He smiled. 'No, I mean, about your life meeting them?'

'Oh. No. I don't feel nervous at all. Just physically ill.'

'It'll be fine, he'll do all the talking.'

'He's not here and I don't think he's coming. I lost my job today and Life isn't talking to me.' I swallowed then, realising how deep I was in it.

His eyes widened. 'Anything I can do to help?'

Everybody was sitting around the table when I poked my head inside the room. Father wasn't at the head of the table, which surprised me, instead it had been left free for my life.

'Everybody, I'm very sorry for delaying you; Father, I know you have an important phone call not long from now, we won't keep you from that but I'd like to introduce you to . . .' I opened the door wider and pulled Don inside.

'This is my family. My family,' I looked at Don, 'this is my life.'

He smiled and his dimples took over his face. Then he laughed and I thought there was no way on earth he was going to be able to do this.

'I'm sorry.' He stopped laughing. 'I'm just so honoured to meet you all.'

He held his hand out to Jemima. 'Hello there.'

'Jemima,' she said shyly, taking his hand.

'Nice to meet you, Jemima.'

Don moved on and my mum hopped up out of her seat. My grandmother didn't budge, just held her hand out limply.

'Victoria,' she said.

'Lucy's life,' he said.

'Yes.' She looked him up and down and pulled her hand away.

'I'm Riley.' Riley stood up and gave him a firm handshake. 'I have a jacket just like that.'

'That's a co-inky-dinky,' I said, ushering Don on to my mum.

'Yes, I left it just out . . .' Riley looked out to the closed door in the direction of the hallway. While Don and my mum shook hands, Riley pulled the curtains open. He looked out the window, saw Don's van and gave me a warning look. I gave one right back and he just looked from Don to me and shook his head and took his seat. Everybody was so busy watching Don, and greeting Don, that they missed our exchange.

'This is Lucy's father, Mr Silchester,' Mum said to Don.

Don looked at me while he made his way to my father. I pursed my lips and tried not to laugh, nervously, while he did the same. Then he took his seat at the head of the table.

'You have a lovely home,' he said, looking around. 'Is this oak?'

'Yes,' my mum said, excitedly, 'We call it the Oak Room.'

'We're a creative bunch,' I said and Don laughed.

'So tell us, how are you and Lucy getting along?' Mum asked, hands clasped together.

'Lucy and I,' Don looked at me, and my heart quickened, 'are getting along just famously, thank you. She's incredibly energetic,' he said and Riley slid down in his chair slightly. 'So it takes a lot to keep up with her but I'm just crazy about her,' he said without taking his eyes off me.

I couldn't stop looking at him.

'Isn't that lovely,' Mum whispered, not wanting to break the spell. 'To be in love with life, I can see it on her face. Isn't that something?'

I snapped out of it then when I realised Mum was staring at me.

'Yes, well . . .' I cleared my throat while I felt all eyes on me and my cheeks blazed. 'Why don't we tell him a little something about us?'

'Well, Mr Silchester and I are renewing our vows,' Mum said, all excited, 'Isn't that right, Samuel?'

My father said a long, lazy and unenthusiastic yes. Don quite understandably assumed it to be a joke and laughed, but as it wasn't his laugh was misguided and misplaced.

Mum said, a little embarrassed, 'It's our thirty-fifth anniversary this year and we thought it would be a nice way to celebrate.'

'Congratulations,' Don said politely.

'Thank you. I've asked Lucy to be my brides-maid. I do hope you will come.'

Don looked at me with amusement. 'I'm sure Lucy is very excited about that.'

'Pardon my ignorance on this matter, but how long do you plan on staying around for?' Mum asked.

'I'd like to stay around for quite a while,' Don said and I felt his eyes on me again. 'But that's up to Lucy.'

I quickly looked at Riley, who winked at me, and despite my plans to get back with Blake, I couldn't help but smile.

Edith entered with a trolley of bowls and a giant tureen of soup. She handed out the bowls and began ladling. 'Courgette and pea,' she said to Don, then fired me a warning look to let me know she wanted no part of this.

'Mmm,' I said, exaggerating. 'My favourite. Thanks, Edith.'

She ignored me, serving up the soup and leaving me until last.

The intercom buzzed again.

'That will be the carpet cleaner,' Mum said and looked to Edith. 'Edith?'

'I'll show him in to the drawing room,' Edith said, giving me an alarmed look.

I was slightly concerned. If Life had indeed decided to show up, he would not be happy being led into a room with a dirty carpet to clean or with the fact that I'd told a majestic lie. I'd really done it now. But it couldn't be him, he had deserted me, had left me alone to deal with my family; he would be a lazy foolish Life to back out of that enormous lesson. Unless he sensed a lie, of course, which would mean it was the perfect time for him to arrive, so that I would learn an even greater lesson.

'Have you been to Lucy's workplace?' Philip asked and my heart sank.

'Yes,' I interrupted, 'and actually, funny you should mention that, but I have some news.' I tried to make it sound positive; gift-wrapping bad news. I needed to say it all in case Life stormed in trying to get me back for this gigantic lie.

'You got a promotion,' Mum anticipated excitedly, her voice almost a screech.

'Actually, no.' I looked at Don nervously for moral support, then back to my mother. 'As of today, I no longer work at Mantic.'

She made an *oh* shape with her mouth.

'Where do you work instead?' Riley asked, waiting for the good news.

'Eh . . . Nowhere yet.'

'I'm sorry to hear that but they've been haemorrhaging money for years, more job cuts were always on the cards.'

I was grateful to Philip for saying this.

'Did they offer you a redundancy package?' Riley asked, concerned.

'Actually, no, because I left. It was my decision.'

My father slammed his fist down on the table. Everyone jumped, the cutlery and condiment bowls all rattled on the white linen.

'It's okay sweetheart,' Philip said to Jemima,

who was wide-eyed and looking at her father in terror – at least I guessed it was terror because her face wasn't moving much apart from her eyes. I put my arm around her protectively.

'Is this your doing?' Father demanded of Don.

'Maybe we shouldn't talk about this now,' I said gently to my father, hoping he'd pick up on my tone.

'I think this is the perfect time to talk about it,' he boomed.

'Jemima, come with me,' Philip said and he brought her out of the room, to my grandmother's tutting. When the door opened I saw Edith letting Life into the house. Life looked in and saw me, just as the door was closing.

'Well, answer me,' Father said patronisingly to Don.

'We're not in the courthouse now,' I said, under my breath.

'Don't you dare speak to me like that in my house.'

I ignored him, I kept eating my soup but everybody was silent and nobody moved an inch. Father rarely lost his temper, he was rarely tipped over the edge but when he was, it was mighty. He had been tipped over the edge now, and I could hear it in his voice; the anger was building too and though I tried to keep calm, I couldn't help but feel my nerves grow.

'He had nothing to do with it,' I said quietly.

'And why not? Shouldn't he be responsible for your decisions?'

'No, because he's not actually my—'

'No, that's okay Lucy,' Don interrupted. I don't know if it was because he was afraid or if it was because he wasn't but when I looked at him I saw no fear at all, just annoyance and the desire to protect.

'What exactly is your role here?' my father asked.

'My role,' Don looked at me, 'is to make her happy.'

'Nonsense.'

'And when she's happy she'll find the right path,' Don said. 'I wouldn't worry about Lucy.'

'I've never heard such absolute nonsense. This is drivel. If, in fact, you are to help her on her right path, aren't you failing?'

'And how well do you assess your abilities in your role as her father?' he said, anger in his voice. He was protecting me but he didn't know what he was up against. He'd barely met me but I felt he knew me better than anyone at this table. My eyes widened. I can't believe he said that. I couldn't look at anybody, I didn't know what anybody was thinking.

'How dare you speak to me like that,' Father shouted and stood up. He was a tall man, and he seemed to be a giant beside us all at the table now that he was standing.

'Samuel,' Mum said quietly.

'Lucy left her job because she wasn't happy,' Don continued. 'I don't see any harm in that.'

'Lucy is never happy with work. Lucy is lazy. Lucy will never find anything to which she will feel the need to apply herself. She has never applied herself. She has walked away from everything which, and everyone who, has ever been of any use in her life. She wasted the good education we provided for her, she is living like a pig in a home the size of this room, she is a disappointment and a disgrace to the family name – as, clearly, seeing as you are her life, are you.'

Silchesters don't cry. Silchesters don't cry. Silchesters don't cry. It was a mantra I had to repeat in my mind after each nasty word was spoken but I knew my paranoia was right, it was everything that I thought he felt about me and now he was saying it. To me and to the person he thought was my life but was actually a man that I had feelings for. It was beyond humiliating, it was beyond hurtful, it was the worst thing I think I had ever heard or endured. Worse than Blake leaving me, worse than losing every job I'd ever worked at.

'I am tired of her behaviour, her constant failure to apply herself. We come from a long line of successes. Here in this very room Philip and Riley have shown themselves to be competent men and hard workers, whereas Lucy here has failed, time and time again, to reach the heights that we have given everything within our abilities for her to reach. Sheila, I have stood back and let the course which you have so believed to be right be carried out, but it is clear to see that when left to her own devices Lucy cannot find direction, so it is left to me to find it for her.'

'Lucy isn't a child,' Don said. 'She's a grown

woman. I think she's well able to make her own decisions.'

'And you, sir,' my father raised his voice even more, so that I was sure it must be echoing through the valley, 'are no longer welcome in my home.'

Silence. I could barely breathe.

His chair scraped across the wood as he pushed it back from the table. 'It was lovely to meet you,' he said gently. 'Thank you for your hospitality. Lucy?'

He was asking me to leave with him and I wanted nothing more than to get out of the room but I couldn't look up. I just couldn't face anything or anyone. If I stayed still, maybe they'd forget I was there. I felt hot tears about to fall and I couldn't do it, not in front of him, not in front of anybody, not ever, ever, ever.

'I'll show you out,' my mother said, her voice a whisper. Her chair didn't scrape on the wood, she lifted it just the appropriate amount in order to prevent that and she quietly left the room. When the door opened I saw Life in the hallway, ashen faced. I had let him down too.

'Lucy, in my office now, we need to make a plan for you.'

I couldn't look at anybody.

'Your father is talking to you,' my grandmother said.

'Father, I think you should allow Lucy to finish her dinner and you can discuss it after,' Riley said firmly.

Allow Lucy. Allow *me*.

'Edith can warm it, this is of importance.'

'Actually, I'm not hungry,' I said quietly, still looking down at my plate.

'You're not a disappointment, Lucy,' Riley said gently. 'Father is worried about you, that's all.'

'I meant what I said,' Father said, but he was sitting down now and his voice was no longer booming.

'None of us think you are a disgrace. Lucy, look at me,' Riley said again.

I couldn't. Mum returned to the room but she didn't sit down; she stayed at the door testing the environment, sticking her toe in to feel the temperature before diving in again.

'I'm sorry,' I said, my voice trembling, 'if I have been such a disappointment to you. Edith, thank you for dinner, sorry I can't stay.' I stood up.

'Sit down,' my father hissed. It was sharp, like a whip. 'Sit down at once.'

I paused, then continued to make my way to the door. I couldn't look at Mum as I passed her by and gently closed the door behind me.

Life and Don stood beside one another in the hallway staring at me.

'Sorry I'm late,' Life said. 'The taxi got lost. Did I miss anything?'

'Should I tell him where the Persian rug is?' Don asked.

They both had wicked glints in their eyes but gentleness in their tone. They were trying to cheer me up. They at least made me smile.

CHAPTER TWENTY-TWO

'Don, I'm so sorry,' I said straight away, ignoring my life for now. 'It was a stupid stupid idea of mine.' I was still shaken up. 'I have no idea why I thought that would work.'

'Relax,' he said and I felt his hand on my back, rubbing me comfortingly. 'Right after this you're coming to my parents' for dinner to pretend to be the long-term currently pregnant girlfriend that I've been pretending to have.' I looked at him with fear. 'Just joking,' he smiled. 'Though that would make their lives.'

The door to the Oak Room opened and all our heads turned. Mum appeared, her hand still on her chest as if that motion alone would bring her breath back, as if it was keeping all her emotions in check, caging her heart in so that it wouldn't move, wouldn't feel, would only pump to keep her alive and expressionless, and emotionless, and appropriate. 'Lucy, sweetheart,' she said, then took in the two men standing before her and after all her practising she said to Life, 'Oh, hello. You must be the cleaner.' The irony.

'Actually, *I'm* the cleaner,' Don said, remembering then to take off Riley's jacket which was covering the magic carpet emblem on his T-shirt. 'He's Lucy's life.'

'Oh,' she said taking him in, hand still on her chest. She didn't seem embarrassed for mistaking Life for the carpet cleaner but she must have been.

'Mum, this is Don,' I said. 'Don is a friend. He's a kind friend who decided to step in at the last minute because our guest couldn't make it and I didn't want to let you all down. I'm sorry, Mum, I didn't want to tell you that he couldn't make it today, I could sense that you were excited.'

'I'm sorry about that in there,' Don said, humble and contrite.

'It was my idea, I'm sorry,' I apologised, still feeling shaky, feeling a little bit faint, wanting to just get out of there but not knowing how.

'We should get you some tea,' Edith said, suddenly at my side, which meant she'd been standing listening.

'Yes, that's a good idea.' Mum finally spoke and I wasn't sure if she needed it more for her or for me. 'I'm Sheila, Lucy's mum,' she said, holding her hand out to my life. 'It's a pleasure to meet you. And Don,' she smiled warmly, 'it's been lovely to have you in our home. I'm sorry the welcome was not warmer as it should have been, but you are

335

still cordially invited to the wedding renewal ceremony.'

It was unbearable having to listen to the polite chit-chat that was now taking place. Edith was shaking hands with Life and Don and offering them tea and discussing biscuit types and from the way that Mum was talking I knew that she was trying to figure out if it was appropriate for Don actually to clean her carpet or if she should let him go. Then Life and Mum were talking about flowers for the ceremony and Don was looking at me. I knew this not because I was looking at him but because I could sense it from the corner of my eye. And all the while these conversations were going on I could hear my father's words, loud and succinct in my head.

Life came closer to me. 'You told a really big lie.'

'I'm not in the mood,' I said quietly. 'And anything you can say can't make this moment any worse.'

'I'm not trying to make it worse. I'm trying to make it better.' Life cleared his throat and sensing something important Mum ended her conversation with Don and Edith.

'Lucy feels that she's never good enough for any of you.'

There was an uncomfortable silence and I felt my face flush but I knew I deserved it. A big lie deserved a big truth. 'I have to go.'

'Oh, Lucy.' Mum looked at me, devastated, but then something snapped in her; the Silchester switch was flicked and she gave me a bright smile. 'I'll see you to the door.'

'You didn't deserve that,' Life said from the passenger seat as we drove through the Wicklow mountains and back towards the motorway.

It was the first thing he'd said in the fifteen minutes we'd been in the car, in fact it was the first thing either of us had said since we'd got in the car. He hadn't even tried to turn on the radio, which I appreciated because there was already enough noise in my head. It was mostly the sound of my father's voice, his words being repeated over and over again and I was very sure there was no way that he and I could ever come back from that. He had said all that he said without difficulty, without emotion; sure, there was anger but it wasn't driven by anything like hurt that would lead him to say things he didn't mean. He meant every word of it and I bet he would back it up until the day he died. There was no going back. I hadn't wanted Life to travel with me but he had insisted and I had wanted to get of there so urgently, I didn't care if a Bengal tiger was in the back seat.

'I got what I deserved, I told a lie.'

'You deserved that alright, I mean, you didn't deserve what your father said.'

I didn't respond.

'Where are you going?'

'I'm not in the mood for deep psychological conversation, please.'

'How about geographical then? You missed the turn for the motorway.'

'Oh.'

'I assume we're going to Wexford now?'

'No, we're going home.'

'What happened to finding the love of your life?'

'Reality happened.'

'Meaning . . .'

'He's moved on and I need to too.'

'So are you going to call Don?'

'No.'

'Oh, so now you're not good enough for anybody.'

I didn't answer but I was shouting *yes* in my head.

'What your dad said isn't true, you know.'

I didn't say anything.

'Okay so I may have lost my temper with you earlier and I also may have said some unfair things.'

I looked at him.

'Okay, I *definitely* did say some unfair things but I meant them.'

'What kind of an apology is this?'

'It's not one. I'm just saying you shouldn't have left your job before you had secured another one but that's all, anything else your father had to say was untrue.'

'I can't pay my rent. I don't even know if I have enough money to get us to Wexford in this heap of crap even if I did want to go. I haven't got enough money to pay Don, which I most certainly am going to do. I should have stayed in the job for financial stability. I should have been looking for other work while in that job. That's what I should have done. That would have been the responsible thing to do.'

He was silent which meant he agreed. I hadn't been paying attention to the road, I took a wrong turn and found myself on a road I didn't recognise. I did a U-turn and took the next right. Again it was unfamiliar territory. I turned in someone's driveway, went back to the road. Looked left and right. I rested my head on the steering wheel.

'I'm lost.'

I felt Life's hand on my head. 'Don't worry, Lucy, you'll find the right path, I'm here to help you.'

'Well, have you got a map? Because I mean, geographically, I'm lost.'

He quickly removed his hand from my head and looked left and right. 'Oh.' Then he glanced at me. 'You look tired.'

'I am. I didn't get much sleep last night.'

'Too much information. Let me drive.'

'No.'

'Let me drive. You can lie down in the back seat and I'll drive us home.'

'I can't stretch my arm in the back seat, never mind lie down.'

'You know what I mean, have a rest. Switch off your mind for a while.'

'Can you drive?'

He reached into his inside pocket and retrieved

more paperwork. He offered it to me. I didn't take it; I was too tired to read.

'It allows me to drive any vehicle as long as it's in keeping with the assistance and development of your life.'

'Any vehicle?'

'Any.'

'Even motorbikes?'

'Even motorbikes.'

'Tractors?'

'Even tractors.'

'Quad bikes?'

'Even quad bikes.'

'What about boats, can you drive boats?'

He looked at me with exhaustion so I gave up. 'Fine. He's all yours.' I got out of the car and tried to settle down in the back.

And so Life was in the driving seat.

I woke up with a crick in my neck, a headache from where my head had been pressed up and repeatedly thudded against the cold hard glass with every vibration and bump in the road, and my neck was stinging from where the seat belt had continuously rubbed against my bare skin. It took me a moment to realise where I was. In the car, with Life in the driving seat, and he was singing to Justin Bieber in a high-pitched voice that would rival any six-year-old boy who had just been punched in the balls.

It was dark outside which wasn't particularly

unusual as we had left Glendalough at eight p.m., and though it would take a normal car without psychological issues less than an hour to get to my apartment, it took the complex Sebastian longer. On a June summer's night it wouldn't become dark until ten so I was expecting a certain amount of darkness but not this. This was pitch black, which meant we had been travelling for a lot more than an hour, and I couldn't see any lights apart from the occasional small oval in a porch or a square of light from a window in the distance, which meant we were not in Dublin city. Then we stopped moving but the engine kept running. We had arrived somewhere only we weren't anywhere. I looked at Life, he had his iPhone out on the dashboard and was looking at his sat nav. Alarm bells rang. Seeming satisfied he indicated to nobody, because there wasn't anybody; the car crept forward again and we maintained a steady speed once more. I leaned forward then and spoke in Life's ear.

'Where are we?'

'Jesus!' he shouted, startled, and he momentarily lost control of the wheel as he turned around to see who was shouting at him. The car went veering to the left, he quickly grabbed the wheel and swung it to the right, stopping us from dropping into a ditch just in time, only he pulled it too far to the right and sent us flying over to the opposite side of the road. Despite my seat belt I went flying to the left like a rag doll, and then was pushed forward into the seat ahead of me as we nosedived into a ditch.

Then we were still and it was silent, apart from Justin Bieber who was singing about his baby, baby, baby.

'Uh-oh,' Life said.

'Uh-oh,' I repeated, pulling the seat belt away from my body so it was no longer threatening to amputate me. 'Uh-oh? We are stuck in the middle of a ditch, in the middle of nowhere, what the hell do you think you're doing?'

'You gave me a fright,' he said, his pride wounded. 'And anyway, we're not in the middle of nowhere, we're in the middle of Wexford.' He turned to me. 'Surprise. I'm helping you follow your dream.'

'We are stuck in a ditch.'

'Ironic, isn't it?' He fumbled with his phone.

I battled with the seat belt to try and free myself from this downward position but it was stuck. 'Can you reverse us out of this?' I asked, full of frustration. The belt finally clicked, and unprepared, I went face first into the headrest in front of me, squishing my nose. I looked out the window. The only thing giving away our position was a house in the distance; I could see a few windows diagonally lit from my position.

'You can't reverse out of a ditch. At least not in this car. I think the problem was that I came off the motorway too early. Now let me see . . .' he mumbled to himself while he fumbled with the sat nav again.

I pushed open the door. It opened a tiny slit but

something behind the door on the other side prevented it from opening fully. It was so dark I couldn't see out the window so I wound it down and stuck my head out. It was a tree that had come down and now lay there, a pile of complicated branches and dead leaves blocking my path. I reached up to the roof and pulled myself out of the car and onto the window ledge and then I tried to figure out how to get the rest of my body out. I tried to twist and take one bent leg out the window but it was complicated. I removed one hand from the roof to assist in squeezing my bent leg out of the open window. It wasn't a good idea, because I lost my grip and I went flying backwards, out of the car and straight onto the tree, which hurt, a lot more than any pain I'd felt recently. Silchesters didn't cry, but Silchesters did curse and scream to the high heavens. I heard a car door bang shut and Life was above me, looking down at me from the top of the ditch. He reached out his hand.

'Are you okay?'

'No,' I grumbled. 'How did you get out of the car?'

'I just went out the other door.'

Oh. I hadn't thought of that. I reached out and Life pulled me out of the ditch.

'Did you break anything?' he asked, spinning me around and checking my back. 'Apart from the tree, that is?'

I jiggled around a little, shimmied a bit, tested out all my joints. 'I don't think so.'

'If you can do that, trust me, you're okay. Physically, anyway.' He surveyed the car with his hands on his hips. 'We're not far from the B&B that I booked, we could walk it.'

'Walk? In these shoes? And we can't leave the car here in the ditch.'

'I'll call the AA on our way to the house.'

'We're not asking for help, we can do this ourselves. You and me. Come on.' I whipped him into action and soon I was behind the wheel of the car while he tried to push us. Then when that didn't work, he was behind the wheel of the car and I was pushing. And when that didn't work we were both pushing. And when that didn't work we took our bags from the boot and trudged down the country road following Life's iPhone sat nav. When I say *road* I use the term loosely – it was more of a track or a trail, a surface for farmyard animals and tractors to travel, not for a wedge-heeled wrap-around-dress-wearing woman with an aching back and twigs in her hair. We were walking for forty-five minutes before we found the B&B, which we realised was overlooked by a brand-new Radisson Hotel on the motorway. Life looked at me apologetically. The B&B was a bungalow with old-style carpets and wallpaper and smelled of air freshener; it was old-fashioned but it was clean. Because I hadn't had any microwave dinners for lunch and I had sipped only a few spoons of courgette and pea soup which my palette had been too stunned to taste as my father shouted insults

344

at me, I was ravenous. The lady of the house rustled up some ham sandwiches and a pot of tea which hit the spot, and a plate of biscuits I hadn't seen the likes of since I was ten years old. I sat on the bed with rollers in my hair painting my toenails. The words my father had spoken rattled around in my head, which felt hollow and empty – a perfect barren place for such words to echo around for all eternity.

'Stop thinking about your father,' Life said.

'Do you read minds?' I asked.

'No.'

'Because sometimes you say exactly what I'm thinking.' I looked at him. 'How do you do that?'

'I suppose I pick up on what you're feeling. But it would be obvious for you to be thinking about your dad. He said some harsh things.'

'Father,' I corrected him.

'Do you want to talk about it?'

'No.'

'So your parents are rich,' Life said, talking about it anyway.

'Wealthy,' I said automatically, not even thinking, it was an immediate response.

'Pardon?'

'They're not rich, they're wealthy.'

'Who told you to say that?'

'Mum. I went to a summer camp when I was eight and the other kids kept saying I was rich because they'd seen me roll up in a BMW or whatever we had at the time. I'd never even thought about it before, money was never an issue, never a thought.'

'Because you had it.'

'Maybe. But I ended up using the word myself at our annual winter solstice breakfast with the Maguires. I said that we were rich and my parents looked at me in such a way I knew never to use the word again. It's as if I swore or something. It's a dirty word, to be rich.'

'What other rules did they put in your head?'

'Lots.'

'Like . . .'

'No elbows on the table, no shrugging or nodding . . . no drinking poitín with nine men in a barn.' He looked at me. 'Long story. No crying. No emotion whatsoever, no expression of oneself. You know, the usual.'

'Do you follow them all?'

'No.'

'Do you break them all?'

I thought about the crying rule, which was never technically a rule, just a learned habit. I just never saw them cry, not even when their parents died; they were as stoic and as still, and appropriate as always.

'Only the important ones,' I said. 'I will never give up my God-given right to drink with nine men in a barn.'

Life's phone beeped.

He read it, smiled and texted back immediately.

'I'm nervous about tomorrow,' I revealed.

His phone chirped again and he went straight to it, ignoring my big revelation. He smiled again, texted back immediately.

'Who's that?' I asked, feeling oddly jealous that I didn't have his full attention for once.

'Don,' he said, concentrating on texting.

'Don? My Don?'

'If you want to be psychotically possessive about another human being, then yes. *Your* Don.'

'That's not psychotic, *I* met him first,' I huffed. 'Anyway, what is he saying?' I tried to look at his phone, but he moved it away from me.

'None of your business.'

'Why are you texting him?'

'Because we get along and I've a lot of time for him. We're going for a drink tomorrow night.'

'Tomorrow night? You can't, we'll still be away and anyway, what are you thinking? Isn't that a conflict of interest?'

'If you're referring to Blake, I have no interest in him, so no, there's no conflict.'

I studied him. His body language had changed; he'd stiffened his spine and turned himself away from me.

'You really don't like him, do you?'

He shrugged.

'What happens if me and him, you know, get back together?' The very thought made my stomach churn and sent butterflies flying everywhere. I thought of his perfect lips kissing me all over. 'How would you feel about it?'

He screwed his mouth up and thought about it. 'If you were happy, it wouldn't bother me, I suppose.'

'You would have to be happy then, wouldn't you? Because when I'm happy, you're happy? But if I was with him and you weren't happy, well then, that would mean I don't really love him, wouldn't it?'

'It wouldn't mean *you* don't love him. It would mean that in some way, it's not right and not meant to be.'

'I'm nervous. First I was nervous about seeing him again. I mean, it's been so long and apart from the TV shows I haven't been anywhere near him. I've never passed him in the street, never bumped into him in a bar. I've never heard his voice or, oh my God, what if he doesn't want me here? What if he takes one look at me and is happy he walked away? What if he really loves this girl and wants to spend the rest of his life with her?' I looked at Life, appalled and terrified by all the new thoughts. 'What if after all this time, I'm still not good enough?' My eyes filled up and I quickly blinked them away again.

'Lucy,' Life said gently, 'if it doesn't work out it's not because you're not good enough.'

I had a hard time believing that.

CHAPTER TWENTY-THREE

I didn't sleep very much that night. Life wasn't snoring but it kept me awake all the same, haunting me with questions and fears and wholly unhelpful thoughts. By the time I woke up I had come to the conclusion that if all did not go well today, then all of my father's accusations would indeed be validated. Getting back together with Blake somehow became my sole aim to fixing everything. It was losing him that had caused me to go off track in my life, so if I could get him back I would find my way again. Despite the fact that Blake didn't have a formal job, my father had always liked him, and as alien as the thought seemed now, he actually attended some of the dinner parties in our converted bread-factory loft. Father liked Blake's can-do attitude, his drive, his ambition; he knew that Blake would always have an interest in something and would do everything to succeed. He liked that he had goals, that he climbed mountains, ran marathons, that he achieved personal physical feats. And even though he didn't like that I wasn't a doctor or a lawyer or a nuclear physicist, he at least used to like my attitude too. But then I'd changed and the things he'd loved about me were gone and then so was his love.

Despite being awake most of the night I was last to get up and showered, and I wandered down the hall, following the voices. At the back of the house, in a bright and airy conservatory which served as the breakfast room, Life sat at a table shared by four others, with a plate before him piled high with food.

'Morning,' he said, looking up at me before shovelling baked beans into his mouth.

'Whoa,' I said, and stopped dead in my tracks at the sight of him.

He looked to the others self-consciously before he continued eating the rest of his fry-up. There was two of everything on the plate.

I pulled a chair out beside him and sat down, saying good morning to everyone. The three boys and girl were the college-student type, no older than twenty, no younger than seventeen, and the surfing kind, the boys with long hair, the girl with short. The chat was moving at a hundred miles an hour as they teased each other and passed insulting remarks across the table at one another. There was no more than ten years between us and I felt like we were living on different planets.

I leaned in close to Life so that the others

couldn't hear me. 'What the hell happened to your face?'

He looked at me with annoyed eyes, and finished eating. 'Not just my face, my whole entire body.' He pulled the neckline of his new T-shirt down and the red blotches continued. 'It's a rash,' he said.

'No shit.'

'Stress. From you tossing and turning all night, convincing yourself everything in your world will be further defined from this moment.'

'Wow.' I studied his face. In addition to the rash, he still had the massive boil on his chin from when Don didn't call. 'Some of the red bits have purple bits.'

'Don't you think I don't know that?' he hissed. His entire face went momentarily even redder as if he was about to choke.

'All this is because of Blake?'

'Blake, your job, your father, your family . . .'

'Don?'

'Don is the only person who cheers me up and because you've dumped him it makes me feel worse.'

'I haven't dumped him.' I meant we had nothing to dump, but Life misunderstood.

'No, you've just put him on hold while you check out another line like you're some kind of 1950s switchboard operator.'

I frowned. 'Fine, you go out with Don then if he makes you so happy.'

'I am,' he snapped. 'Tonight. So you'd better

talk quickly with Blake because I'm not hanging around another night.'

'Don't worry, I can try to cover up your rashes with powder.'

'This isn't about the rashes,' he hissed again, his face going purple.

He was more like the Life I'd met on the first day; tragically we were going backwards. The lady of the house asked me what I'd like to eat. I eyed up Life's breakfast. 'Something healthy,' I said critically. 'I'll have the granola, please.'

'Microwaved?' he said loudly, making a point.

'I'm going to start cooking again,' I said defensively.

He snorted. 'I've filled your fridge with fresh fruit and vegetables every few days; they've all gone rotten and I've had to throw them out.'

'Really?'

'You wouldn't have noticed, you were only opening the freezer.'

'Are you guys going to the adventure centre too?' the girl asked.

Life rudely ignored her, not in the mood to talk to anyone unless it was to torment me.

'Yes,' I smiled, excited for Blake. 'You're all going there?'

'Second time this month, but it's Harry's first.'

I could tell which one was Harry because the blond beside me went red as they all jeered and jostled him, ruffling his hair and leaving him even more dishevelled looking.

'Harry's terrified of heights,' the girl explained for me, with a bright smile. 'If he dives, Declan has promised to shave his eyebrows.'

'And his balls,' the redhead said and it was Declan's turn to look slightly embarrassed as they all jeered again.

'Have you been taking lessons?' It was a question for Harry.

'No, his mom's been shaving his balls all his life so he knows exactly what to do,' the cheeky redhead said and they all laughed again, Harry included this time.

'We're doing a tandem skydive,' the girl answered me.

'What's that?' Life asked, starting on a chocolate croissant. I glared at him but he stuffed it in his mouth.

'Tandem skydiving is when two people fall through the sky attached to one parachute system,' I explained. 'You just need to do twenty minutes of training before the skydive.'

Life made a face. 'Who in their right mind would want to do that?'

Harry looked like he agreed with Life but wouldn't say.

'We used to do it all the time.' I smiled at the memories of Blake and me hurtling towards the earth together, and wanting to get back up in the air as soon as we'd landed.

'How romantic,' Life said sarcastically. 'It's a pity the parachute didn't fail to open.' He reached into the basket for a chocolate muffin. Again my glare did nothing to stop him. 'So what? I'm depressed.'

'Well, you need to snap out of it because you're going to need every ounce of energy you have to help me.'

'You can get a lift with us if you want,' the girl said. 'We've got Declan's mum's camper van. There's plenty of room.'

'Great, thanks,' I perked up.

It was a five-minute drive from the B&B to the adventure centre. My stomach lurched every few seconds. I was quite uneasy and not just because I was precariously perched on a pile of surfboards, which were bouncing around and fit to fall despite Declan's very careful driving, though the others were shouting at him to speed it up. Harry was sitting beside me, pale as could be.

'It'll be fine. If anything, this will help you overcome your fear of heights.'

He looked at me doubtfully, then, when the others were busy slagging each other about Declan driving like an old man he said quietly, 'What if I get sick in the air?'

'You won't,' I said confidently. 'There's no sensation of sickness. Skydiving is a constant so it doesn't turn your stomach like going over a bump or a hill.'

He nodded, then a moment later he asked, 'What if the parachute doesn't open?'

'It will and anyway there are two parachutes,

and both parachutes will have been meticulously maintained by highly qualified staff. I know the guy who runs the place and he's perfect, I mean he's a perfectionist.'

He looked a little more relieved but not completely. 'How well do you know him?'

I thought about it, then said firmly, 'I haven't seen him for almost three years but I'm in love with him.'

Harry looked at me like I was a weirdo and mumbled, 'Yeah well, people can change a lot in three years.' Then he left me to think about that while he joined the other two who were pretending to snore as Declan carefully rounded the corners.

'Well, that told you,' Life said, sitting on a half-inflated banana boat across from me. Despite his crankiness he looked good in a new pair of jeans, trainers and a polo shirt. I'd managed to take down some of the redness in his face with powder but he was still a bit blotchy. He looked like he wanted to say something.

'Out with it.'

'Oh, nothing.'

'Tell me.'

'It's just that poor little Harry there is terrified of going up in a plane and you've just given your word that Blake is "perfect".' He rolled his eyes.

'So? Blake is the most safety-conscious guy I know.'

'He's also a liar. Pity you didn't tell him that.'

I ignored him the rest of the way.

The centre was actually a very modest building.

'It's a Portaloo,' Life said, stepping out from the camper van and joining me.

'It's not a Portaloo,' I said, annoyed, surveying Blake's new business. It was more of a Portakabin. In fact, it was two. One was clearly the registration and checking-in room and the other was changing and toilet facilities.

'Is this what your dream looked like?'

It wasn't but I ignored him. At least Blake had actually done something he wanted to do unlike most of the people in the world. Unlike me. The nerves were still there but I was excited; I kept that paused image of Blake and Jenna clinking glasses in Morocco and I held onto it as a driving force. That was why I was here; to break them up, to make him see me and realise he loved me again. I'd changed a lot in our two years, eleven months and twenty-one days of being apart and I wanted him to see that.

I followed the excited Fantastic Four – or at least the Thrill-Seeking Three and a Petrified Harry – into the cabin. There was a sweets and crisp dispenser, a tea and coffee dispenser and chairs lining the walls.

'That's good, maybe I can see the doctor about my rash while I'm here,' Life criticised once again.

The walls were covered in framed photographs of Blake, some of which had been blown up and super-sized. They were taken from his TV show and made him look like Ethan Hunt from *Mission*

Impossible, freeze-framed in a muscle-bulging action sequence, all biceps and abs and rock-solid bum cheeks: Blake jumping out of aeroplanes, Blake white-water rafting, Blake climbing Mount Kilimanjaro, Blake's muscles popping from his skin as he climbed the Rocky Mountains, Blake having a shower under a waterfall. My eyes lingered on that one for a while as I checked out his amazing body, as did all the eyes of the young women in the cabin. It was only then, when I looked around at the rest of the clientele, that I realised it was mostly women, mostly young women, mostly beautiful, tanned, toned, pretty women. It put me on the wrong foot momentarily; all these young things were here to see Blake the TV star, he probably got this attention all the time, in every bar, in every town and city, in every country. They probably all threw themselves at him; he could have his pick, he could have them all at once and just to torment myself, I had an image of them all together, him in the middle of all their young naked bodies writhing all over him. I might have been ten years older than them all but I used to have his naked body writhing all over me too, whenever I wanted, and that made me feel better.

I was scanning the walls of Blake's achievements when I saw her. Her. Jenna. The bitch. From Australia. She was sitting down at a little makeshift desk sorting through application forms and IDs and taking money and generally running the place. I felt like the RoboCop, zoning in on her and running through her vital statistics; her strengths and weaknesses as a human being, even worse, as a woman. Hair: natural blonde and plaited in a bohemian casual way along her hairline. Body: toned, tanned, long limbs – but not as long as mine, she was more petite. Eyes: brown, big and honest, puppy dog-like, every man would want to take her home – but she had a small scar in the middle of her eyebrows. Clothes: a white vest that made her tan stand out and her teeth glow, a pair of jeans and trainers. I was wearing the same except I'd chosen a baby blue vest because I'd been wearing that colour when we'd met and he'd commented on how much it made my eyes pop – the colour, not the actual eye, that only happened when I ate shellfish.

'Take a picture, why don't you,' Life said to me, standing beside me and noisily opening a packet of salt-and-vinegar crisps he'd got from the dispenser.

'That's her,' I said.

'The girl from Morocco?'

'Yes,' I whispered.

'Really?' He was surprised. 'Maybe there's something to your psychotic paranoid tendencies after all.'

'It's called instinct,' I said, sure now that every time I was paranoid about something, including the guy in my building being part of US witness protection, was completely and utterly true.

'Still, they might not be together,' he said, popping a crisp into his mouth.

'Look at her,' I said bitterly, disgusted, 'She's exactly Blake's type.'

'And what type is that?'

I watched her interacting with the group, with a wide smile, dimpled cheeks, laughing and joking, showing concern and helping those who were worried.

'The nice type,' I said bitterly. 'The bitch.'

Life almost choked on his crisp. 'This is going to be fun.'

She glanced up then, as if her internal radar had warned her about an enemy nearby, and looked straight at me. Her smile didn't fade but her eyes hardened, lost their shine momentarily, and I knew that she knew what I was here to do. I knew that she had feelings for Blake, I'd known since the beginning, ever since we'd met in a London bar when Blake had signed the TV deal and she'd asked him if he'd like *ice* in his drink. A girlfriend always knows, can pick up on the vibes, and now here I was, and she was possibly the girlfriend and she knew.

'Lucy?' She came towards me, her eyes flicking to Life beside me and seeming to relax a little. She needn't relax.

'Jenna, isn't it?'

'Yeah.' She seemed surprised. 'I can't believe you remember me, we only met the one time.'

'In London.'

'Yeah. Wow.'

'You remembered me.'

'Yeah, well, that's because I heard about you all the time,' she smiled.

Heard. Past tense.

'Well, welcome,' she said, looking at Life shyly. She was sweet. I was going to destroy her.

'This is my friend Cosmo.'

'Cosmo, cool name. Nice to meet you.' She held out her hand and he wiped his salt-and-vinegar-greasy fingers on his jeans before shaking it.

'Is Blake around today?' I asked, looking around.

'Yeah. Doesn't he know you're coming?'

Translation: *Is this arranged? Are you getting back together? Should I be worried?*

I smiled sweetly. 'I wanted to surprise him.'

'Wow. Great. So, I'm sure he'll be really stoked to see you but he's very tied up at the moment. He's getting ready to train the first group of divers. Are you guys part of this group?'

'Yes. Yes, we are.'

Life looked at me as if there wasn't a hope in the world of him diving with me but I appreciated that he didn't say anything.

'How long have you been working here for?'

'The past month, ever since it opened. Blake was very kind to give me the job. We wrapped on the TV show and after that I just didn't want to go home, you know? I love it here.'

'It's a long way from home.'

'Yeah, it is,' she said, rather sadly. 'But we'll see.'

'We'll see?'

'Yeah. We'll see what happens. Right, well, I'd

360

better get this group ready and I've to bring a coffee to Blake, he always likes it first thing.'

I could tell her a thing or two about what else he liked first thing. I smiled tightly and watched her as she clapped her hands to get everybody's attention, then issued polite orders, made a funny joke, and then, after she had herded everybody into the correct positions and they all knew what they were doing, she ran out of the cabin with a steaming hot coffee in a styrofoam cup.

'You're on your own, sweetheart,' Life said, stuffing another crisp into his mouth.

'You're afraid of diving?'

'Of course I am,' he said. 'Especially if she's preparing your parachute.' Then he chuckled and wandered off to turn his nose up at more of Blake's photos.

I assured Life that he didn't have to do the dive but in order to see Blake I had to go along with the day's schedule. He had driven me here so that I could make a go of things, so he knew his role was to go with the flow. I didn't want to hang around for hours waiting for Blake like a stalker, because clearly I wasn't that.

I wasn't.

Life and I followed the group outside onto a grassy area. It was only ten a.m. and already it was warm. Before us was two miles of runway and to the right was the airplane hangar. As basic as the set-up was I was proud of Blake for following his dream, for achieving it. It felt bitter-sweet that it was without me, that it wasn't me about to take the training class, that it wasn't me sitting in the cabin sorting through applications and greeting customers. He had taken my dreams – *our* dreams – and moved on without me. Here I was, a mere spectator standing among a gaggle of girls waiting to see him as if he was a pin-up star, which of course he was now. If you subscribed to *Love to Travel* magazine. Which I did. There were nine of us in total. The four from the B&B, three fans of Blake's, and Life and me.

'Where is he?' one blonde asked her friend and they both looked at each other and giggled.

'Are you going to ask him for his autograph?'

'No,' she said, 'I'm going to ask if I can have his children.' They both cackled again.

Life looked at me, his eyes dancing like he was laughing at me. Since we'd arrived at the 'Portaloo' he seemed to have got his spark back, but I wasn't sure it was for all the right reasons. The door to the hangar made a large booming sound as it was unlatched and began to open. It slid back slowly, revealing the plane inside, then when the door was midway open it revealed Blake standing in front of the plane, dressed in an orange jumpsuit, the top unzipped and falling down around his waist, revealing a tight white vest that showed his protruding muscles beneath. He was too far away to see his face but the body, his shape, was recog-nisable from space. He looked pumped and ready for action, he looked amazing, then he slowly started to walk towards us, like a scene from *Armageddon*. His parachute was attached to his waist and he pulled it along behind him, the weight of it so great that it was like he was walking against a gale-force wind. Sometimes the parachute material would catch the wind and it would pick up behind him, ballooning slightly and then falling to the ground again.

'Oh. My. God,' Life said, finally pausing from eating his crisps.

I felt proud of Blake, and proud that Life could see him like this. People were drawn to him, he had an aura, this was a perfect example.

'What a gobshite,' Life said and threw his head back and laughed.

I looked at him in surprise. Then the three lads and girl from the camper van started laughing and I was angry.

Harry looked at me in disbelief. 'Is this the fella?'

I ignored him. The other women in the group were cheering, whooping and clapping, delighted by the opening introduction. I joined in with the polite applause, the cheering I did on the inside in a soprano High C. Blake smiled and looked at the ground shyly in an *aw shucks, gee whizz, you guys* kind of way. Then he detached his parachute and walked the rest of the way to the group with his groin wrapped up in a harness as if he was gift-wrapping his sizeable manhood. He finally reached the group.

'Thanks, guys,' he said, beaming, raising his hands to calm the applause. It had the desired effect and there was silence.

Life chose that moment to finish eating his crisps and crumple the packet into a ball. Blake's head turned as Life noisily stuffed the crisp bag into his jeans pocket. Blake looked at him and then at me. And then his face broke into the largest smile. My stomach did a triple Axel jump, the crowd roared and I stepped up to the first position on the podium, accepted my flowers, dipped my head for the gold medal and listened to the national anthem while second and third scowled and plotted ways to break my legs.

'Lucy Silchester,' he smiled, then looked back at the curious group. 'Ladies and gentlemen, meet the love of my life.'

CHAPTER TWENTY-FOUR

From the corner of my eye I saw Jenna slip back inside the cabin. It was possibly the happiest moment of my life and I would have punched the air with delight were it not a ridiculously sad thing to do. Blake told them to take a moment to chat amongst themselves while he came over to me, his arms spread wide, ready for a hug. I fell into his arms and my head naturally went to his chest, my right cheek resting against him, his arms wrapped around me tightly as he kissed the top of my head. It was the same, it was all exactly the same, we slotted together like a jigsaw puzzle. Two years, eleven months and twenty-one days since I'd seen him, since he'd sat me down, after we'd made love the night before, and said that he was leaving me.

All of a sudden anger rushed through me as I remembered how he'd brought me breakfast in bed and then sat at my feet and began explaining his complicated, turbulent mind. He had been so awkward, so uncomfortable, so unable to look me in the eye that I thought he was about to propose. I was *afraid* that he was going to propose and then when he was finished I would have done anything for him to have proposed. And then while I lay in bed with a heavy tray of food and coffee resting on my thighs he stood before the wardrobe, scratching the back of his head, and tried to figure out what clothes he should pack for his new single life. If indeed it was a single life he was headed to, and if he hadn't been seeing Jenna behind my back for the first few weeks of filming the travel show. And then on the same day that I had lost my boyfriend, I had gotten drunk and lost my career and my driver's licence, shortly afterwards my home when we put it on the market.

He hugged me tight two years, eleven months and twenty-one days later and all the love I had felt for him, every single day since then, vanished and was replaced by anger. My eyes opened suddenly and I saw Life looking at me; he was smiling, enjoying the sight of us embracing. Confused by my sudden emotional shift, I let go of Blake and peeled myself away from him.

'I can't believe you're here,' he was saying, his hands holding on tight to the tops of my arms. 'You look great, this is great.' He laughed and I let the anger settle as I relaxed under his gaze.

'Blake, I want you to meet a special friend of mine.'

Blake was slow to turn away from me, he seemed

a little disconnected then. 'Yeah, sure. Hey, how are you doing?' He shook Life's hand quickly as if he was doing me and him a favour, then returned his gaze to me. 'I'm so happy you're here.'

'Me too,' I laughed.

'How long are you staying for?'

'I just popped by to say hi. I wanted to see the dream realised.'

'Stay and do the dive with us.'

'OK. We'd love to.'

He looked confused by the *we*; then he glanced at Life quickly again and back to me and said, 'Oh, yeah, sure.' Then he made his way back to face everybody on the grass and he started the lesson on how to position the body when free falling. I was an expert on that.

'Sorry about that,' I said to Life as I observed him on the ground copying the positions.

'No problem,' he said. 'He looked really pleased to see you. That's great, Lucy.'

'Yeah, it is,' I said nervously. 'So are you going to do the dive?'

'No,' he said, moving to the new position, 'I just like the view from here.'

I looked ahead of him to the cute blonde girl with her bum in the air and I rolled my eyes. 'Come up in the plane at least.'

'No way.'

'Are you afraid of flying too?'

'No, it's the hurtling towards the earth at astronomical speeds that terrifies me.'

'You don't have to dive. Honestly, just come up there with us, I want you to see. It's a twenty-minute flight, the views will be nice and then you can come back down with the pilot the old-fashioned way.'

He looked up at the sky to make the decision. 'Fine.'

I followed Blake to the aeroplane hangar to help gather the equipment.

'Does your girlfriend not do the dives too?' I asked him, trying to keep my tone casual and uninquisitive when really my sanity and lifelong happiness depended on his answer.

'Girlfriend?' He looked at me, confused. 'What girlfriend?'

I almost danced on the spot. 'The girl doing the paperwork in the other cabin,' I said, not wanting to say her name out of fear that he'd think I was a stalker who'd been following her around for years, despite the fact that she and I had talked an hour ago. 'The girl who works on your show. There she is.'

We looked out and saw Jenna leading everybody to another area. She was all smiles and she said something and everybody laughed, including my life, which bothered me.

'Oh, her. That's Jen.'

Jen, not Jenna. I hated her even more.

'Why did you think she was my girlfriend?'

'I don't know. She just seemed your type.'

'Jen? You think?' He looked at her thoughtfully,

and I didn't like what he was thinking. I tried to get his attention again but short of clicking my fingers in front of his face I wasn't sure what else to do. I stepped in front of him, side-stepped kind of casually to block his view of her, which worked because he looked away and concentrated on the equipment. We were quiet for a while. I hoped he wasn't thinking of Jenna. I desperately tried to think of something to say to make him change his thoughts but he got there first.

'So is he your boyfriend?'

'Him? No,' I laughed. 'It's the oddest thing, actually.' I had to tell him the truth, I was *excited* to tell him the truth. 'You'll love this, you're so into this kind of thing. I received a letter from him a couple of weeks ago from the Life Agency, have you ever heard of it?'

'Yeah.' He stopped with the equipment and looked at me. 'I read an article when I was at the dentist about a woman who'd met with her life.'

'Was she standing beside a vase full of lemons and limes?' I asked excitedly.

'I don't know.'

'Well, anyway, *he's* my life. Isn't that kind of cool?'

I expected him to be impressed, he used to be so into that kind of thing, reading book after book about self-development, self-empowerment, self-searching and anything and everything to do with oneself. He used to always talk about different religious theories, reincarnation, life after death, so many exploratory searching works about the human soul that I knew this would be the ultimate for him. Meeting Life in the flesh; I was so sure he thought he'd never see the day when I would reach such depths. I was so sure he would be so enthusiastic about it that I spoke with more passion than I did about anything, because he was into that kind of thing, because I wanted him to know I was too, that I had changed, that I had new depths he didn't even know about, that he could love me.

'He's your life?'

'Yes.'

'And why is he here?'

From the questions he might have seemed interested, but believe me, he wasn't. It came across more like, *he's* your life, and tell me again *why* is he here?

I swallowed, wanting to back-pedal, but I couldn't and I felt it would be disrespectful to my life not to sell him properly after he'd driven me here for a surprise and gone along with my little 'get Blake back' adventure. 'The idea is that we spend some time together, to get to know one another. When people are busy with work and friends and other distractions, sometimes we lose sight of the important things. Apparently I'd lost sight of me.' I shrugged. 'But not any more. He's everywhere I look. But he's funny. You'll like him.'

He nodded once, then went back to his equipment. 'You know I'm going to do a cookbook?'

That was an unusual key change but I went with it. 'Really? That's great.'

'Yeah,' he lit up. 'It came about because of the show I do — have you seen it, by the way? Lucy, it's such a ride, it's the best thing I've ever done. Anyway, we were going to so many different places, experiencing so many cultures and just the tastes and smells and sounds were so inspiring that whenever I came home after travelling I wanted to replicate what I'd tasted.'

'That's great, you always loved cooking.'

'Yeah, and I don't just replicate it, that's the idea of the book, I give it my own twist. The Blake twist or the Blake taste. I think that's what we'll call it. *The Blake Taste*. The publishers love it, they say it could even transfer onto the screen so I could have a separate show from *Wish You Were Here* just based on the food I eat when travelling.' He had lit up, his face was animated, his words were hopping a mile a minute, he was so excited he could barely get them out in the right order. I watched him, fascinated that I was seeing him in the flesh, that he hadn't changed one bit, that he was still the passionate, energetic, beautiful man he had always been. 'I'd love for you to taste some of my recipes, Lucy.'

'Wow, thank you, I'd love that,' I beamed.

'Would you?'

'Of course, Blake, I really would. I'd like to get back into cooking myself, actually. I just kind of stopped. I suppose I got out of the habit. I moved to a smaller place, the kitchen isn't as good as the one that we—'

'Oh, man, that kitchen,' he shook his head. 'That was some kitchen, but you should see the one I have now. I'm using this amazing oven; it's a built-in multi-function stainless-steel PyroKlean oven. It offers you forty different programmes for fresh and frozen foods and you just enter the weight of the food and the oven automatically selects the best setting, then it controls—'

'—the cooking time and switches off when the meal is done, using the residual heat to save energy,' I interrupted.

His mouth dropped. 'How did you know that?'

'I wrote it,' I said, proudly.

'I don't understand, you wrote what?'

'The instruction manual. I work at Mantic. Or at least I did until yesterday. I translated the manuals.'

He continued to look at me in such an unusual way that I had to turn around to make sure it was me he was looking at, at all.

'What is it?'

'What happened to Quinn and Downing?'

'I haven't worked there for years,' I laughed. Then, though I tried to keep it casual, I added more seriously, 'Didn't Adam tell you anything about me over the past few years?' I meant it. I thought that everything I was doing was going back to Blake, I thought he knew everything about me and I knew nothing about him. For the past

372

few years I'd made decisions and created lies thinking they'd be working their way back to him, and he didn't even know what had happened on Day One, the day that he left me and I lost my job.

'Adam? No,' he said, confused, then smiled and his face lit up again. 'So let me tell you about this Moroccan pie—'

'He thinks I cheated on you,' I interrupted his recipe. I didn't plan to say that, never ever in all of my conniving thoughts and pre-planning plans; it just came flying out of my mouth.

'Huh?' He had been about to talk about saffron and this had put a spanner in the works.

'They all do.' I tried to keep the tremor out of my voice, the tremor not of nerves but of anger; it was building again and I was fighting hard to keep it under wraps.

'Blake,' called a guy who stuck his head in the door. 'We have to get a move on.'

'Coming now,' Blake said and he picked up the equipment. 'Let's go,' he grinned. My anger once again dissipated and I found myself with a mushy smile on my face.

The plane held six people, which was three groups. Harry was strapped to Blake, and the young fertile lady who wanted to have Blake's babies was strapped to another instructor named Jeremy – the one whose timely arrival had stopped me from exploding at Blake in the equipment room – and she was staring at Harry with jealousy over having pulled the short straw. Life was wearing an orange jumpsuit with goggles over his eyes; he was sitting on the floor between my legs with his back against my front, and every now and then he looked at me with absolute disgust and terror.

He turned around again as we took off. '"The view will be nice,"' he hissed at me.

'It is a beautiful view,' I smiled calmly.

'"And you can land with the pilot,"' he said angrily. 'You tricked me. You lied to me. That's one big lie,' he said with venom in his voice.

'You don't have to jump,' I said, trying to be relaxed, but really I was worried. I couldn't afford for Life to tell a humongous truth. Not here, not now, not with Blake so close that our feet were touching.

'Then why am I attached to you by an umbilical cord?'

'You can pretend to have a panic attack. We can go back down if you want, I just wanted to, you know, do this one more time with him.'

'Pretend? I won't need to bloody pretend,' he said, then faced front again and ignored me for the rest of the journey. Harry was absolutely terrified looking and was green in the face; I could see his body trembling. Our eyes met.

'You're going to love it. Just picture Declan with no eyebrows.' He smiled, closed his eyes and took deep breaths. Blake and I watched one another as the plane left the ground and we went up to the sky. We couldn't stop ourselves from smiling; he shook his head again out of disbelief that I was there. We climbed up to two hundred feet. We flew for twenty minutes and finally we were ready for action. Blake opened the door and wind blasted inside as the countryside below was revealed to us like a patchwork quilt.

Life uttered a tirade of unrepeatable expletives.

'Ladies first,' Blake shouted, moving aside for Life and me.

'No, no, you go ahead,' I said firmly. 'We're going to go last.' I tried to give Blake warning eyes to hint that Life was afraid but Life had turned around again to stare at me.

'No, I insist,' Blake said. 'Just like old times.'

'I'd love to but . . . he's a bit nervous, I think it's better if we watch first. Okay?'

Life was fuming. 'Nervous? I'm not nervous. Come on, let's go.' He started shuffling on his bottom to the edge of the plane and I was pulled along with him. I was flabbergasted but wouldn't argue with him, so I checked that the tandem harness and parachute were safely secured and we moved to the edge of the plane. I couldn't believe Life was doing this, I had been expecting us to go back down with the pilot. I had been disappointed all the way up and now I was ready, adrenaline was pumping.

'Are you ready?' I shouted.

'I hate you,' he shouted back, in a shrill voice.

I counted him down. On three, we were out the

door, free falling through the sky and up to the speed of 200 km per hour in just ten seconds. Life was shouting so loudly, one long scream of terror all the way down, while I felt alive. I whooped happily alongside him so that he knew it was okay, that this was not a mistake, that we were supposed to be twirling around like snowflakes, not knowing what direction we were going in. Then finally we adopted the free-fall position, and we floated and fell for a total of twenty-five seconds, experiencing the ultimate rush; the wind in our ears, in our hair, everywhere, loud and cold and wonderfully terrifying. When we reached 5,000 feet I deployed the main parachute and once it was open, suddenly the mania and the rush of the wind in our ears was gone. Everything was quiet, everything was blissful and wonderful.

'Oh, my God,' Life said, breathless and husky after his fit of screaming.

'Are you okay?'

'Okay? I almost had a heart attack. But this,' he looked around, 'this is amazing.'

'Told you,' I said, so pleased to be sharing this moment with my life. I was so happy I was fit to burst; the two of us hung there in the air, suspended like the two freest souls in the universe.

'I didn't mean it when I said I hated you.'

'Good. Because I love you,' I said, out of nowhere.

He turned around. 'I love you too, Lucy,' he beamed. 'Now shut up talking, you're spoiling my experience.'

I laughed. 'Do you want to steer?'

Life took control and steered the parachute and we moved around the sky, flying like a bird, taking the world in, feeling happy, feeling alive, feeling united and complete. Our perfect happy moment. The flight lasted four minutes and finally I took control again for landing. We adopted the landing position, legs and feet up, knees together. I slowed the parachute and we touched down for a soft landing.

Life collapsed on the ground in a fit of exhilarated laughter.

Released from the parachute and from me, Life jumped up and ran around in circles as though he were drunk, whooping and laughing.

'That was absolutely incredible. I want to it again, let's do it again, can we do it again?'

I laughed. 'I can't believe you did it!'

'And let him see that I was weak? Are you joking?'

'What are you talking about?'

'*Blake*. Who else? I don't want that idiot seeing me back out of anything. I want him to know I don't care what he thinks of me, I'm tougher than he thinks.'

'What? I don't understand. Why are you trying to create a battle with him?'

'I'm not creating anything, Lucy. It's his issue. Always has been.'

'What are you talking—'

'Anyway, never mind,' he said, smiling again and doing a celebration dance. 'Woohooooo!'

Feeling happy about Life's exhilaration but confused as to its source, I watched him with mixed emotions. Surely, in order for my newly rediscovered love for Blake to be fair and right, both Life and I should be on the same page when it came to our feelings. I wanted us all to get along, not for Life to be preoccupied with one-upmanship, but perhaps this was the natural course of things. Blake had hurt me, had wounded my life, and though I was on my way to forgiving him and was able to accept responsibility for my side of the relationship's failure, Life needed more time. But what did that mean? What did that mean for Blake and me? Usually after parachute jumps I felt exhilarated, just as Life did, and everything became clear, but suddenly my headache was back, the one I got when I had deep emotional thoughts about issues I'd rather sweep under the shagpile of my mind. A jeep was headed towards us across the field. A lone woman sat behind the wheel and as she got closer Jenna's face came into view. My heart twisted in the same way it used to when I thought of her, even though I knew for sure, without doubt, they weren't in a relationship.

'You look like you want to kill someone,' Life said breathlessly, finally stopping his whooping and standing beside me.

'Funny that,' I said, watching Jenna come closer, with two hands gripping the sides of the wheel, staring at me intently. I wondered if she was going to stop.

'Be careful, Lucy, she's a nice girl. Anyway, I thought you said they weren't together,' he said.

'They're not.'

'Then why do you still hate her?'

'Habit, I suppose.'

'Just like loving him,' Life said, looking up to the sky. Then he left me alone to view Blake floating down like the perfect pumped-up angel and ponder that bombshell.

CHAPTER TWENTY-FIVE

Blake and I were face to face in the people carrier. He had his back to my life who had declared he was 'riding shotgun', then persisted to gabble excitedly to Jenna who was behind the wheel. Occasionally Jenna would break from my life's full attention to the rear-view mirror to check I wasn't misbehaving, and each time she played taxi mom, our eyes met and she quickly looked away. She knew, and I knew, and we both knew that we both knew; an ex-girlfriend and a girlfriend in waiting, we were like two hawks circling our prey, wary of one another, wondering who was going to go in first for the kill. The no-longer-green-in-the-face Harry and the girl who wanted to have Blake's babies were engrossed in their own little adrenaline love fest, talking a mile a minute about the experience they'd just had, going over each second of the dive, each following up the other's description with an overenthusiastic 'Me too!' I sensed Blake had just lost his chance of a surrogate, if indeed he ever needed one. Jeremy, the second instructor, was staring out of the window, cool and uninterested by anything inside, outside or around the general vicinity of the jeep, but apart from him everybody was on a high. My heart? It soared. My adrenaline pumped for different reasons from the others; mine was because I was in love, but instead of enjoying it, I was having a full-on debate in my mind about whether it was a habit or not. These moments with Blake were precious and crucial, I had waited a long time to be this close both physically and emotionally, and I was destroying it by developing new thoughts which I had more than enough time to create while I wasn't with him. Plenty of hours alone on the couch with Mr Pan, in a club, pub, restaurant or family occasion, to ponder the foundations and authenticity of my love and yet I chose now, *now goddammit*, to have a crisis of the mind. It was frustrating, *I* was the most frustrating human being on the planet.

Blake and I watched one another; there was a smile on his face as bright as my new bathroom light bulb which, given, on first read is a lame and unromantic simile, but when plunged in darkness for a year whilst on the toilet, a new light bulb is a very welcoming and enlightening thing to have, not to mention useful. Jenna said something in the front seat, Life howled with laughter and while Blake was before me smiling at me, promising a million tomorrows – or at least a tonight which I would gladly take, I wasn't fussy – their growing bond over the past five minutes bothered me to distraction. Life's disgusting rash was gone, he was delirious with happiness and as much as I tried to convince myself it was Blake's doing, the reality felt very far away. He'd hit it off far more with Jenna than with the love of my life, and it wasn't for his lack of trying either. I had seen it first-hand on the first day we met how Life could have greeted Blake – he could quite simply have been a bastard – and I was so thankful for Blake not to have seen that side of him. Whatever possibility of a future would we have together if Blake hated my life? And who would I choose? A new thought, which scared me. I wanted to slap my own face. Stop *thinking*, Lucy, it's never done anybody any good.

'Just like old times,' Blake said suddenly.

Something about that irked me. I analysed it as Life had programmed me to do to everything, it seemed, and it wasn't him that bothered me. It was neither his expression, nor his tone, it was the mere sentiment itself. Yes it did feel like old times but there was a large pile separating us, it was the *unsaid all* swept under the mat between us, getting so high that I could barely see his face. But I didn't want to pull back the rug, I didn't want to go backwards by delving into the compost heap of our past problems. I wanted to stay right here in the car in the airfield with the unsaid all still hidden away, suspended in time where everything was still and quiet and blissful, like we were floating down to earth with a great big parachute tying us together.

'Are you staying around?'

I wasn't sure if he was asking me to, or asking if I planned to; there was a difference. I played it safe.

'I have to go back today. He has to meet somebody later.'

'Who?'

'A guy called Don,' I replied, confused as to why he'd ask and then I realised what he'd meant, he'd forgotten about the presence of my life again. 'My life,' I said firmly which took him back. '*My life* is meeting someone called Don.'

'But *you* can stay, can't you?' He gave me a mischievous smile, one of his best, and I couldn't help but break my momentarily hardened exterior. 'Come on,' he laughed, leaning forward and squeezing just above my knees where he knew I was ticklish.

Jenna looked in the rear-view mirror. Our eyes met. I couldn't help but laugh, not at her, which she might have assumed, but because Blake's fingers were wrapped around the ticklish part of my thigh and I couldn't keep a straight face.

'Jer's having celebration drinks tonight.' He continued tickling while I battled him off, laughing. 'He's thirty.'

'I wish,' Jeremy said, smiling, still looking out the window.

383

'Happy birthday,' I said but he still didn't look at me. He was one of those people who made you feel like they either didn't know or didn't care that you were in the room and if they ever did acknowledge your existence it was bizarrely score one to you, and twenty years later they'd tell you they'd always had a crush on you but never had the courage to say anything and you'd tell them, *What? I didn't even think you liked me?* And they'd say, *Are you crazy? I just never knew what to say!* At least that's what happened with Christian Byrne who confessed to me in a bar four months ago, the coolest guy in our tennis camp when I was fifteen, who spoke to and kissed practically every girl in the dorm apart from me. And after all that time and after the confession, I still couldn't kiss him because he'd gotten a girl pregnant and they were getting married because he felt it was the right thing even though it had caused him to end up in a dodgy strip club on Leeson Street at four in the morning and confess his love to a girl he hadn't seen for fifteen years. I was in the club with Melanie, in case inquiring minds wanted to know.

'We'd love to go if you don't mind,' I said to Jeremy.

Jeremy didn't react. Jeremy didn't know or didn't care that I was talking to him. Jeremy secretly loved me, he would discover this soon enough but by then it would be too late because I would be back with Blake. Their friendship would suffer because he wouldn't be able to stand seeing his best friend with the woman he loves so he would have to quit his job and move away, try to find another love but he never would, he'd eventually find someone but it wouldn't be his one true love; he'd get married and have children but each time he and his wife would finish making love and she'd fall asleep, he'd lie awake until late in the night always thinking of the woman he left behind in Bastardstown, Co. Wexford. Me.

'Course he doesn't mind,' Blake answered on his behalf. 'It's in the Bodhrán at six o'clock. We'll go as soon as we get out of here. Come,' he said, playfully prodding at my legs again, one poke with each word. 'Come, come, come.'

'Okay, okay,' I laughed, using all my strength to catch his fingers to stop him from tickling me, but he was stronger and he grabbed my hands and we clasped fingers and sat like that, leaning in towards each other, staring at each other. 'I'll come,' I said.

'You bet you will,' he joked quietly, and my heart actually had a conniption fit.

'We can't go,' Life said as we lay on the floor in the back of the camper van, looking up through the skylight to the perfect blue sky we had merely moments ago fallen through. The camper van was still parked in the car park and we were waiting for the others to join us after Declan, Annie and Josh had finished their dive. Harry was somewhere using clever wordplay to figure his way into the underwear of the girl who wanted Blake's babies.

'Why can't we go?'

'Don!'

'Screw Don!' I said, immediately feeling guilty, but I was more than frustrated that my life was missing the point.

'You already did that.'

'But *Blake* has invited me out, the whole reason we're here. Can't you at least be happy for me?'

He thought about it. 'You're right. I'm very happy for you. Ever since *Sunday night* this has been exactly what you wanted so you stay here and sell yourself out to Blake, the man who broke your heart, and I'll go back to Dublin to meet Don, the nice guy you just slept with, who invited *me* out for a drink.'

'Why don't you two just do it and get it over with,' I snapped.

'That's very mature,' he said calmly, 'but again, you already took care of that. Me? I'm just interested in the friendship. We're meeting in the Barge at eight tonight so that's where I'll be if Mr Theologian decides to leave you hanging while he goes in search of greener pastures again.'

'You don't believe in us,' I said sadly.

'That's not true. I don't believe in him, but who am I to stop you?' He thought about it. 'Oh, yeah, I'm your *life*. Do you think most people in a personal crisis would listen to their life or do they do as you do, drag them around from county to county searching for geological happiness?'

386

'What does that shit even mean? *Geological happiness*?'

'Most people look for fulfilment and happiness *within* themselves; you, on the other hand, physically move to another county thinking it will help things.'

'That woman ate and loved and prayed herself through three continents and she got happy,' I snapped then I sighed, calmed down. 'I just want you to see what I love about him.'

'I've seen what you love about him, all strapped up in a very tight harness.'

'Seriously, please, for once.'

'Seriously? I've seen what you love about him and I'm meeting Don for a drink.'

I wanted to try one more time. 'I just think that there are issues between you and him that I don't entirely understand. He hurt you, I can see that, he tore you down and now you're trying to protect yourself but at least give it a chance. If you don't, you'll be forever wondering was he the one that was supposed to bring me eternal happiness and in turn, bring *you* eternal happiness?'

'I don't believe in eternal happiness, just occasional spurts.' But he'd softened.

'I know you don't want to let Don down but it's just a pint. He's a grown-up, he'll understand.' He looked slightly persuaded but just to be sure I added the final nail in the coffin. 'Plus Sebastian is lying in a ditch and God knows how long it will take to fix him so there's no other way to get home.'

'Okay,' he said, resigned to his fate. 'I'll stay. I'll call Don, but that'll be it. He knows where I am and he'll think I've chosen Blake over him and he'll never want to see me again.'

I patted him in sympathy.

He lay there and we both stared out the window in the roof at the passing clouds in the perfectly blue sky. And then the doors burst open and Declan stood at the end of the van and paraded his parts from the lost bet, and they were considerably bald.

The bodhrán is an Irish frame drum with a goatskin head and the other side open so a hand can hold the drum and control the pitch and the timbre while the other hand pounds it with a cipín. The Bodhrán in this instance was a pub five minutes away from the B&B, which even at seven p.m. was heaving, and inside was a live session of traditional Irish music. We had arrived late because Declan had broken out in a rash in his nether regions which was so itchy he insisted on driving twenty minutes out of our way to the nearest pharmacy to buy a lotion and some talcum powder; he tipped the latter into the top of his trousers and then gyrated his hips in all kinds of directions to make sure it hit the right areas.

Harry, winner of the bet, should have been happy with his friend's new-shorn issues, but was instead annoyed because he was meeting the girl who wanted to have Blake's babies and he was afraid that someone else would get there first. I

388

laughed at his immature impatience at thinking that being just twenty minutes late would ruin his chances, but then I thought of Jenna and I joined in on bullying Declan to put his foot down and show Wexford what his mum's camper van was made of. Harry's irritation had rubbed off on me, which in turn had rubbed off on my life who was none too pleased with having to break his date with Don. His own disgusting rash had returned and he and Declan were taking it in turns passing the powder back and forth while Annie and I were taking turns passing the cider back and forth. Josh was lying down in the back smoking hash and blowing smoke rings. I hadn't drunk cider since I was their age but it was thrilling spending time with them and it had given me a new lease of life, though it had given Life a rash. I think it was that for the first time in a very long time, I didn't have to worry about stumbling upon a lie I had told. They didn't know anything about me, they didn't care, and I could be myself. I hadn't been myself for a long time.

When we arrived at the pub, it was still a beautiful summer evening and the wooden tables and benches outside were crowded. I quickly scanned the place for Blake; Harry quickly scanned it for the girl he wanted to have his babies and surmised that they were inside. He took the lead, I followed. He needn't have worried, because she had kept a free seat beside her; her friend thumped her leg when she saw us and despite the dead leg as a warning, the girl lit up when she saw him. I looked around the packed tables for Blake. The band were singing 'I'll Tell My Ma', and everyone was whooping and cheering and I pushed my way through the moving bodies to find him. I saw Jenna sitting at the table beside Harry and his love and there was an empty seat beside her. My heart pounded, hoping it hadn't been for him, even though I knew they weren't together. It was just . . . habit. My eyes found him at the bar surrounded by a gang of guys, telling a joke, centre of attention as usual. It was word-perfect, he had them all captivated, I watched him, Life watched him, then he got to the punchline and everybody exploded in laughter. I did, Life did too. I felt like pushing my face into his and saying, *See?*

Blake saw me then and excused himself and rushed towards me. Jenna watched us.

'Hey, you came,' he said, wrapping his arms around me and kissing the top of my head again.

'Of course I did,' I beamed, not wanting to look at Jenna but hoping she'd seen it all. 'You remember my life,' I said, moving aside so they could be face to face.

'Yeah, sure,' Blake said.

'Hey,' Life said casually. 'I realise this must be very weird for you,' he said, surprising me with his maturity, 'so let me buy you a drink.'

Blake looked at him warily, then at me, then back at Life.

'To break the ice,' Life added.

Blake took his time deciding, which really

annoyed me. I couldn't understand what *his* issue was. Don had had breakfast in bed *butt naked* with me and my life; Life had even found his underwear for him, which Mr Pan had somehow managed to line his basket with, he'd even eaten breakfast with Life – *cooked* him breakfast – while I showered. I wasn't comparing Don to Blake – I wasn't – it was simply their reactions I was contrasting. In Blake's defence, because I had to try to justify his behaviour, there was a history between him and my life, more emotions, more complexity than the simplicity of a one-night stand, we'd had a five-year love affair, *of course* he was going to be uncomfortable. Or. Shouldn't it have been the other way around?

'Yeah, okay' Blake finally caved in to whatever battle he'd having. 'Let's have it over here.' He guided Life and me away from the rest of the gang to a quieter part of the bar behind a stained-glass divider.

'Well, this is nice,' I said nervously, looking at Life who was clearly insulted and beginning to prickle again. 'At least we can talk in private here.'

'So what are you having?' Life asked Blake.

'Guinness.'

No please. I looked from one man to the other; there was something I was clearly missing.

'Blake, you know he's my life, don't you?' I asked quietly once Life was distracted at the bar.

'Yeah, I know,' Blake said defensively.

'He's not a boyfriend, or an ex-boyfriend, or anybody to feel threatened by.'

'Threatened? I don't feel threatened.'

'Good, because you're acting oddly.' I sighed. 'What's going on?'

'How do people usually react to this?'

'With interest,' I said immediately. 'Usually the people that love me are interested in my life. They are happy, excited to meet him. They usually ignore me so that they can talk to him. You know? At least, apart from my father, that is.'

He lit up. 'Hey, how is your father?'

Another inappropriate key change but I'd go with it. 'Father and I don't speak.'

'Why not? What happened? You were so close.'

So much had changed. 'We were never *close* but what happened is that I changed, he didn't like it. He didn't change, I don't like it.'

'Have you really changed?' Blake asked, studying me.

I swallowed. His face was so close to mine. Stupidly, my answer depended partly on whether he wanted me to have changed or not but mostly because I didn't know the answer. I'd changed since I'd met my life, sure enough, but had he helped me become again the person I was before Blake met me, or had he helped me move on from the person who was stuck in the rut after Blake, making me a new person entirely? It was confusing and I almost felt like breaking away to confer with my life on the answer. But I couldn't because that was odd behaviour and because Blake's lips were almost touching mine and I never ever wanted to ever have to move away.

'Because everything feels the same,' he said. 'Everything feels right.' Our lips were so close they were almost brushing. My body tingled all over.

Then I felt something cold on my chest and I looked down and saw a pint of Guinness attached to Life's hand.

'Your drink,' Life said. 'Enjoy.'

Our moment was lost, stolen from me by my life.

'So,' Life said, handing me a glass of white wine, and holding a bottle of beer in his hand.

Nobody jumped at the conversation-starter bait so he tried again.

'That was really amazing today,' Life said enthusiastically, genuinely trying hard. 'I've never experienced anything like it. Is the rush still the same every time you do it?'

'Yeah, it can be,' Blake nodded.

'Even though you had to dive how many times today?'

'Three times. We'd three groups.'

'Wow. I'd love to do it again, absolutely,' Life said. 'I'd recommend it to anyone.'

'Great. Good, thanks. Let me give you this,' Blake rooted around in his back pocket, 'in case you do want to recommend it to anyone.' He handed Life his card. It had his face on it. Life studied it, a small smile tickling on his lips, and I crossed my fingers and hoped he wouldn't say anything catty. He looked at me and smiled instead. Blake caught the smile. It was so awkward between us all, I wanted it to be over. Enough already. I tried hard to think of something to say, but all thoughts failed me, which was ridiculous as all I'd been having all day were thoughts. Thoughts upon thoughts and now I had none. We all stood in silence in a little triangle, searching our brains for something to say. Nothing. We had nothing.

'Do you want me to introduce you to some people?' Blake asked Life, finally.

'No, it's okay, there's a few people I recognise from earlier.' Life jumped at the opportunity to get away. 'Lucy, if you need me, I'll be over here.'

'Okay,' I said, feeling annoyed and uncomfortable at the same time.

Then the music went up a notch and as 'Whiskey in the Jar' started everybody was lifted a bit and the noise went up to a level where conversation was impossible.

'Come on,' Blake said, taking my hand and leading me through the crowd. I saw Jenna looking at us with such a forlorn expression that a minuscule part of me felt a tiny bit of guilt. Ish. The madness lessened as he led me through the throng; the crowd thinned out, in size and in stature, as we moved to where the old thin men were propped up on the bar, eyeing up the newbies. We passed by the reeking toilets, then went by the back of the bar where the red and black chequered tiles were faded and sticky from spilled drinks and out towards a fire exit door held open by a beer barrel. I followed him, then when we were outside I looked around for the beer garden. 'Hey this isn't—' but I didn't get to finish because his lips were on mine, he was somehow kissing me and removing my glass from my hand and then his hands were back on me again, on my hips, on my waist, running upwards to my chest and neck and through my hair. My hands immediately went to his chest, his shirt was open all the way to four buttons down, revealing nice man cleavage, and my hands rested there as they always had, feeling smooth waxed skin. It was perfect, everything I had daydreamed about in my Saturday and Sunday lie-ins till one p.m. I could taste the beer on his tongue, could smell the shower gel from his recent shower, could remember everything that was ever good about our relationship. Then we finally pulled away to catch our breath.

'Mmm,' he said.

'Have I still got it?'

'*We've* still got it,' he murmured, then kissed me again. 'What were we doing all this time not being together?' He kissed my neck, and I froze.

All this time. I wanted to say something but every sentence I ran through my mind sounded bitter and angry, so I shut my mouth and waited my anger out. He stopped kissing me, then led me to the grass in the sunlight and we sat down. We laughed, not about anything in particular, but for the fact that here we were, together after all this time.

'Why did you come?' Blake asked, moving a hair from my face and putting it behind my ear.

'To see you.'

'I'm glad you did.'

'Me too.'

We kissed again, falling short of the kiss-a-thon record I'd had with Don, then I mentally boxed myself for comparing them again.

'We were interrupted earlier, weren't we?' he asked, casting his mind back to the equipment room in the airfield.

Finally, the moment had come, to talk about it. I took a sip of my wine and prepared.

'Oh, yeah,' he said, remembering. 'My Moroccan pie. *The Blake Taste.*'

I thought he was joking but he wasn't. He started explaining the old recipe and then went into further detail about how he had altered it. I was in so much shock that I couldn't hear his words, nor think of any of my own. At least five minutes passed of me not saying anything and he had moved onto another recipe, describing fully in detail how he marinated and seasoned and simmered things for forty days and for forty nights, or at least it seemed that way. 'So then you take the cumin and you—'

'Why did you leave me?'

He had been so engrossed in his own little world that he was completely taken by surprise.

'Lucy, come on.' He became defensive, 'Why do you have to talk about that?'

'Because it seems appropriate,' I said, voice trembling and hoping he wouldn't hear it, though it was obvious. 'It's been almost three years.' He shook his head and pretended he couldn't believe it had been that long, 'And I haven't heard anything from you and here we are just like old times and it seems like the elephant in the room. I think we should talk about it. I need to talk about it.'

He looked around to make sure nobody was in earshot.

'Okay. What do you want to talk about?'

'Why you left me. I still don't understand it. I don't know what I did wrong.'

'You didn't do anything wrong, Lucy, it was me. I know it sounds corny but I just needed to go do my thing.'

'What thing?'

'You know . . . my *thing*. Travel and see places and—'

'Have sex with other people?'

'What? No, that's not why I left.'

'But I was travelling with you, everywhere, we were seeing places all the time. I never once told you you couldn't do what you wanted to do or be who you wanted to be. Never once.' I was battling with staying calm so that I could have the conversation; if I was in any way emotional he wouldn't be able to cope with it.

'It wasn't about that,' he said. 'It was just . . . me, you know. Something that I needed to do. You and me, we were so serious so young. We had the apartment, the – you know, five years,' he said, not making sense to any other human ear but making perfect sense to mine.

'You wanted to be alone,' I said.

'Yeah.'

'There wasn't anybody else.'

'No, Jesus, no. Lucy—'

'And what about now?' I asked, terrified of the answer. 'Do you still need to be alone?'

'Ah, Lucy.' He looked away. 'My life is complicated, you know. Not to me, to me it's so simple, but for other people it's . . .'

Alarm bells rang in my head. I felt myself physically move away from him, not so much that he would notice, but so much that I would. I felt myself move away in a lot of ways.

'. . . spontaneous and exciting and full of adventure and I like to keep moving and experience new things. You know,' he lit up, 'there was this one week when I went to Papua New Guinea . . .' and he was off.

For ten minutes I listened to him talk about his life and by the time he was nearing the end I knew why I was here. I was sitting on the grass beside him, listening to this familiar man sounding like a perfect stranger, and in a matter of minutes I was feeling completely differently about him. I was seeing him as somebody else, less of a god and more of a friend, a silly little friend who'd lost his way and found himself besotted with his life, his life and not anybody else's and certainly not mine because mine was inside drinking beer and listening to traditional music on his own after I'd dragged him all the way here. I suddenly wanted to leave Blake and be inside with Life. But I couldn't, not until after I'd done what I came here to do.

He finished talking and I smiled, calm and serene, a little sad but feeling at peace, finally. 'I'm really happy for you Blake,' I said. 'I'm happy that you're happy in your life and I'm proud of you for all you've achieved.'

He looked a little confused, but pleased, and looked around. 'Do you have to go now or something?'

'Why do you ask?'

'They sounded like parting words.'

I smiled again. 'Maybe they are.'

'No,' he groaned. 'We were doing so well.' He moved in closer to me again, tried to kiss me.

'This isn't going to work, Blake.'

'Ah, Lucy, don't.'

'No, no, listen to me. It's nobody's fault. It's not my fault. I didn't do anything wrong, I know that now, it's just the way it is. Sometimes things just don't work. You and me, we worked for the amount of time that we worked, then we didn't any more. We can't go back, and, frankly, I can't see what we can be. I've changed.'

'He did that to you?' he said, looking towards the bar.

'No. You did. When you left.'

'But I'm here now and we're so good together,' he said, reaching out to me.

'We are,' I laughed. 'We are so good together

when we're not talking about what counts, and my life counts, Blake, my life is important to me.'

'I know that.'

'Do you? Because he's in there, having a pint on his own and I don't think you're the slightest bit interested in him. You haven't asked one question about me since I've seen you, not one.'

He frowned while he thought about it.

'That might be okay for someone else, it was okay for me for a while, but not now.'

'So you're leaving me.'

'No, no,' I laughed and gave him a stern look. 'Don't pull that trick. No one is leaving anyone, we're just not starting anything.' There was a silence and before he made a move to leave and became forever become lost to a world I had no access to, I spoke again. 'But I'm glad you brought that up, because that's why I'm here.'

'Why are you here?'

I took a deep breath. 'You need to tell our friends that you left me.'

CHAPTER TWENTY-SIX

'I'm sorry, I need to do what?'

From the way he was looking at me I knew that he'd heard exactly what I said. I wasn't being asked to repeat it for hearing's sake but so that I would know there was no way in the world that was ever going to happen. That's when our friendly break-up, or our not-getting-back-together moment became less so.

'I'd like them to know that I didn't break up with you,' I said easily, trying to keep my tone casual but firm so this could be as non-conflicting as possible.

'So you want me to just call them all up and say, Hi, by the way . . .' He finished the sentence in his head, carried the scene out. 'No way.' He shifted uncomfortably on the grass.

'You don't have to call them all up and make a big song and dance about it, Blake, in fact you don't have to say anything at all, I'll tell them. My thirtieth is in two days and we're going out for dinner and I could just tell them then, no big deal, no fireworks, just tell them and then if they don't believe me, which they probably won't, they'll probably call you up and that's when I'd need you to back me up.'

'No,' he said immediately, eyes fixed ahead of him. 'It was years ago, it's history, let's just leave it there. Believe me, nobody cares. I don't know why you want to bring it all back up.'

'For me. It's important to me. Blake, they all think I cheated on you, they—'

'I'll tell them you didn't, that's ridiculous,' he said protectively. 'Who said that?'

'All of them, apart from Jamie, but that's not the point.'

His jaw set as he thought hard. 'You didn't, did you?'

'What? No way! Blake, listen to me, they think I'm the bad guy, that I broke your heart, that I ruined your life and—'

'You want me to be the bad guy instead,' he said angrily.

'No, of course I don't, I just want them to know the truth. It's as if they blame me for all the changes in our lives. Not everyone, mostly Adam—'

'Don't mind Adam,' Blake said, calming then. 'He's my best friend, he's the most loyal human being on the planet, but you know what he's like, he's intense. I'll tell him to lay off you.'

'He makes comments all of the time. There's

always an atmosphere between me and him, and Mary for that matter, though that doesn't bother me much. He makes things difficult for me; if he just knew that he was misinformed then he'd stop. He might even apologise.'

'You want an apology? So that's what this is about. I'll talk to him, I'll tell him to calm down, to stop being so intense, that things between us just fizzled out naturally and you were the strong one to finally point it out and end it, that I'm fine about the whole thing, that—'

'No, no, no,' I said, not wanting to get sucked into another story. 'No. I want them to know the truth. We don't have to tell them why we said what we said, we'll tell them it's private and we never want to talk about it again. But at least they'll know. You know?'

'No,' he said firmly and stood, wiped the grass from his jeans. 'I don't know what you and him came here to do. Trick me into becoming some kind of bad guy to our friends but I'm not falling for it. I'm not doing it. The past is the past, you were right, there's no point in going back there again.'

I stood too. 'Wait, Blake. Whatever you think this is, you're wrong. This is not some kind of act of sabotage, in fact it's the opposite. I want to fix things, more specifically I want to fix my life. I thought that meant finding you, and in a way I was right but just not exactly the way I thought it was supposed to be. Look,' I took a deep breath, 'it's as simple as this. A few years ago we told a lie. What we thought was a small lie, but it wasn't. It's okay for you because you're away all the time, you're travelling the world and you don't have to live with it. I have to live with it every day, every single day. Why did I walk away from something that was perfect? They ask me all the time. But I didn't. Truth is, something that I thought was perfect was taken away from me, and I never wanted perfect again. I wanted middle of the road, stuff I didn't care about so that I couldn't lose anything I really loved ever again. I can't live with the lie any more. I can't. I need to move on but in order for me to do that I need you to help me do this one thing. I could tell them myself but it needs the both of us. Please, Blake, I need you to help me do this.'

He thought hard, staring at a pile of barrels with his jaw firm and square, his eyes intense. Then he bent over and picked up his pint from the grass and looked at me, but only for a second. 'Sorry, Lucy, I can't. Just move on from it, okay?' And he left me and disappeared into the black hole in the pub, swallowed up by the songs and cheers from inside.

I fell back down, exhausted, on the grassy slope we had been lying on moments earlier, and went through the conversation in my head over and over again. There was nothing I could have said differently. It was dusk now, the half-light of a summer night, when shapes and shadows threatened more sinister things beneath. I shivered. I heard footsteps around the corner, coming from the direction of the lively beer garden. Life appeared then, he stopped when he saw me alone, didn't come any further, just leaned his shoulder against the wall.

I looked at him gloomily.

'We can catch a lift back to the B&B in five minutes if you want.'

'What, and not stay until the end? Have you not taught me anything?'

He gave me a small smile, a congratulation for effort. 'Jenna's heading back to her holiday cottage. She's thinking of moving out.'

'Of the cottage? Good for her.'

'No. Out of Ireland. She's going home. To Australia.'

'Why?'

'I don't think things quite worked out for her the way she'd hoped.' He looked at me knowingly.

'Fine. I'll be ready in five minutes.'

He made his way to me and groaned like an old man as he lowered his body to the grass. He clinked his bottle to my glass. 'Sláinte,' he said, then lifted his face to the stars. We had a moment's silence while my head still rang with Blake's words. There was no point in following him inside for round two, I knew that his mind couldn't be changed. I looked at Life; he had a smile on his face as he watched the stars.

'What?'

'Nothing,' he grinned even wider.

'Come on, tell me.'

'No. Nothing,' he tried to stop smiling.

I gave him a dig in the ribs.

'Ow.' He flexed his stomach and sat up beside me. 'Just that he has his face on his business card.' He chuckled like a girl.

He annoyed me at first but the more he laughed, the more I wanted to join in, which I eventually did.

'Yeah.' I finally took a breath. 'That was a bit sad, wasn't it?'

He snorted, an actual pig snort, which sent us both into a fit of giggles.

Life had jumped in the back of the jeep, forcing me to take the front seat beside Jenna. She was subdued, there wasn't the big smile that greeted us that morning, though she wasn't rude – I doubted there was a rude bone in her body.

'It's been a long day, hasn't it?' Life asked, capturing the mood in the jeep and breaking the silence.

'Yeah,' she and I said simultaneously in a tired tone. We quickly looked at each other then away again.

'Did I hear something about you and Jeremy in the pub? Whispers of romance?' Life stirred it up.

Jenna's cheeks had pinked. 'Oh, there was a party . . . it was nothing, well, it was something, but it's nothing. He's not . . .' She went quiet, swallowed hard. 'It's not what I want . . . so.'

That explained her status change on Facebook. We rode the rest of the journey in silence. She pulled into the B&B driveway and we thanked her and jumped out. She turned the car around and we stood there to wave her off.

Life glared at me.

'What?'

'Say something,' he said impatiently.

I sighed, watched her, a tiny little blonde thing in the big jeep, then I jogged over and knocked on the window. She hit the brakes, and lowered the window. She looked tired.

'I heard you might be going back home.'

'Yeah, I am.' She looked away. 'Like you said, it's a long way.'

I nodded.

'I'm going home in the morning.'

She looked up, suddenly eager to hear more. 'Yeah?'

'Yeah.'

'That's too bad.' She was too polite to say it cattily but it wasn't altogether convincing either.

'I'm not . . .' I struggled to think of how to phrase the sentence. 'I'm not coming back,' I said simply. She studied me, trying to understand what I'd said. Then she did. 'Just thought you should know.'

'Right.' She gave me a brighter smile, battling with it not to take over her face. 'Thanks.' She paused. 'Thanks for letting me know.'

I stepped back from the car. 'Thanks for the lift.'

I went back to the house and heard the wheels on the gravel. I turned back once, saw the window closing, the smile on her face, and the jeep drove back down the long drive. It paused at the exit, then she indicated right, back the way we'd come.

I'd been holding my breath all that time and as soon as she turned, I let it out. My heart twisted again and for a moment I panicked. I wanted to call her back, take it back, I wanted to go to Blake, take *him* back, live the way we had always lived together. But then I remembered.

Habit.

CHAPTER TWENTY-SEVEN

I awoke to a fully dressed Life watching me from an armchair, which was spooky to say the least. He looked concerned.

'I have some bad news.'

'We are gathered here today to mourn the loss of Sebastian,' Life said as we stood in a scrapyard staring at my poor car that had been brought here by the medics.

'How long have you known about this?'

'Since yesterday, but I didn't want to tell you then. Didn't seem right.'

'Does he really have to go? Can we not keep him going for a bit longer?'

'Afraid so. A team of mechanics couldn't bring him back. Besides, you'd be better off buying a new car with all the money you spend on fixing him.'

'I'm loyal.'

'I know.'

We took a moment of silence then I patted Sebastian on the roof. 'Thank you for bringing me to all the places I wanted to go to and for taking me away from them again. Farewell, Sebastian, you have served me well.'

Life passed me a handful of soil.

I took it from him and threw it on the roof. We took a step back and the clamp was lowered and Sebastian was lifted up towards the heavens.

And then promptly dropped and crushed.

A car horn broke into my thoughts and we turned to see Harry hanging his head out of the camper-van window. 'Brazil Nuts here is itching to leave. His mum is having a hissy fit and needs the van for some Irish-dancing feis.'

I was quiet on the way home as was Harry. He was beside me, texting the entire time, and in the moments he was waiting for the next reply, he read the previous ones.

'Harry's in love,' Annie teased.

'Congratulations.'

His cheeks pinked, but he smiled. 'So what happened with your man?'

'Oh. No. Nothing.'

'I told you people can change a lot in three years.'

I didn't want a young college boy to think he knew more about the evolution of the human race than I did, so I smiled at him and spoke rather patronisingly. 'But he didn't change, he was exactly the same.'

He rolled his nose up at that, disgusted that Blake's little entrance yesterday was the norm and not the result of some knock on the head he'd received in the past three years of my not knowing him. 'You changed then,' he said matter-of-factly and then went back to his phone to text the girl he wanted to have his babies.

I was even quieter after that conversation; I had a lot to think about. Life was all chat but finally realised after my delayed mono-worded answers that I didn't want to talk so he left me in silence. I had lost a lot on this trip: not just the love I thought I'd had, and my beloved car, but also the hope that I could redeem myself – my dream to stop living in a web of lies woven entirely by myself seemed to be an unrealistic one, or at least was going to be more of a battle than I had thought. I felt like I didn't have anything or even worse I felt like I had nothing: no job, no car, no love, a dilapidated relationship with my family and my friends, and more worryingly, with my best friend. All I had was my rented studio-flat across from a neighbour who probably never wanted to speak to me again and a cat that I had left alone for two nights.

I looked to my other side. But I had my life.

Life leaned forward as soon as we reached the inner city. 'Can you let us out here?'

'Why here?'

We'd gotten out on Bond Street, the heart of the Liberties in Dublin, one of the most historical

411

and central areas in the city where most of the original streets, including the one we found ourselves on, were still cobble-locked. Behind the black gates of the nearby Guinness Brewery, smoke pumped into the air as the scientists in white lab coats inside concocted our greatest export.

'Follow me,' he smiled proudly. I followed him down the cobble-stoned road, the old walls beside us towering above us as they hid working factories side by side with derelict buildings and walls of bricked-up arched windows. Then, just when I thought we were in the middle of a lesson of the heart that would go a little something like talking about all the problems that had come to people before, perhaps to the very people who lived on this street, yet they had recovered from it – perhaps sealing up their windows in a mass form of self-healing – and that hearing this would somehow make me feel better about myself, he took out a set of keys and made his way to a random door in a wall full of bricked-up windows.

'What are you doing? What's in here?' I looked around, waiting for somebody to stop us.

'I want to show you something. What do you think I've been doing all the time I was sneaking away from you?'

I frowned, then had an image of Life cheating on me with a younger prettier version of me, parading as her Life in order to get close to her, sitting with her family at Sunday lunches, trying to keep up with the stories of her growing up and under the beady eyes of her possessive father having to act like he knew them all already, while all the time feeling guilty for pretending to the well-adjusted woman who was now questioning herself that she needed a life intervention, yet also feeling torn inside about what he was doing to me; exhausted from the double lie.

Life was staring at me. 'You look angry. What are you thinking about?'

I shrugged. 'Nothing. So what is this place?'

Inside, it was a converted warehouse, a large open space with high ceilings and exposed brick-work, dusty from new renovations. We stepped into an elevator and I waited for us to catapult through the ceiling and soar into the sky over rooftops while my Willy Wonka Life showed me all that was mine to keep. But that didn't happen. We got out on the seventh floor and Life led me down the hall to a light-filled square room, boxes everywhere on the floor and a window which looked over the city: flats and terraced houses dominated the view immediately below, St Patrick's Cathedral and the Four Courts were visible in the distance with their bright green copper roof and dome respectively, and out towards Dublin Bay, building cranes filled the sky alongside the Poolbeg red-and-white striped 680-foot-high chimneys. Then I waited for the lesson. But it didn't come.

'Welcome to my new office,' he beamed. He looked so happy, so far removed from the man that I had met a fortnight ago that it was difficult to believe he was the same person.

I looked at the boxes cluttering the floor, most of which were still taped closed but some of which had been half-emptied revealing the files inside. Black marker on the outside of the boxes declared 'Lies 1981–2011', 'Truths 1981–2011', 'Boyfriends 1989–2011', 'Silchester Family Ties', 'Stewart Family Ties'. There was a box for 'Lucy's Friends', with files divided into individual headings of 'School', 'College Degree', 'MBA', 'Miscellaneous' and a file for each of my previous jobs, not that I had made or taken many friends with me from them. There was a box marked 'Holidays' with separate compartments for each trip I'd taken, with the date. I surveyed the floor, the dates and random moments jumping out at me and sparking off memories I'd long lost. These boxes contained my entire life – on paper – all my dealings with every single person I had ever met; Life kept a report of them all, analysing them and studying them to see if the victim of bullying in the school yard had anything to do with a failed relationship twenty years later, or whether it was the contrary; a successful day at work; and if an unpaid bill in Corfu had anything to do with a drink in my face in a Dublin club – which I mention because it turned out it had absolutely everything to do with it. I imagined him then as a kind of a scientist and his office his laboratory, where he'd spent the days before I met him, and would continue to spend

414

the rest of my days, analysing me, experimenting with philosophies and theories as to how I'd turned out the way I did, why I made mistakes, why I made good decisions, why I succeeded and why I faltered. My life; his life's work.

'Mrs Morgan thinks I should get rid of all this and just have everything in these little USBs but I don't know, I'm old-fashioned, I like my written reports. It gives them character.'

'Mrs Morgan?' I asked, in a daze.

'You remember the American woman you gave the chocolate bar to? She offered to help me put everything on computer but the agency won't fork out for it so I'll get round to doing it at some stage. It's not like I've anything else to do.' He smiled. 'As you probably remember from our first meeting, I've a lot of the important stuff on the computer already. Oh, and you'll be glad to know I got a new one,' he said, patting a brand-new PC on his desk.

'But . . . but . . . but . . .'

'That's a very good point, Lucy, and one I argued countless times.' He smiled softly. 'Has this become weird to you now?'

'No, but I suppose I'm just realising, I really am your *job*? Just me?'

'You mean, do I do nixers with other people's lives?' he laughed. 'No, Lucy. I'm your soulmate, your other half, if you will. You know that old-fashioned theory that there's another part of you elsewhere . . . that's me.' He waved awkwardly. 'Hi.'

I don't know why I was finding it all so weird now, I'd read about all of this in the magazine; as well as giving us a schedule of her new diet and toning exercises which was displayed in a separate box complete with photos of the food – porridge, blueberries, salmon, a piece of broccoli for those who weren't yet acquainted with the food types – the star interviewee had also gone into extreme detail about how the entire 'Life' system worked. So I knew, I had no cause to be surprised, but seeing it all at play here in an office, so *ordinary,* seemed to take the magic out of it, not that I believed in magic – thanks to my Uncle Harold's overemphatic declarations of stealing my five-year-old nose but my only ever being able to see his fat yellow thumb between his fingers. It looked nothing like my nose; my nose did not have a dirty fingernail and carry the stench of cigarettes.

'How do you know I'm the right person for you?' I continued. 'What if there's some depressed man named Bob sitting on his couch now eating chocolate sandwiches and wondering where on earth his life is, and it's you, and instead you're here, with me, and it's all just a big mistake and—'

'I know,' he said simply. 'Don't you have the same feeling?'

I looked at him then, dead in the eye, and I immediately softened. I knew. Like I'd known when I looked at Blake every day for five years. There was a connection. Every time I looked at Life in a crowded room where nobody and nothing made

416

sense to me, I knew that he was thinking exactly the same thing as me. I knew. I just knew.

'What about your own life?' I asked him.

'It's getting better since we met.'

'Really?'

'My friends can't believe the change in me. They keep thinking we're going to get married even though I'm always telling them that's not how it works.' He laughed, then there was an enormous awkward moment as I felt, oddly I'll admit, like I'd just been dumped.

I looked away, not wanting him to pick up on my confused feelings, but just ended up feeling dizzy as my life literally flashed before my eyes. 'Lucy and Samuel 1986–1996'. That was a fairly thin file. My father and I had had a relatively normal relationship then, if you considered it normal seeing him once a month for Sunday lunch when I came home from boarding school. The following years' files grew thicker for a bit – when I was fifteen years old with a head as stubborn as his we'd begun to lock horns – and then somewhere in my early twenties they got thinner again – I was away for long periods of time, studying in university, which pleased him. The file for the last three years was thicker than any other. There was a file for the relationship I had with each member of my family. I wasn't even the slightest bit intrigued to see what was inside them. I had lived it, I knew what had happened, I'd rather remember them with the certain bias and misinterpretation

417

that time, age and hindsight had brought me. Life continued speaking as normal, still excited and proud of his accomplishment and not at all realising my discomfort.

'I'm still going to keep all of these papers though, even when I've inputted them into the computer. I'm kind of sentimental about them. So, what do you think?' He beamed again at his office, delighted with his achievement.

'I'm so happy for you,' I smiled, feeling sadness. 'I'm so happy that everything is working out for you.'

His smile lessened then as he sensed my mood but I didn't want him to. I didn't want to selfishly turn this special moment for him into being about me.

'Ah, Lucy.'

'No, don't. It's okay. I'm fine.' I brightened up, plastered a fake smile on my face. I knew it looked fake and I knew I sounded fake but it was better than the truth. 'I'm really happy for you, you've come a long way, but if you don't mind, I have to go now. I have . . . em . . . an appointment with this girl I met at the gym who . . .' I sighed, I couldn't lie, not any more. 'Actually, no, I don't have an appointment, but I have to go. I just have to go.'

He nodded, the wind taken out of his sails. 'I understand.'

It suddenly felt awkward.

'Maybe you can meet with Don or something,

tonight?' I asked, more hopeful than I realised, but then Life's face fell.

'No, I don't think that would be a good idea.'

'Why not?'

'Not after last night.'

'You just missed a pint, it's hardly a big deal.'

'It was to him,' he said, serious then. 'You chose Blake, Lucy. He knows that. It wasn't just a pint. It was a decision you had to make. You know that.'

I swallowed. 'I didn't really see it that way.'

Life shrugged. 'It doesn't matter. He does.'

'But it doesn't mean you and he still can't be friends.'

'Doesn't it? Why on earth would he want to spend time with me when it's you that he wants? Blake was the opposite, he wanted you, not your life. And Don, Don can only have your life but not you. Ironic, isn't it?'

'Yeah.' I smiled weakly. 'Well, I'd better go. Congratulations, really, I'm so glad for you.' I couldn't hide the sadness and the words sounded so hollow. So I left.

I bought a tin of cat food and a microwave cottage pie in the corner shop near my block. As soon as I stepped out of the elevator on my floor I froze and then wanted to get back in. My mum was standing outside my door, her back to me as she leaned against the door, and looking as though she had been there for a very long time. My first instinct as I said was to get back into the elevator

419

but immediately after that I thought that something was terribly wrong. I rushed towards her.

'Mum.' She looked up and as soon as I saw her face I felt sick. 'Mum, what's happened?'

Her face crumpled then and she reached out to me. I held her in my arms and comforted her, thinking that's all she needed but then I heard a sniffle, then another, then a squeak and a whimper and I realised she was crying.

'It's Father, isn't it?'

She wailed even more.

'He's dead, is he dead?' I panicked.

'Dead?' She stopped crying then and looked at me in alarm. 'What have you heard?'

'Heard? Nothing. I'm just guessing. You're crying and you never cry.'

'Oh, he's not dead.' She rooted in her sleeve and pulled out a snotty tissue. 'But it's off. The whole thing is off.' She started crying again.

In shock I put one arm around her shoulders and scrambled in my bag with the other for my keys. I ushered her into the apartment. It smelled clean from the carpets and I was so thankful I'd got the job done and changed the light bulb. Mr Pan, who'd already heard our voices at the door, was waiting there eagerly; he rushed in and out of my legs with excitement, unable to contain himself.

'He's absolutely unbearable,' Mum cried. She entered the flat and it was only then that I realised she had quite a sizeable bag in her hand. She barely looked around, just sat up at the breakfast counter on a high stool and put her hands to her head. Mr Pan jumped up on the couch, then to the counter and slowly crept towards her. She reached out and started rubbing him without thinking.

'So the marriage is over?' I asked her, trying to take in this alien who had invaded my mother's body.

'No, no,' Mum said dismissively. 'The *wedding* is off.'

'But the marriage is on?'

'Of course,' she said, wide-eyed, surprised I'd even mention such a thing.

'Okay let me get this straight.' I sat down beside her. 'He is so unbearable you will not renew your vows but you'll stay married to him?'

'I could marry that man once, but I could never marry him twice!' she declared confidently, then she groaned, and collapsed on the counter. Suddenly she popped her head up again. 'Lucy, you have a cat.'

'Yes. This is Mr Pan.'

'Mr Pan,' she smiled. 'Hello, beautiful.' He was in heaven under her touch. 'How long have you had him?'

'Two years.'

'*Two years?* Why on earth wouldn't you tell us that?'

I shrugged, rubbed my eyes and mumbled. 'It made sense at the time.'

421

'Oh, dear, let me make you some tea,' she said, sensing a problem.

'No, you sit down. I'll do it. Go make yourself comfortable on the couch.'

She looked at it, a large brown suede L-shaped couch that took over the entire room.

'I remember this,' she said, then she looked around and took in the rest of the room as if suddenly realising she was inside for the first time. I braced myself but she turned to me with a smile. 'How cosy. You're absolutely right. Your father and I are rattling around that big house like marbles.'

'Thanks.' I filled the kettle. Her phone started ringing; she clamped her handbag shut tighter to quiet it.

'That's him. He's relentless.'

'Does he know where you are?' I tried to hide my amusement.

'No, he does not, and don't you think of telling him.'

She walked to the window trying to figure out how to get around to the couch but on seeing it was shoved up against the windowsill she went back the other direction searching for a way in.

'Mum, what on earth happened?'

Once at the other end of the couch she found it was lodged against the kitchen counter. So she did what any normal person apart from my mother would do and she lifted her leg and climbed over the back of the couch.

'I married a selfish beast, that's what happened. And go ahead and laugh, I know you think we're two old farts but there's life in this old fart yet.' She made herself comfortable on the couch, kicking off her black patent pumps and tucking her feet close to her bum.

'We're out of milk,' I said guiltily. Usually Mum served me tea on a silver tray in her finest bone china. This was not adequate.

'Black is fine,' she said, summoning the mug of tea towards her.

I climbed onto the couch with the mugs in hand and sat on the opposite part of the L. I put my feet up on the coffee table. Never had we both sat together like that before.

'So tell me what happened?'

She sighed and blew on her tea. 'It wasn't one thing, it was a great many things but his behaviour with you was the straw that broke the camel's back,' she said feistily. 'How dare he speak to my daughter like that. How dare he speak to your guest like that and I told him so.'

'Mum, he always speaks to me like that.'

'Not like that. Not like that.' She looked me dead in the eye. 'Up until then he was being his usual bastard self' – my mouth dropped – 'which I could deal with but then, no, that got to be too much. It's this blasted wedding. I wanted to organise it to bring us together, so that we could become closer. I wanted him to put a bit of thought into the last thirty-five years of our marriage and help celebrate it with me. Instead, it's turned into an ostentatious fanfare full of people I honestly don't even like.'

I gasped again. It was like one revelation after another, and it was my mother's mind which intrigued me so much more than the state of their marriage which didn't much concern me. They were grown-ups, it was ridiculous of me to think it had been a bed of roses for them over the past thirty-five years.

'And his mother.' Her hands went flying to her hair as she mock-pulled it out. 'That woman is worse now than on our wedding day. She gives her tuppence worth on every little detail, which frankly means jack shit to me.'

Jack shit?

'Honestly, Lucy, she is so rude and you are so funny with her.' She leaned forward and placed her hand on my knee. 'I wish I could think of the things you say to her.' She chuckled. 'What was the one about the breastfeeding, my lord, that was the best one yet, I thought her dentures were going to fall out of her head.' Then she turned serious again. 'I said after my wedding that I would never organise anything again – she had her paws all over every aspect of that day just like my mother did – but this wedding, I wanted it to be *mine*. All mine. A lovely memory to share with my children.' She looked at me softly and reached for my hand again. 'My lovely daughter. Oh, Lucy, I'm sorry I'm unloading all of this on you.'

'Not at all. Keep unloading, I'm really enjoying it.' She looked surprised.

'I mean, I can't believe you're saying all of this. You're usually so composed.'

'I know.' She bit her lip and looked guilty. 'I know,' she whispered, almost afraid, and placed her head in her hands. Then she bolted upright in her seat and said firmly, 'I know. And that is exactly what I need to be from now on. Unlike me. I've been like me my whole life. I wish I was more like you, Lucy.'

'You what?'

'You're so gung-ho.' She punched the air. 'You know what you want to do and you don't care what anybody says or thinks. You were always like that, even as a child, and I need to be more like that. You see, I never knew what I wanted to be – I still don't know. All I knew was that I was supposed to get married and have babies just like my mother did and my sisters did, I *wanted* to do that. I met your father and I was his wife, that is who I was. Then I had my children.' She reached out to me again, I assumed so I wouldn't take offence at what she was saying. 'And then I was a mother. That's who I was. A wife and a mother but I don't know if I was or if I am of any real value. You and the boys are all grown up, so what am I now?'

'I always need you,' I protested.

'That's sweet,' she said, rubbing my cheek affectionately, then she let go. 'But that's not true.'

'And you're a wonderful grandmother now too.'

She rolled her eyes, then looked guilty again. 'Yes, of course and that is wonderful, believe me it is. But that's me doing things and being things for other people, I'm Jackson and Luke and Jemima's grandmother, I'm your and Riley's and Philip's mother, I'm Samuel's wife, but who am I to me? Some people have always known what they're good at. My friend Ann always knew she wanted to teach, and that's what she did, moved to Spain and met a man and now they drink wine and eat charcuterie and watch the sunset and teach every day.' She sighed. 'I never have known what I wanted to do, what I was good at. I still don't know.'

'Don't speak like that. You're a wonderful mother.'

She smiled sadly. 'No offence, my darling, but I want to be more.' Then she nodded to herself as if in agreement with a silent thought.

'You're angry now,' I said gently. 'Understandably. I couldn't spend three minutes with Father never mind thirty-five years. But perhaps when you've had a chance to cool down, you'll be excited about the ceremony.'

'No,' she said firmly. 'It's off. I mean it.'

'But there's only a month to go. The invitations have already gone out. Everything has been booked.'

'And they can all be cancelled. There's plenty of time. There will be a small fee for some of it – the dresses will always be nice to have and the boys can always do with smart suits. I don't care. I'll send a personal note to everybody to let them know it's cancelled. I am not marrying your father a second time. Once is enough. I have done what people have wanted me to do all of my life. I have been responsible and dutiful and appropriate at all times and on all occasions but to celebrate *my life* – thirty-five years of marriage with three beautiful children – I do not want an event at City Hall filled with everyone from the law world. It is not fitting. It does not represent what I have accomplished in my life, but merely what he has in his profession.'

'What would you like then?'

She looked at me in surprise, but she didn't answer.

'Don't you know?'

'It's not that, it's just that nobody ever asked me.'

'I'm sorry I haven't been helping you. I've been so selfish.'

'Not at all. You've had an exciting adventure with your life. That's important, believe me,' she said wistfully. 'How is that going, by the way?'

'Oh,' I sighed, 'I don't know.'

She looked at me for more and after everything she'd said, about not feeling like a good mother, I couldn't hold back.

'I lost my job, my car got scrapped, I've hurt a perfectly good one-night-stand, Melanie's not speaking to me, neither are the others, my neighbour thinks I'm evil, I went to Wexford to tell Blake that I loved him and wanted him back but realised when I got there that I didn't and now my life is moving on without me. So, that's my life in a nutshell.'

Mum put her delicate fingers to her lips. The corners of her mouth twitched. She let out a little high-pitched, 'Oh.' Then she started laughing. 'Oh, dear, Lucy.' Then she couldn't stop.

'I'm glad my life amuses you,' I smiled, watching her fall back on the couch in hysterics.

Mum insisted on staying the night with me, partly because my birthday was imminent but mostly because she didn't want to interrupt Riley and his boyfriend no matter how much I told her he wasn't gay. While she was showering I hid Mr Pan in an oversized handbag and brought him to the park across the road. Fresh air was supposed to help and so I prayed for the wind to pick up and to blow the thoughts out of my head. My neighbour, Claire, was sitting on a bench in the playground, with the buggy beside her.

'Mind if I join you?'

She shook her head. I sat beside her with Mr Pan on my knee. Claire looked down at him.

'I'm sorry I thought you were—'

'I know,' I interrupted. 'It's okay.'

He began to struggle and so I let him free to roam.

We sat in silence.

'He loves the swings,' she finally said, watching them. 'I've never heard him laugh so much as when he's on them.

'I used to love the swings too,' I said and we fell back into silence.

'How is he?'

'Pardon?' She snapped out of her trance.

'Conor. Yesterday you said he was sick, how is he now?'

'He's not getting any better,' she said distantly.

'Have you brought him to a doctor?'

'No.'

'Maybe you should.'

'Do you think so?'

'If he's not well.'

'It's just . . . I hate doctors. I hate hospitals even more but with Mum sick, I just have to go. I haven't been since . . .' She trailed off, looking momentarily confused. Another few minutes passed before she spoke again. 'My mum is improving.'

'That's great news.'

'Yes,' she smiled. 'It's funny, it takes her going through all that to unite us all again.'

'In my apartment the other day, that was your husband?'

She nodded. 'We're not together but . . .'

'You never know,' I finished for her.

She nodded. 'He's not sick sick.'

'Your husband?'

'No, Conor. He's not sick, he's just different.'

'In what way?'

'He's quieter.' She turned to me then, her eyes – wide and worried – were filled with tears. 'He's much quieter. I don't hear him so much any more.'

We returned our gaze to the unmoving swing and I thought of Blake and the sounds of our memories that were getting quieter, and the feelings I had for him, which felt further and further away from my heart.

'Maybe that's not such a bad thing, Claire.'

'He loved swings,' she said again.

'Yeah,' I replied, noting her use of the past tense. 'I loved swings too.'

CHAPTER TWENTY-EIGHT

'Mum, are you awake?'

It was midnight. Mum was in my bed and I was on the couch and I was wide awake.

'Yes, dear,' she replied instantly, wide awake. The bedside lamp went on. We both sat up.

'Why don't you have a garden party, at the house? Invite close friends and family, keep the flowers you've ordered and the caterers you've booked.'

Mum thought about it, then clapped her hands and beamed. 'Lucy, that's a wonderful idea.' Then her smile faded. 'Problem is, I have to marry your father again.'

'Good point. Well, that's one thing I can't help you with.'

She turned the light off and we lay in silence, both of our minds on overtime. I took my phone from the coffee table and stared at my screen saver. Don's eyes still dominated the screen. I couldn't stop thinking about him. I wanted to contact him to apologise but I didn't know what to say. I had been so disrespectful to him, had clearly chosen Blake over him and then cowered away from dealing with it by leaving it up to my life to tell him. I put the phone back on the table but as if she read my mind, Mum asked out of nowhere, 'What happened to your boyfriend?'

'Blake?'

'No, not him, the young man who came for dinner on Monday.'

'Oh. Don. He wasn't exactly my boyfriend.'

'Wasn't he? You had such chemistry. And I just loved how he defended you in front of your father. Wasn't that something?'

'Yeah,' I said quietly. Then, 'What do you mean, we had chemistry?'

'The way you looked at each other, you both looked like you were caught in a spell.'

My heart flipped.

'Your father and I used to be like that or so people said. You know, we met at one of Daddy's parties. I was still in school and your father was doing an internship with Daddy.'

'I know, you told me.'

'Yes, but I never told you how he chatted me up.'

'Father chatted you up?'

'Of course. I'd brought a friend along with me to the party but she went to the bathroom and so I was alone and this austere, serious-looking young man with a moustache approached me. He had a glass of water in his hand and he said to me, "You look lonely, would you like some company?"'

'That was his chat-up line?' I smirked.

'Yes,' she giggled. 'But it worked because as soon as he sat beside me I was never lonely ever again.'

I swallowed, my eyes filled up. I turned on my side again, picked up the phone to look at Don's eyes and immediately knew what I had to do. It was time to tell a few truths.

Life arrived later than usual the following day, letting himself in with his own key at lunchtime, lost behind a bundle of multicoloured 'Happy Birthday' balloons. 'What on earth is happening in this building, it smells like – oh, my God.' He stopped and looked around.

I didn't stop, kept doing what I was doing which was rolling out pastry. My arms were tired and beads of sweat had broken out on my forehead but things had never been clearer in my mind. Everything in my life was crystal clear now, I knew what I had to do. The more pastry I rolled, the more I knew my fate.

'Are you having a nervous breakdown?' Life asked, with mock concern. 'Because if you are, I'll have to go back to the office and file some serious paperwork. And I'm just done with filing your nervous breakdowns. Typical,' he huffed.

'No, the opposite, in fact. I'm in the midst of a

moment of enlightenment,' I said, still busy with the pastry.

'Have you been reading books again? I told you not to do that. They give you notions.'

I kept working.

'Well, happy thirtieth birthday.' He kissed my head. 'I bought you balloons but my real present was to give you the morning away from me. Priceless.'

'Thank you.' I admired the balloons briefly, then got back to work.

'Have you taken a break at all, crazy lady?' he asked, moving a plate of muffins to the floor and sitting at the counter.

I finally paused for a moment to take in the scene and he had a point. Every available surface in the flat was filled with cupcakes and pies. On the hob more fruit bubbled in a pot: rhubarb and apple. I'd made blueberry muffins, apple tart and pecan and caramel pie slices. After spending the night sending out text messages to spread the word, I had gone to the supermarket early that morning in a quest to find food for my mother. It had been a few years since I'd been to the supermarket, a real one, not a fancy newsagent that had serviced my dinner-for-one appetite for the past two years. I had passed by the food and been pulled directly to the baking section and once there my mind had come alive, as though it had been dormant for quite some time and then there was an explosion of thoughts. Not just ideas, I always had them, but of actual decisions. I'd decided to make a chocolate biscuit birthday cake for myself but then as soon as I'd started, I couldn't stop, it was as though baking was therapy enough for me, things were becoming clearer in my head.

'The more I knead, the more I realise what I need,' I told Life, as I frantically worked the dough. 'I need to knead,' I giggled.

He looked at me in amusement.

'But I also need to speak to my friends, I need to speak to Don, I need to get a job – a proper job, a job that I kind of like, a job I'm qualified to do, I need to finally move on.'

I pushed a blackberry and apple crumble towards him, then I checked my mobile. Everybody else had returned my message but still no response from Don.

'Wow. Enlightenment is an understatement. So you're ready to make changes?'

'Ready is my middle name.' I continued to work the dough, like a woman on a mission.

'Actually, it's Caroline but I know what you mean.' He leaned his chin on his hand and watched me lazily but I could tell he was as pumped as I was. There was a change in me, things were finally moving. 'I received your text message at midnight last night.'

'Good,' I said, lifting the pastry from the counter, resting it on a plate and gently smoothing it down to fill the shape of the dish.

'I take it you sent a similar message to all of your friends?'

435

'Yep.'

'Did they even know it was your birthday? Why didn't they plan something for you?'

'They wanted to plan it months ago but I told them not to. I told them I'd be in Paris with my mum.'

'Is everybody attending this birthday dinner for the surprise announcement?'

'Yep. So far, everybody but Don.'

'And are you going to fill me in on what your little announcement is going to be?'

'Nope.'

He didn't seem to mind.

'So what do you plan to do with all this food?'

'I can give some to the neighbours.'

He was quiet. Then, 'You watched that movie last night, didn't you?'

'What movie?' I tried to act confused.

'Lucy.' He stood up from the stool, losing his patience. 'What are you going to do, open up a cupcake shop like the girl in the film?'

I pinked. 'Why not? It worked for her.'

'Because it's a movie Lucy, they make life-changing decisions in twenty-second montages. This is your *life*. You don't have the first idea about starting up a business, you don't have any money, no financial acumen, no bank would give you the start-up money – you just like fannying about with pink icing.'

I snorted childishly. 'You said fanny.'

He rolled his eyes.

'Well, maybe I'll sell them at the market along the canal today.' I said it as though it was a new thought, but really, apart from the adrenaline of clarity urging me on, I had the excitement of selling them at market at the back of my mind. I was being pro-active, creating work for myself when I didn't have any, it's what everybody was saying to do these days, surely my life would be proud.

'That's a great idea.' He lit up and I immediately sensed the sarcasm. 'Do you have your trader's liability? Have you registered as a food business and complied with HSE/EHO standards?' He looked around the flat. 'Hmm. I wonder. Have you got your own stall? Booked a place to display your goods?'

'No,' I said quietly.

He opened his bag and then threw down a newspaper onto the counter. 'Get real, read this.' It was opened on the jobs page but all I could concentrate on was the fact that the corner of the page had landed in cream. Then he dunked his finger into the bowl of icing and licked his finger. His eyes lit up. 'Mmm. Maybe you could open a cupcake restaurant after all.'

'Really?' I perked up, feeling hopeful.

'No,' he scowled at me. 'But I'm taking this with me.' He lifted a tray of cupcakes and brought them to the couch.

I smiled. 'Oh, by the way, did Don call you?'

'No, sorry,' he said gently.

'Okay. Not your fault.' Then I got back to work.

Life was scoffing cupcakes and shouting at the *Jeremy Kyle Show* when there was a knock on the door. I opened it and immediately slammed it closed again. Life paused the television and looked at me in alarm.

'What's wrong?'

I panicked, trying to motion to the door and act out *landlord* in sign language. He didn't catch on so I ran around the apartment trying to catch Mr Pan who thought it was a game, while all the time my landlord's knocking turned into banging. Eventually I scooped him up and locked him in the bathroom. Life looked at me with a cupcake paused midway to his open lips.

'Am I next? If you want some time alone you should just say.'

'No,' I hissed. I answered the door to my landlord who was red in the face with anger at being ignored.

'Charlie,' I smiled. 'Sorry about the delay, I just had some things lying around. Personal woman things of a personal nature.'

His eyes narrowed suspiciously at me. 'Can I come in?'

'Why?'

'It's my apartment.'

'Yes, but you can't just storm in here unannounced. I live here. I have rights.'

'I've heard reports that you've a cat in here.'

'A cat? Me? No! I'm completely allergic to cats, my arms get all rashy and scratchy and I hate the little buggers. Cats – not my arms – I've been working on them for years.' I showed him my muscles.

'Lucy,' he said in a warning tone.

'What?'

'Let me in so I can take a look.'

I hesitated, then slowly pulled the door wider. 'Okay, but you can't go into the toilet.'

'Why not?' He stepped in and looked around like the child-catcher.

'Her mother has diarrhoea,' Life said, kneeling up on the couch. 'She wouldn't take very kindly to you breaking and entering.'

'I'm not breaking and entering, I'm the landlord. Who are you?'

'Not a cat. I'm her life.'

Charlie looked at him dubiously.

Thankfully, the baking had gotten rid of the cat smell that I never noticed because I was so used to it but that the cat-catcher would sniff out in an instant. Then I remembered Mr Pan's bed and litter box.

'What's going on here?' Charlie asked, surveying the plates of baked goods which dominated every surface.

'Oh, that? I'm just baking, why don't you taste some?' I guided him to the furthest point of the room where he'd have his back to me and handed him a spoon. Then I rushed around the corner to kick Mr Pan's bed under mine. He turned around just as I'd finished. He narrowed his eyes suspiciously and pointed the fork at me.

'Are you up to something?'

'Like what?'

'Have you a licence to do this?'

'Why would I need one? I'm just baking.'

'There's an awful lot of food in here. Who are you going to give it to?'

'She wants to open a cupcake shop,' Life said.

Charlie's eyes narrowed. 'I saw that in a film last night. That was in New York, it would never work here. And if the guy really wanted her back he should have done it before she became a success, instead of bursting into the shop in front of all the customers. I didn't trust his motivations.'

'Really?' I settled down on the back of the couch, happy to have the debate. 'Because I thought they were perfect for each other and the fact that her friend and his friend got together too really showed that—'

Mr Pan started miaowing in the bathroom. And then my mum breezed in the open door and I knew I was royally screwed.

'What is this wondrous smell? Oh, Lucy, how fantastic! If I ever eventually decide to marry your blasted father will you please bake my cake? Wouldn't that be splendid?' Then she noticed Charlie and thinking she was being welcomed into my world of secrets and friends she held her hand out. 'Oh, hello, I'm Lucy's mother. It's lovely to meet you.'

He looked at me with interest. 'So who's in there?'

Mum took back her hand, as though she'd been stung.

'In where?'

'In the toilet?'

'Oh . . . that's . . .' I couldn't lie in front of my life. He owed at least three truths at this stage, but I didn't need to think of anything because Mr Pan mewed again, loudly and perfectly audible.

'Why, that's Mr Pan!' Mum said, astonished. 'However did he get in there?'

'He's a family friend,' Life said casually, taking another bite of a cupcake.

'In fact, look what I got for him today.' She rooted in her shopping bags and came out with a pink tutu. 'He strikes me as the feminine type, for some reason, *always* sitting in your shoes.'

'A very small family friend,' Life added.

'So you do have a cat,' Charlie said, tucking into more pie.

'Oh,' Mum said, suddenly realising what she'd done.

I gave up.

'Get rid of him, Lucy,' Charlie said. 'Pets aren't allowed in this building, you know that. I've had complaints.'

'I can't get rid of him,' I whined. 'He's my friend.'

'I don't care what you think he is, he's a cat. Get rid of him or else move out. Nice to meet you, Mrs Silchester, and . . .' he looked at Life. Then at me. 'You.' He gave me one last warning look. 'I'll be back around to check on you,' he said and then left.

'Well, happy birthday to me,' I said glumly.

Mum glanced at me apologetically. I opened the bathroom door and finally released Mr Pan. He stared from one face to another, knowing something bad had happened.

'No job, no boyfriend, no friends and no place to live. You've really done wonders for me,' I said to Life.

'Just thought I'd do a little decluttering for you,' he replied, then resumed watching Jeremy Kyle. 'He talks to them like they're imbeciles. I should take notes.'

'You don't have to lose your lovely home,' Mum said. 'I'll take Mr Pan, I'd love to have him at the house. Imagine all the space he'd have.'

'But I'd miss him.' I picked him up and cuddled him. He jumped out of my arms, disgusted by the loving gesture.

'All the more reason to visit,' Mum said happily.

'You're not selling it to her, Sheila,' Life piped up. 'And how could you possibly leave all this behind?'

'I love my apartment,' I huffed. 'Two years and seven months I managed to keep you a secret, Mr Pan.'

Mum looked like she felt even more guilty.

'Today is obviously the day to end all secrets,' Life said, serious for once.

Mum clapped her hands excitedly. 'Let's get ready!'

Mum dressed in the bathroom to protect her modesty while I stripped off in front of my life.

'What are you wearing?' he asked.

I surveyed the curtain pole.

'That one?'

He scrunched up his nose.

'The pink one?'

He shook his head.

'The black one?'

He shrugged. 'Try it on.'

I stood up on the windowsill in my underwear and reached for the dress.

'So how do you feel about reaching thirty?'

'The same as I felt yesterday when I was twenty-nine.'

'That's not true.'

'No, it's not true,' I agreed. 'I had an epiphany last night, which was nurtured this morning at the supermarket. I really should go there more often, you know. As soon as I was looking at the raisins I knew exactly what it was that I had to do. But it had nothing to do with turning thirty.'

'No, it had everything to do with the magical supermarket.'

'Maybe it's the way it's all laid out. So structured. So decisive, so matter of fact, so fruit over here and veg over there, and hey, you ice cream, you're cold, you go over there in the fridge with the other cold—'

'Lucy,' he interrupted.

'Yes.'

'That dress makes you look fat.'

'Oh.' I lifted it back over my head.

Life was lying on the bed in a smart summer suit, propped up by my pillows and his arms behind his head.

I tried another dress.

'Your mum seems excited about tonight.'

'I know,' I frowned. 'I think she thinks I'm going to admit to winning an Olympic medal or something. I don't think she quite gets what I'm revealing.'

'What did you tell her?'

'The same as everyone else.'

'That you'd like to invite everybody for "a celebration of the truth",' he said, grandly reading my text from his phone, '"and P.S. if you're getting me a present please just give me cash, love, Lucy".' He raised his eyebrow. 'Charming.'

'Well, there's no point beating around the bush, is there? I need money.'

'This really is a whole new you. I can see your nipples,' he commented.

'Believe it or not, some men actually want to see my nipples,' I huffed, but took it off anyway.

'Not this man.'

'You must be gay,' I said, and we laughed.

'Speaking of gay, how do you think Blake is going to feel about this little gathering?'

'I think by the time Blake hears about it he'll be very pissed off,' I said, getting frustrated as I became tangled in my dress. Finally, with my head trapped inside I pulled the zip down the back and it fell over my head and body. My hair was a static

444

mess, I had to dislocate my arm sockets to zip my dress to the top.

'Let me help,' Life said, finally moving from the bed. He zipped me up. He smoothed down my hair, fixed the front of the dress, gave me the once-over. I waited for him to tell me to invest in some of Philip's plastic surgery or something. 'Beautiful,' he said and that made me smile. 'Come on.' He smacked my arse. 'The truth shall set you free.'

For the first time in two years eleven months and twenty-three days I was first to the dinner table in the Wine Bistro. Life sat one side of me and there was an empty seat to the other side because I hoped. I just hoped. Mum sat beside the empty seat. Riley was next to arrive and brought a bouquet of flowers, a doormat, a three-bean salad and an envelope. I laughed at the gesture, then went straight for the envelope and didn't even read the card before shaking it and counting two hundred euro in four fifty-euro bills. I whooped. Life rolled his eyes.

'You are so obvious.'

'So what? I'm broke, I have no pride.'

Riley greeted Life by bowing at his feet and kissing his hand. 'Mum, I didn't know you were coming,' he said, greeting her next and going for the empty chair beside me.

'I'm expecting someone,' I said, putting the three-bean salad on the chair.

'I'm staying with Lucy,' Mum said happily, pulling out a chair for him on the other side of her.

'Oh, yeah,' Riley laughed, thinking it was a joke.

'Your father's a bastard,' Mum said, sucking on the straw of her vodka, soda and lime.

Riley looked at her in shock, then at me accusingly. 'Have you brainwashed her?'

I shook my head.

'So I take it he's not coming?'

Mum snorted.

'And Philip?'

'He's doing emergency reconstructive surgery on a little boy who was in an accident,' I said, bored.

'Oh, please.' Mum waved her hand in the air. 'Let's not all pretend we don't know Philip is doing boob jobs.'

We both looked at Mum in surprise. Life laughed, enjoying it all.

'Who are you and what have you done with my mother?' Riley asked.

'Your mother is on a much needed break. Sheila, however, is back on duty,' she said forcefully, then she giggled and leaned into me. 'Did you like that?'

'Brilliant, Mum.'

Jamie and Melanie arrived and I stood to greet them. Melanie hung back a little so I hugged Jamie first.

'Happy birthday.' He squeezed me tight, crushing my ribs. 'Melanie has my present for you, we integrated, the present company wasn't doing well so we merged.'

'You forgot, didn't you?'

'Completely.'

'Sorry I didn't return your call last week.'

'Hey, it's fine, it was no big deal, I just wanted to see if you were okay. Hey, Melanie just told me that guy is your life?' Jamie's eyes were wide. 'That's crazy. I read about that in a magazine once. Wait till Adam hears about it. That's what we're here for, isn't it?' he asked, but he didn't wait for the answer before moving off. 'Where do I sit? Beside you, Mrs Silchester?'

I heard Mum giggle behind me.

Melanie's eyes widened. 'Your mum's here?'

'A lot has happened since I've seen you last.'

'Sorry I haven't been in touch.'

'No, I deserved it. It's fine. Melanie, I'm really sorry.'

She just nodded her forgiveness. 'Sorry that I told Jamie he's your life, you know what I'm like with secrets. Oh, my God, speaking of secrets, Jamie just told me that he's still in love with Lisa. Shit, I've just done it again.' She clamped her hand across her mouth.

I barely had time to take it in as Lisa and David arrived next, Lisa waddling with only weeks to go to her due date. People had to pull their chairs in so she could manoeuvre around the tight restaurant, her swollen belly knocking against the backs of people's heads as she went through sideways, which was actually a pointless task because she would be narrower if she'd walked straight on. They were both awkward after our last meeting but I gave Lisa a warm hug and silently whooped

447

when she handed me a sealed envelope. It held promises of treasures within.

David joined the table and sat beside Jamie. Jamie stood up. 'Wow, Lisa, you look amazing.' David glared at him, Melanie pretended to choke and they turned her attention on her, slapping her back. She stopped when I suggested the Heimlich manoeuvre. Then Chantelle arrived with a strange man in tow, or at least a stranger to us, I didn't know what he liked to do in his spare time.

'Hey, birthday girl.' She gave me a kiss and handed me an envelope, probably not even remembering our last encounter. 'Everybody,' she said so loudly that the entire restaurant could hear, 'this is Andrew. Andrew, this is everybody.'

Andrew's cheeks blazed red, to the same colour as his hair, and he gave the table an awkward wave. Chantelle in her usual loud and self-centred voice proceeded to fire names at him as if he was hard of hearing, which he could never remember even if he wasn't completely overwhelmed by meeting so many new faces all at once. Then finally, Adam and Mary arrived; Mary sullen and dressed in black, Adam looking like he felt every accusation he'd ever thrown at me was about to be vindicated. I couldn't wait; though to reveal that I'd been lying about mostly everything for the past few years was hardly a win for me. They handed me an envelope and a potted plant and I didn't even pretend to be happy about it; I could guess that the card contained nothing but courteous words inside and not a banknote in sight.

I remembered the cake I'd brought with me and took it to the fake French waiter.

'Hi,' I smiled.

He barely looked at me.

'It's my birthday today.'

'Mm-hmm.'

'And I brought this cake for myself. In fact, I baked it.' No response. I cleared my throat. 'Could you please bring it to the kitchen, so we can have it for dessert?' He tutted and took it from me, then turned on his heel. 'I'm sorry,' I called out and he paused and turned back around again. 'I'm sorry for all the things I said to you. In French. They were never *bad*, by the way, just random, and I knew you didn't understand.'

'I am French,' he said threateningly, in case anybody else heard.

'Don't worry, I won't tell anybody. I'm not perfect, in fact I've told lies myself. Lots of lies. But tonight I'm going to tell the truth.'

He looked at the group and then back at me and spoke quietly in his Irish accent, 'Only French speakers needed apply, the ad said.'

'I understand.'

'I needed the job.'

'I completely understand. I need a job too and I speak French – are there any going?'

'Now you're trying to steal my job?' He looked horrified.

'No, no, no, not at all, I'm not trying to do that. I mean, I would work *with* you.'

449

He looked at me as though he would rather I stick daggers in his body.

I made my way to the table and the chatter suddenly died. The seat beside mine was still empty and I looked at my watch; there was still time. I sat at the head of the table and all eyes were on me. I didn't blame them, I had summoned them here with a dramatic text about truth and then swiftly followed it with a demand for money and now the red light was on. Time for action. The waiter came to the table and slowly began pouring water. I was going to wait until he was gone, but he was moving so slowly I got the sense he wasn't budging until he heard what I had to say.

'Okay, thank you for coming. It's not a big deal, but it's a big deal to me. Something happened and it changed the current course of my life which something happened to again and now it's taking another course.' Chantelle looked confused. Andrew, who had never met me, looked uncomfortable as if he shouldn't be there, but Mary nodded in complete understanding. 'And in order for me to move on, I need to share it with you.' I took a deep breath. 'So—'

On that note the restaurant door opened and my heart lifted, hoping, hoping, hoping . . . but Blake stepped inside.

CHAPTER TWENTY-NINE

'Blake.' My voice was a barely a whisper but they all heard me and turned around to stare at him. Blake looked around the room and his eyes fell upon our table and then on me. We shared a look: his was angry, mine was pleading for understanding.

'So that's who the seat is for!' Melanie squealed. 'Are you guys back together?'

There were murmurs of surprise and intrigue and excitement but then the door opened again and Jenna arrived in the restaurant, and everybody turned to me in confusion. I looked angrily at Adam, assuming that it was he who had invited Blake without telling me, but his face was as shocked as mine. His friend had surprised him too. Everybody stood up to greet Blake; their hero had arrived.

'You didn't tell me you were coming,' Adam said, giving his friend a handshake, seeming put out.

'I'm just up for the night. Adam, this is Jenna,' Blake said, stepping aside and pushing Jenna into the limelight. She seemed overwhelmed by it all and incredibly embarrassed to be at my thirtieth birthday celebrations and so she should have been. She looked at me half-apologetically and half-jubilantly as she wished me happy birthday and apologised for not having brought a gift.

'I'm sorry,' she said, her voice a whisper. 'I thought he was just coming in to say hello to someone.'

'Yes.' I pasted on a smile, though I did genuinely feel sorry for her. 'He does that.' As soon as she moved on to meet the others, I felt a hand on my arm tugging me.

'Don't do this,' Blake said, in a low voice.

'Blake, you don't even know what I'm trying to do.'

'I know you're looking for a few fans and you need a bad guy. I know exactly what you're doing. Just listen to me, don't do it. We can figure out another way to sort things out with them.'

'Blake, it's not about *them*,' I said through gritted teeth. 'This is about *me*.'

'And what you're about to do is about me too so I think it's fair that I have a say, don't you?'

I sighed.

'Looks like we need two more chairs,' Riley said, all gameshow host trying to keep the atmosphere up.

I looked at the empty chair beside me, looked

at my watch. It was a half an hour late, Don wasn't coming. 'No,' I said sadly, 'just one more chair, he can have this one.' Everyone moved up a place and mum was beside me.

Blake sat at the head of the table directly opposite me with Jenna next to him. She was at the corner beside Andrew, and they were like two spare tools together who empathised with each other.

'Well, look at this,' Chantelle boomed, 'just like old times. Apart from him,' she referred to Andrew. 'I was dating Derek back then.' She pretended to retch. Andrew went puce again.

'So what did I miss?' Blake asked the table but looked at me.

'Nothing yet,' David said, bored.

'Lucy was just about to share something important with everyone,' Life said, looking pointedly at Blake. 'Something that means a lot to *her*.'

'No, it's okay,' I said quietly, drained. 'Forget about it.'

'Okay,' Blake jumped in, 'because I've a bit of important news myself.' All heads swiftly turned to him as if it was a tennis match. 'I just heard that my deal came through for my new cookbook and TV show.'

There was a collective cheer, mostly from our friends; my family and my life weren't overly enthused but they were polite – apart from Life who booed but only so that I could hear. It wasn't an entirely overenthusiastic cheer from the rest of the gang either, but I'm not sure if Blake noticed, and if he did he was ignoring the signs to shut up and had begun talking about a fish course he'd designed from sardines he'd eaten in Spain which were cooked on a hot stone under a scorching summer sun. Adam was looking a little concerned by Blake's interruption, as it appeared to everyone to have been an obvious one. Jenna was the only person who seemed rapt; everybody else listened politely apart from Lisa who looked fit to burst. I don't know if that was due to her personal discomfort or because Blake was talking incessantly about himself. Jamie had given up listening and instead was ogling Lisa's watermelon breasts.

'My word,' Mum turned to me and said quietly. 'He hasn't changed a bit, has he?' From the way that she said it I knew she didn't mean it in a good way and I was surprised, because I'd always thought she'd been fascinated by him and his stories. Perhaps she had just been appropriately polite and attentive. Pockets of conversation had begun to form around the table as people tuned out of Blake's stories – each seemed to lead seamlessly into another – until eventually it was just Blake telling Lisa, and Lisa was not to be messed with.

Finally she yawned. 'Blake,' she held her hand up. 'I'm sorry, can you please stop?' All other conversations died down to listen to her. 'I don't mean to be rude but I don't care any more. I'm uncomfortable and I'm disgusting and I have no patience and I'm just going to say what I think. Before you arrived, Lucy was about to tell us something, something important and we all care because Lucy never tells us anything important. Not any more. No offence, Lucy, but you don't. You didn't even tell us about the weirdo in your office who held a gun to your head, I had to hear it from Belinda Bitchface who lives around the corner from me, do you remember her? She's a single mother with three kids with three different fathers and has the face of a scrunched-up nipple and it serves her right. Don't look at me like that, Mrs Silchester, she deserves it, honestly – if you heard the things she used to do to us when we were at school. Anyway, she told me he had a gun to your head and I was mortified because I didn't even know, and it wasn't just that.' Lisa looked at Blake again. 'She doesn't tell us *anything. Nothing.*'

'It was a water pistol,' I said, trying to calm them all down as they gave out to me for not telling them anything, rattling off everything in my life that they'd heard from other people which I'd never told them about. Blake listened to them all, fascinated.

'Silence!' Lisa finally shouted and again the restaurant became hushed and stared at her. 'Not you, just them,' she gestured at us. 'Let Lucy speak.'

The waiter returned to fill my glass with water and gave me a smug smile. He took his time and moved on to another glass. I stared him down and finally he left the jug on the table and walked away.

'Okay fine. Blake, can I, please?'

'You don't need to ask his permission,' Chantelle snapped. 'We've heard enough about sardines for one night.'

Jamie smirked.

Blake crossed his arms, looked nervous beneath the tough exterior.

'I just want to say that this is for me, it is not to make anybody into the bad guy. Blake had a part in it but I take full responsibility for the rest of it. It's *my* doing – not his.'

Blake seemed satisfied by that.

'So do not attack Blake,' I urged. Then I paused. 'I did not,' I began slowly, 'break up with Blake. He left me.'

Mouths fell open. They stared at me silently, in shock, then shocked faces turned to scowls, and then those faces turned away from me and towards Blake.

'Hey, hey, hey, not his fault, remember?'

With gritted teeth they all looked back at me. Except for Adam; he looked at Blake questioningly and when Blake wouldn't meet his eye he saw it as an admission and his look turned to anger.

'I was very happy in our relationship. I was completely in love. I didn't feel that we had any problems but obviously I wasn't paying enough attention because Blake wasn't happy. He ended the relationship, for his own reasons, which he is perfectly entitled to,' I said forcefully, trying to quash the uprising.

'Why did you say she left you?' Melanie asked Blake.

'*We* decided to say that because I was embarrassed,' I answered. 'Because I was confused and I was worried what people would think and because I didn't have any answers and I thought that if I said I just wasn't happy and I decided to leave him then it would all be much easier. Blake was helping me. He was trying to make it easier for me.'

Blake had the decency to look embarrassed.

'And whose idea was this?' Jamie asked.

'I don't know,' I said dismissively, 'It's not important. The point is that it set off a chain of events in *my* life that—'

'But who suggested the idea first?' Mary interrupted.

'It doesn't matter. This is about me now,' I said selfishly. 'I felt it would be easier to deal with, only it wasn't because you all held it against me, and thought that I cheated.' I looked at Adam. 'I assure you, I absolutely did not.'

'Did *you*?' Melanie asked Blake angrily.

'Hey, I told you not to attack him, it's about *me*.' But no one was listening to me.

'Can you remember who thought of it first?' Jamie asked Blake.

'Look,' Blake sighed and leaned forward, elbows on the table, hands clasped. 'It might have been my idea but it wasn't to back away from any blame, it was genuinely to make it easier for Lucy—'

'And you,' Mum said.

'Mum, please,' I said quietly, embarrassed it was all turning out as Blake had feared.

'So it was your idea?' Riley confirmed.

Blake sighed. 'I guess.'

'Lucy, continue,' Riley said, and that was that.

'Well, that day that he, that *we* broke up we told you all that I'd left him and I was very confused. I was very sad and very confused. I had a day off work, I'd taken it off because, Blake, remember we were supposed to go strawberry picking with your niece in . . .' I looked at Blake and he looked genuinely sad. 'Anyway,' I changed the subject, 'I had a bit to drink at home. Quite a bit.'

'As you should,' Lisa said, looking at Blake angrily.

'And work phoned me and told me to collect a client from the airport. And I did.'

Mum looked shocked.

'Dad knows this, by the way. That's why we had the argument. And Riley, whatever you heard about that day from Gavin is correct. And for the record, he isn't cheating on his wife with a man. I lost my job and I lost my driving licence but I couldn't tell anyone that.'

'Why not?' Melanie asked.

'Because . . . well, I tried to. Chantelle, do you remember?'

Chantelle looked like a deer caught in headlights. 'No?'

'I called you and told you I'd gotten really drunk

458

the day before and you asked me why and I said because I was upset and you said why the hell should I be upset, I was the one who left Blake.'

Chantelle's hands went flying to her mouth. 'Lucy, you know better than to ever listen to me. So this is my fault?'

'No,' I shook my head. 'It's really not, but it made me realise that I was locked into this lie and I was going to have to stick to it. I sold the car and started cycling and I desperately needed a job because I needed the money and the only one I could find was at Mantic but I had to have Spanish to take it so I pretended that I did. What was one little lie in a line of so many bigger ones? But then I needed Mariza to help me or I'd lose my job and I couldn't tell anyone, and so I rented a studio flat the size of this table and none of you were ever there because I was ashamed that everything had fallen apart and that my life was so crap and all of you were doing so well. I was embarrassed, that's all, but then I grew to like my life and it was just me in this bubble where only I knew the truth, but then my life contacted me – this man to the right of me, who helped me see that I'd tied myself into a big knot and that the only way to get out of it and move on was to tell you the truth because it's all connected – every little truth is connected to a big lie – and in order to tell you one I'd have to tell you them all and I couldn't, so I didn't, so I either didn't tell you anything or I told you a lie and I'm sorry for that. I'm really sorry. And Blake, I'm sorry to drag you into this but I had to. It wasn't about you, or turning you into the bad guy, it was about me and turning everything into what it should be.'

He nodded, full of understanding, looking sorry and sad all at once. 'I had no idea, Lucy, I'm so sorry. I honestly thought at the time that it was the best thing.'

'For you,' Mum repeated.

'Mum,' I said, annoyed.

'Anything else?' Life asked and I thought about it.

'I don't like goat's cheese.'

Lisa gasped.

'I know, I'm sorry, Lisa.'

'But I asked you five times!' she referred to a dinner party she'd held two months ago where she'd singled me out at the table for pushing the cheese around my plate. 'Why didn't you just say?'

I think everybody at the table understood why I hadn't said, even a *goat* would have eaten that cheese and Lisa would have eaten me if I hadn't eaten it. Still, it didn't explain why I'd ordered it most times we'd eaten out in an effort to prove her theory wrong, and as a result I hated it even more.

'Anything else?' Life asked again.

I thought hard. 'I have been babysitting my neighbour's invisible baby? Is that it? No? Oh. Oh, yes, and I have a cat. I've had him for two and a half years. His name is Mr Pan but he prefers Julia or Mary.'

Life finally appeared satisfied – but the others stared at me with shocked expressions trying to take it all in. There was a long silence.

'So that's it, guys, my life in a nutshell. What do you think?' I asked nervously, waiting for them to stand up and storm out or throw drink in my face.

Adam turned to Blake and said angrily, 'So *you* left Lucy?'

I sighed and pushed away my salad, appetite gone.

'What's wrong?' Melanie asked, eyes wide. 'Did you lie about liking salad too?' She smiled then and we both had a private chuckle while everyone turned on Blake and gave him the abuse they'd been giving me for almost three years.

'I'm sorry, could you all please be quiet,' Jamie finally spoke up, and everyone hushed. 'I think that even though it should go without saying, I should say it anyway. I think I can speak on everyone's behalf – well, almost everyone,' he threw a look at Andrew, 'because I think it's clear to see you've never liked Lucy –' we laughed as Andrew reddened again – 'when I say, Lucy, I can't believe you felt you couldn't tell us any of this before. It would never have changed our opinion of you – we've always known you're a disaster no matter what.'

Everyone laughed.

'No, seriously, Lucy, we would have been your friends no matter what dumb job you had or no matter where you were living. You know us better than to think we care about any of that crap.' He genuinely seemed insulted.

'I suppose I did know that, but the lie got too big and then I was afraid I'd lose you all when you found out I was a psychotic lying freak.'

'And that's a very valid point,' Jamie said sombrely. 'But it's not going to happen.'

'I second that,' Melanie added and everybody else joined in, apart from Andrew, Jenna and Blake, of course, who was too busy feeling the most uncomfortable he'd ever felt. Life was silent as he observed it all, making mental notes for the next file for his new office. I caught his eye and he winked, so for the first time in two years eleven months and twenty-three days, I finally relaxed.

'Now down to the important stuff,' Riley said. 'Did nobody else hear what I heard? Lucy, you said you have a neighbour who has an *invisible* baby? Is that by any chance—'

'Never mind that,' Lisa butted in. 'She hates bloody goat's cheese!'

And willing to face whatever punishments were coming their way, they all started to laugh. After what felt like a very long time, Lisa joined in.

Riley dropped Mum home to Glendalough; she'd drunk too much at dinner and had come over all emotional and drunk-dialled Father. He wanted her home immediately, partly because he missed her but mostly because he was embarrassed she was out in public in that state and especially with me.

The others had insisted on bringing me to Melanie's club to celebrate my birthday and the truth; but I was exhausted, drained from the revelations, and I just wanted to go home and spend time with my life and my cat. When I'd announced this Melanie had blurted out, 'Ah, you can't even stay until the end of your own birthday party!' which told me she still definitely had issues with my Cinderella timekeeping. Blake had sloped off before dessert, taking a relieved Jenna with him, so it was in Life's hands to walk the birthday girl home.

I thought we would stay up half the night analysing everything about the big reveal. It had been years in the lead-up and now that it was over, dealt with, I almost didn't know what to do with the big hole in my mind where the stress of it had once been. When I snapped out of my thinking, I realised I was walking alone and Life had stopped suddenly under the street-light outside my apartment block. I turned to him, feeling that hole in my head quickly being replaced by a new worry. He shoved his hands in his pockets. His demeanour had all the ingredients of a goodbye and suddenly my heart both drummed and ached. I hadn't thought about not being with him after I had fixed everything, partly because I never thought I was going to fix anything but mostly because I couldn't bear to think about a day going by without spending time with him.

'Aren't you going to come in?' I asked, trying to keep the shrill tone out of my voice.

'Nah,' he smiled, 'I'll give you a break.'

'I don't need a break, honestly, come in. I've about twenty cakes I need help eating.'

He smiled. 'You don't need me, Lucy.'

'Of course I need you, you don't expect me to eat them on my own,' I said, deliberately misinterpreting him.

'That's not what I meant,' he said gently and gave me that look. *That* look. That *goodbye my best friend, I'm sad but let's pretend to be happy about it* look.

I felt the lump in my throat swell to astronomical sizes but I had to keep my tears in check. Even if my mum had broken the Silchester rules, I wasn't about to start or we'd all fall like dominoes, and the world needed emotionally retentive people, it was imperative to our life cycle. 'Of all people, I need you.'

Life sensed my desperation and did the honourable thing and looked away to give me a moment to compose myself. He looked up to the sky and breathed in slowly and then out. 'It's a beautiful night, isn't it?'

I hadn't noticed; if he'd told me it was day I would have believed him. I studied him and it struck me then how beautiful he was, how handsome and strong, how confident and secure he always made me feel, always there for me no matter what. I had an overwhelming urge to kiss him. I lifted my chin up and leaned in to him.

'Don't,' he said suddenly, turning to me and placing a finger on my lips.

'I wasn't going to do anything.' I backed away, embarrassed.

We were silent.

'I mean, okay, I was, but – it's just that you look so handsome and you've been so good to me and . . .' I took a deep breath. 'I really love you.'

He smiled, dimples forming in both cheeks. 'Remember the day we first met?'

I scrunched up my face and nodded.

'You really hated me then, didn't you?'

'More than anyone I'd ever met. You were disgusting.'

'So I've won you over, it's mission accomplished. You couldn't stand to be alone and in the same room as your own life and now you actually *like* me.'

'I said I love you.'

'And I love you,' he said and my heart surged. 'So we should celebrate.'

'But I'm losing you.'

'You just found me.'

I knew he was right, I knew that as much as I was feeling he was my everything right there and then, it wasn't romantic, it wasn't physical and it just wasn't possible; that would make for an entirely different magazine interview. 'Will I ever see you again?'

'Yeah, sure, the next time you mess up. Which, knowing you, won't be too long away.'

'Hey!'

'Just joking. I'll check in on you now and then, if you don't mind.'

I shook my head, not able to speak.

'And you know where my office is, don't you? So you can visit me whenever you like.'

I nodded again. Pursed my lips, felt the tears almost come, *almost* come.

'I came here to help, and I helped. Now if I stay, I'll only get in the way.'

'You wouldn't be in the way,' I croaked.

'I would,' he said gently. 'There's only enough room for you and the couch in that flat.'

I tried to laugh but couldn't.

'Thanks, Lucy. You helped fix me too, you know.'

I nodded, couldn't look at him. Looking at him would mean tears and tears were bad. I concentrated on his shoes instead. His new, polished shoes that didn't match the man I'd first met.

'OK, so it's not goodbye. It's never goodbye.'

He kissed me on the top of my head, the only part of me I'd let him see. It was a long kiss and then I rested my head on his chest, feeling his heartbeat racing as fast as mine.

'I'm not leaving until you're safely inside. Go on.'

I turned around and walked away, every footstep loud in the silent night. I couldn't turn around at the door, I had to keep looking forward, the tears were going to come, they were going to come.

Mr Pan looked groggily up at me from his bed, acknowledged me and then went back to sleep; it occurred to me that this was the end of the life that I had lived with him here in our bubble. Either he had to go or we both did. That made me sad too but he was a cat and I wasn't going to cry over a cat so I toughened up and felt good that I had beaten the tears, I was stronger than them, all they meant was that you felt sorry for yourself and I wasn't sorry for myself. All I wanted to do was bury myself under my duvet and not think about anything that had happened that night but I couldn't, because I couldn't reach the zip on the back of my dress. I hadn't been able to close it earlier; Life had done it for me. I just simply couldn't get my arms around to reach it, any angle I tried. I contorted my body in different directions trying to reach the zip but it wouldn't work, I couldn't reach. I was sweating and panting, angry beyond belief that I couldn't get the stupid dress off. I looked around the apartment for something to help. Nothing. No one. It was then I realised I was well and truly alone.

I climbed into bed with my dress still on. And I cried.

CHAPTER THIRTY

I lay in bed for a week – at least it felt like a week but it was probably no more than four days, which was still good going. The morning after my birthday I had eventually waited until I'd heard sounds in Claire's apartment to knock on her door for help with my dress. It was answered by her husband in his boxers and with tousled hair, which told me enough; that she'd had to finally let go of something too and now Conor's memory was free to be celebrated.

There were no disruptions from Life arriving unannounced at inappropriate times, no envelopes landing on my newly cleaned carpet. I had plenty of messages from my friends asking me to go out, arranging to meet, apologising, trying to make up for lost time, trying to take advantage of my new-found truthfulness, and I didn't ignore them but I didn't go out to meet them either and I certainly didn't lie. I told them that I wanted and needed to be alone, I wanted to enjoy living in my little bubble for a little longer, and for the first time in my life it wasn't a lie. Mum had taken Mr Pan to Glendalough and while I missed him I knew he was in a far better place; it wasn't fair to him to be cooped up in here and it was either live with Mum or live with me in a cardboard box under a bridge, and I doubted I'd fit the brown suede couch in a shopping trolley with the rest of our possessions. The choice wasn't that difficult in the end. I likened it to a spring clean; as soon as I'd started decluttering, the rest of the baggage was falling away easily.

Sometime in the four-day hibernation retreat I'd actually gone shopping for real food that had to be prepared and cooked. As out of practice as I was, I had to remember that real food took organisation and had to be prepared before hunger hit. On top of cleaning the three-year-old muck from my summer festival Wellington boots, if I collected enough stamps at the supermarket I would get a free rug; it would take me a year of real food shopping but it was an incentive to keep going back. I'd bought lemons and limes and filled a small vase in a nod to my friend in the magazine. I'd rather I never had to work again, I still hadn't found a *passion* for anything, that nauseating word I kept hearing people say to me, and even though I had no idea what I wanted to do with my life – an unrealistic cupcake shop dream aside – I was starting to get on the right way of thinking. I would try and find something that marginally interested me and which paid the bills. Progress. However, my birthday money wouldn't last for ever, in fact it was paying next month's rent so I needed a job quickly. I showered and dressed and made sure I was perfectly prepared with a fresh cup of coffee as I sat at the breakfast counter to read the newspaper Life had flung at me on my birthday. I hadn't actually looked at it when or since he'd thrown it down on the counter – I was too distracted by the blob of cream the corner page had lifted from my sponge cake – but as soon as I began to read, I was lost. Circled in red in what I assumed must be a suggested responsible job in the middle of the jobs page was in fact an advertisement for a flatmate in the property section. I was annoyed that Life was suggesting I leave the flat that he knew I loved more than most things in my life and I was about to crumple up the page and throw it away when a thought occurred to me. He wouldn't ask me to leave the apartment. I read it again. And again. And then when I realised what it was, a smile formed on my lips and I wanted to give Life a big kiss. I ripped out the page and jumped off the stool.

I hopped off the bus with a spring in my step but quickly it went flat. Momentarily lost, I finally found my bearings when I spotted Don's beacon, a bright red magic carpet atop the Magic Carpet Cleaner van. It made me smile; the superhero's car.

I took out my pocket mirror and got to work, then I buzzed the intercom.

'Yes?' Don answered, out of breath.

'Hello,' I said, disguising my accent. 'I'm here for the interview.'

'What interview?'

'The flatmate interview.'

'Uh. Hold on . . . I don't . . . who is this?'

'We spoke on the phone.'

'When was this?'

I could hear paper rustling.

'Last week.'

'Maybe that was Tom. Did you speak to someone called Tom?' I tried not to laugh as I heard him mentally cursing Tom.

'Is he the fella moving in with his girlfriend?'

'Yes,' he said, annoyed. 'What did you say your name is?'

I smiled. 'Gertrude.'

There was a long pause.

'Gertrude what?'

'Guinness.'

'Gertrude Guinness,' he replied. 'I can't quite see you on the screen.'

'Can't you? I'm looking right in it,' I said, holding the palm of my hand flat over the camera at the intercom.

He paused again. 'Okay take the lift to the third floor.' There was a buzz and the main door unlatched.

In the elevator mirror I fixed my eye patch and

made sure all my teeth apart from the front ones on the top and bottom were blacked out. Then I took a deep breath, thinking, here goes everything. The elevator doors slid open and there he was standing at the open door, leaning against the doorframe, arms folded. When he saw me I knew that he wanted to be mad but he couldn't help it, and he smiled, then he threw his head back and laughed.

'Hello, Gertrude,' he said.

'Hello, Don.'

'You must be the hideous toothless woman with an eye patch with ten kids that I spoke with on the phone.'

'Your wrong number. That's me.'

'You're crazy,' he said softly.

'About you,' I said cheesily, and he smiled again, but then it faded.

'I was led to believe you and Blake were back together. Is that true?'

I shook my head. 'Didn't you get my message about dinner last week? I wanted to talk to you.'

'I did. But . . .' He swallowed. 'I told you I don't want to be second choice, Lucy. If he didn't want you back then—'

'He did want me back,' I interrupted. 'But I realised it's not what I wanted. *He* wasn't what I wanted.'

'Is that true?'

'I don't lie. Not any more. To quote one of the most beautiful sentences that was ever said to me, "I don't love you."' He smiled, and feeling encouraged, I continued. 'But I think that I easily could and that I probably very quickly will. Though I can't promise anything. It could all very possibly end in tears.'

'That's so romantic.'

We laughed.

'I'm sorry I messed you around, Don. It will be the first and probably the last time I ever do that.'

'Probably?'

'Life is messy,' I shrugged, and he laughed.

'So are you really here for a flatmate interview?' He looked uncomfortable.

'Yes,' I said sombrely. 'We've met three times now and slept together once, I think it's time we both took the plunge and moved in together.'

He paled slightly.

'Hell no, Don, I love my little hovel and I'm staying put and I'm nowhere near being emotionally secure enough to live with another human being.'

He looked relieved.

'I am here for *you*.'

He pretended to think about it, at least I hoped he pretended.

'Come here, you.' He reached for my hands and pulled me close. He gave me a lingering kiss, which left his mouth covered in the eyeliner I'd used to blacken my teeth. I decided not to tell him, it was more fun that way. 'You know, we've actually slept together *twice*,' he corrected me. 'Which is a horrible number,' he rolled up his nose with disdain. '*Two.*'

'Yuck,' I played along.

'But three,' he brightened. 'Three, is a number I like. And four? Four is a *great* number.'

I laughed as he tried to pull off my eye patch.

'No, I like this, I'm keeping it on.'

'You're nuts,' he said warmly, kissing me again. 'Fine. On one condition.'

'Which is?'

'Everything comes off except for the eye patch.'

'Agreed.'

We kissed again. Then he pulled me inside and kicked the door closed.

EPILOGUE

Saturday 6 August in Glendalough was a stunning day as meteorologists had predicted, and one hundred members of our parents' family and close friends milled around the grass with champagne in their hands, enjoying the sun on their skin as they happily chatted and waited for it all to begin. The back lawn of my parents' home had been transformed for their vow-renewal ceremony with one hundred seats separated by a white aisle leading to a white hydrangea-adorned trellised archway. Nearby was a marquee filled with ten tables of ten, for which the dozens of shades of green mountainside provided the backdrop. A single white rose sat in a tall vase in the centre of each table and at the top of the room was an enlarged photograph of the day the vows had first been said, thirty-five years ago, before Riley and Philip and I had come along.

As I walked around the side of the marquee I

spied Father dressed appropriately for the summer setting in a white linen suit, and talking with Philip. I hid behind a blue and pink hydrangea bush to eavesdrop, momentarily thinking father and son might be having a moving moment, but then I remembered this was real life, not the film about the girl with the cupcake shop who had reunited with her father. At the same time as I had the realisation, Philip turned away from Father, red faced and angry, and stormed off in my direction. Father didn't even bother to watch him leave; instead he sipped on his glass of white wine which he held by the stem, firmly between his finger and thumb, and watched the view in the distance. As Philip passed the bush I grabbed his arm and pulled him into the shrubbery.

'Ow, Jesus, Lucy, what the hell are you doing?' he asked angrily, then once he'd calmed, started laughing. 'Why are you hiding in a bush?'

'I was trying to witness father-and-son bonding time.'

Philip snorted. 'I've just been informed I've brought embarrassment on the family.'

'What, you too?'

He shook his head disbelievingly, then had the sense to finally laugh about it.

'Is it about the boobs?'

He laughed. 'Yes, it's about the boobs.'

'I'm afraid Majella in *that* dress gave it away for you.'

Philip laughed and reached out to my hair to remove a leaf. 'Yeah, but it was worth it.'

'"The gift that keeps on giving",' I said and he laughed loudly. I punched his arm and he clamped his hand over his mouth. I felt like we were kids again, hiding from a pending family day out to a museum or our parents' friends' house where we would be ignored and would have to sit politely alongside the adults being seen and not heard. We both looked at Father looking out to the distance, away from the crowd of people who'd gathered there for him.

'He doesn't mean it, you know,' I said, trying to make Philip feel better.

'Yes, he does. He means every single word and you know it. It's just in him to be miserable and judgemental to everybody in his life apart from himself.'

I looked at him in surprise. 'I thought that role was just especially for me.'

'Don't think so much of yourself, Lucy. I was born before you, I've given him at least a few more years worth of disappointment than you have.'

I tried to think back to a time when I'd witnessed Father bearing down on Philip but couldn't.

'He's fine when you're doing what he wants but if you divert in any way at all . . .' he sighed and it was filled with resignation. 'He wants the best for us, he just has no idea that the best for us in his eyes and the best for us in reality are not one and the same.'

'So Riley is still the golden child,' I said, bored. 'We'll have to take him out.'

'Done. I just told Father he was gay.'

'What is it with you and Mum? Riley isn't gay!'

'I know that,' he laughed. 'But it'll be fun listening to Riley get himself out of that one.'

'I've already got a bet on with him that he can't say "transcendent elephant" in his speech. He's not having a good day.'

We laughed.

'He'll pull it off, he always does,' Philip said good-naturedly, then pushed himself out of the hedge and back on the path. 'Shouldn't you go up to Mum now?' He glanced at his watch.

I looked at Father again. 'I will in a minute.'

'Good luck,' he said, dubiously.

I deliberately made my presence known so as Father wouldn't get a fright when I appeared.

'I already saw you in the bush,' he said, not turning around.

'Oh.'

'Though I won't enquire as to what you were doing. God knows, you won't find a profession in there.'

'Yeah, about that . . .' I started, feeling the adrenaline of anger surge through my body again. I tried to control it. I got straight to the point. 'I'm sorry I lied to you about how I left my job.'

'You mean about how you were fired?' He looked down at me, through the spectacles at the end of his nose.

'Yes.' I gritted my teeth. 'I was embarrassed.'

'So you should have been. Your behaviour was

despicable. You could have found yourself behind bars. And they would have been right to do it, you know.' He left a long pause after every sentence as if each was a new thought and nothing at all to do with the previous one. 'And there would have been nothing I could have done about it.'

I nodded and counted to five, keeping my anger at bay.

'It's not really about the drink-driving, though, is it?' I finally said. 'It's me. You have a problem with me.'

'Problem, what problem?' he mumbled, already irritated that I'd pointed out a weakness in him. 'I have no *problem*, Lucy, I merely want you to rise to the challenge, show responsibility and make something of yourself, instead of this . . . idleness . . . this nothing that you so much want to be.'

'I don't want to be nothing.'

'Well, you're doing a ruddy good job of it, regardless.'

'Father, don't you realise that no matter what it is that I do, you won't be happy, because you want me to be what *you* want me to be, and not necessarily what I need to be, for me?' I swallowed.

'What on earth are you talking about? I want you to be a decent human being,' he snapped.

'I am one,' I said quietly.

'One who offers something to society,' he continued as if he hadn't heard me, and set off on a rant about responsibility and duty, each sentence beginning with, 'One who . . .'

I counted to ten silently in my head and it worked; my anger and hurt had subsided and on the day that it was, after the conversation I'd had with Philip, I didn't feel as uptight about his lack of approval as I usually did. Though I believed in self-development and evolution for all of the human race, I knew I would never be able to change him or his opinions of me, and as I would never want to try to please him, an eternity of locking horns was in our future. However, deliberate attempts to displease him would no longer be on my to-do list, at least not intentionally, but one can never predict how the subconscious works. I suddenly felt light, the very last lie to myself undone; Father and I would not ever be friends.

I tuned back into his rant '. . . so if you've nothing further to add we should end this conversation immediately.'

'I've nothing further to add,' I grinned.

He wandered off to Uncle Harold whom he despised and who could not take his eyes off Majella's chest.

Mum was in her bedroom preparing when I knocked on the door and entered. She turned around from the full-length mirror.

'Wow, Mum, you look amazing.'

'Oh,' she wafted her eyes. 'I'm being so silly, Lucy, I'm nervous,' and she laughed as her eyes filled. 'I mean, what have I got to worry about? It's not as if he's not going to show!'

We both laughed.

'You look beautiful,' she said.

'Thank you,' I smiled. 'I love the dress. It's perfect.'

'Oh, you're probably just saying that to please the fussy old bride.' She sat down at her dressing table.

I pulled out a tissue and gently dabbed at the corners of her eyes where her tears had smudged her make-up. 'Believe me, Mum, I don't lie any more.'

'Is Don here?'

'He's outside talking to Uncle Marvin who asked me in front of Father if he'd just seen me in an infomercial for Magic Carpet Cleaners. Father almost dropped dead.'

'It was your finest work,' Mum said with mock pride.

'It's been my only work,' I said, worried.

'You'll find something.'

I paused. 'Don asked me to work with him.'

'Cleaning carpets?'

'His dad is having back problems. Don has had to do all the work himself for the past two weeks and he needs help.'

Mum looked concerned at first, the old Silchester adage of respectability the first thought in her mind, but then her new thoughts kicked in and she smiled supportively. 'Well, that will be handy, won't it?

Having a daughter who can clean up after herself for a change. Are you going to take the job?'

'Father won't be happy about it.'

'When have you ever done anything to please him?' Mum looked out of the window. 'Look at him. I'd better put him out of his misery and get down there.'

'Nah, leave it another ten minutes, let him sweat it out.'

Mum shook her head. 'You two . . .' Then she stood up and took a deep breath.

'Before you go down there, I just want to give you a present; a proper present this time. Remember you said that you never felt you were good at anything, that you never knew what it was you were supposed to do?'

Mum looked embarrassed, then resigned herself to the fact. 'Yes. I remember.'

'Well, it got me thinking. Apart from being the best mother in the world, and the best bread maker, I remembered how you used to draw pictures for us to colour in. Do you remember that?'

Mum's face lit up. '*You* remember that?'

'Of course I do! We had colouring books wherever we went because of you. You were so good at that. So, anyway.' I ran out to the landing and returned with an easel and its accessories all wrapped up in a red bow. 'I got you this. You're lots of things to lots of people, Mum, and when I was a child, I always thought that you were an artist. So, paint.'

Mum's eyes filled again.

'Don't, you'll ruin your make-up. I preferred it when you didn't cry.' I grabbed another tissue and dabbed at her eyes.

'Thank you, Lucy,' she sniffed.

Riley knocked on the door. 'Are you ladies ready?'

'For now and for the next thirty-five years,' she smiled. 'Let's go.'

Walking down the aisle behind my mother who was arm in arm with Riley was the most positive emotionally charged day of my life. The two of them walked before me towards a dapper Philip and the proudest-looking Father I'd ever seen, and I could see the young awkward apprentice who had promised Mum she would never be lonely again in the older man who had never broken that promise.

Melanie winked at me from the pews, beside her Don made a face to make me laugh and to my utter surprise and delight as I looked ahead of me, beside my grandmother who was checking Mum out from head to toe, I saw Life in the front row, healthy, groomed, handsome but most of all unmistakably happy. He smiled at me proudly, and I was so excited and moved to see him there. It had been just over a month since we'd said our goodbye – for this phase anyway – and even with Don to keep me company I'd missed him every day. As the vows were said, I couldn't help bu look at my life and smile as if we were mentally saying the vows to each other; for better for worse, in sickness and in health, till death do us part.

As long as you're around, your life is too. So just as you shower love and affection and attention on the husbands, wives, parents, children and forever friends who surround you, you have to do so equally with your life, because it's yours, it's *you*, and it's always there rooting for you, cheering you on, even when you feel like you can't do it. I gave up on my life for a while, but what I've learned is that even when that happens and *especially* when that happens, life never ever gives up on you. Mine didn't. And we'll be there for each other until those final moments when we will look at each other and say, 'Thanks for staying until the end.'

And that's the truth.

Thank you David, for your unshakable support and belief in me, without which I couldn't have written this book with as much joy and love. Robin, you are yummy and I adore you; this is the one book I'll allow you to scribble on, enjoy the moment. To Mimmie, Terry, Dad, Georgina, Nicky, Rocco and Jay, thanks for your constant love and support.

Thank you to my agent Marianne Gunn O'Connor for your guidance and encouragement – you're partly to blame for making my life so exciting. Thank you to my editor Lynne Drew for your advice and skill which make every story a better one. Thanks to HarperCollins, a great big machine made up of such fantastic, hardworking people. I am honoured to be working with you. Huge thanks to Pat Lynch and Vicki Satlow. Thanks to Aslan for allowing me to use the lyrics for 'Down on Me'.

I'd like to thank my girlfriends. In the interest of world peace, you shall all remain nameless, but thanks for your friendship and most importantly, for sharing your personal stories late into the night and early hours of the morning, all of which have been an endless source of inspiration for this book. Relax, just joking . . . I never listen anyway.

And finally, I'd like to thank my Life. It's been really nice meeting you, please stick around.

Cecelia's Facebook fans from around the world share their thoughts and dreams

Which one key event made you re-evaluate your life?

※ Being a military wife. You can't take anything in life for granted, not even time together

※ Finding out I have an illness which can't be cured, but can be managed

※ Losing loved ones and having children

※ My parents passing away

※ Having my second child which made me stop working for several years

※ The fact that I was short-tempered and weak at maintaining relationships!

※ Being given a second chance – it's a wake-up call to anyone

- Being diagnosed with breast cancer at 27 and losing my mother at 35

- I re-evaluate my life every night. We don't actually need a special event to make us do it

- Moving to a foreign country. Relearning how to speak!

- Meeting my new partner and starting a new life after I had given up. I now live a lovely stress-free time at my age (57) in Ireland

- Moving abroad and meeting my now husband . . . I believe it shouldn't always take bad events in our lives to make us stop and re-evaluate. Always make time to take a step back once in a while and look at your life from a different perspective. We often get stuck in routines/ruts and don't realize until it's too late!

- After my son was stillborn in May this year, I wished that I had cherished every aspect of my pregnancy. It made me realise that everything happens for a reason and has really made me rethink what is important in my life

- Finishing reading *Thanks for the Memories* when I was about to get divorced . . .

- Being a father. It opened my eyes to how amazing life really is. My daughter has not

only changed my life, but she has made me
be alive

- My friend is in the Navy, when I hear about
his day, the trivial day-to-day things don't
compare. I'm more grounded and
compassionate then before

- Just when I thought I lost everything is
when I found everything that matters

- My mum being such a brave person, after
having breast cancer for the second time,
and still fighting! Realised women can be so
strong, especially mothers

When you're lost, how do you find yourself?

- By writing a song

- Isolation, contemplation and a talk with myself

- Friends help me find my way

- Friends and family, or else I stick my swimsuit and goggles on and swim

- Drink tea

- By thinking to myself how good I really have it by comparison of those who truly suffer, and to remind myself not to be so selfish

- I find myself reading a really good book

- I go for a long walk with my dogs in the countryside and talk to my Mum and Dad . . . I lost them almost 10 and 2 years ago respectively and I find that I always get answers to whatever it is that got me there in the first place

- Good long walk on the beach or the forest . . . Always clears the head!

- Do something that takes you back to

childhood . . . like granny's baking! Makes you think back to simple times as a child and reminds you who you are

* I jump in a big bubble bath, chilled playlist on the ipod and a good girly book. Takes me to a place away from my troubles and when I finish they don't seem so bad

* My friends and my kids help me find myself! A quick, or not so quick, phone call to a mate usually works and my kids' laughter!

* Walk, talk, think of what advice my nana would of given me, cry, give myself a shake and finally realize its never as bad as you think

* I sit in a quiet place and ask for guidance from whoever may be listening to me . . . And sure enough I get it

* Thinking, reading, listening to what's around me, sometimes you can be in a place where you least expect someone or something to put you back on the map!

* I have a memory box for both my parents who have sadly passed away, I go through each box and smell my mum's perfume, look through her purse and with my dad I smell his hat and read the cards he sent to me before he died. This always gives me a

great sense of who I am and where I came from.

- I take each hour and each minute as it comes

- Reading books, listening to music, playing the piano

- I write my feeling down on a sheet of paper. It might sound weird but it really makes me feel better when I feel kind of stuck and it often helps me to find some answers that I have been looking for a very long time for

- Watching the sea